HERVÉ LE CORRE

AFTER THE WAR

Translated from the French by
Sam Taylor

MACLEHOSE PRESS
QUERCUS · LONDON

First published in the French language as *Après la guerre* by
Editions Payot & Rivages in Paris, 2014

First published in Great Britain in 2016 by
MacLehose Press
An imprint of Quercus Publishing Ltd
Carmelite House
50 Victoria Embankment
London EC4Y oDZ

An Hachette UK company

Copyright © 2014, Editions Payot & Rivages
English translation copyright © 2016, by Sam Taylor

The moral right of Hervé Le Corre to be
identified as the author of this work has been
asserted in accordance with the Copyright,
Designs and Patents Act, 1988.

Sam Taylor asserts his moral right to be identified as
the translator of the work.

All rights reserved. No part of this publication
may be reproduced or transmitted in any form
or by any means, electronic or mechanical,
including photocopy, recording, or any
information storage and retrieval system,
without permission in writing from the publisher.

A CIP catalogue record for this book is available
from the British Library.

ISBN (HP) 978 0 85705 383 1
ISBN (TPB) 978 0 85705 389 3
ISBN (Ebook) 978 0 85705 382 4

This book is a work of fiction. Names, characters,
businesses, organisations, places and events are
either the product of the author's imagination
or are used fictitiously. Any resemblance to
actual persons, living or dead, events or
locales is entirely coincidental.

Laois County Library
Leabharlann Chontae Laoise

Acc. No. 17/2395

Class No. F

Inv. No. 14154

10 9 8 7 6 5 4 3 2 1

Designed and typeset in Haarlemmer by Libanus Press
Printed and bound in Denmark by Nørhaven

AFTER THE WAR

I

A man is on a chair, hands tied behind his back. Wearing only a vest and underpants, he sits motionless, jaw slack, chin on his chest, breathing through his mouth. A thread of bloody spit dangles from his smashed lips. With each breath his chest heaves, though it's hard to tell if he is sobbing or retching. The arch of his right eyebrow is cut, and blood trickles into his swollen eye, a blackened egg. A huge bruise bulges from his forehead. Blood from his face has dripped onto his undershirt. There's blood on the floor too.

The room is lit only by the lamp suspended above the pool table, which shines in a tight, yellowish cone and leaves everything else in the shade: four circular café tables with orange chairs around them, a scoreboard, a storage cabinet. There are wall lights, with little green lampshades, but apparently no-one thought to turn them on.

Around the man on the chair stand three other men who smoke cigarettes and, for the moment, say nothing. They are slightly out of breath too; their breathing comes in fits and starts, slowly returning to normal. One of them in particular – a tall, fat man – coughs violently, almost choking, as he drops his cigarette butt to the floor and crushes it under his heel. His shirtsleeves are rolled up, revealing powerful biceps. The shirt he wears is tight around his protuberant belly, the buttons threatening to burst open at any moment. He has curly black hair that gives his round face the look of an ill-tempered angel. Lips pursed, he frowns, his pale eyes with their large pupils trained at this moment on the back of the neck of the man slumped in the chair.

"Alright, so what do we do?"

The other two stare dreamily at the man's inanimate body, as if they have not heard this question. The oldest of the three steps closer to the unconscious man. He leans down to examine the swollen face, snaps his fingers near one of the ears.

"We have to wake him up. He can't take it, this twat."

He stands straight and slaps the man on the top of his head.

The man flinches, his good eye opening wide.

"You know where you are? You know why you're here? Do you remember? Hey, I'm talking to you! Can you hear me?"

With a groan, the man nods. Maybe that's the word yes forming at the back of his throat.

"You know Penot? Yeah, of course you know him. All we want is the bloke who killed him. That's all. So tell us where Crabos is and we'll let you go home. You understand?"

The fat man sighs. He clears his throat then spits on the ground. Breathing more easily, he lights another cigarette. The click of his American lighter. The third man is sitting on a chair now, elbows leaning back on a table, his legs stretched out, ankles crossed. He looks at his watch. The only sound is the victim's laboured breathing.

"We're wasting time," he says. "Fuck's sake, it's nearly midnight. He's not going to talk."

"Yes, he is. Aren't you, eh? Grab his head!"

The man gets up from his chair, removes his jacket, rolls up his shirtsleeves and wraps his arm around the man's neck, choking him with the hollow of his elbow. The oldest one lights a cigarette and takes a deep drag, watching the tobacco flare red, then steps closer to the man, who is now trying to scream, the sound muffled by the vice-like pressure of the arm around his throat.

"Where is Crabos? It's obvious he'd have murdered Penot the first chance he got, given what Penot did to his brother during the Occupation. We know it's him, or one of his mates. So fucking tell us, or we'll torture you until you're fucking dead."

He moves the cigarette close to the man's right eye.

The man gasps that he doesn't know, the words sputtering out in a spray of blood. Then the end of the cigarette is crushed into the skin just below his eye and he screams. The man holding him struggles to stop him shaking his head, and his body convulses so that the chair moves, the legs scraping quietly on the wooden floorboards. The fat man comes to his rescue, flattening his hands against the victim's temples with the vexed expression of a man who is wearied and annoyed by this type of routine obligation.

"Shut your mouth," he says. "And answer Albert, unless you like having only one eye."

He pronounces these words without raising his voice, in a tone of impatient advice. His hands are posed on the man's bloody head like a helmet, with his thick fingers as the visor.

The man called Albert removes the cigarette from the victim's face and takes another drag. The stink of burned skin and flesh. Smoke floats under the pool-table lamp, thick and nonchalant. He makes a sign to the other two and moves in again. He holds the tobacco embers close to the corner of the man's eye.

"Listen, if Penot was here, he'd already have given you a manicure. He always did that to poofters like you when he sniffed one out, and then they'd have to use more nail polish for a while! And your prick would already be plugged into the mains. So, you see, in a way it's better that he's dead. But we know how to make people talk too. We have other ways. We'll work you over with a flick-knife, like a pig."

The man in the chair shakes his head. He moans that he's done nothing wrong, that it's not him. That he doesn't know anything. Tears roll endlessly down his cheeks.

"Stop fucking whining, you're getting on my nerves. Just tell me where I can find Crabos or I'll stub out my fag in your eye, you cunt. I'll use you as an ashtray all night long if I have to."

The two others immobilise the man the way they did before. They are calm, methodical. Diligent. They betray no impatience, no anger. Only a faint weariness can be read in their glistening faces.

The man tries to put up a fight, but his struggle is futile given the straitjacket of arms and hands holding him tight. A couple of eyelashes are already sizzling and the air smells of scorched hair. All three of them are startled by the scream the man lets out. Albert takes a step back, holding his cigarette between thumb and index finger. The man groans and gasps and chokes, his throat filled with phlegm. He has given up his struggle now, too preoccupied with the important task of breathing. Then suddenly he shouts out, throwing his torso forward so violently that the chair almost tips over:

"Rue du Pont de la Mousque! He's spending the night at Rolande's place with his tart. He'll go to Spain tomorrow for the winter. He hasn't stayed in his own flat for the last week; he says it's not safe cos the others are looking for him after what happened to Penot."

He slumps, breathless, head down. His chest jerks as he gobbles up air, his lungs whistling like burst tyres.

"That gives us a bit of time," says Albert.

He gestures to the fat man, who takes a flick-knife from his trouser pocket, unfolds the blade and stands there looking at the steel gleam, turning it over in his hands so it catches the meagre light from every possible angle. The man on the chair weeps silently, mouth twisted. Then, in a whiny voice, he manages to say that they shouldn't do that to him, that he's told them what they wanted to know.

The fat man cleans one of his fingernails with the point of the knife. He sniggers.

"Do what?" he asks, in mock surprise. "You think we're going to butcher you here? You think we're going to mess up these nice floorboards with your filthy blood? And who'd clean up afterwards? You? The old lady would go bananas if we got her pool room dirty."

"That's enough, let's get out of here. Francis, go and fetch the car."

Albert throws him the keys. Francis uses a large handkerchief to wipe the blood from his hands and forearms, then puts on his jacket, followed by a coat that he's picked up from a table.

The street lies somewhere behind the station, pockmarked with large cobblestones and cut across in many places by train tracks where diesel locomotives sometimes rumble through, towing freight wagons. No-one around. In the distance, the sounds of metal creaking, a dog barking. They shove their prisoner into the back of the car. He is crying.

They drive, Albert at the wheel, Francis next to him. On the back seat, the fat man and the man they tortured. No-one speaks. Someone called the fat man Jeff, a little earlier, when they were starting the car. They talked to the other man but never used his name. They tied his hands behind his back before making him sit down. They never gave him time to get dressed, so now, wearing only underwear on the imitation leather car seats, he is shivering and sniffing and his teeth are chattering. His name? It will probably appear, a few days from now, in the local news section – or maybe even on the front page – of the *Sud-Ouest* newspaper, after his body has been discovered and identified.

On the other hand, it is important to understand why Albert insisted on driving: the car, an almost new 403, belongs to the judicial police department, of which he is the head.

Commissaire Albert Darlac.

They slow down in a dark street on the north side of the city, in a district full of factories and workers, trapped between the marshland with its flooded paths and the muddy river that flows northward. Riverside poverty. They turn on to a concrete track that leads to the submarine base near the docks, left behind by the Germans. You can sense its gigantic mass absorbing the night and condensing it into impenetrable darkness. They stop on a rutted part of the track next to a wasteland invaded by thistles and bram-bles. Francis and the fat man open the car's back doors and drag out their victim, who falls to his knees in a puddle of water. Francis picks him up like a rag doll, standing him back on his feet and cutting the rope that binds his wrists. Then he pushes him in front of the car, where he's illuminated by the headlights.

"You're free to go. Now fuck off!"

The man trembles and moans. He doesn't move. He stares at them uncomprehendingly, trying to read the truth in their faces but seeing there, probably, only the night. He hugs himself tight in this frozen darkness, then begins to walk cautiously – because he's barefoot – along a path that can just be made out amid the scrubland.

Jeff, the fat man, takes a Luger pistol from the inside pocket of his pea coat, silently loads the breech, then moves forward and aims at the back of the man, who is panting and groaning a little further up the path, as his feet are hurt by the thorns and other junk that litter this squalid wasteland. When the gunshot rings out, Darlac and Francis flinch slightly because the noise rebounds from the concrete walls of the monstrous blockhouse, amplifying the detonation and seeming to spread its echo all across the city.

The man is thrown forward by the impact and he trips, one knee to the ground, and yells out in pain, then stands up again and tries to run. He goes two or three metres, shrieking, and his figure is about to disappear into the darkness, beyond the headlight beams, when the fat man fires again and they see a pale shape fall and then the dried-out vegetation moving, collapsing, where he crawls perhaps, or fights against what is killing him. They hear the rattle of his breath, muffled groans, the sounds of leaves rustling, dead branches snapping.

Jeff walks over to him, holding his gun down at his side. His massive body waddles.

"What the hell are you doing?" Darlac asks.

"Nothing," Jeff replies, without turning around.

He fires three more shots and looks at what lies at his feet, which the other two cannot see.

Albert Darlac starts the car and puts it into reverse. Francis gets in just before it begins to move. They watch Jeff running towards them in the headlight beams. He's heavy but so quick, so agile as he opens the door on the fly, yelling angrily.

"Fuck's sake, Albert, what're you playing at?"

Darlac does not respond. He manoeuvres the car onto the cobblestones of the street.

Behind him, the fat man wheezes, coughs, mutters.

"He had to die, didn't he? So what's the problem?"

"Couldn't miss your chance, could you? Gets you hard, does it? You're a fucking lunatic! You like that, do you, a nice bit of red meat?"

Half turned to the back of the car, Darlac bellows at the fat man as the car rattles over the cobblestones. His gloved hands gripping the steering wheel tightly, he shakes it as if he means to yank it free. Francis, shrinking imperceptibly into his seat, looks through the windows at the empty boulevards moving past in the dimly lit night. Suddenly there is silence inside the car. The only sound is Jeff breathing through his nose like a sulky child, trying to contain his rage.

"You didn't ought to talk to me like that," he says at last in a quiet voice, as they drive past the wall of the Chartreuse cemetery.

"'I didn't ought to?' I'll talk to you how I want. You obey, and that's it. We kill this piece of shit, and that's how it goes. One bullet, nice clean job, leave him to rot, end of story. So calm the fuck down, or I'll send you back where you came from!"

The fat man says nothing. He looks down, his hands touching.

"You're a hard bastard," Francis says. "Christ, people don't say stuff like that."

"A hard bastard, am I? We're doing this to make sure that Destang wanker doesn't declare war and set fire to the whole fucking city. And this twat goes and does that? He was out of line, and you know it. He's not following the rules anymore."

Leaning against the door, Francis sniggers.

"Oh, there are rules, are there? First I've heard of it. The only fucking rule I know is the law of the jungle – you don't mess with the lion. And right now, the lion is us."

"True. But you still do things a certain way. What we left behind there is the work of a weirdo, a psychopath, not the work of serious men. People won't respect us if we leave that kind of shit lying around."

Francis nods. Jeff sniffs. Everyone goes silent. Then, as they approach place Gambetta, they look at the people coming out of the Rio cinema in little groups, then at those rushing into the square in the cold. Here the city has a little light, a little life. Cafés with tables outside, the neon signs of the cinema. They take the cours de l'Intendance down to the docks, the street still packed with cars and pedestrians. They have to wait at a red light at the corner of rue de Grassi. Some women pass, laughing. Francis lowers his window and calls out to them. They turn towards him, giggling and nudging each other.

"I'd do one of them. Just a quickie, you know, take her up the arse . . ."

The car starts up again and he winds the window up, shifting awkwardly in his seat. They have to take a detour via the stock exchange to reach rue Saint-Rémi. At the corner of rue du Pont de la Mousque, Darlac parks the car on the pavement and they get out, the doors banging shut at almost exactly the same time. They run towards the blue hotel sign, lit by the feeble glow of a single bulb. In the small lobby, the manageress, Rolande, wakes up as they arrive, weary eyes peering out from folds of wrinkles. With a sigh, she asks them what they want.

"Police," says Darlac, holding up his I.D.

She puts her glasses on the end of her nose and compares the photograph with Darlac's face.

"And them?"

Husky voice. Tobacco, alcohol, a vile life.

The commissaire nods. In unison, they show their red, white and blue cards.

Darlac spots a telephone behind her.

"Don't touch that or I'll shove it down your throat. Got it?"

The woman shrugs.

"Oh, stop it, Darlac, I'm terrified. What do you want?"

"Crabos."

"Don't know him. Seafood isn't my thing."

He slaps her so hard he knocks her off the chair and sends her flying into a little table behind, overturning an ashtray filled with cigarette butts and two phone books. All of this comes crashing noisily to the floor. Darlac bends over the counter, leaning on his crossed arms.

"Crabos," he repeats. "Don't make us get nasty."

The woman sits up a little bit, leaning against the partition and pulling her dress down over her thighs. She stares at the three men and wipes her split lip with the back of her hand. Blood trickles down her chin.

"Room eight. Second floor."

She gets to her feet, still leaning against the wall, out of their reach. Darlac nods at the telephone and Jeff goes behind the counter, rips out the wires and ties them around the woman's neck.

"I won't make it too tight, this time. There you go – pretty as a bollard!"

Francis laughs.

The woman doesn't move. She is short of breath, face frozen, mouth open and full of blood. Tears roll down her cheeks, blackened by mascara.

"Take a good look in a mirror, you bitch. This can't be the first time someone's given you a good slap!"

Darlac smiles as he contemplates this humiliated woman, with her necklace of black wire hanging heavily over her chest. Then, with a click of his tongue and a look of contempt, he walks towards the stairs, followed by the two others. They climb the stone steps almost soundlessly, their shoes squeaking faintly and Jeff wheezing a bit. On the second floor, they move slowly through the dark corridor, but the floorboards betray them at every step. Illuminated only by the stairwell lamp, they can hardly see each other. Darlac gives them the sign to stop moving and takes a pistol from under his armpit. For two minutes they remain like that outside the door of room eight, devoured by the darkness. Only the dimmest glimmer of light catches the skin of their faces. They are like immaterial creatures, shaped by the night. There is no sound but the rhythmic creaking of a mattress down the hallway. Pointing towards the source of this noise, Francis makes a floorboard creak.

"Sounds like they're . . ."

"Shut up!"

Whispering, faces close together. Then Darlac taps Jeff's shoulder. The door and the walls vibrate as the fat man smashes his shoulder against the wood. The lock is torn free when he bangs the sole of his shoe into it, as if he's about to climb the wall. Darlac charges into the darkness and instantly a body flies at him from his left, grunting as it pushes him into a wall, and a woman starts screaming. When the light comes on, he is sitting on the floor, trapped in the corner formed by a wardrobe and the wall, and a beanpole of a man is hitting him haphazardly, too close to put any real force into his punches, too quickly to aim properly. Darlac thrusts the barrel of his gun under the man's chin, and the man puts up his hands, gets to his feet, steps backwards. Crabos is thin as death, a skeleton in pyjamas, his grey hair dishevelled. Jeff backhands him, and the beanpole is sent flying against the sink, knocking over a chair and smashing into the pipework. You half expect the stickman to snap in two or collapse into pieces.

The woman lying on the bed has stopped screaming. because

Francis has pressed a pillow over her face. She's naked. She's arching her back, twisting her body and kicking out, legs wide apart, and Jeff has a good look on the sly. For a few seconds the silence is total. Throughout the brothel, people have stopped breathing so they can hear what happens next. Francis lets go of the pillow and the girl sits up, pulling the sheet over her and hiding the lower part of her face. She is very young, quite pretty, no make-up.

Francis holds his large, beringed hand above her head and quietly advises her to keep her mouth shut.

Darlac goes over to the sink and grabs Crabos by the collar of his pyjama top. He drags him to the middle of the room like a faggot of dead wood then lays him on a bedside rug, grey with encrusted dust, which might have been trodden upon fifteen years ago by Kraut boots between patrols of the port. His pyjama top has come open, the buttons torn off, and you can see his shoulders, his shoulder blades, his collarbone, you can see the vertebrae in his spine, you can see his ribcage, his skeletal frame covered by the pale cloth of his skin, pulled so tight you think it might tear. Darlac has seen this before, after the war, on stretchers in the concourse of the gare Saint-Jean: all those people who had failed to recover despite the best efforts of the doctors and who were being taken home, ravaged by dysentery and despair, to see if they would decide to start living again.

He had looked at them curiously, those bodies that seemed barely alive, the immense eyes rolling back in their sockets as if from the bottom of an open grave. There had been something there that he hadn't understood, that he would perhaps never understand, because he had been requisitioned to check these people's identities just as, three years earlier, he had established and then zealously checked the identities of those same people during round-ups, had pushed healthy families out of their homes, seeing their eyes full of dread but alive and shining with all sorts of emotions, had slapped full cheeks and shoved powerful shoulders, had ordered buses and trucks to set off and had gone back into those buildings to search the empty apartments, to begin the inventory and the pillage.

Darlac remembers all of this as he presses his gun into the hollow temple of Bertrand Maurac, aka Crabos, aka THE Crabos, so called by all the bastards in the gangs and in the police, because three cancers in fifteen years had not managed to finish him off, each one ending in spontaneous remission, but had left him this almost empty husk where perhaps even death himself could no longer find anything to scythe. The commissaire stands up and tells Jeff to keep an eye on him. The fat man stands in front of the Crabos, arms dangling. A whale contemplating a shipwreck reduced to its frame.

Darlac puts his pistol in his shoulder holster and walks over to the bed. He tears away the sheet that was covering the girl, revealing her naked amid this crumpled chaos. Instinctively she curls up in a ball, then seems to relax and lies on her side, leaning on an elbow, one leg bent at the knee as if she's posing for a painting. Doing her best to act tough.

"How old are you? You look too young to be whoring for the walking dead here."

"I'm twenty-two. And I wasn't whoring. We're friends."

Darlac turns to the Crabos.

"So you have friends, do you? Do you know anyone you haven't fucked over or who hasn't fucked you over? Do you know anyone who doesn't want you dead, anyone who wouldn't want to turn you into a lampshade before the cancer gets you? Well, fucking introduce them to me so I can shoot them in the fucking head!"

"You'll find out for yourself who they are and just how many friends I have, you ugly twat. When they take care of you, you'll be in so much pain that you'll offer up your whore of a mother to take your place."

A cracked voice. A larynx operation. Hollowed-out throat between two bluish tendons.

Jeff turns his fat, squarish face towards Darlac. Forehead gleaming. He balls his fists. Darlac watches the Crabos, whose eyes stare up at him from that skin-covered death's head, lips slick with spit, then he sighs and blinks and mutters, "Leave it," and turns back to the naked slut on the bed.

"Twenty-two, are you? Got your papers with you? What's your name?"

"Arlette. I'm sixteen."

"Where are your parents?"

"Don't know, don't care."

"Fair enough. A life of prostitution and homelessness it is then. Get dressed sharpish, and let's get out of here. You've got three minutes to cover your arse."

He turns back to the Crabos, who is still sitting on the floor.

"You too. You're coming with us. Get dressed. Chop-chop!"

The man gets up. You can see his skeleton moving under his skin, poking and rolling. It looks as if it must hurt. He bends his dragon spine to pick up his things, and covers his body in clothing. Little by little, the horrors of his carcass are hidden beneath layers of fabric.

"My parents, they live in Saint-Michel. Rue Saumenude, number thirty-four," the girls says, now wearing a blue raincoat over a black dress. "They have five kids, and there's no room for me anymore. And my dad doesn't want me in his bed now cos he says I'm too old."

"Your dad's a fucking idiot," says the fat man. "He doesn't know what he's missing."

Francis shrugs, then looks at his watch. He does that all the time. Looking at his watch. Like a stationmaster.

"We have to get out of here, Albert."

Darlac pauses to think, his eyes on the girl.

"You go in the Crabos' car and take the girl to the Couchots' place. Tell Emile to keep her warm and leave her in peace. No work or anything. She doesn't go out, she doesn't speak to anyone. I'll go to see them later and we'll work out what to do with her then. Right now I'm going with Jeff and this bag of bones, and we're going to have a little chat."

They clatter downstairs, pushing their prisoners in front of them, and pass a couple who get out of the way by shrinking back against the stone wall. Some four-eyed git in a hat and a Russian whore who looks away when she spots Darlac, then watches him walk away from behind. As soon as they hear the men's footsteps in the lobby, she pushes her john ahead of her as if the stairs are on fire.

They walk past the manageress without a glance. She holds a handkerchief to her mouth and pretends to ignore them too. At the corner of rue Saint-Rémi, they are surprised by a cold wind blowing up from the river, and all of them hunch their raised collars up over their necks. The girl looks tiny surrounded by these shadowy men, and for a few seconds no-one says a word, no-one moves, as if the icy air has turned them to statues or they're afraid of the night.

Darlac thinks. He looks far ahead, out towards the docks, staring unflinchingly into the east wind. No-one moves. His two henchmen watch him, awaiting his orders like soldiers in a commando unit.

"Where's your car?"

The Crabos answers him through gritted teeth, shivering under his sailor jacket.

"Place du Parlement. It's a grey Chambord."

Understanding what they want, he rummages inside his pocket, brings out the keys and hands them to Francis. They go their separate ways without a word. The wind whistles in their ears, and when Darlac and Jeff collapse onto the seats of the 403, they sigh with relief, while the Crabos shrinks against the inside of the door, eyes closed and arms crossed. Darlac takes the wheel.

"Where are we going?" the Crabos asks.

"Spain. Isn't that where you wanted to go?"

"Who told you that?"

"Same bloke who told us where you were dossing. Lulu de Kléber. You know him? Lucien Potier."

"Right. That cunt. I guessed as much."

"He won't be snitching on anyone else," Jeff remarks.

The Crabos sits up in his seat.

"You . . ."

Darlac quickly gives Jeff a warning look to shut him up. Silence. They drive past the docks and the Pierre Bridge. The city is empty, its darkness punctuated by dimly glowing bulbs hung from wires over the streets.

"Why did you do that?"

"So you know we're not pissing about. We didn't like what you did to Penot. So we put a few holes in that piece of shit Lulu. This way, you don't have to."

"I should have slaughtered Penot in '46, when I found him. But we had an arrangement with Destang back then. The business had to start up again on a sound basis. But for this one, I'm not your man. I didn't do anything to that arsehole, even if I'd happily piss on his rotting corpse now. And I didn't ask anyone else to do the job, because it's nothing to do with me anymore. Can you get that into your thick cop's head?"

He goes silent, out of breath now. Gives a little cough. Wipes the sweat from his forehead.

Darlac turns towards him, leaning on his seat.

"What's up with you? Cancer back, is it?"

"What do you fucking care?"

Darlac shrugs.

"I don't. If you piss off to Spain to die, I'll happily pay for your train ticket. First class."

"Oh yeah? Well, make it a return ticket. I'll die here because this is where I'm from and this is where my folks died."

They start up again, driving straight then turning at the Grand Théâtre to head south to the docks.

"Where are you taking me?"

"We'll drop you at the station. Don't you want to go to Spain?"

The Crabos wipes condensation from the window and looks out at the city as if he doesn't recognise it.

"Have you got a fag? I left mine in the hotel room."

Jeff starts fumbling around in his coat pocket, but Darlac flashes him a look from the corner of his eye, so the fat man stops moving. Neither of them says a word.

The Crabos shivers. He raises his collar and shrinks against the back of the seat.

"Why don't you kill me?"

"You'd like that, wouldn't you? I bet you're too weak to even take a shit now. No. You never set foot in Bordeaux again. Do some pimping in Valencia or sell hash in Algeciras or die in Toledo. Or just go fuck yourself, for all I care. But catch your train, cos I don't want to see you or even hear about you here anymore. You'll be fine for money down there, I'm sure – you'll get your postal orders, and you must have some put aside already. The judge will slap an arrest warrant on your head tomorrow morning. You're black-listed in Bordeaux now, shithead. We've got you for pimping – and now you're an accessory to murder too. And that's without even mentioning the drugs. Come back, and you'll have me and Destang on your back – and believe me, if Destang gets hold of you first, you'll end up in the river, chopped into so many fucking pieces that the prawns will have you for breakfast. And listen, when you're down there, you call me, you give me your address, and you keep me informed about everything that's moving between France and Spain. Whores, drugs, all of it. If I don't hear from you, we'll take care of your daughter. It must be expensive, that fancy boarding school she goes to in Nice? Well, I know some people who'll give her work. You can't put a price on a good education, can you?"

The Crabos mutters a shitload of swear words as he bangs his head against the window.

"Why don't you just kill me?"

Darlac lights a cigarette. He blows smoke out through his mouth, through his nose, with a long weary sigh, just as he pulls in next to the kerb.

"I just told you why. Besides, you're already dead. Alright, time to piss off now."

They are parked opposite the gare Saint-Jean, outside a café that spills too much light inside the car, the brightness broken up by the fast-moving shadows of people walking past. The Crabos watches all this with astonishment, his mouth half open. He slowly opens the door and gets out, but remains standing there for a few seconds, one hand still resting on the door handle, looking around him at the bustle of the night. Then he softly closes the door and they watch his frail figure move away along the pavement, very slowly, step by step, as if he might collapse at any moment.

2

He stops suddenly in front of the gates of the port, his bicycle between his legs, and remains there, stunned. With his balaclava and his sheepskin coat with the collar turned up and the mittens on his hands gripping the handlebars, only his eyes are visible. He observes the blaring traffic of cars and trucks, intoxicated by the din they make, grinding his teeth as axels groan and bodies shake over the large cobblestones of the cours de la Martinique. He feels the dull rumble in his legs as a train trundles slowly past endless rows of warehouses, accompanied on foot by a man swinging a lantern in his hand. The city buzzes and trembles in his flesh.

He looks at all this as if the landscape had appeared suddenly out of darkness and he was now encircled by a film set that had miraculously materialised. His eyes are wide with amazement. His frozen figure is painted black in this night that is already fading before the vast pale gold gleam rising over the Garonne, above the blanket of mist that lies on the water. Above all these early morning stirrings, the greyish-green street lamps, hung from wires, are blown casually about in the weak north wind, their dim lights fading. The young man hunches his shoulders.

His name is Daniel and he is twenty years old.

Often, as now, he finds himself wondering what he's doing here. The feeling can come over him anywhere. At dances, in buses, at the cinema. In the midst of noise and chatter. In spite of friends and laughter. When it happens, he stops whatever he's doing and looks around unseeingly, listens uncomprehendingly to the humans that surround him. Their agitation, their frenzied trample, their crazy trajectories like insects caught between window and curtain. In these moments he feels horribly light, transparent, barely even existent, dissolved in the air, with beings and objects passing through him as if he's a ghost, a revenant that no longer knows where it has returned from, only that it's terrified to have left there.

Or he freezes and looks up at the dawn sky, clear and faded, rubbed clean by a cold wind. This pure emptiness, crossed occasionally by a rushing bird, tightens his heart and renews, each day, the wonder of the light that lifts up the lid of night. In these instants of happy contemplation, time seems to suddenly contract, to become as dense and painful as a bullet.

And then the feeling leaves him, of course. Because life is all around, so strong and noisy.

Above the warehouses, he can see the jibs of cranes bending over boats. They look like iron witches rummaging through the upturned bellies of those lumbering monsters that the river has thrown against the wharf. It's high tide, so he can make out the top of a forecastle, the glimmers of the gangway, the mast bristling with aerials and the black-and-blue chimney bearing the arms of the Delmas-Vieljeux company. Some days the tide was so high that he imagined they might all drift into the city, their huge prows slicing into stone, digging out canals in place of the dark streets.

But the cold is penetrating deep into his flesh and his stomach suddenly feels as if it's full of snow, so Daniel shakes himself, smacking his arms, ridding himself of his dark thoughts and the frost that has settled over him. Then he starts pedalling over the cruel cobblestones, insides shuddering, arms stiff as he grips the handlebars, manoeuvring his way between train tracks and cobbles and potholes. The bike jingles as it jumps, and even the bell, which hasn't worked for months, sometimes chimes amid the spluttering uproar of traffic. From time to time, the little bag he carries over his shoulders, containing his overalls wrapped around his lunch box, slips down his back and he has to hitch it up again. He rides past the port, no longer even seeing that interminable parade of warehouses behind miles of fences; head down, eyes watering from the cold, he charges blindly ahead until he reaches the station.

The pavements are packed with people encumbered with luggage, lifting up heavy suitcases that bang against their legs, walking lopsidedly, knees buckling, arms aching from the weight of large bags that they try not to drag on the ground. Or they carry a child wrapped up in a dark, unwieldy package that they constantly have to lift up with a shrug of a shoulder or a jut of a hip to stop them slipping out of their grip. They cross the street and hurry towards the main concourse, occasionally grumbling at someone who's dawdling in front of them or another who's trying to push past. All these bow-legged figures, hobbling and tottering, unsteady shadows that you half expect to see swallowed up in the great mouths of their suitcases that suddenly yawn open, the locks knackered. A herd of crippled beggars, emerging from the pale bluish morning, limping along as they try to storm this profane cathedral. It looks like some of them will be catching the last train, so pathetic is their staggering progress.

Against the current though, you can see a few solitary fellows, hands free or buried deep in pockets, who come out through the large glass doors and stop in the greyish glimmer of morning to light a cigarette then slowly start walking again, indifferent to the crush of people going the other way, upright, light-footed figures amid all this broken-backed turmoil, towering ghosts.

Daniel imagines them driven to despair after leaving a loved one forever, roaming lost all day long through a city they don't recognise. Or walking towards a vengeance that obsesses them, tortures them like some incurable pain. Every morning, as he rides his bike, the glimmerings of a cinematic melodrama pass through his mind, but he never takes the time to develop the plot.

Then he sees soldiers passing, in khaki coats and side caps. Twenty or so, walking two by two, spines curved by the weight of their suitcases. Ahead of them are two gendarmes, rifles on shoulders. Daniel slows down to let them cross. They will take the train to Marseille. Get the boat tonight to Algeria. Heart heavy. Friends already gone. Hot over there. Death everywhere. So it's said. So they say. Apparently. Words dancing. Patrols, ambushes, reprisals, massacres, mutilations. Everyone knows someone who's died, or someone who's lost a son or a brother and who curses the politicians and is starting to hate that race of cutthroats who slaughter the beautiful children we deliver to their knives.

Daniel knows he'll be leaving next month. Can't be long now till he gets his marching orders. He doesn't know what he'll do over there. Or what will be done to him.

He starts riding again, pressing hard on the pedals to move over the cobbles. He passes the bars, already packed, and thinks what a pleasure it would be, just once, to stop here and order a café au lait and a croissant at the counter . . . Or to daydream in a booth, there in the warmth, over a mug of hot chocolate. What extravagance! In rue Furtado, he sees the Neiman sign over the garage and, standing beneath it, Norbert, the apprentice, smoking a cigarette and stamping his feet. They shake hands. Daniel asks him how he is but Norbert doesn't reply, eyes down, face consumed by the shadow of his cap.

"What's up with you?"

Norbert shakes his head as he looks at the garage. He tosses his cigarette and it sizzles in the gutter.

"Show me," Daniel insists.

His eye is half closed, black, the arch of his eyebrow swollen, ready to burst. His cheek too is bruised.

"Shit, what did you do?"

Norbert shrugs then starts to sob. No tears, just big jolts that tear at his chest. Choking with sadness and rage.

"Was it your dad?"

The boy nods.

"Come on, we can't stay out here, we'll freeze to death. Let's light the stove."

Daniel takes two heavy keys from the pocket of his sheepskin and unlocks a small door that opens within the garage door. While Norbert switches on the lights, he takes out the sign, puts it by the side of the road, then goes back into a corner of the workshop where they have a camping stove connected to a gas cylinder, a sink, and a cupboard where they keep their lunch. He cleans the Italian coffee-maker, gets it ready and places it over the gas fire. He rubs his hands near the blue flame. He's shivering, now he's stopped cycling, so he doesn't take his balaclava off yet. The cold is heavy and dense, accumulated under the high steel girders in the garage. They should light the wood burner, but the boss is the only one who knows how to do it: he rummages around inside it for ten minutes, moaning about how he's going to smash this piece of shit up with a sledgehammer and get another one, and then, just like that, it starts purring like a great big pussycat.

Norbert busies himself in the glass-walled office where they keep the orders and invoices. There's a paraffin heater in there: he fills it and lights it, sniffing as he wipes his nose with the back of his hand.

They drink their coffee in the smell of the gas, sighing with pleasure as they blow on their bowls. Norbert puts three sugars in his and swallows it in big gulps, hands cupping the bowl to warm them. Then they smoke a cigarette, blowing the smoke away as far as they can, leaning back in their chairs and talking about the day's workload. Testing the valves on a 202, the brakes on a Juvaquatre, and fixing the electrics in a Traction that the old man's been struggling with since yesterday. And that's their morning.

Daniel watches the kid with his swollen face, his one good eye sparkling darkly, the self-satisfied way he smokes his Gauloise, acting like a movie star.

"You should see a doctor about your eye. Maybe go to hospital."

Norbert shrugs then lowers his head.

"Nah, it's nothing. Anyway, it's not the first time."

He says these words almost into his jacket and his voice dies there. For a moment, they don't speak. They crack their necks, stretch their backs. The cold settles over them again. Sometimes there's the sound of metal creaking in the garage. A train horn in the distance, down towards the station warehouses.

"What happened with your dad?"

The kid stares at his feet as he rotates them slowly. He blows smoke and contempt through his nose.

"It's always the same thing . . . He started yelling as soon as he got home cos he reckoned it was cold. Said my mother hadn't put enough coal in the stove. He'd been drinking, so of course he got pissed off about it, and then he got his feet caught in the straps of my little sister's satchel which she'd left in the hall, and that got him fuming. He grabbed her by the hair to make her tidy it away and he started calling her a whore: you're a little whore like your whore of a mother, he was saying. So my mother started moaning, going on about how he couldn't call a little girl, his own daughter, a whore, and he asked her if she wanted some. After that they started yelling and it all kicked off. I tried to stop him, and since he's stronger than me and he's got hands like shovels, well . . . this is the result. I played dead so he'd stop beating me and he eventually tired himself out; he could hardly even stand anymore cos he was so drunk. I protected my face, but after that he started kicking me, so my back took the worst of it. It's black and blue, you should see it . . . Thank God I was still wearing my leather jacket. Anyway, at least my mum and sister were able to go next door, to Mrs Jiménez's house, like they always do . . . So they got a good night's sleep, and Mrs Jiménez has a bathroom . . ."

He shakes his beaten-up head, then takes a drag on his cigarette and blows the smoke out noisily.

"One day I'm going to stab him in the fucking belly and let him die on the floor, holding his guts. He'll regret it then, the cunt."

"And so will you, when you're in jail. Because of that bastard . . .

He's not worth ruining your life over. You're talking shit."

"You're the one who's talking shit. My life ... What do you know about my life? You're not there, every night, wondering what's going to happen next, how it'll end up. You don't know what it's like, the fear, not daring to say anything, not even daring to look at each other cos he thinks we're plotting against him. There are evenings when I hope he won't come home at all, that he's been knocked down by a truck, or that the wheels of his bike have got stuck in the tram tracks just as a bus is coming. Or that he gets so pissed that he falls in the river. I dream up stuff like that and it makes me feel so good, you wouldn't believe it. We won't ever be happy in our house until that bastard's dead and it's just my mum, my sis and me. You have no fucking idea. Cos he'll kill us one day, you know: either my mother, or my sister, or me. So, yeah, it'd be better if I did it to him before he does it to us."

Daniel nods his agreement. It's true: he has no idea. It reminds him once again that the world is a circus where the animals have been set free, it's an overcrowded storeroom on a boat tossed by a stormy sea, a greasy-spoon café populated by brutes, lost innocents and fallen women, run by a manager who's wedged behind the cash drawer, one hand on the rifle he's got hidden under the counter. And he doesn't know why and he doesn't understand this stubborn misfortune that never lets up and always kindles in his heart a powerless rage or that dreamy melancholy that sometimes isolates him for a brief while inside a glass cage.

Silence. The stove ticks metallically. Then Daniel stands up, takes off the balaclava that he'd already rolled up to his forehead like a hat and starts unbuttoning his sheepskin coat.

"Maybe we should do some work. That might warm us up a bit, don't you think? The old man'll be here about eleven, and he'll have a right go at us if we haven't finished the 202 by then: I think the bloke's supposed to come and pick it up this afternoon."

They put on their overalls as fast as they can, blowing into their hands and stamping their feet. They're in a rush to get into the work-shop, to switch on the overhead lights and plug in the inspection lamps. They talk loud, amid a booming blur of tools and sheet metal, perhaps in an attempt to scare off the arctic monster that prowls nearby and holds them tight and blows its icy breath in their faces. Norbert starts an engine with a hand-crank and jumps into the front seat to slam down the acccelerator pedal. The engine coughs, pops, stalls. The kid disappears under the bonnet, muttering insults, and becomes locked in a struggle there, groaning with the effort. Fuck, he says several times, voice muffled by anger. Looking at him with his arms tensed and his feet slipping on the concrete, you'd think he was strangling someone. Bollocks, he whispers, through gritted teeth.

"What's up?" asks Daniel.

"Nothing. The distributor. Forget it."

He forgets it. From where he is – by the workbench where he's put the cylinder head, to remove the scraps of melted piston from the steel – Daniel can see only the kid's feet, which are sometimes both off the ground as if he's being swallowed by the huge mouth of the open bonnet, digested in the entrails of the engine.

They take a break around ten, as they do every morning. Coffee. Norbert digs into the tips box then runs to the bakery to fetch *pains au chocolat* while Daniel gets everything ready. There's a big puddle of pale sunlight out in front of the garage, so he pulls aside the heavy sliding door to let the light in and smokes his cigarette, blinking in this unexpected brightness.

The first they see of the man is the shadow that he throws. There in the winter sunlight, at the centre of this icy glare. He stands immobile, a leather helmet on his head, leaning against the handle-bars of a large motorbike. The lower part of his face is wrapped in a roughly knitted red scarf. Daniel sighs, drains his bowl, then leaves the office, flicking ash from his cigarette. He's expecting to have to calm down a worried client who's come to see if his car will be ready tonight, and who'll act as though they'd promised it would be ready yesterday. He greets the man and asks what he can do for him.

The man does not reply. He stares at Daniel. His eyes shine. He pulls down his scarf and his mouth exhales hurried little clouds of steam that show how fast he's breathing. He does not move a muscle, as if the cold was about to freeze him into a solid block of ice like those mammoths in Siberia. Then he starts talking about spark plugs and ignitions, about his machine that broke down not far from here, on the cours de la Marne. His voice is hoarse.

"If you could take a look at it," he says, still without moving.

Daniel explains that the boss won't be there until noon, and he's the one who knows about motorbikes. At the moment he's on his own with the apprentice, they've got loads of work on their hands, and as he says this he points behind him at the chaos of cars piled up in the garage.

The man nods, hesitates. He seems about to leave, then he asks if he can leave the bike there, if they might have time to look at it by tomorrow or even the day after. He can make do, after all: he can take the bus.

"Do you live far away?"

"Not really. And I like walking. Don't worry about it."

The man's voice quivers and dies away, as if he's short of breath. Or as if he's about to start crying. Daniel stares at him and the man blinks and smiles weakly, and suddenly a whole mesh of wrinkles appears on his face, like those veils that old people wear to funerals. It is impossible to guess his age. His body seems vigorous, straight-backed, probably quite sturdy. But his face is an old man's, crumpled like an old newspaper in which only bad news has been printed. And his eyes – black or navy blue? – must have read all that news before blubbering over it. He's shaking now. The handlebars are vibrating between his hands.

"Leave it here," Daniel says. "Come back tonight, if you can. If it's just the ignition, it shouldn't take long to fix it."

32

"That's very kind of you. Yes, I'll come back – about six o'clock, is that alright?"

Still his voice sounds out of breath.

Daniel shows him where to park the bike. A Norton. Probably picked up after the war. The man takes off his helmet, hangs it on the handlebars, thanks Daniel again and walks away, taking a cap from his pocket and putting it on his head. Without knowing why, Daniel goes out onto the pavement to watch him disappear towards the pont du Gui, the bridge that crosses the railway tracks. The slender figure moves unwaveringly. Daniel is surprised by that quick, determined gait. He would have expected to see the man's silhouette staggering in this ice-sharpened sunlight. A shiver makes him move again when the man vanishes at the corner of the street, and suddenly everything is empty, and silent, and he finds it unbearable.

3

One day, I died. We were walking on this road and we were sleeping as we walked, and we fell and others picked us up so our legs started moving forward again and we held up other men who tripped because they were falling asleep and sometimes they didn't get back up again so the soldiers threw them by the roadside in the mud or the snow and they pushed us ahead, hitting us in the back or the back of the neck with their rifle butts. Sometimes they did it so much that a man would fall and that gave them a good reason to kill him, holding him on the ground with their boot and putting a bullet in the back of his neck. Many of the men had broken fingers from trying to protect themselves and afterwards they couldn't even eat the few scraps of bread that still circulated along the line and that we would soften in puddles of water or in the snow. The ones with the smashed hands couldn't even undo the string that held their trousers up when they wanted to shit during breaks so we helped them, when we could, when the cold hadn't frozen the wet knots, or they relieved themselves crouching down, hiding their faces with their black swollen hands as if they were ashamed. As if any of us could still feel that emotion, by this point. Or maybe it was a sort of reflex, a buried and very distant memory of what we had been before being reduced to these bodies kept upright only by the stubbornness of their skeleton, these bodies for which every step taken, every heartbeat torn from nothingness constituted a victory without hope.

I don't know what they had to be ashamed of. I watched them gasping and sobbing in their hands and I didn't understand. We'd seen so many dead on the latrines during the night, their bony arses inside the fetid holes as if sucked there, their bodies caved in, already stiff and dry and cold, frozen by the ice in their final suffering. We had seen so many of them. We never dared touch them, content just to be able to get up and walk after emptying our bellies so we could flee far from what awaited us.

Those men with the fractured hands, we also helped them to eat and we took a little mouthful of their mouthful, and they didn't say anything and neither did we. We hadn't said anything for a long time, in fact, because we were too tired and our dry mouths and our swollen tongues and our sore gums transformed every word we spoke into a torture, as if we'd swallowed burning oil.

Either that or we talked in whispers. We would murmur encouragements into each other's ears, enjoining those who couldn't get up anymore to walk and to live, because it all went together, because walking was falling onto the other foot, the only way we knew to stay upright. We promised them imminent breaks which never came, we told them we'd be arriving soon in another camp, we whispered it all close to their sharp faces, gently patting their bones that shivered under threadbare cloth amid the screams and kicks of the S.S.

How many days?

Maybe several lifetimes. Interminable lives on the verge of ending. I relived mine, step by step. My dying mind, just alive enough to push what remained of my being to walk, to breathe, because it seemed possible to me that I might forget to breathe, so exhausting was this effort, because the cold and the damp that invaded my lungs with each inhalation were like an enemy intrusion, a commando attack intended to further undermine my empty fortress, my mind that no longer thought but was full of forgotten memories that crossed it now like fish wriggling at the bottom of a drained pond.

Childhood, happiness, sunlight. The laughter of drinkers in the little café that my parents ran. The train to Arcachon. Sitting between them, I stared through the window, on the lookout for the first pines that, for me, marked the happy lands bordered by the sea. I could still feel the two of them against me, their hands on mine, their kisses. But also the autumns and the endless rain and the chestnut trees in the school playground. Faces appeared before me. Names. Lost for over fifteen years.

The memory of a fight in the toilets, broken up by the teacher who dragged us back to the classroom by our ears. Smells. Wet stone, mildew in the cellar where we kept the bottle racks and the beer barrels. The cologne my father sprayed on himself on Sunday mornings before taking me, sometimes, to the Marché des Fossés on the cours Victor-Hugo, among the onlookers and the smooth patter of the hucksters and the scent of candyfloss and boiled sweets.

Intoxicated by the smell and the colours of my life, I walked on through the stink of corpses and shit that we gave off, all of us, uniformly grey, from our heads to our feet, skin pasty beneath the grime, a battered troop shuffling through the endless abattoir that was this path in a world so grey even the snow couldn't whiten it, on the lookout for the distant black lines of fires like so many landmarks stretched horizontal by the wind. Surprised and terrified when one of us collapsed puking blood, because of the sudden flash of colour and because that scarlet was death carried within them like a monster and delivered in a final rattle.

And one day, I died too.

I fell on the hard, dirty snow, packed solid by thousands of feet. I was on all fours and trying to breathe, to pump in air as if I might have been able to reinflate myself and get back on my feet, but each time I had the impression I was emptying myself even more. I was on all fours and I felt my arms trembling, incapable of holding up my body, and the cold was burning my hands and knees. I had seen so many do the same and whom we'd tried to carry a few metres further, hoping that they would start walking again but whom we'd let go in the end because we didn't have the strength to help them anymore. We had to leave them behind because there was always a guard or an SS officer who would come up to us screaming, pushing men out of the way with the point of his bayonet or whirling his stick, and who would start kicking the man lying flat on his belly or beating him with a club. Sometimes he would kill them on the spot or he would have them carried to the roadside and leave them there, maybe already dead.

Someone grabbed me under the arms and lifted me up, whispering that we were going to get in more trouble, and I was surprised to hear them speaking French; I don't know why, there were other French men in the camp, and in our line, of course, but since we'd been walking we'd said so little that whenever we talked to someone we used, I think, a sort of pidgin made up of a few dozen words borrowed from German and French or Italian, or Polish. Survival words, essential words, without sentences or grammar. Something like the sounds that animals make to each other.

I heard the guard yelling and straight away we were pushed in the ditch before I even got to see the face of the man who'd been helping me and I fell flat on my belly, the other man on top of me, on a soft layer of snow piled up there, almost comfortable, and I thought how lucky I was to be able to die without any further suffering. Two gunshots exploded overhead, and in the moment when I felt a bullet in my shoulder, the man who had lifted me up suddenly became heavier and I was pushed down into the snow and I turned my head a little so I could take a few more breaths, then I had the impression of being pushed further down and all I felt then was the cold, nothing else, not even pain. The cold, and nothing more.

I was suffocating. I lifted my head and I spat out water and bits of ice and I cried out in order to breathe. The man's corpse was crushing me and I couldn't move at all now, couldn't feel any part of my body, as if I were nothing more than a severed head. I was lying in the melted snow and I thought I was going to die of cold under this corpse that was pressing me down into the ground so I would stay with him in death. I concentrated on my hands. One was trapped beneath me but the other one was above my head and I was able to wriggle my fingers. They came back to life and then I could move my arm. It was at this moment that I heard the man moaning and it didn't even surprise me. As the living were already dead, the dead could easily be resurrected from one hell to another. I asked him to get up because I was dying underneath him but he continued to groan, his head between my shoulder blades. I tried to push down on my free arm but I had no strength and sometimes I couldn't even get enough breath in my lungs and I was suffocating so I started wriggling as much as I could, twisting myself under that dying body and I insulted him, you fucking piece of meat, go and die somewhere else, I spat insults at the man who had helped me, supported me, carried me, who had taken the two bullets that should have killed me.

I don't know how long I spent twisting like a worm in that frozen mud. The man's body suddenly tipped over and I found enough strength to crawl away from him, as if he might jump back on top of me. I sat up, leaning against the embankment, and looked at him. He had lifted himself up in a strange way, his back arched against the edge of the ditch, eyes wide open, mouth gaping and full of bloody spit. I went over to him and felt for the artery in his throat so I could take his pulse, but all I felt beneath my fingers was a tangle of knotted strings around the bones protruding under his skin. I closed his eyes, my teeth chattering. I was now nothing more than shivers and the cold took hold of me and I felt it spreading through my stomach and paralysing me inch by inch. As the man's jacket was dry, because it had been lying on me, I took it off him and put it on, but his trousers were covered with shit and mud so I had to get up to try and find another pair.

Trembling, I took a few steps, my heart in a panic and my chest filled with pain. I rubbed my sides but that was worse: I no longer knew where it hurt and I felt that crazy pounding under my fingertips, making my skeleton vibrate with those heavy beats that would surely smash it to pieces. The injury to my shoulder was nothing in this cage of pain. Just a hole that had gone through me above my collarbone. I began walking again and found a bit of breath and only then did I lift my eyes from the paved road and look around me.

The light was unbearable. Everything was white, all the way to the horizon, dusted with fresh snow and encrusted with ice. The sun fell from above, hitting this whiteness and making it sparkle, blinding. The sky was a pure blue so deep and clear that I expected to see a few stars in the middle of the day.

The road was empty. Rows of footprints covered by snow trailed off

westward, millions of hollows turning blue in the harsh sunlight. The
traces of ghosts. In the still air, the silence was absolute. I could feel my
heartbeat thudding against my skull, but that could only be a distant
echo of life, because I was dead. I knew it in that instant. I would never
return from this frozen earth, I would never leave this corpse-lined path.
I would never rediscover life. I was walking down this road, on this cold,
powdery ground, among the dead men abandoned by the roadside,
with nothing to hold onto, with no physical substance. I was now the
only one who could see me, who could experience the material reality of
my spectre. For everyone else, I was disappearing into the transparency
of the air. Their gazes would pass through me without ever guessing at
my existence.

Sometimes the night would open around me and then only those
wandering souls I passed randomly would recognise me, their eyes dead
with horror like mine, their mouths wide open in their final breath like
me as I suffocated, surrounded by the living. But I would glide on forever,
unperceived, amid calm executioners and traitors turning their backs
on the past, and they would never know who killed them nor from what
hell came stealing this shadow who stared and smiled at them.

I could barely walk and I was making myself promises that were
impossible to keep but it was the only thing I was capable of believing
in, so I clung to that as to a shaky handrail on a collapsed staircase.

4

When the light comes on again, while the murmur of conversation rises around him, Daniel remains seated for a few seconds longer, watching the silent white screen. He blinks as if he were in the dust and blinding sunlight of Tombstone, and he clicks his tongue like Doc Holliday when he's thirsty and he sees the street flooded with light bordered by wooden sidewalks where figures on rocking chairs sit motionless in the shadows. Inside his head, men are still running, leaping, falling during the gunfight, shots are still echoing, the cocking levers of Winchester rifles still snapping into place. The seats bang softly into seatbacks as people stand up and he feels these muffled thuds in his back, savouring this solitude in which he lets the film percolate through him, burning itself into his memory. His friends often ask him how he manages to remember so many details about the films he sees, the names of actors and directors, things they pay no attention to. He replies simply that he likes all that stuff and that, if he could, he'd go to the cinema every day and write books about it, write reviews in newspapers. The others think this is too much: write a book? Oh yeah, and what else? Him, the mechanic from rue Furtado, the kid who grew up here in Bacalan, this workers' suburb on the edge of the city and the marshes?

He doesn't dare tell them how he used a folding ruler to make a little rectangular frame that he keeps in a pocket and that he often looks between those right angles at people and things and that nothing then exists except what he sees there, a sharper, deeper image, something stronger and more singular. He doesn't dare tell them – because they'd think he was crazy – that he frames women walking down the street and they are more beautiful that way, that the city itself, enclosed in this geometry, becomes a place of intrigue where anything might happen, mysteries appearing suddenly from the corner of that street, the middle of that square, behind that window, in that car driving past too fast . . .

He hears the lid of a lighter snap open somewhere above him, and immediately afterwards a cloud of smoke with the smell of Virginia tobacco pours down on him. Alain hands him a pack of Camels.

"So are you staying to bury the dead or are you coming with us?"

"Where are the others?"

"Outside, where do you think? It's stuffy as hell in here."

Daniel takes a cigarette from the pack and Alain lights it for him with his Zippo.

"Let me see," says Daniel. "Where'd you get that?"

He weighs the lighter up in his hand, opening the lid with a flick of his thumb, turning the wheel. Smell of oil, good strong flame.

"From a sailor, on the docks. I worked there five days last week and got chatting with a wop. He told me he had loads of 'em. He's from Naples, and down there they buy and sell anything American, he said. Apparently the Yank soldiers have these in their kitbags.

"You couldn't get another one, could you?"

Alain shakes his head. Then throws Daniel the pack of Camels.

"Here. You can keep these. He gave me two cartons. His boat left yesterday and he won't be back till February – they're going to Senegal and then Tunisia. Next time he comes he might be selling bags of couscous or wooden statues."

They leave the cinema laughing, arm in arm, and bump into an old granny who yells at them, waving the handle of her umbrella.

"Oh, don't bother saying sorry! That's young people for you these days! Just a bunch of yobbos! I'd send the whole lot of 'em to Algeria . . ."

"My son is there at the moment," says a woman behind her. "That's young people for you these days, as you say. The things we do to them. Sending them off to war, as if the last one wasn't bad enough. So let them have a bit of fun, and shut your face!"

41

The granny turns around but says nothing, dumbstruck, mouth gaping idiotically. She holds her handbag and her brolly tight to her side.

"I'm going there in February, if that makes you feel any better," Daniel tells her. "I'm just waiting for my marching orders. So stick it up your arse."

The woman goes purple-faced. A man appears from behind her and grabs the younger man by the arm.

"What did you say to my wife? Say it again."

"Oh, that's your wife, is it? Well, tell her from me that she can stick it up her arse, if she didn't hear me the first time. And so can you, dickhead. How's that for you?"

The people around them have stopped and are watching in silence. A dark little crowd, faces pale under the lobby's bright lights. Who knows what they're thinking. Maybe they're expecting a scrap. Another duel, minus the sunlight, on this winter night whose cold air they can feel blowing through the open doors. The man grabs Daniel's collar and shoves him, yelling "What? What?", eyes bulging from their sockets, spit drooling from his lips. He's shortish but well-built, fists as big as his thick-skulled head, and Daniel retreats, not knowing how he's going to get rid of this moron because right now, pushed backwards, off-balance, he can't even give him a good kick in the balls. Alain gets in between them. He grabs the man by his collar and blocks the way so he has to stand on tiptoes to face him down, like a cock on its spurs.

"So you're too bloody scared to take me on your own, eh, you queer?"

Alain lets go of his collar, pushing him back slightly. The people around them are leaving now, perhaps disappointed by the punch-up. The man gives up but remains standing in front of the two youngsters, his face white with rage, forehead shining with sweat.

"Fuck off then, you little poofters! You won't have to worry about the Algerians cutting *your* balls off!"

Daniel takes another step forward, but Alain drags him towards the exit. "Come on," he says. "Just ignore those twats."

Their friends are waiting for them on the pavement, under the awning, although even here the cold drizzle reaches them, blown there by the wind. Irène and Sara, whispering to each other a little further off, and big Gilbert, who comes towards them.

"So? What're you up to?"

His black moustache smiles, his eyes growing round under his mass of hair. Too tall and wide for his tight raincoat, his long legs poking out from his ill-fitting trousers. A thick blue scarf wrapped around his ears. He always says he doesn't give a toss if he's badly dressed when girls politely mention it to him. You could make an effort, they tell him. You're a handsome bloke. Look at you. Like a bloody scarecrow. And he smiles, red-faced, clowning around because he's the centre of attention, all these girls crowding around him, pulling at the sleeves of his jacket or his turtleneck sweater. They all know he's skint though, with his half-mad mother and his three sisters to feed, even working overtime every day as a docker, and they know that his clothes are hand-me-downs from an uncle who's not rich either but is a lot shorter and punier than Gilbert. It's actually because of this unshakable poverty that he's been spared Algeria. Family to support. He has broad shoulders and strong arms, but sometimes his burden gets too heavy and they can tell it's hard for him.

Alain tells the story. Sara wants to go and explain things to the old lady, and she looks through the crowd to try and find her. She shakes her head and mutters to herself. Daniel shrugs.

"Shall we go?"

They start to walk, pressed close together, their shoulders bumping occasionally. Sara insinuates herself between Gilbert and Alain and hangs on to their arms, her legs suspended above the ground, betting them they can't carry her all the way home like that, while Daniel and Irène walk just behind them, not saying a word.

43

"Can you believe it? Having a go at Daniel about that! If there's anyone who actually wants to go to Algeria, it's him! We should have beaten the shit out of that wanker!"

Daniel walks over and stands in front of him.

"What did you say?"

"Nothing," says Irène, taking his arm. "He didn't say anything. And you – why don't you give it a rest, eh? You really think this is the time?"

"I didn't say I wanted to go, I just said I was going. That it doesn't really bother me. At least I'll get to see what it is."

"We already know that," says Sara. "It's an imperialist war. You think they're going to let Algeria go, after what happened in Indochina?"

"Your father was in a war, wasn't he? You talk about it all the time!"

"Careful what you say about my father, Daniel. Yes, he went to war to fight the fascists. Yes, he died and I'm proud of that even if I'm sad that I never got to know him, that I don't even remember his face. And Maurice and Roselyne fought the war too, in their own way, I have no problem with that. But Algeria . . . who are you fighting against?"

They have stopped in the middle of the street, gathered in a circle, and their breath and the words that they speak look like smoke in the cold air as if they were pouring in a blaze from their mouths. The street has gradually emptied. People pass them by, grumbling because they're in the way.

"Yourself, that's who you'll be fighting against," says Irène in an undertone, as if talking to herself.

Daniel seeks out her eyes in the shadows of her face.

"Why do you say that?"

"You know."

"Stop trying to sound clever, with all your philosophy. Just cos you passed your exams."

"She's right," Sara says. "Men often go to war to find them-selves, to discover their limits. You see that in plenty of films – you should know, you love them so much. But this war you want to see is a real one. Errol Flynn won't be there, just a bunch of morons and shit. What did they see in Palestro[1], huh? Are any of them still around to tell people about their adventures?"

"So? What do you think I should do then, you and your big mouth? You think I should desert? Or jump on a boat like Alain wants to do? Anyway, it's my life: I'll do what I want with it."

"Works for me," says Alain. "We'll enrol as novices on a pas-senger–cargo ship going to French West Africa and we'll get to see the world! And at least we won't have our balls cut off by bicots[2]."

"What? Shit, you can't say stuff like that," says Irène. "It's a dis-gusting way to talk."

Sara has walked ahead a few steps and now turns around.

"So we've got one who wants to go but doesn't really know why and another who's refusing to go but sounds like a stupid squaddie. I'm sick of talking with you lot."

"Alright, calm down," says Alain. "I shouldn't have said that. But everyone talks like that, so . . . You know me though! You know I'm not a racist!"

"What about you, Gilbert? Don't you have an opinion?"

Irène has turned towards the beanpole, who shrugs.

"Me? Well, I'm just going to stay here, safe and sound, while the

1 The Palestro gorge: located 50 miles south-east of Algiers; this is where a French army patrol was caught in an ambush by the resistance fighters of the Algerian A.L.N. (National Liberation Army) on 18 May, 1956. Twenty-one soldiers died in the attack, and their bodies were found horribly mutilated. The attack caused outrage in France, and the Palestro Ambush, although far from the only such attack, became the symbol of this war's cruelty, and crucially gave credence to the image of the insurgents in French public opinion as "barbarians" fighting against the "pacifying" efforts of the French Army (*c.f. L'Embuscade de Palestro* by Raphaelle Branche, Armand Colin, 2010).
2 Racist slang term for North Africans.

others go and get shot at, so . . . But I think our friends are both pretty brave, each in his own way. I don't know . . ."

They are silent for a few seconds. The rain starts falling more heavily.

"Well, I've got some new Yank records," says Alain. "We could listen to them while we have a beer. What do you think?"

Smiles all round. They rub their hands, pull their collars up and set off the other way, towards Alain's house. But Daniel does not move. He is watching them walk away when Irène turns around.

"Aren't you coming?"

"Nah. I've had enough of this crap. I'm going home to crash out."

The others call out to him. Come on, Frank Sinatra, Dean Martin, how can you say no to that?

He says goodnight and turns around, ignoring their protestations. He hears them behind him, worrying about him. What's up with him? Irène says something in reply then their voices vanish in the distance and the wind. Once he is around the street corner, all is silent again, except for the low insistent hiss of the rain in the gutters. He walks quickly, almost running, and the night protects him, deeper and darker here on this street bordered by rumbling factories that glimmer and smoke. He turns onto rue de New York, his fingers already clasping the set of keys in his pocket. Breathlessly he climbs the three steps, trembles as he searches for the lock and almost dives into the hallway, banging the door shut behind him. He stays like that in the blackness, leaning against the wall, the cold raindrops trickling down his neck, over his face.

He starts thinking about them. It comes over him sometimes. Especially his mother. She is merely a silhouette, a shadow, the timbre of a voice. A woman singing. What about him? He would come along sometimes, smiling, happy. He sniffed all the time. He can no longer remember his face. All that remains to him now is that photograph in which he can barely recognise the couple who stand hand in hand on the cours de l'Intendance in August 1936, the date marked in purple ink on the back. Here in this darkness he summons their faces, but his cinema does not respond and the screen remains dark, flickering only with a few stray images from the film. The Earp brothers and Doc Holliday walking down the street and the dust kicked up by their boots. The tormented look on Kirk Douglas' face. Guns swaying against their thighs. They are walking towards him and maybe they are going to appear at the end of the hallway, the door swinging behind them for a long time, letting in waves of sweltering Arizona sunlight. Daniel is almost panting with the effort of trying to remember his parents' faces and he can feel himself falling slowly to the bottom of a well, from where daylight, seen through the opening, will soon be no more than a quivering star. And he knows that the two of them, leaning on the rim, are staring down at him.

The kitchen door opens and Roselyne pokes out her head, wide-eyed. The pale light gives her a tired look, a grey face.

"Ah, I thought I heard the door. What are you doing in the dark?"

"Nothing. Just thinking."

"Irène isn't with you?"

"No, they went to drink coffee and listen to records at Alain's place."

She nods, smiling vaguely. She pulls the woollen shawl more tightly around her neck, then takes a handkerchief from the pocket of her dressing gown and rubs his hair with it.

"Look at you. You're all wet. Was the film good?"

"Yeah, it was good. A Western."

"Ugh, I hate those!"

He holds her shoulders and kisses her on the forehead.

"I know . . . What about you? Why are you still up?"

"Couldn't sleep, so I made myself a herbal tea. Maurice fell asleep on his book and started snoring. Do you want anything?"

Daniel does not reply. He holds his hands over the stove. Drops of water fall from his hair and crackle on the burning steel. He becomes more peaceful as the well disappears from his mind and he finds the open air again.

"I'm going to heat up some coffee."

He pours a few drops into the saucepan then takes a cup and some sugar from the sideboard while it warms up. When he sits down, Roselyne stares at him.

"What were you thinking about, all alone in the dark?"

He stirs the sugar into his coffee, fully absorbed by what he's doing so he doesn't have to look at her. The clink of the spoon against the cup. Occasional murmurs of wind in the chimney.

"You don't want to tell me?"

"What am I supposed to say? It's always the same thing. When it comes over me, there's nothing else I can think about."

She tries to take his hand, sliding hers onto the oilcloth, but he gently shrinks away.

"Have you talked to your sister about it?"

He shakes his head.

Silence falls between them. They sip their too-hot drinks. Roselyne watches Daniel, a mocking smile in her eyes. He does not look at anything. Maybe the sideboard, standing in front of him, and the frosted glass doors, their panes decorated with floral swirls. He feels either sad or bitter, he's not sure which.

"Anyway, she's not really my sister."

"She's just like your sister. We raised you together. She was only two when you arrived."

Roselyne suddenly stops talking, and a smile spreads across her face.

"That is one of my happiest memories, you know: seeing the two of you there with me. Your parents had been arrested but, back then, we didn't know where they were being taken, although there were rumours, of course. Germany, Poland . . . People talked about prison camps, but everyone thought they were like the P.O.W. camps where soldiers were kept. But anyway, we had to face up to the truth.

It was hard; we forgot what normal life was like. Irène called you Dada straight away, remember? That went on for years. She used to follow you around all the time to start with; she didn't understand why you couldn't go out like her. Once, I remember, we were in the butcher's – this was in January '44 – and she started yapping away about Dada. That butcher was a nasty piece of work: he used to sell meat on the black market to the Krauts. I didn't know how to stop her talking. She was going on about how she talked with Dada all the time, how she played cards and Ludo with him because he got bored in his room that he could never leave, how he spent too long in the toilets . . . just a whole load of stuff, and I could imagine her spilling the beans completely at any moment and I had no idea how to stop her. And that bastard started questioning her, casually, you know, like 'And what's he like, this Dada? Is he nice? Why doesn't he go out? Is he ill? What sort of stories does he tell? What's his real name?' He knew there must be something fishy going on and he wanted to figure out what it was, like a dog sniffing around a bush. She was only three or four at the time, and you remember what a chatterbox she was – she used to drive us all crazy! And then suddenly she stopped talking and she looked at that bastard and giggled and she said: 'He's silly, that man, he's getting it all mixed up. A teddy bear can't go out in the street or he'll get wet, and he can't tell stories, I just said that so he would sleep in my bed. Dada is for Danilou. That's what they call him in the forest.' You should have seen the bloke's face, and him holding a packet of meat in the air. All the people in the queue were laughing at this little girl and the way she talked, addressing everyone in the shop, her eyes wide as saucers. As a recompense, he gave us an extra fifty grams of beef trimmings. When we got out of the shop she held my hand and said, 'Did you see how I got out of that? It was good, wasn't it? He wanted me to tell him about Daniel, did you see?' She'd understood completely. War makes children grow up faster but it doesn't neces-sarily make them more intelligent; otherwise human beings would all be geniuses. But that kid: she knew exactly how much danger you were in, she knew that there were bastards all over the place with big open smiles like gas chambers. She never asked many questions about the Germans, or what was happening in the news, but she listened to everything, and observed, she watched us talking with Maurice at the dinner table with that serious look on her face and sometimes I'd catch her looking at me with those huge eyes as if she wanted to swallow me whole. I was so afraid for those eyes and I wondered what world they would see later. Anyway . . . She started hopping about on the pavement again and I was worried like always that she'd trip over a cobblestone, but I felt happier then than I'd felt in a long time."

"I used to listen to you too. I stayed in my little room but I heard everything. And I used to listen out for any noises on the stairs. I thought they'd come back and we'd all go home and life would go on like before. Or I'd look through the window. I used to stand on a chair and pull back the curtain to see as far as I could. And sometimes my heart would leap because I thought I'd seen Mum crossing the street. I wonder if Irène understood the situation better than I did. She knew they weren't coming back, that it was all over. That was why she used to hug me sometimes without saying anything and I'd let her even though it annoyed me."

Daniel lights a cigarette and gets up to fetch a clean ashtray from the sink.

"Camels, huh? Let me have one."

"Do you smoke? Alain got them from a bloke on the docks."

She lights her cigarette and closes her eyes as she takes a drag.

"It's going to make my head spin, but it's really nice!"

They smoke in silence, smiling occasionally, each in their own thoughts. Daniel feels good here, with this woman who raised him and who has blown away the dark night that was closing around him like a toxic cloud. This is his home, these people his family. With eighteen-year-old Irène and her green eyes that sometimes don't dare meet his, that turn away and hide themselves the way a woman might cover up a suddenly bared shoulder.

"I miss them too, you know, even after all this time. Your mother was like a sister to me. See, we can't get away from the subject of brothers and sisters, can we? Anyway, I sometimes imagine that she's going to come home too, that she's standing outside the door at that very moment, so I wait a few minutes to see what happens. It's a strange sensation: it seems so definite, I'm sure that she's going to walk in. There's a knock at the door and I open it and there she is, smiling at me but looking so terribly tired after all they put her through, after all she must have seen . . . So we fall into each other's arms and we start crying and laughing at the same time and then we talk for hours . . . How many times have I stopped what I was doing in the hope that my daydream was about to come true!"

"What about my father?"

"We've already talked about this . . . When he was there, with the two of you, he was an extraordinary man. Always so cheerful, and gentle. He'd come back with presents, toys, sometimes money. And Olga, your mother, would welcome him back the way people greet a cat who's spent three days outside in the rain and who's been fighting with other toms. She would dote on him and he'd promise that he wasn't going to do it again, that he was going to stay with you at home, that all his stupid behaviour was a thing of the past. For a long time she believed what he told her. I think she wanted to believe him. She must have liked the lies somehow. Maybe she loved men who were like tomcats, I don't know . . . She suspected there were other women, of course, beautiful women, unclean women . . . Maurice and me, we knew what was going on, but we never dared talk to her about it. But we should have done, me especially . . . Then again, would it really have changed anything? Anyway, one day, in place Pey-Berland, she saw him in the arms of another girl, saw him kiss her and laugh with her. I remember the day she came here in tears, with you in your pushchair, just a baby."

Roselyne suddenly stops talking and looks up at Daniel, as if surprised to see him there, across the table, as if just emerging from a daydream.

"Why am I telling you all this? You know it already."

Daniel had let his cigarette burn down to his fingers while he was listening, and the burn of it on his skin wakes him from the trance in which he was floating. He stubs out the butt in the ashtray and the smoke drifts away like the transparent images that came to his mind before, leaving only the smell of tobacco, already overpowering. He seeks out the woman's hand and she moves it towards his and they touch their fingertips together without looking at each other, without speaking.

"It helps me," he says quietly. "Like this, they still exist a little bit."

Roselyne smiles sadly at him.

"We should go to bed, don't you think?" she asks.

They overcome their tiredness at the same time, pushing themselves up from the table. Roselyne goes into the hallway before Daniel, then turns around and strokes his cheek.

"Sleep well."

"Goodnight."

He hears the door creak softly behind him and Maurice's muffled snoring. Then he switches off the light before entering his room. The window looks out over the little garden where a faint light, falling from the low sky and worn away by the wind, attaches itself to the pane along with the rain. He takes off his damp jacket and his shoes and lies on the bed in his clothes. His mind is a confused place, full of strange entanglements. Brambles, ivy, suffocating flowers. He stares up at the invisible ceiling and that is, perhaps, how he falls asleep, listening to the distant sound of a badly closed shutter rattling somewhere in the winter night.

5

The young girl nods at the surly-faced woman who watches over the pupils as they exit the school, dressed in navy-blue skirts and white socks, all wrapped up in dark coats. She moves away from the stern-looking herd that is slowly dispersing along the high walls, behind which ring chapel bells, then almost immediately crosses the boulevard to the bus shelter. The large satchel she wears over her shoulder bangs against her hip as she walks, forcing her to twist her body and limp slightly. She drops it on the ground as soon as she arrives beneath the sign and pulls her fawn leather gloves more tightly over her fingertips. She stares out through the noisy crowds of cars and trucks, then glances at the time on the little gold watch that she wears on her wrist.

The man is about two metres away, casually watching her. His eyes shine darkly as they linger on the young blonde girl's delicate face and green eyes, then turn away as soon as she looks up at the traffic, the houses, the leaden sky, with a calm, virtuous expression. He too, from time to time, scans the horizon to check whether the bus is arriving, then turns his gaze back to her. He keeps his hands in the pockets of his long and rather worn charcoal-grey coat, his collar turned up, and stamps his feet to keep away the cold and hunches his shoulders as he blows into the scarf he wears wrapped around the lower half of his face.

When the bus arrives, the young girl gets on first and he lets the other two people waiting in line go before him too, a birdlike woman carrying a shopping basket and a bearded old man in a sailor's cap. On the bus, he leans against a steel pole, one hand hanging on to a leather strap, and watches the girl out of the corner of his eye as she sits next to a sleeping man. Two weeks ago she gave him the slip by getting off three stops early and he had to run until he was out of breath to glimpse her entering a house on rue Georges-Mandel. She was meeting a boy called Philippe who studies law in place Pey-Berland. It had taken him two telephone calls to ascertain that. He doesn't know if the information will prove useful, but its possession makes him feel stronger, more secure.

Today, she gets off as expected by the local sports ground and crosses the boulevard towards rue d'Ornano. He follows her on the opposite pavement. She never turns around, walking quickly, one hand gripping tightly to the strap of her bulky schoolbag. She turns into rue de Madrid, so he quickly crosses the road but lets her get further ahead as he knows where she's going. As soon as she's disappeared around the corner of the street, he breaks into a run and sees her rummaging in her bag outside her front door. He walks up to her and she turns to face him, holding up a steel key, then emits a feeble scream when he grabs her throat with one hand and squeezes her larynx between his fingers just enough to make her choke and her face turn purple. He is still holding her when she slips down onto the doorstep, arms flapping, eyes bulging, mouth full of slobber and a tearful groan. He bangs her head against the door and tears her satchel off her and opens it and throws it into the middle of the road, where textbooks and exercise books go flying, pages whipped by the wind.

Behind him a window is flung open and a woman starts screaming, "Help! Stop him!" but he doesn't run away. He leans over the suffocating girl, keeping hold of her throat, and grabs her by the coat collar.

"Tell your father, little girl. Tell him I've returned and I'll return again."

Then he strides quickly back the way he came, hands in his pockets, while a door is opened and someone screams. Women's voices talk about calling the police, quick, does anyone have a telephone?

54

On the boulevard, he takes another bus, packed, overheated, the windows covered with condensation, where the passengers are crammed together, elbow to elbow, almost standing on another man's feet, his mouth with its rotten teeth next to a snotty nose, an arm against a cheek, and sometimes eyes staring into yours, people who would kill you if they could just to free up a bit of space. The dark mass of humans rammed inside this bus sways and leans in time with the vehicle's braking and accelerations and he feels the weight against him of bodies hanging from straps like slabs of meat and suddenly he is suffocating, and mouth open he tries to gulp down air but his panic-crushed chest remains empty and his throat is tightening, so he has to force a way through, slide between two shoulders, dig an elbow in the ribs of some twat who's staring at him not getting out of the way or moving at all and he gasps, "Let me past, please, let me out!" and he stretches out like a gymnast on the parallel bars or a diver, above the steps that lead down to the accordion doors marked EXIT, and as soon as they open he jumps outside and staggers over to a wall where he leans, catching his breath, coughing out a few sobs that shudder through his body. Then he walks for about twenty minutes through empty streets, walking quickly, running almost, like a fugitive desperately trying to distance himself from whoever is pursuing him, and all the demons and ghosts that hang on his coat-tails.

He lives in a little apartment on rue Lafontaine, not far from the Marché des Capucins, in a quarter where, for many, Spanish is the language of defeat and exile alike. An entrance hall, a small kitchen lit by a fanlight overlooking a narrow courtyard, and a bedroom. Minimal furniture. A table, two chairs, a sideboard left by the previous tenant, a shelf filled with books. A bed, bought new, is his only luxury. The sheets smell clean, washed every week for 200 francs by a neighbour. He sniffs them every night when he goes to bed, every night he fills his nostrils with this odour of soap and lavender. Then sleep comes quickly and he can abandon himself to it without fear.

It's the best moment of the day, that slow dive, cheek pressed against cool cloth. The nights belong to him now. He knows that the nightmares will wake him in sweat and tears; he knows that he will scream, thinking that he can feel the icy presence of a corpse next to him, and that he'll have to turn on the bedside lamp to check that he's alone in his scented sheets; he knows that this will probably never end, but this moment, this solitude, this exquisite pleasure as sleep takes him in its soft warm embrace . . . how he savours these things, grunting like a happy animal.

He puts a few lumps of coal in the stove, stirs things up with a poker, then goes to sit down on a chair without unbuttoning his coat. There, he gets his breath back, looking around unseeingly, his mind filled with the girl's terrified eyes and the way he felt as he squeezed her throat between his fingers. All-powerful and cowardly. How easy it was, how weak she was, knocked backwards in her panic, utterly defenceless. In that moment all he thought about was her father going home that evening and hearing the kid tell him what happened between sobs. Of the fury that would possess him but also the fear that would start to gnaw at him secretly, questioningly. It was only just beginning.

He could have killed her. Left her dead on the doorstep. He thinks about that now. A few extra seconds, a bit more pressure on her windpipe. He'd seen a kapo do that one night. A Ukrainian insomniac who couldn't even knock himself out with alcohol and who used to roam the latrines at night, killing any prisoners he found with his bare hands and then boasting about it the next morning, explaining that it calmed him down and that he could sleep afterwards. He had seen him throw a man to the ground, leaning over him and holding his neck between the fingers of one hand, apparently without effort, until the man's groaning stopped. He had waited, slumped against a wall, bent double over the mess of his intestines, until the criminal walked away and then he had gone inside to empty his bowels, swallowing a wail of pain and fear. The next day . . .

The images assail him with the brutality of a decisive attack. Pushing them back, he gets up and stamps his feet to shake off the cold that is numbing him so he can dive back into the icy darkness of the nights in that place, into their murmur of groans, coughs and screams, those nights, both endless, as he would wait until it was time to get up again to be sure he was still alive, and so short, because sleep seemed only to steal a little more of his strength and to leave him stricken, fleeing like a silent thief.

He lifts his coat collar, walks up to the stove and holds his hands over the cast iron hotplates, listening to the metal clicking as it expands. He thinks he can't do this anymore, that he'll never make it, that he'd be better off dying, now, once and for all. Then he goes over to the sink and spits out the vile taste that has started flowing in his throat.

6

Commissaire Albert Darlac holds her hand and the young girl sighs wearily as she repeats for the fourth time that she's fine, that she was scared, that she was attacked by a mad old man who will not come back. She is lying on the green velvet sofa, in her socks, a big red cushion under her head.

Elise. Fifteen years old. He is not sure he loves anyone else in this world. When he looks at her, when he touches her, he knows that not everything inside him is dead, he knows he is not just a collection of organs stewing in bitter juices, moved only by the desire to dominate and corrupt.

He in turn tries to smile but it is a grimace of pain and fury that reveals his straight teeth lined up like a cartridge belt. Some rabid dogs smile that way. He turns to the doctor, who is putting the stethoscope back in his briefcase.

"She's fine. Not even a bruise. I'm going to prescribe her something to help her sleep tonight, and tomorrow it will all be over. I'm not worried."

Darlac gets to his feet and sighs, stroking his daughter's chin, then moves over to where the doctor stands.

"I'm not worried either. Because I'll get the bloke who did this very soon, and as for bruises, he'll have them for quite a while cos I'm going to give him a new face. Even his fucking mother won't recognise him in the morgue."

He says all this in a low rumble. The doctor bursts out laughing.

"There you go with your fancy words. You'll never change."

"I should bloody well hope not."

A woman appears, quite tall, slim, blonde with dark, lively eyes, dressed in a houndstooth suit. Pretty face. Annette. The wife of

Commissaire Darlac. She is carrying a silver tray. Cups, coffeepot, porcelain sugar bowl. She places this on the dining-room table. The doctor ogles her quite openly and she gives him a movie-star wink: batted eyelid, discreet pout. Then she sashays towards the entrance hall and announces that coffee is served. Two voices reply to her and almost immediately afterwards two detectives enter the living room.

"So?" Darlac asks.

The two men approach the table, rubbing their hands. They look similar: same dark hair, same grey coat. As if they came out of the same cop-making mould. One of them wears tortoiseshell glasses, which he is constantly nudging up his nose. He is the one who replies to the commissaire.

"Apart from the woman who lives across the road, no-one heard or saw anything before she started screaming. We've got a pretty precise description that matches the one your daughter gave us. A man of about forty-five, very short grey hair, with marks – maybe scars – on his face. Quite tall, pretty quick and agile. He went towards rue d'Ornano afterwards, and he wasn't running. Nothing else."

They thank Madame Darlac, who has served them coffee, and awkwardly hold the cups by their fine handles as if they might explode between their fingers at any moment. They lift their drinks, pinkies in the air, and sip noisily, burning their lips and tongues, and their eyes go from Darlac's daughter to his wife, probably trying to make out a resemblance.

"Your coffee is very good, madame."

Madame smiles, sitting next to her daughter and rubbing her feet.

Silence, for a moment. Darlac stands in front of the French window, smoking and loudly sighing, knocking the ash from his cigarette onto the floor. The others contemplate his wide back, his shoulders squared off by the cut of his jacket.

"It's going to snow," ventures the chief's wife.

He shrugs.

"If that's all you have to say, you can take the cups back to the kitchen. Your coffee is wop juice. Disgusting."

The two detectives and the doctor eye the bottoms of their cups as if trying to discern traces of poison. Madame clears away the cups, gathers up the little spoons and lifts the tray in a sure, silent movement, not even the faintest tinkling, when they were all expecting to see her trembling under the blow of her husband's insult, his contempt. She crosses the room, staring straight ahead, an indecipherable half-smile playing on her face, her gait as supple as a ballerina's. A strange beauty, wounded perhaps, or frighteningly tough. The three men who watch her go past can no longer breathe in this rarefied atmosphere.

Darlac turns swiftly, stubbing out his cigarette in a plant pot.

"Alright, men, while we wait for it to snow, we're going to get our arses in gear."

He gestures with his chin at the kitchen door.

"If you want a souvenir, I have photos. You ought to like these. Backstage shots of the Revue Tichadel.[3] Signed by the artist, no less."

The two coppers lower their eyes and smile stupidly.

"Ask Dr Chauvet. He gets to examine her. What do you think, doc? Nice photos?"

"Very suggestive," says the doctor, with a bawdy wink. "Tichadel was better backstage than onstage!"

Darlac is already wearing his coat and clicks his fingers to make his men follow suit. He turns towards the doctor, who has sat down to write out a prescription, and points to his daughter dozing on the sofa.

"Get her back on her feet. Anyone who lays a finger on her is dead, so make sure you take good care of her."

3 Music-hall show with powerful singers and half-naked female dancers that was staged in Bordeaux, at the Alhambra Theatre, during the New Year holidays.

His voice is hollow, not much more than a croak. Chauvet nods, glancing at the girl.

"She doesn't need taking care of, just protecting, but she's got you for that. You know you've always been able to trust me, don't you?"

Darlac's face contorts as he puts on his hat.

"Of course," he says, then goes out to join his men in the car parked on the pavement and the slammed door shakes on its hinges behind him.

As soon as the engine is running, he gives his orders, doing his best to lean back in his seat and relax. Go and check out the lunatic asylums in case some psycho's escaped or been set free, go through the file of paedophiles and rapists living in or near the city. He doesn't buy this theory of a maniac or nutter who happened to do this in front of his – Commissaire Albert Darlac's – front door. Of course not. And neither do the two detectives, who keep their mouths shut because no-one discusses anything with Darlac, because there's no point even trying with someone as brutal, as stubborn, as plain nasty as him. And also because they don't give a shit. They nod in agreement, exchanging little glances that the commissaire doesn't see, too busy writing things in his notebook or scanning the streets with a menacing look as if the attacker might suddenly appear on a street corner.

As soon as they get out of the car, the two cops lift their hats and slip quickly away, explaining that they have work to do.

"That's right, you twats," he mutters. "Go to work with your arses safely planted in your chairs."

As he enters his office, the telephone starts ringing.

"Commissaire Divisionnaire Laborde. I have to see you. Straight away."

It's a bad line, crackling. The voice metallic. Like a dog barking in a cistern.

Darlac slams the phone down, swearing loudly and removing

his coat from his back as if it was an enemy.

Commissaire Divisionnaire Laborde. The name whirls inside his head and his heart pounds with rage, anger and disgust. He lights a cigarette and opens the window to let in the cold, the damp, anything that might cool down the fevered hatred that has taken hold of him. He exhales and balls his fists as he looks out at the grey sky, the gloomy courtyard, the grimy façade on the other side of rue Abbé-de-l'Epée. The city is filthy, soiled by the sooty winter drizzle, turned cancerous by the humid summer heat. It stinks of diesel oil, saltpetre in airless stone cellars, the putrid mud of the brown river, the fish and vegetables displayed on market stalls. He has the impression that all these smells have come and mingled together in the police-station courtyard and are blowing into his face all the rottenness that has submerged the city and the country since the end of the war, this fetid breath carried by all these mouths that have been allowed to open.

He stubs out his cigarette in an already overflowing Cinzano ashtray and spits in the bin and bangs shut the window in a racket of loose panes.

The commissaire divisionnaire is on the phone and signals him to sit down, but Darlac prefers to remain standing, if only to avoid obeying this son of a bitch. He stands in front of a corkboard pinned with office memoranda. Just above it is a large photograph of De Gaulle in Bordeaux, in September '44. The big man, come to bring his Commie partners into line, is standing in front of a microphone, surrounded by Resistance leaders but also by a few collaborationists already in new jobs whom the purge will pass over, later, like a very small cloud, barely even a shadow: real shits these, fake Resistance fighters, cops, civil servants, military leaders who organised the round-ups, countersigned the arrest requests, carried out vicious tortures, anticipated and exceeded Kraut orders, but who sensed the tide turning in '43 and invented acts of bravery for themselves, fabricated alibis, saved a few Jews and kept evidence of this heroism so that when the moment came, when the juries gathered and the firing squads lined up, the wimps and weaklings would come and testify in their favour. They were there – not all of them, of course – watching the crowds behind the Dickhead of State, wondering perhaps which of their victims would remember them, and maybe already regretting that there were still survivors of all the massacres who could tell the tale and point their fingers at the executioners.

Darlac remembers how, in that emotional, joyful crowd, there were men walking round wild-eyed, hands in pockets probably gripping the butt of a gun, F.T.P.s[4] champing at the bit, others with gaunt and closed faces, survivors of clandestine networks betrayed then dismantled, dumbstruck by the sight of these scum all bragging on the podium. They had sent a few detectives out to spy on those bitter men and forestall any acts of temper or desperation, because in the streets bedecked with bunting and flags, in those days of jubilation, there roamed singular sorrows, solitary griefs that no-one took the time to see.

Behind him, Commissaire Divisionnaire Laborde speaks quietly then goes silent then taps on his desk with a pencil before starting to speak again, and Darlac becomes absorbed in his examination of the photograph and its parading bigwigs and he feels once again all the contempt in his heart for the rabble mooing the "Marseillaise", swept up by those patriotic urges and those vague desires for vengeance when they had spent four years grovelling under the boot in pain and hunger and denunciation. You can do whatever you want with people. All it takes is for them to be hungry or scared and to have something to hate, because hating gives them the illusion of existing. Yesterday it was the Jews. Today it's the Arabs. Algeria is remoulding the French people around a common enemy defined by a murderous vocabulary all its own: the *frisé*; the *bronzé*, the *bicot*,

4 Francs-tireurs et Partisans was the name of the French internal Resistance movement founded in 1941 by the leaders of the French Communist Party.

the *crouille*, the *raton*. Sneaky shits, sure, but poor, weak, alone. Not like those tough, well-armed Kraut soldiers who inspired such fear and respect. Bastards, yes, but at least they were upfront about it. You could see them coming a mile off. The French don't like powerful adversaries: their instinct is always to make peace with them, thinking that they're being really clever.

That is why Darlac never understood the Resistance. Perhaps because he never saw what they were supposed to be resisting. He was bored and disgusted by politics. Marquet, the mayor, a former radical, who became a Petainist and collaborator; the communists, who signed a pact with Hitler then called the people to sabotage, setting off bombs and derailing trains. He couldn't stand people who lived their lives according to ideas. Puritan patriots. Passionate nutcases. Lunatics. Oh, they have spirit, of course. And balls. Even the women. He hesitated, for two or three months. He felt the same courage as them, without really knowing what use it was. Love of nation? Honour? Liberty? No. Maybe the adventure of it would have amused him, the secret. Like in those films with Jean Gabin. Evening, in the mist, a fugitive's destiny, taking in his arms a woman with the most beautiful eyes in the world.

But on the other side were money, power, sex and comfort. And anyway the Germans seemed invincible and their helmeted order covered up the chaos, like the dense canopy of giant trees, where the great birds live, stretching over the primitive jungle. Afterwards they lit up the forest, but he realised that it was down there on the ground, in the seething mire, that he felt at his ease. He collected what fell from the branches above or what was created by decomposition. He didn't climb in the trees. He didn't play the wise monkey or the screeching, colourful parrot. He knew his place in the vast hierarchy of the world and he knew to what profit he could put it. That knowledge was the only kind that mattered to him.

"Great moment, wasn't it?"

A faint shudder. Darlac turns around. The chief super is sitting back in his chair, legs crossed. He watches with his very hard, very pale blue eyes as Darlac sits down. Even in the shade, beyond the halo of light emitted by the lamp, those eyes have a gleam of their own.

"I was there. We all were, or almost. You wanted to speak to me?"

"How is the Crabos?"

"Why are you asking me about him?"

"To find out what's happening."

"Apparently he buggered off to Spain. Good riddance. He won't be around to piss us off anymore."

"He wasn't really up to much though, was he? A few girls, his bar on rue de Bègles . . . And seriously ill, from what I've heard. Cancer again."

"He'll die in the sun. It's better than in the shade. He was smuggling in a bit of heroin and opium, but anyway . . ."

The chief smiles.

"I don't give a shit about drugs. We need to have a proper talk, Commissaire Darlac. Alright? We know each other and we're not going to hide anything from each other. Understood?"

Darlac sighs. Nods. Shifts around in his chair to make sure it's solid, because he knows it's in for a good shaking. Turbulence. An air pocket. Just wind, when it comes down to it. This idea forces him to suppress a smile. Still, it's not going to be fun.

"What were you doing on rue du Pont de la Mousque on Monday night?"

"My job. I was looking for the Crabos, in fact."

"Did you find him?"

"Yes."

"So why didn't you tell me that when I asked you about him, just now?"

"What was the point? He's gone to Spain, as I told you. The matter's been dealt with. The bloke's half dead anyway – who cares what happens to him?"

65

"So why go looking for him? And also, four days ago he was still in Bordeaux, wasn't he? It's not like he went off to eat paella two years ago, is it?"

"You know perfectly well why I wanted to see him. For the same reasons as you. Because he might have been able to give me information about Penot's death. And because we found one of his men at the submarine base the day before yesterday. Three bullets. Sloppy work. There's been a lot of that recently."

Laborde sighs. He picks up his pencil and starts rapping it against the edge of the table again. He thinks, is about to say something, shakes his head, then looks Darlac in the eyes and starts to speak:

"We'd agreed that we didn't give a shit about Penot. That piece of shit. One of Poinsot's[5] henchmen. No-one knows why he wasn't executed after the Liberation like his boss."

"We're sure he was involved in that robbery in Bayonne last year. He was working for Destang, and consequently against Crabos, who went round telling everyone that he was going to kill him. So we had to give a shit, as you put it."

"Crabos' brother was a communist. He was tortured by Poinsot and Penot, then sent to the camps. He died out there. Everyone knows that. We're not going to go out of our way to catch someone who nailed a former torturer, are we? Unless . . ."

Darlac waits for the next words, rigid in his chair. The chief

5 Pierre Napoléon Poinsot: commissaire divisionnaire, head of the S.A.P. (Political Affairs Section) in Bordeaux until January 1944, at which date he was appointed to run a subdirectorate of the French police's intelligence services in Vichy. A notably zealous and efficient auxiliary to the Gestapo. When the German army retreated, he took refuge in Constance. Arrested during an attempt to flee into Switzerland, he was put on trial by a special court in Riom and executed on 1 July 1945. His department, in the offices of the Gironde prefecture, specialised in tracking down Resistance members, particularly communists, whom he hated, and it systematically used torture in interrogations. It is estimated that close to a thousand people were shot or deported on his orders.

stares at him, hard, elbows on his desk. He waits too, and his blue eyes darken to steely grey. In the background, there is the sound of a typewriter, the keys rattling in short bursts, and a telephone ringing unanswered. These familiar noises vibrate the air between the two cops, slowly boring into each of them like a form of Chinese torture.

Laborde is silent, his eyes trained on Darlac, a half-smile on his lips. Then, pressing his hands flat on the desk, he says in a hollow voice:

"Anyway, I don't want to see your fat arse near rue Saint-Rémi anymore. Particularly if you're harassing people who are useful to us."

"Ah, right, the hotel boss . . . I thought she was a bit high and mighty, that bitch."

Silence. The chief opens a drawer and pretends to rummage around inside it. Darlac shifts in his chair.

"Is that all?"

"Why? You want to request a transfer to Oran? You've got it."

Darlac takes this in silence. He stands up. Behind him, he hears the chief's hollow, almost muffled voice:

"Watch yourself . . . And your men. The war is over. The Liberation – you've heard of that, I suppose? So change your methods, or don't get caught."

They try to outstare each other. Neither backs down. Finally, Laborde shrugs and silently laughs.

"Get out of here. And keep being careful."

The commissaire divisionnaire immediately starts reading a file, with a little wave of the hand to dismiss Darlac.

In the corridor, Albert Darlac realises that he is soaked in sweat, his breathing ragged. He runs downstairs to his office. There, he opens the window again and takes two or three deep breaths, arms outstretched and fists balled. Then, from a drawer, he takes a leather shoulder harness weighed down by a large black pistol, which he removes from its holster. The steel ridges are smooth with use. A Colt 1911, a gift from an officer in '45. He takes off his jacket, puts on the harness and slips the gun under his left arm.

Then he stares at himself in the frame of the open window. His reflection in the glass is dark, thick, faceless.

When he leaves the car park, the night is already there, grey, soaked with water, scattered with vague glimmers. The rain seems to extinguish this drab city, while elsewhere it lights up the streets with splashes of colour and makes the wide avenues gleam. Murky figures roam the pavements. He shivers in the front seat of his 403, hands tensed on the wheel. Wondering if he has a fever, he lights a cigarette, but its harsh taste instantly makes him feel sick and he tosses it through the open window. He drives like that, with the windows rolled down, through the confusion of narrow streets packed with cars and trucks and bicycles veering close to his wheels. Ghosts, hunchbacked and screeching. They scream insults at him and he barks back abuse and threats.

He parks near a little bar cum wine cellar on place Nansouty, then he walks, bent under the wind, and the cold seeps in through his coat. Inside the little bistro, narrow, low-ceilinged, full of barrels and shelves packed with bottles, it smells of wine and cork. At the back, next to a glass door marked "PRIVATE", a couple sits at a table, two glasses of red between them. The man and the woman are sitting up straight in their chairs, almost stiffly, smoking and looking at each other, not saying a word. It is impossible to guess their ages. Emile Couchot, the landlord, pours wine from a barrel into bottles that he puts into a crate. He nods at Darlac then goes back to what he's doing, one hand on the tap. The cheap wine foams inside the bottle. The man rams in the cork, banging it down with the palm of his hand.

"'Ere you go," he says to the couple when the sixth and final bottle has been filled. "You'll 'ave a ball with this. I'll put it on the tab."

He walks up to Darlac, wiping his hands on a tea towel.

"You 'ere for the kid?"

Darlac nods.

Couchot goes behind the counter. Two men enter and say good evening to no-one in particular. They sit down and order a Monbazillac. One of them puts a toolbox down next to him and it makes a metallic noise.

"Trains still going the right way, lads?" the landlord asks them.

"Yeah, you'd think they were on rails," one of the men replies.

They all laugh. Emile pours the golden wine into two glasses, fills a bowl with peanuts from a machine, and takes all of this over to the railway workers.

"Missus not here?"

"She's making soup."

"Didn't spit in it, did she?"

"Nah, that's only for the special clients."

They laugh again. The man and the woman at the back of the room turn their way and smile as they watch them with an expression halfway between envy and weariness. Same puffy skin, same red watery eyes. A pair of corpses. Their frayed, skimpy clothes are the same colour as the wall they're leaning against: grey, brown. But you can't camouflage poverty.

Darlac turns his back on all this and looks behind the bar at the lines of bottles and the barrels with their *appellations contrôlées* marked in chalk. He wishes all these losers would just leave. The couple of derelicts. The pair of union workers. The pistol weighs heavy under his armpit and he thinks that he could kill them all now and they'd have no idea what was happening to them and what he saw in their eyes would be the ultimate expression of their deep stupidity, that ignorant contentment with little that holds up their pathetic existences.

Couchot comes back behind the counter and asks him what he's drinking.

"Nothing. I have to see the girl."

"I wanted to talk to you about that actually. But you should drink something first. I got a Saint-Emilion, look . . ."

He takes a bottle from under the counter and uncorks it. The wine flows into a glass with a gargling noise.

Darlac sniffs it, takes a mouthful and swishes it around his mouth, then slowly swallows it. Emile watches for his reaction, leaning close, the bottle still in his hand.

"Not bad. What did you want to tell me about the girl? Is there a problem?"

"No, no, it's just that . . . Well, basically, she tried to run off yesterday, and it was a pain in the arse stopping her, and then afterwards she went a bit mad and I 'ad to calm her down with a couple of slaps, the bitch. We put 'er in a room upstairs, but she 'as to go outside to use the bathroom, and, you know, we 'ave to be careful. So it's not easy, is what I'm saying. Not easy at all."

Darlac says nothing. He inhales the bouquet of his wine, observes it in the gleam of a lamp.

"You see what I'm getting at?" Couchot asks. "I mean, it's a big responsibility!"

Darlac sighs. Shakes his head.

"That's why I thought of you. Cos you don't shirk your responsibilities. There are loads of other places I could have stashed her. But I came here cos I know I can count on you. It's disappointing to me to hear you talking like this. But never mind . . ."

Darlac pats him on the shoulder, trying to force a smile. The way you pat a stupid mutt after you've belted it for running away. A way of showing it who's boss, who metes out punishment and reward.

"Where's Odette?"

"Making supper. She's got the key."

Darlac pushes open the glass door. The dead-eyed woman looks up at him with her swollen face and he has the impression that he's seen her before, a long time ago, when she was younger, fresher, but decides he doesn't give a shit because this is what she's become: not much. He crosses a storeroom crammed with crates and barrels and racks, the air thick with that same odour of damp and cheap wine. Without knocking, he enters a shockingly bright kitchen where a tall woman with almost red hair turns, startled, towards him, a knife in one hand and an onion in the other. A billycan of soup is warming up in front of her.

"You scared me!"

"Where is she?"

"In the back room. The key's on the hook, there, near the door."

She turns away. He grabs the key and remains standing there, in the doorway that leads to the staircase, to watch her. Narrow black skirt, tight over her hips. Mauve sweater. A grey apron tied behind her neck and her back. He looks down at her slender legs, sheathed in stockings, the black line of the seam running up the middle. She always loved lingerie. And for a long time he loved taking it off her. But that's an old story. Everything has grown old.

"We never see you anymore," the woman says without turning round.

She wipes her eyes with the back of her hand and sniffs because of the onion.

"You can see me now, can't you? Don't tell me you miss me."

"I wouldn't tell you that. But let's just say you used to come round more often, before."

"Before what?"

"How's Annette? Still doesn't dare ask for a divorce?"

She is talking over the soup. He watches her hands moving left and right to pick up what she needs to season it.

"I'm the one who should ask for a divorce. She still doesn't know how to make coffee. And every year she loses a bit more of her charm."

"Ever the gentleman. And your daughter?"

He hesitates for a moment. Odette turns around. Her mascara is running, she looks muddled. With a snigger, she says: "I wonder what she's been up to . . ."

"Shut your mouth. Don't even mention her."

He starts up the stairs as the woman's laughter rises behind him. When he opens the bedroom door, the girl is lying on the bed, poorly lit by a bedside lamp with a wonky shade, her coat acting as a blanket. She puts a romance novel down on the bedside table and watches him approach. He grabs a chair, sits close to her and removes his overcoat.

"You recognise me?"

The girl says yes with a bat of her eyelashes.

"Arlette, isn't it? Arlette what?"

"Darriet."

He writes it in his notebook. The kid is sitting up now, leaning on an elbow. She has big black eyes and long thick lashes.

"How long have you been a whore?"

"Six months. I left home on 14 July. Not hard to remember. A friend of mine introduced me to this bloke and—"

"What bloke? Who was it?"

"I only know his first name. Robert. He took me to meet men, he said I could make a living that way. It was fine with me, anyway. Anything was better than going back to my father. I'd rather anyone fuck me than him."

"What's he like, this Robert?"

"Blond. Glasses. Tall. Two fingers missing on his left hand. He's got a Parisian accent."

He writes this down in his notebook. Who is this man? Someone new? Where did he come from?

"So how does he treat you, this Parisian bloke?"

"He puts me up in a room, behind the cours de l'Yser. Not far from his place."

"And where would that be?"

She shakes her head. She pulls her coat around her, shoulders hunched, suddenly shivery.

"Answer, or you'll go to prison. Vagrancy, prostitution. Or we'll take you back to your bastard of a father. In both cases, you won't have a choice."

"He'll kill me . . ."

"No. He won't kill anyone, cos we'll get him first."

The girl stares into Darlac's eyes. They are only about a metre apart. Presumably she's trying to figure out if he is trying to dupe her.

Darlac says nothing. Almost holds his breath. No point forcing it. Don't shake the tree too hard: if the fruit falls, it'll go to waste. He smiles. Now he's coming up with agricultural proverbs! He enjoys moments like this, watching creatures struggle in his hands, creatures he knows he will later crush.

"Rue de Bègles, number twenty-eight. It's his missus' place. Blandine, she's called."

Blandine. Darlac remembers the images they showed at school of the Christian martyr thrown to the lions. Only nuns would give names like that to orphans whom they rule with an iron fist then kick out the door – sometimes literally onto the street – as soon as they're eighteen. They must do it on purpose, those twisted sisters. THE Blandine. The Venus of the F.F.I.[6]. She arrived in Bordeaux following a column of irregulars from the Landes who had taken her under their wing to help make the most of their R&R time. After a month, she had set up a discreet and highly republican and patriotic brothel between the Saint-Pierre church and the docks where young men went with their weapons standing to attention. A Resistance member who insulted her was instantly ejected by pros who knocked a few of his teeth loose with their rifle butts. That was how she got to know the Crabos, a handsome man at the time,

6 French Forces of the Interior – the name given, in the later stages of the war, to the French Resistance movement.

and who considered himself an honourable crook because he was swindling for the right side.

"Where do you work?"

She keeps her eyes lowered, fiddling with the material of her coat.

"The men come to us in an attic room, above a bar run by a mate of Blandine's, on the cours de la Marne. It's clean. No more than two or three a day. Sometimes old men who can't do it anymore. With gold watches and waistcoats. Who pay more cos I'm young. Blandine told me there are some of 'em who like little girls less than ten years old, but she says they're perverts and she won't have anything to do with blokes like them. I reckon they're the same ones, but they make do with me."

She says all this in a monotonous drawl, not looking at Darlac. When he finally sees her eyes again, they are huge and black and sad.

The commissaire looks away. He knows all about these sob-story whores who try to suck you in with their big, poor-me eyes all wet with tears. He can't stand them. They scare him, like those stray mutts who you look at or pat on the head and who start following you round and won't leave you alone even if you kick them.

"And Crabos?"

"Who?"

"The bloke you were with the other night. The corpse on legs."

"Oh, yeah. Bertrand. What about him?"

"Tell me how long you've known him. Who you've seen him with. If I like your answers, we'll get you out of here, we'll protect you. Far away from all this shit."

"He was different. He respected me. We talked a lot."

Darlac sniggers like a creaking door.

"You don't seriously expect me to believe that? You're saying he took you to dodgy hotels to chat about the weather? You were naked in a bed the other night, weren't you? Or did I dream that?"

"Oh, is that what you're interested in? You want me to tell you?

Well, guess what, he never fucked me. He can't anymore, because of his disease. He hasn't got the strength. So he asks me to take my clothes off and to sleep next to him. Holding him. He takes me in his arms. He touches me a bit – he likes that. And we talk, sometimes. He tells me about his childhood, stuff like that. Me too. We go to the hotel to keep up appearances, as he says. He doesn't want people saying he's not a man anymore. He's very kind. He pays for my meal and he gives me money so Blandine can take me to the cinema."

The kid stops talking and seems to go into a daydream. Suddenly she looks twelve years old, with her pale, sweet face. She lets out a big sigh as she plays with her fingers.

"He wanted to take me to Spain with him. By the sea, near Valencia. He wanted me to leave Bordeaux. He said I didn't belong here, that I deserved more than this."

"And you believed him?"

"You have to believe in something."

She sits up on the bed and her knee brushes against Darlac's. They are still about forty centimetres apart. Darlac watches her. He sees her as a lost child who has cried a lot and whose tears will dry up until she is merely a robot body with a heart of stone. But the touch of her leg against his leaves a tactile print, a feeling of pins and needles that doesn't go away even after he rubs it with his hand. His head is spinning so he stands up suddenly, knocking his chair to the floor, and the girl looks up, frightened, then curls up on her bed, against the wall, arms wrapped around her legs.

"Am I going to stay here a long time?"

She says this in a single breath. He remains standing in the darkness, arms hanging at his sides, and the girl looks for his eyes, finding only two dark hollows without a hint of sparkle.

"Don't you like it here? Odette and Emile treat you well, don't they?"

She shrugs, then picks up her coat and pulls it over her.

"I should take you back to your parents. You're a runaway, and in the eyes of the law you should be living with them. How old are you really? Sixteen? Eighteen?"

The girl curls up in an even tighter ball. Covered by her coat like that, she looks like an unformed creature that cannot extricate itself from the darkness. Small. On the verge of disappearing.

"Seventeen and a half."

"And already working for six months . . . How do you . . ."

"It was that or have my father on top of me. At least all these other bastards, I don't know them. They do what they want and they go away and I scrub myself with soap afterwards."

She says this very quietly, very fast, eyes staring at the wall in front of her.

Darlac watches her. He sees the back of her neck, the top of a shoulder, pale curves in this dark corner. He picks up his overcoat and puts it on without taking his eyes off the girl.

"I'll come and get you in two or three days. I know someone who can get you earning cash, and you won't need to get screwed in an attic. In ten years you can retire or you can buy a bar or a clothes shop or something, it's up to you. Or I can take you to the police station and we'll let a judge decide."

"Yeah, that'd be great. So he can lock me up in a boarding school with a bunch of bloody nuns or dyke warders. Thanks a lot."

She lifts her black, shiny, staring eyes to his. For the first time since he entered the room.

"Alright then. As you please."

Silently he closes the door behind him while the kid lies down in the foetal position, then he walks downstairs, touching his penis through the cloth of his trousers, which has gone stiff from being close to that beauty so plain and unembellished, that body so young and slender, and he doesn't know what's come over him.

Back in the empty room, amid the stench of cold tobacco, he

leans on the bar and Emile walks up to serve him another glass. Darlac waves it away.

He lights a cigarette.

Emile, looking pensive, wipes glasses. The commissaire busies himself examining part of the wall that is covered with labels, full of prestigious names and long-ago vintages.

"I'll come and get her in three or four days," he says, stubbing out his cigarette in an ashtray. "Take good care of her. And feed her, for God's sake. She looks like a ghost."

Emile tidies away the clean glasses and pours himself a Lillet. He lifts his glass to the cop and drinks half of it before sighing loudly.

"Only because it's you," he says. "I don't know where you got this girl from. Maybe there are blokes looking for her, and I wouldn't want them to find her here. That's not on, you know, nicking other people's girls."

Darlac shrugs. Plays with his lighter. Flicks it on and then blows it out again several times.

"Course it is. Happens all the time. You don't know what it's like in the jungle."

He heads towards the exit, then changes his mind and turns back to the landlord.

"Alright, I'm sorry. I was a bit harsh. I had a shitty day and I took it out on you."

Emile shrugs. Doesn't matter. Don't worry about it. He's used to it. Maybe he even likes it.

Out on the pavement, in spite of the shock of the drizzle in his face, Darlac starts laughing loudly, alone on the street. He laughs so hard it makes him stagger like a drunkard as he walks towards his car.

7

Daniel helped the boss with the hoist so he could lift up the dead Traction engine, the pistons rusted in place. They had to clean off the cobwebs that covered it, not to mention the bloodless, curled-up spiders that turned to dust between their fingers. Afterwards, they each went back to their separate tasks. Repairing the ignition on a 4C.V., then the brakes on an Aronde. The boss kept the Traction's engine for himself. Right now, Daniel can hear him unblocking the nuts with the aid of a hammer, breathing loudly and grunting over his workbench.

He doesn't talk much, the old man. His name is Claude Mesplet. He's a stocky fellow, black-haired, with dark, almost grey skin. Thick arms. Legs like tree trunks. Never smiles. Or only with his eyes. A brighter gleam, a few deepened wrinkles. Only laughs when he's drunk. He has to drink a lot for that to happen, and it's quite impressive. Daniel has seen this several times, at New Year's Eve parties, when they were kids, him and Irène, with Roselyne and Maurice. Times like that he would drink while he was talking, while he was cutting meat, pouring wine, serious and thoughtful, his smile constantly lighting up the corners of his eyes, being tender with Marguerite, his wife, whom everyone called Margot, and especially with their son, Joseph, who watched the table from his wheelchair, drool dribbling down his chin, hitting the table sometimes with his claw-like hands and grimacing smiles at anyone who turned to look at him. Smashed up before he was even born, his mother kicked repeatedly in the belly, in '43, during four days of interrogation with Poinsot.

Just before midnight, it would happen, suddenly. Claude would begin to laugh. You couldn't tell that he was rat-arsed. He wasn't the type who forgot how to walk after a few drinks. No hesitation in his movements. Even pissed, he could screw in platinum screws, dead straight, without a wall plug, with his eyes closed. He'd just begin to make a sort of convulsive squeaking noise, as if to himself, that he would try to suppress to start with, drowning it with another mouthful of booze. Then anything might set him off. A cork popping, a glass knocked over. One of Maurice's cruel jokes. Roselyne telling a story about the factory. A kid looking at him. And then a cascade would pour over the table. The kind of sound that swept everyone along in its torrent. And Joseph would laugh with them too. He laughed just like they did, until he was in tears. It was a joyful way to start the year, when they hugged each other tight and wished each other the best in life.

He always has that serious, preoccupied expression on his face, Claude. Daniel calls him that, by this first name, even though he addresses him as *vous*. And Claude talks to him always in that calm voice, never shouting, even when a big diesel is running or when Norbert is straightening sheet metal with a sledgehammer. He speaks in a deep, husky voice that can somehow be heard through any racket. Within six months, Daniel knew the job. Claude had entrusted him with its secrets like a magician teaching his apprentice. In a quiet voice, often late at night or early in the morning before the garage opened. To start with, the technical terms, pronounced in an undertone over an engine whose occult workings and diabolical traps they described, sounded like a wizard's incantation. Then, little by little, Daniel had taken up this chant, with snatches of it sometimes strangely illuminating the dark mysteries of grease and metal.

For the moment, the two of them have their heads inside the bonnet and the clanking of their tools does the talking for them. The cold is on their backs like a factory foreman railing at them to work faster. If they keep moving, at least they can shake those huge icy hands off their shoulders for a few seconds; if they keep busy, they can avoid thinking about it, can pretend they don't care about that haunting presence. Then there's something with the connecting rods, a problem that's causing everything to short-circuit. It requires a certain patience, but it's also intriguing. You wonder how you're going to repair it or come up with some ingenious solution that won't cost the client a fortune. You wipe your dirty hands and you put your grey matter to work. Thinking warms you up.

Norbert has gone to buy bread for their snack. Apparently he scared the woman at the bakery yesterday, with his bloody eye and his face marbled with bruises, and she felt so bad she gave him a *pain au chocolat.*

Claude always pays for the bread. Often he brings some pâté or the remains of a veal blanquette that the three of them share. He shares everything, the old man. A rare species, one of a dying breed. Daniel is well aware of this. He often talks about him to his friends, who sneer: "A boss is a boss, and that's all. He'll fuck you over eventually." He has trouble contradicting them. There's no shortage of examples. Everywhere he goes, he hears talk of this daily battle in the workshops, against the management minions, engineers, middle men, little Hitlers let loose among the machines, sniffing out workers who turn up late, barking about productivity, teeth bared, and how the men often feel like giving those sneaky, yapping little mutts a good kick in the teeth. "We're going to make those bastards pay soon, believe me. We'll shove it down their throats." That was what Herrero, a loudmouthed Party member, said to him one day. "Thorez[7] is showing them the way, and eventually the people will see the light and follow him."

Funny that he is thinking about that now, as he grapples with a nut, trying to fix a starter. The way? What way? Last night he dreamed that he was following a narrow path through a steep-sided rocky valley. He knew there were other men with him, but he

7 Maurice Thorez, leader of the French Communist Party from 1930 until his death in 1964.

couldn't see them. Suddenly, someone jumped him and cut his throat with a knife. He woke up clutching his neck, feeling for the wound with his fingers. Algeria. It's the first dream of this kind he's had. He puts it down to the news report they saw the other day at the cinema, showing a patrol advancing carefully under a burning sun. It should also be said that, every evening, when he gets home, he goes to look at the kitchen table to see if the papers from the army have arrived, summoning him to the slaughter. And every evening, Roselyne says to him: "No, don't worry, there's nothing there." Except he does worry, because one of these days, inevitably, there will be something waiting for him on the table. And when that happens, maybe Roselyne won't dare say anything at all.

Around ten o'clock, they eat their snack. Potted meat, saucisson. The fresh bread smells good and crunches softly when they cut it, making them salivate. They don't speak. They just reach out to the desired object, pass it on to whoever asks: knife, pâté, bottle of water. No alcohol here. Never. No wine, no beer.

According to the boss, booze is – after the bourgeoisie – the worker's worst enemy. His beloved poison. One of those opiates that keep the people stupefied in poverty. Daniel thinks he's exaggerating a bit, but he doesn't really care because, apart from the occasional beer, he doesn't drink anyway. He hates wine, says it smells too strong. The odours of cheap wine and cork that he sniffs sometimes rising from the wine cellars in the Chartrons district, as he cycles through, have put him off for good. He hates drunkards, and he thinks if they love their poverty, then let them wallow in it like they do in their vomit. He doesn't really understand what the boss means when he talks about the opium of the people. Take Norbert's father, for instance. No-one makes him drink until he can't stand up every day; no-one makes him get so drunk that he terrorises his wife and kids. The booze will kill him one day, and the sooner the better, before his son sticks a carving knife in his gut. His head smashed open on a pavement somewhere, or flattened

under a truck's wheels, his bicycle wrapped around him, the handlebars buried in his guts.

There are people who love their misery, who cultivate it, while
others, who only ever wanted to live happy and peaceful little lives,
are thrown into hell.

Something happens to interrupt his thoughts, as he lies under a
sump filled with oil. At first he doesn't understand what it is, and
then he notices that the boss has stopped working at the bench and
he sees his feet moving towards the door that opens on to the street.
Someone is waiting at the threshold. Against the light, Daniel can
make out the legs of two men facing each other. As Norbert is in the
back of the garage, using a hammer to straighten out a bumper, he
can't hear what they're saying, so he gets to his feet and recognises
the man the boss is talking to: the man who left his motorbike here
the day before yesterday. Dressed the same way, hands in the pockets of his sheepskin coat, the lower part of his face covered by his
scarf. Staring with the same intense yet absent gaze. His eyes like
chasms. He gestures with his chin at the motorbike standing further
off on its kickstand, and Daniel can tell that he is speaking almost
without opening his mouth. The old man replies, waving his hands
around, shrugging, probably explaining that they have a lot of work
and that he won't be able to fix his bike for several days yet. The man
nods and his gaze flickers momentarily over the boss' shoulder,
searching the garage, and Daniel crouches down to avoid being
seen. He can't bear the thought of meeting those eyes, in which
everything seems to be absorbed and to be lost, can't even bear the
feel of their gaze upon him.

Norbert stops hammering and Daniel shrinks even further, as if
the silence has suddenly exposed him, and he watches all this
through the windows of a Simca. He hears, "Sorry, that's the best I
can do," and the stranger nods thoughtfully. The two men don't say
anything else. They look at each other and their breaths mingle in
the cold air in fleeting little clouds. Mesplet shakes his head then

pulls it back between his broad shoulders, arms hanging at his sides. Norbert starts making a din again and Daniel wants to wrench that damn hammer out of his hands so he can try to hear any other scraps of conversation that the two men might share. For now, they look like two statues, frozen in place by ice. The stranger doesn't blink; he is absolutely still. Only the steam issuing from his mouth proves he is still alive. The boss stamps his feet, presumably growing impatient. Suddenly, without a word, the man turns on his heel and leaves. Daniel goes out onto the pavement and lights a cigarette, watching him walk away like he did the other day, the man's tall, thin figure, his stiff-legged stride.

"Who's that? What did he want?"

The boss does not reply. He stares unwaveringly at the long silhouette.

"Nothing," he says finally. "He just wanted to know if we'd fixed his bike. Bloke's a pain in the arse."

He scans the end of the street, where the man disappeared, as if fearing that he will reappear at any moment.

"He looked annoyed. Do you know him?"

"I told you, forget it. Anyway, since when do I have to tell you what I say to clients or what they say to me? Don't you have any bloody work to do? Oh, you do? Well, do it then, and keep your mouth shut. I'm not paying you to stand out here and chat."

Daniel gets the message. He signals to Norbert to make sure he doesn't rub the boss up the wrong way with his sometimes depressing questions or his corny puns about dirty screws and not being able to fit his nozzle in the tank. All three of them work alone all morning, taking no notice of each other.

And then, around noon, the boss suddenly drops what he's doing with the Traction, washes his hands, changes his clothes and announces that he has some shopping to do and he might be gone all afternoon. He tells Daniel to close the shop before six, there's no point working overtime, they're not in any hurry, tomorrow is another day, etc. There's just old Mr Gomez who's coming to pick up his 2C.V., and it's ready, the invoice is on the desk.

As soon as he's gone, they close the big door and sit close to the stove. Norbert's mother couldn't make his lunch today, so they share Daniel's. A dish of mutton and flageolet beans that they warm up. And, as Roselyne always makes too much, there's plenty for both of them, taking turns to dig in with a spoon and then soaking up the last of the sauce with bread.

"What's up with the boss?" Norbert asks, mouth full.

"If anyone asks, just say that you have no idea."

The boy swallows greedily. As always, he hardly chews his food at all, as if afraid that someone will steal it from his mouth.

"You don't have any idea either. Was it the bloke who brought the bike?"

"For fuck's sake, yeah, just go and warm up the coffee."

Norbert marches off and fiddles around in front of the camping stove.

"All the same, he's a strange-looking bloke. I saw him earlier. He gives me the creeps. Don't you find him scary?"

Daniel feels a shiver run through him.

"No, why?"

Fear? No. It's more like he's going to faint. A sort of dizziness.

Fear is what he felt grip his throat at six years old, on a rooftop, sitting against a chimney, in the cold wind of a night that never ended. Fear is why he pissed himself when he heard the stampede of cops on the stairs, yelling out orders and hammering on doors, and when his mother held him close to her, moaning, telling him to be a good boy, wetting his face and neck with her tears and whispering words that he now can't remember, just before his father hoisted him through a fanlight onto the roof and handed him a bit of bread in a paper bag and told him to wait there until someone came to get him.

The fear of feeling the house collapse beneath him. Or of falling off the roof as he leaned over to see if someone was coming. The fear of seeing night fall in silence as the birds fell asleep before Papa and Maman came back to take him in their arms and put him in bed, rock-a-bye baby, on a rooftop . . .

The fear that they will not come back.

He's not afraid anymore.

So this man with his wrinkled, tormented face, with his eyes that search you or that seem always to be trying to see through you to something unattainable, he senses that he has come much further than all those sailors you see on the docks, shoulders and feet rolling, the great swell of the ocean still in their legs, because the ground is moving too much and can only be brought under control, the floor moored safely to the walls, by a few beers and a bottle of Scotch.

But him: stiff and thin and sharp-edged, like a statue made of sheet metal or glass. And those eyes, absent or hollow, that seem to want to pull you down into the depths of his whirlwind. Daniel met his gaze for only a few moments, but he cannot rid himself of that sensation of vertigo.

They go out on the pavement to drink their coffee and breathe the fresh air, almost mild as it blows in off the ocean before the rain arrives, and they smoke their cigarettes leaning against the iron door, feeling at peace and watching people walk past: workers going to the station warehouses, a few women weighed down by shopping bags. They hear a hooting train, the brakes of another train squealing. This din is carried on the wind from the south, along with metallic noises that they normally don't hear.

While they talk, Daniel watches the end of the street because it seems to him that the man will reappear and walk straight towards him, staring into his eyes the whole time and forcing Daniel to follow him. This is exactly how he feels and when a figure turns that corner his heart shivers.

All afternoon, he is startled each time someone passes the door, whenever a faint shadow crosses the threshold of the garage. So he dives inside bonnets, he crawls under chassis, he bangs scrap metal sticky with black oil, he tries to wear himself out so he won't think about it anymore, but nothing works. It is Norbert, at quarter to six, who yells out that they should call it a day, that he's had enough. Besides, they can barely see what they're doing by the feeble light of the bulbs hanging from the girders. Without inspection lamps, they have to grope around just to find an engine. So they push shut the big iron door, yelling in accompaniment to the awful grating noise it makes.

The rain is falling now, in a cold dust over the city, and Daniel takes a roundabout route through the drizzle of lights absorbed by the night, almost crashing a dozen times on the slippery cobblestones or getting knocked over by trucks whose drivers don't see him. As soon as he can, after the cours du Médoc, he gets his head down and rides fast, maybe hoping to cleave through this wet fog and see it part before him like the Red Sea in *The Ten Commandments*, which he and Irène went to see on Sunday afternoon, dubbed in French in the large screening room with its columns and gilt decorations. But no miracle occurs and he arrives at the house swaddled in cold and damp.

And Irène is there, as it happens, and she enfolds him with her huge green eyes and takes him in her arms in spite of the rainwater seeping and dripping from him. And he regrets that he cannot feel the shape or the warmth of her body because of his icy wrapping.

On the table, leaning against a glass, there is an envelope with red, white and blue bordering. Roselyne, standing in front of the sink, does not dare turn around.

After the meal, they talk about it in hushed voices, sitting in front of their empty plates. Normally Roselyne would clear the table as soon as dinner was over, but tonight she leaves everything where it is. Maurice has taken out a bottle of Armagnac and pours some into his own glass before offering it to Daniel, who watched him do it. It was good, the smell and the taste of the alcohol mixed with the remains of the coffee. The fire in his mouth was gently doused before descending in a blaze through his oesophagus and into his stomach. Then the flame began purring like a fire in a stove and the warmth rose up to his face.

He glides into intoxication and listens as they talk but says little himself because he feels as if he no longer knows what to say or think or do. In a few weeks, he will be at war. He has seen epics, marching columns, ambushes, heroic charges, men running low on ammo but not giving up, hand-to-hand fighting with knives or bayonets or rifle butts, lost patrols, battles in the jungle, faces glowing with sweat or covered with mud. Men cut down amid roaring gunfire and yowling bullets, scarlet-painted corpses thrown back into the arms of their friends, men who ignore their fear or cowards who redeem themselves at the end through self-sacrifice, loyal officers, generals who speak to the men like their sons and pinch their cheeks, I know you're suffering, lads, but back home everyone is proud of you, and you have my trust because I know you will give everything, won't you? Thank you, general, you can count on us, and the commander pretending to be friendly with his clear gaze and his greying temples. He's seen it all in films, running all over Bordeaux since he was fourteen years old, and when he came out of the cinema he always felt bigger, his shoulders broader, and he took on the nonchalant and totally relaxed look of someone who's seen it all and seems to trail bravery and horror in his wake.

In a few weeks, he will be at war. He might kill, he might die. This is the most important thing that has happened to him since. Since when? In fact, he doesn't know if anything has ever happened to him before. He knows he is missing something and he feels it there, deep in his guts, between his sternum and his stomach. Like a hole. A ball of nothingness. Sometimes it hurts, twists in knots, it's bitter and he spits it out or pukes up a few gobs of phlegm. War. Suddenly he is scared. But he wants to go and find out what he is scared of, despite everything that sickens him.

A bit like when children dare their friends to do things: walk as far as possible along the edge of a pavement, blindfolded. Smoke cigarettes from the wrong end. Ride down a flight of steps on a bike without braking. Put your hand in a fire.

Of course, Maurice has told him stories about his own war, in '39, the waiting period in the Ardennes, cleaning machine guns, exercising, drills, and that bastard of a cabot-chef who yelled all the time and made them crawl in the dirt or run through the rain for the slightest misdemeanour. And then the first bombardments, in the distance, that approaching rumble, and staying up for nights on end, on patrol with fear in their guts, holding those old rifles from the first war that jammed so easily, and the first stiffs they'd found, two kilometres from there, four men all collapsed in a heap, blood and innards mixed, already stinking, he told Daniel all this, once only, on a night like this in fact, his voice trembling and his body utterly still while he spoke except for his fingers as they held his glass, his eyes wandering to the three of them sitting around the table, perhaps not even seeing them because it was all coming back to him, descending over his head like a mourning veil as behind each word poured images, smells and screams.

He described the winter, terrible, the frostbite, men huddled in holes around fire pits, the east wind that flushed them out of their shelters, roaring and biting, then blew on their green-wood fires turning them to smoke, the snow that fell for days on end, so thick and dense that they didn't even see when a regiment of German tanks came upon them.

He didn't fire a shot except for hunting, because for a long time the only warnings they got were those given by sentries who were sleep-dazed or drunk on hooch when they opened fire on deer who came early in the morning to break the crust of ice in the hope of finding grass.

The war approached them: they heard the rumble of artillery fire, felt it shake the earth sometimes with its heavy tread; they saw trucks full of corpses driving past, battalions retreating; they dived to the ground as German fighter planes flew overhead, seeming not even to notice them or perhaps simply ignoring this superfluous rank and file, already beaten. And then one day a colonel had given them the order to withdraw, to run away even, otherwise two Panzer regiments would roll right over them the next day, so they left and found themselves on sun-blasted roads, dying in their winter coats, pursued by columns of smoke that rose in the east. They were told to hand over their weapons and their kits and not to hang around but to go home because there was nothing more they could do here, that they would be demobilised later.

Bogged down in the melting snow, it took Maurice two weeks to get home. He helped bury people machine-gunned by Stukas by the side of the road, he pushed carts, he helped a bourgeois family by fixing their broken-down car in return for a lift – a hundred kilo-metres at an average of ten an hour through the crowds, sitting crushed in the back seat against an old granny in a state of shock, distraught and delirious, or sitting on the roof, his bloody feet macerating in his squaddie's boots.

He arrived at the house one morning and Roselyne screamed with terror and hid in a cupboard because she didn't know it was him, bearded, stinking, covered in grime and blood, eyes crazed with weariness, because this creature could not be him, would never again be him, just some stranger that resembled him, returned from who knew where and capable of who knew what. He talked to her, leaning against the wobbly door, whispered sweet nothings to her, their secret words, like a code. He pronounced this open-sesame in a breathless voice, on the verge of fainting. Then he said, almost in a moan, that life would go on, because nothing was over, not the war or any other battle, not even a scrap of happiness torn from the brambles that had overrun everything, and so she opened the door and fell into his arms, unconscious and heavy, and him with no strength left, carried her, staggering, over to the bed.

Daniel listens to them as they advise him to try to land a cushy job somewhere, maybe in an office, or in Logistics, Maurice suggests, with your job you should hide out in a truck engine, like that you won't have to walk into the wolf's mouth. And there are people who like war, you know, so just leave it to them. Especially when it's a war against the Algerian people, Irène adds. Most of the conscripts don't know what they'll be doing there or why they're being sent. This isn't your war, Daniel. It's not our war.

Yeah, of course, he mutters, stunned by the chaos in his head. He would like to pour himself another Armagnac to send himself even further into the cotton-wool torpor that is muffling his brain, but he doesn't dare, and anyway he dislikes drunkenness: he always feels sick, during and afterwards, tortured by the feeling that he is going to die, to puke up his heart and soul.

Bang, bang, bang. Someone at the door. They all jump. The sound echoes in the hallway. At this time of night? In weather like this? They look at each other.

"It must be Alain," says Irène.

Daniel turns to her. Why Alain? Roselyne lowers her eyes.

He stands up and rushes into the hallway, grabbing his sheepskin as he goes. Behind him, he hears Roselyne asking:

"Where are you going? Have you seen the weather?"

Alain is on the pavement, his cap pulled down over his eyes. Daniel closes the door softly behind him.

"Got any cash?"

"I got paid yesterday. What about you?"

"I'm O.K."

They walk for a while without speaking. The last bus goes past just before the swing bridge and they watch its red tail lights fade into the distance along with the blurred glow through its steamed-up windows. A few street lamps shine weakly on the docks, and a few lit-up portholes are visible between the warehouses. The wind pushes them, bowing their necks. North-west. Daniel glances up at Alain, fag in his mouth, face shadowed by the visor of his cap.

"So?"

Alain shrugs. Sighs. Takes a drag on his cigarette and blows smoke out in front of him. It vanishes quickly.

"So I'll get pissed . . ."

He shakes his head, as if to rid himself of the thoughts inside.

"Fuck. Shit," he adds. "I won't go."

"How will you manage that? You'd be a deserter."

They fall silent. Each lost in his own thoughts.

After the dockers' employment offices, they make out a few luminous signs. They continue at the same pace, their shoulders bumping occasionally as they walk unsteadily over the slanting cobblestones. Outside a bar called Le Havre, they wait while two men emerge, laughing and speaking in a foreign language, then walk away hesitantly, heads bowed, clapping each other on the back and spitting on the ground.

"I'm going to find a ship," Alain says suddenly.

"You're mad. It'll never work."

"We'll go to the Escale. My uncle told me I could find a bloke he knows there. He used to go there pretty often when he was sailing. I've told you about him, haven't I?"

Of course Daniel had heard all about Uncle Auguste, the family hero, the globetrotter with clothes and scars from all over the world who had weathered every storm, unfrozen the Baltic, drunk every bar dry before destroying it, knocked men out like a kid sending skittles tumbling at a funfair, visited every brothel between Copenhagen and Dakar, fucked all night long with ugly bloaters and beautiful women, spraying his dick with Polish vodka or Russian champagne to cool it down . . . Everyone in the neighbourhood knew the stories about him. Back when he would still leave his house, tall and straight-backed and handsome, in spite of his scars – glassed in a brawl in Liverpool or Tangiers or Rotterdam, he couldn't remember, and it changed all the time anyway – and sometimes he would sit at the bar in Mauricette's, on rue Achard, at six in the morning, his worn-out woollen hat on his head, and recount his own legends to anyone who'd listen. There was always some bloke to get him started on his drunken epics, and he would be off. But the poor sod knew how to tell a story – his dramatic timing had improved as his memory had faded – and the evenings when he turned up, the men who hung around there after eight o'clock, instead of going home and dozing off in a chair as they listened to the radio, preferred instead to let this woollen-hatted liar, who had, all the same, seen places they had never even dreamed of going, sweep them away on his words, and they sat silent and motionless over their drinks, by turns sneering and impressed.

He's renting some hovel in the Cité Pourmann now, Auguste, where he lives as a hermit surrounded by African masks, the walls lined with magic necklaces and amulets brought back from his travels. He's been there ever since a half-whore kid emptied his bank account and his heart and left him there, in the middle of his exotic museum, so she could get screwed by some little thug from the Saint-Pierre neighbourhood.

Alain pushes Daniel by the shoulder and they enter the thick, dark warmth of a bar, peopled by shadows and voices and rugged faces around formica tables under red or black lampshades, and they walk up to the counter where they climb onto bar stools. The woman standing behind the counter is a Jayne Mansfield-style blonde in skintight black jodhpurs and a mauve sweater sparkling with a few silver threads. She watches the two boys sit down at the bar but doesn't move, just continues smoking a cigarette, elbows on the bar, chatting with a small, thin, black-haired, shifty-looking man who keeps shooting sideways glances to spy on and weigh up everything that breathes in his vicinity. The two of them smile like wolves, teeth bared but eyes impassive. When the woman isn't talking, her mouth subsides, pulling her face down, bitter little creases at the corners of her lips.

At the other end of the bar, two girls perched on stools talk with a bearded colossus who leans towards them because he can't understand what they're saying and they laugh as they repeat things into his ear and the man shakes his head and laughs in turn, taking advantage of the situation to put a hand behind their back, which they gently push away.

Alain has turned around to have a look at the roomful of customers, chatting and sometimes laughing.

"There's a table free over there."

"Why did we come here?"

Daniel examines the labels on the countless bottles ranged on shelves, amazed by the apparently infinite variety of drinks for pissheads.

"You think we're supposed to serve ourselves?" Alain asks out loud.

"Just try it and see what happens," hisses the blonde, her cigarette between her teeth.

The short-arse she's talking with turns his dark, dangerous gaze on Alain.

"What's up with him? Does he want some?"

"Forget it," mutters Daniel. "We'll go somewhere else. This place is full of cunts. Come on . . ."

He has already hopped off his stool when he sees the little big shot from the bar moving towards them. He's got a crooked smile and you can tell he's a nasty piece of work, a Rottweiler of a bloke, full of dirty tricks. Suddenly an empty bottle appears in his right hand.

Alain does not retreat. Daniel puts a hand on his shoulder and the two of them face up to him.

"What can I serve you, gentlemen?"

The man moves the bottle in a circle in front of him, the neck held tightly in his fist. He's still smiling, sturdily set on his short legs. Silence in the bar. Hard to tell if anyone's even breathing anymore. The two girls and their giant have moved back towards the jukebox, behind the wide leaves of a big ficus plant.

When the glass explodes on the corner of the bar, a sort of gulp tightens every throat in the room. The blonde walks up, dishcloth in hand.

"Come on, Christian. Let those wankers leave."

"No, they're not leaving like that. What do you think? Did you hear the way they talked about me? Look at them trying to act tough, those fucking queers! I'm just going to take care of them nicely. Those little shits will remember Christian Penot. They'll go home crying to their whore of a mother, begging her to sew up their faces."

Then a man walks in and leans on the bar between the threatening dwarf and the two boys, saying excuse me to all three without looking at any of them. Straight away, he orders a double whisky. He's dressed in a grey wool coat and he places his hat on the bar, after first, with a very absorbed air, pushing away a few shards of glass with his fingertips. Jayne Mansfield watches him, open-mouthed, mechanically wiping a glass, chest swelled with surprise. Her eyes seek out Penot's, but he is sticking out his neck and standing on tiptoes as he addresses the intruder.

"Hey, what's-yer-face, can't you tell you're in the way? We're in the middle of a discussion here."

The man ignores him. He asks again for his whisky.

"Fuck off somewhere else, you twat. Do you understand or do I need to draw you a picture?"

Without turning round, almost without moving, the man elbows him in the face. Penot takes three steps back, staggering on his heels, then crouches down, his face covered by his hand, blood pissing between his fingers. The blonde starts yelling. She's waving a crank over the beer pumps and around her neck fake gemstones rattle as they clatter into each other. She says she's going to call the cops but doesn't, then starts uttering insults, her big mouth flapping. Around

94

the room, people are getting to their feet. Chair legs scrape on the floor, glasses are knocked over. The stranger walks up to Penot, who's still holding his broken bottle, and crushes his wrist underfoot. The dwarf lets go of the bottleneck, and the man kicks it away.

"You know who I am?" the man asks, leaning over him.

Penot shakes his head. He's holding his nose, and above his cupped hand his eyes roll, wide-eyed with panic. A kick in the ribs forces a squeal from him.

"So you don't know who I am, huh? But I know you. I even know where you live. I know about the little girls too. See? I know. There are loads of people who know. Once they get past ten or eleven, you think they're too old, don't you?"

Penot closes his eyes. His face is covered with blood.

"But the cops turn a blind eye because you're a snitch, right? And then there's your brother, who was a pig, and a right bastard too, during the Occupation. So they don't care, do they? They let you get away with the shit you do to little kids. But now your brother's had his throat slit, they won't have so many reasons to cover for you, will they?"

The man kicks him in the ribs with the point of his boot.

"Now fuck off. And you'd better take care, if you don't want to end up like your cunt of a brother."

Penot starts to get up as the blonde hands him a wet dishcloth to wipe his face. She helps him to his feet and accompanies him to the door, murmuring a few words of consolation. She is taller than him in her high heels, and looks like an adult cuddling a child who's banged his head into a door.

"It's alright, it's over. There'll be no scrap tonight," the man tells the other customers. "That piece of shit just needed calming down. The next round's on me."

He rummages in his pocket and pulls out a wad of banknotes that he drops on the counter. People start chatting again, *mezza voce*. No-one dares move very much. And yet there are some big, strapping lads in here, their coat sleeves bulging with muscle, men with chests like percherons. Dockers, sailors, tough bastards. But all of them know a fight between gangsters when they see it: it's as dangerous as a nest of snakes. You'd have to be mad to get mixed up in it.

Daniel's hand is still draped on his friend's shoulder. He does not move. He's wondering who this man is with his greying hair and his impassive violence. Constructing theories, searching his memory. Nothing. The man turns towards them, with a smile of fake friendliness. You can tell he's not the type of man who's often in a good mood, with his long face, his broken nose, his dark thick brows, and those of eyes of his, sunk deep in his face, maybe grey, or blue. Not the kind of man you'd invite for a drink after hitting him in the belly. Above all, he is big, and his shoulders move with the supple solidity of a boxer.

"What are you drinking, lads?"

The blonde picks up the cash without a word then starts pouring. Three whiskies for these gentlemen. After that, she rushes between tables to water the troops.

"Thanks," says Alain, lifting his glass. "We were up shit creek there."

"He'd have slashed your faces. He's a vicious bastard."

"Why did you help us?" Daniel asks. "I mean . . ."

The man squints as he looks Alain up and down.

"You're Auguste's nephew, aren't you? He told me you'd be here. And you must have come here to see me. Anyway, I wasn't going to let that piece of shit shine up his ego by cutting you two to pieces. We all know that cunt here. He's pure poison."

"Is it true what you said about him?"

"What? The little girls? Course it's true. He's already been in the nick for that. It runs in the Penot family, that sort of shit. His brother was one of Poinsot's henchmen here – you know, the French Gestapo. They had their torture chamber on the cours du

Chapeau-Rouge. And that one, he used to get girls for the Krauts, and he'd have them himself beforehand. He's the kind of man who indulges his vices fully when circumstances permit. And during the Occupation, all sorts of filth was permitted. Those bastards were like flowers growing in horseshit."

Daniel tries to remember if Maurice has already told him about this. Poinsot? No, there's nothing. He asks the man how he knows all this.

Jayne Mansfield is back behind the counter, listening as she pours drinks. The man shoots a look in her direction.

"Because I was there. Besides, loads of people know. They just keep their mouths shut."

"Where were you?"

"Never you mind about that."

They drink in silence. Daniel feels himself losing it a bit. Oesophagus burning, eyes blurred with tears. He watches Alain, who's squinting into the bottom of his glass, back hunched, almost slumped on the counter. Behind him, the conversations and the laughter are now nothing more than a murmur buzzing in his head. He feels hot, and he starts sweating in this sticky atmosphere, the air thick with smoke and warmth.

"What about you?" the man says. "What are you doing here? Oh yeah, I forgot: Algeria, huh?"

Alain drains his whisky and takes a deep breath before replying.

"Yeah. We're trying to find a bit of courage before they send us to the slaughter. In three weeks."

The man nods.

"What a pile of shit."

"He told you, my uncle?"

"Yes. But it won't be easy. I know a quartermaster on a Norwegian ship who owes me. He's coming in tomorrow – it's good timing. I'll go and see him. He'll be here three days, the time it takes to unload. Sometimes he takes an apprentice, for a month or two.

You'll be peeling potatoes and cleaning the bogs, but at least you won't get your bollocks cut off. They're going to Germany, Poland, Denmark and England too. No-one will bother asking for your papers there, except in Poland, where you should stay on board. I'll need a photo and thirty thousand francs. That's how much it costs for fake I.D."

Alain turns his back on Daniel and rummages in his pocket for his wallet. Photo, money. He counts the notes. Daniel moves between them so he can hear and see better and maybe be noticed, but neither of them pays any attention to his presence.

"That's quite a bit," he says.

"Don't worry, I've been saving. I wanted to buy a motorbike, but I think that can wait."

The photos and the money vanish into the man's trouser pocket. He checks his watch.

"I'd better get going. The day after tomorrow is Thursday. I'll meet you at six in the evening at the Bambi Bar, a bit further on, near the cours du Médoc. I'll introduce you to that bloke. It's a prossie bar, you'll see, but he likes it, he's a regular there. I'm Jacky, by the way."

He gets up, shakes hands with them both and leaves. Daniel looks around. A panoramic sweep. Surely all this is just a backdrop, with a few extras waiting for the director to shout "Cut!" so they can leave the set and go home? He wishes he had his frame with him so he could contain the scene and give himself the illusion that he is controlling it, but he can more or less imagine what it would look like: a desolate vision, under a wan light. Alain remains motionless, staring vacantly at the mirror behind the bar, where the bottles are multiplied. Further off, Jayne Mansfield is smoking a cigarette and sipping at a glass of port, heavy-lidded, her mascara damp.

Daniel pushes his glass away and turns up his collar.

"I think I've seen enough for tonight. I'm going home."

Outside, the wind blows into his face. It has stopped raining but he shrinks inside himself, hands in pockets, and does not see the sodden city glowing weakly around him, its lights almost extinguished. Alain is running behind him but he does not slow down to wait for him.

"Shit, what's up with you?"

"Nothing. You're not taking the same boat as me. Much good may it do you."

"I'm not going to Algeria. There's no way I'm going to risk my neck for those colonialist cunts."

"You've spent too long listening to Sara. You'll be a deserter."

"No. A conscientious objector it's called. I wouldn't even set foot in that hell. Anyway, Sara's right. We're just cannon fodder, for the government. All wars are the same. What about you? Are you really going? Just like that, unquestioningly? Didn't Irène say anything?"

"We've already talked this to death. You know perfectly well what I think about all that. But what you're doing is pointless. Better just to go there and do what we can."

"Oh yeah? And what exactly do you think we can do, over there? Sabotage the trucks? Block up the missile launchers with pamphlets? Or maybe you're going to gun down your own officers? In three months you'll be like they are. You've seen the others, you know what they say. Either that or you'll go to jail, and you'll be no use to anyone then."

"We can make the others aware that—"

"No. The war – this war – when it gets hold of you, it's as if you've gone mad. It eats you alive. Have you seen the men who came back? Perez? Bernard? You remember what he was saying, Perez, before he left, with that big gob of his? And the blocked trains, and the C.R.S.[8]? What was the point of all that?"

8 The Compagnies Républicaines de Sécurité is the riot control division and general reserve of the French National Police. It was infiltrated by Communists in the late 1940s, just after its inception, but their influence was reduced thereafter.

Daniel cannot think of a reply. Perez, a tough man and a supporter of both the C.G.T.[9] and the Party, had wanted to foment rebellion among the conscripts in order to bring the war to an end. He found himself trekking through the jebel, setting fire to villages, plus other things that he refused to talk about. In fact, he didn't talk much at all anymore, and slept even less, or so it was said.

"I don't know."

Alain grabs his shoulder and shakes him.

"Let's talk about it another time. We're not going to fall out, are we?"

Daniel shoves him away. They burst out laughing then start walking again without speaking. When they cross the swing bridge, Daniel looks over at the ships berthed in the wet docks.

"I hope it works out, your ship. I want to hear all about the ports and the sea. And the girls . . ."

After the swing bridge, they are swallowed up by the darker street and they begin speaking and laughing more quietly, as if in this gloom they dare not make any noise for fear of extinguishing the few sad lamps suspended above the cobblestones.

9 Confédération Générale du Travail, a major French trade union, affiliated to the Communist Party. During the Algerian war, it supported Algerian aspirations for independence.

8

"Do you love me?" She always asked me that, Suzanne, on Sunday mornings when we were lazing in bed in my room on rue Beccaria. "You never say it to me," she would insist. "You're supposed to say things like that, you know." I asked her to shut up and go back to sleep, and afterwards we would go and have a bite at Hortense, a greasy spoon behind the place d'Aligre which on Sunday lunchtimes served the best blanquette in Paris. After that, we would take a walk down to the canal and then come back to bed and make the springs creak again because she liked that, Suzanne, she was always asking for it and she knew what to do to put lead in my pencil. She told me that she learned all that with an American soldier she fell for in August '44 and who, for about ten days, had made her see all the colours, as she put it. "It weren't only Paris what was liberated, I'll tell you that for nothing!" she recalled enthusiastically.

So we fucked until exhaustion set in and about six in the evening she'd have her hand between her thighs pretending she was in pain because we'd been going at it too hard, simpering as she whinged, and then she'd get up to wash herself at the little sink, giving me a good look at what she was doing. Sometimes that got me going again in spite of the fatigue, but she had to go back to her place in the 19th, where she lived with her mother who'd been sent half-mental by the death of her husband in captivity and was constantly threatening to throw herself out of the window and lived like a hermit most of the time in a room with the shutters closed because daylight gave her migraines, or so she claimed. Suzanne looked after this poor woman, terrified by her suicide threats even though, deep down, she didn't really believe them. "Well, I'd better go see if she's jumped," she'd say sometimes in a casual voice as she was leaving, but she didn't hang around all the same, and nothing, not even her insatiable desire for romping in the sheets, would have kept her back a single minute longer.

She worked in a foundry in Aubervilliers, making aluminium saucepans. She spent the whole day in front of a metal-stamping press and at twenty-five she was already half-deaf and she talked really loud just like she screamed really loud when she was coming, and on sunny days, when the window was open, the whole building must have heard her. In fact, I'm pretty sure they must have heard her on the other side of the boulevard, even over the traffic.

We didn't feel anything for each other except a sort of camaraderie, but that did mean we had stuff to talk about and we would discuss politics as we walked through Paris and she would take me to Galeries Lafayette to daydream among the aisles, trying on hats or feeling up lingerie. Sometimes, in a little bistro where we'd go to eat and dance a bit on Saturday nights, we would meet up with her friends from the Communist Party, among them a woman of my age who'd come back from Ravensbrück. Her name was Hélène and she smiled all the time and had a lovely clear laugh, huge dark eyes and brown hair that fell down in waves over her shoulders. She was maybe the prettiest woman in Paris. She should have been in the movies, she'd have shown the stars of the era a thing or two. I didn't dare speak in her presence. I watched her on the sly, trying to understand what made her gaze so sweet, and sometimes our eyes would meet and what I saw then would take my breath away: in those depths, all I could see was pain. Absolute misery.

She knew, about me. The others had told each of us about the other. But we never talked about it. Sometimes an allusion, a news item read in the paper, would bring the monster rising to the surface, but straight away a rush of frivolity would shove its mouth back below the water and once again we'd start to laugh, drink, dance. Life went on, and we had to live.

And in moments like that I desired all women and I wanted to eat everything and drink everything, forgetting myself in this noisy jubilation, letting myself be swept away by this whirlwind in the hope perhaps that it would tear me up from the depths where I'd been thrown years before.

I remember the evening when Hélène asked me to dance. She was a really good dancer. Her long legs lifted her up, sent her spinning with so much grace and power that she never seemed to feel tired. Her partner was a man who must have been her boyfriend at the time, Jacques, a teacher who'd fought in the Resistance in Limousin. He was younger than her and he joked around all the time, a warm and friendly man, and also a skilled dancer. When they took the floor together, people would often move to the sides to watch them. I can see them now in that cellar with an orchestra playing jazz, the crowd clapping their hands in rhythm, the two of them alone in the world and me in my corner unable to stop myself loving that woman and drinking like a fish to drown out the feelings that scared me.

One evening, she came up to me and held out her hand. It was the outdoors dance near the Bastille, and the musicians onstage had embarked on a series of slow waltzes to give the dancers a rest after the javas and tangos. Hélène held me tight to her with her hand on my waist and I let her lead me because I danced like a lump of wood, especially when I'd been drinking. And especially if I was dancing with her. I could feel the fabric of her dress under my fingers, soaked with sweat because she'd been dancing non-stop for nearly an hour. Her hair flew into my nose, my mouth. From time to time, as we spun, I saw Suzanne wagging her finger at us warningly, smilingly, and I responded with exaggerated winks or grimaces. We danced. Hélène's ankles and thighs sometimes touched mine, pushing me and leading me and, furtively, her belly was brushing against my crotch. All I could think about was that body against mine, that skin a few millimetres from mine, damp and warm, and now and then I would look down to glimpse her face with her eyes almost closed and I could think of nothing to say to her, not even a remark about my dancing or some gallant nonsense, the kind of platitudes that usually came so easily to me.

Suddenly she moved even closer to me, held me more tightly. "So?"
she said. "How is it?"

I didn't understand. I thought she was talking about the fact of us
dancing together, as this was the first time we'd done so in the months
we'd known each other. "It's good," I said. "I'd been wanting to for a
while."

The music stopped and people clapped and shouted. Around us,
people changed, swapping partners. "No," she said in an irritated voice.
"I mean you, now. How are you?"

The orchestra started up again and we remained immobile, face to
face, looking at each other and hardly even breathing, mouths open,
despite our breathlessness and the weight that was crushing our chests.
"I don't know. I kind of feel like I'm floating. I just let it take me. Enjoy
it. And sometimes it's like I'm watching myself do it, from afar."

She nodded, looking thoughtful, her eyes darker and deeper than
ever, staring into mine.

"What about you?"

She thought for a few seconds then said: "Me? I dance." And she led
me once again out onto the dance floor and I followed her twirls with my
feet of lead, legs stiff, head hanging heavy.

I saw her maybe another dozen times and we never spoke again, not
face to face like that. Jacques was no longer around. He'd gone back
to his hometown, summoned by the Party to stand in the elections. So
Hélène danced with other men, never more than a dance, and she
chatted and she laughed, and Suzanne and her friends put the world to
rights, convinced that Stalin would not leave the French working classes
alone against strike-breakers, that Maurice, as they called him, would
guide the people of France towards a better tomorrow. I thought they
were right. I remembered the soldiers of the Red Army who found us, the
ten of us, hidden out in the ruins of a farm, reduced to chewing the frozen
meat of a dead cow. I remember their appalled looks when they saw our
moving corpses, in spite of all they must already have seen, and their
kindness and all the little things they did to make sure we'd be less cold,

less hungry, that we wouldn't die. So it seemed to me that those people really could save the world, even if I didn't know from what, because I couldn't see what might happen to us now.

I reckon Hélène thought the same way as me: she didn't speak much, mostly content to share in the general outrage or to nod agreement with that smile which would, in itself, have been capable of changing people's lives had it been plastered to the walls or projected on a cinema screen. Sometimes I met her dark gaze that cloaked a suffering I immediately sensed was just like mine. Several times I tried, as we were leaving, somewhat dazed by the noise, head heavy from too many cigarettes and too much booze, to walk next to her and talk to her but I never managed to say anything and the last time I saw her she took my arm and said: "Life is good, don't you think? The weather's good, and spring is in the air!"

"That doesn't alter the fact that we . . ." I began to reply, but she put a hand to my lips: "We're alive, aren't we? Plenty of others are dead. We have to deal with that. As best we can. Anyway, no-one's listening." Then she moved away from me, lifting her hand above her head and giving me a little wave of goodbye.

That is the memory of her that I keep. The warmth of her skin on my lips. And then that hand waving above her hair, like a wing. And her fathomless gaze and her smile that I try to summon in the evenings when I feel the abyss sucking me down. Because I tell myself that if she was capable of smiling like that, of producing so much light and warmth and spreading it all around her, then I should have the strength to remain, to carry that flame, to stay on my feet and keep moving forward a while longer.

One Friday evening, Suzanne was waiting for me outside my building, something she never did. As soon as I reached her, she collapsed in tears into my arms. The day before, about six in the evening, Hélène had thrown herself under a metro train in the gare de l'Est.

We went to a café, holding each other up because we might easily have fallen, exhausted, there on the pavement. People moved out of our way, as they would have done for a drunken couple. We ordered a cognac and the alcohol brought more tears to our eyes and Suzanne told me what she'd heard from someone who'd been at the same camp as Hélène: how she'd been forced to carry her mother's dead body, among others, to the crematorium. The sort of madness into which she'd sunk, refusing to eat the little they gave her, explaining that, like this, her mother would have more, and the way she started dancing, unsteadily, whenever a kapo entered the block or approached the work commando. Other than that, she remained lucid, continued to help the weakest in spite of her own exhaustion, and would tirelessly discuss the end of the war, analyse the courage of the Soviet people in Stalingrad, dream of what she would do when she returned to France. Apparently she already had it then, that smile which could resuscitate those who were close to death.

"Me? I dance."

Afterwards we stayed there, not saying anything, sitting across from each other and watching the people and the cars passing on the boulevard amid the murmur of conversations and the clinking of glasses.

The day of her funeral – this was June – the burning sun scorched our eyes and the heavy air left the red flags hanging like damp dish cloths from their poles. I remember the silence. The crunch of gravel under our soles. A woman spoke. Her voice was powerful and calm. I don't recall what she said. She talked about Hélène, of course, about her courage and her devotion, probably. All those banal and true things that get said when people like her die. Listening to her, I imagined Hélène on the platform, among the crowd, watching out for the train under which she would throw herself. But I couldn't imagine her face. What her face was like at that moment. When the woman stopped talking, someone started humming the "Chant des Partisans" and then all of us – a hundred or a hundred and fifty of us, standing in that humid heat, dazzled by the pitiless light – we all hummed it while the coffin was lowered into the ditch.

At that moment, I regretted not having taken her by the waist and held her against me to kiss her. I found it unbearable that I would never *again see her shake her hair or feel her drape the black veil of her gaze upon us . . . upon me. I realised then that we must love the living because the dead don't care and will leave you for the rest of your days with your remorse and your grief. Olga, Hélène. I had let them leave without doing anything, incapable of understanding, of living.*

We saw each other a few more times, Suzanne and I. But there was someone in the room with us, watching. Or pacing the floor, from the door to the window. When I mentioned this to Suzanne, she stared around her, panic-stricken, in the silence of that winter afternoon where the only sound was the whispering of the rain. So we didn't dare anymore. Or didn't want to, I don't know which. We shared exactly the same sensation of that presence with us, between us. We felt the same terrified sadness. One night, when I was alone, I saw Hélène, forehead pressed to the window, holding the curtain back with one hand. I sat up in bed, hopeful that she would turn around and give me one of those smiles that would dispel the darkness, but her image was absorbed by the lights in the street.

She came almost every night for a month. I did start talking to her but she never replied, just turned her sad face towards me. I asked her if she could dance, if she could still do that where she was now, but she remained immobile, her hand always holding back the curtain. Then I didn't see her anymore. I woke up at night, about two in the morning, and I scanned the shadows in search of her. I think I even wanted to make out, in the bluish gleam from the window, her long silhouette and the disorder of her curly hair around her face, but it was over: the curtain remained motionless and heavy, only a few vague traces of light from the street penetrating the room. It seemed to me that she was there though, around me. I thought I could see the shadow of her eyes in the darkness. I was waiting for her ghost and I was angry with myself for this superstitious hope. Then she left me. My solitude deepened, bit by bit. Some days I managed not to think about her. My nights tormented me, full of shadows and cries and bodies that I felt on top of me, everywhere, all around, trembling with fever and fear.

I bumped into Suzanne at a protest march the following year. She was pretty and fresh-looking, on the arm of a tall, shy man. We embraced like old friends, happy to see each other, and we told each other what we were up to. She was going to get married. She would invite me, but she didn't have my address. Then a movement of the crowd around us swept her to the other side of the boulevard. I saw her looking for me. I took advantage of this moment to go home, my throat lined with sand, my heart so swollen that I could hardly breathe.

9

They are on the docks, by the prow of the ship, the *Katrina*, a Norwegian passenger–cargo ship that will load up in a few hours, and above them rises the ship's bow in a perfect curve like a sabre. They can't see the river. It is only a black expanse flickering with the occasional hazy gleam, a will-o'-the-wisp perhaps. They can smell its odour of mud and diesel, hear its sound like a mouth sucking at the concrete bank. All five of them stand at the foot of a crane, in precisely the location planned for the meeting, and stamp their feet in the cold. Irène has tied her scarf around her head, and her coat collar is turned up, the lower part of her face gagged with red wool. Sara is wearing a black beret pulled down to her eyebrows, and she's buried inside a reefer jacket that's too big for her because it belonged to her father, a gigantic anarchist who died in Lerida in August '38 during the retreat on the Ebro.

Alain and Daniel look the same from a distance: cap and sheepskin coat. The only difference is the large bag and the suitcase at Alain's feet. Gilbert is sitting on a crate, feet resting on a knot of ropes, and he smokes as he looks out over the dark water.

They have been here for ten minutes. The man had told them eleven sharp, but they're here and he is not. Nor is the boatswain, who's supposed to be in charge of boarding.

They hear men shout then laugh. One of them begins to sing, but his voice breaks up in a fit of coughing. Somewhere an engine starts up, purrs, stops.

Daniel listens to these erratic noises and tries to put images to this soundtrack, but all he can see is their group, the five of them, silent and alone and frozen stiff, and he frames a series of dimly lit close-ups on their darkened faces. He looks for Alain's eyes but sees only a sparkless hollow, extinguished by his own night. He goes up to him and offers him a cigarette.

The flame of the American lighter. Illuminating only the shadow of eyelashes. Alain nods his thanks.

"You O.K.?" Daniel asks.

"I'd better be."

Forced smile. My brother, thinks Daniel, giving him a little punch on the arm.

"Everything will be alright. We'll get through this."

The girls come up to them. The pack of cigarettes is passed from hand to hand. Their faces light up in the glow of the embers, eyes shine but say nothing.

"There's someone coming," says Gilbert.

He gets to his feet and joins them and they all watch the figure walking towards them. It's him. Jacky. Long coat, trilby hat. Tall and broad, with a supple, silent gait.

"Sorry I'm late," he says, greeting them.

He shakes the boys' hands, keeping Alain's in his.

"So? You changed your mind?"

"No. I'm not backing out. I've not spent all that money for nothing."

"The money's nothing. I'll pay you back right now if you want."

"Keep it. I know what I'm doing. This war . . . I'm not going. I've talked about it so many times with Daniel. And anyway I want to leave this place. I can't stand it anymore, I . . ."

He stops talking and breathes in, as if he had been suffocating.

"I want to see what it's like, in other places. But not in Algeria."

Irène walks up to him. She holds his collar and plants a kiss on his forehead.

"*Comme je descendais les fleuves impassibles | Je ne me sentis plus guidé par les haleurs . . .*"[10]

10 "As I was going down impassive rivers | I no longer felt myself guided by haulers . . . ' – from "The Drunken Boat", translated by Wallace Fowlie.

He looks at her, surprised.

"It's poetry: *Le Bateau ivre* by Rimbaud. *Et j'ai vu quelquefois ce que l'homme a cru voir!*"[11]

"Why drunken?"

"You'll find that out for yourself pretty soon!" Jacky says.

He laughs and pats his shoulder. Irène starts to mutter something then changes her mind.

"Maybe by becoming a sailor, you'll put poetry in your life," Sara says. "You'll see sunrises that we've never seen."

He shrugs.

"I couldn't care less about poetry. I just want to get out of here. The war's just an excuse for finally doing it."

They hear footsteps echoing on the gangway, further off. Jacky squints into the darkness to get a better view of the figure now walking on the dock.

"That's Oskar, the boatswain."

A sturdy man walks towards them, hands in his trouser pockets. He's wearing a woollen hat on the top of his head and a pea jacket of no discernible colour. Maybe grey. He says hello to no-one in particular, his voice muffled. Round, smooth face. Clear, almost transparent eyes. Jacky starts talking to him in English, supported by a full range of hand movements and nods. The other man seems to understand him. He stares at Alain the whole time, looking preoccupied because Jacky is jabbering at him.

"O.K.," he says after a while.

Then he smiles at Alain and places a thick, short-fingered hand on his shoulder.

Alain seems to become a little boy again. He looks at the boatswain with fear and respect, eyes shining. His friends are crowded around him, trying to read his face, which is held apart from the night by those incredibly clear eyes.

"Me speak a little French," he says. "Few words. But the cook he

11 "And at times I have seen what man thought he saw!" – Ibid.

is French too so you can ask him. Good bloke, you'll see. You'll help him, at the beginning. Serve the passengers in cabins, and other things. O.K.?"

"*Oui*," Alain says, but the word gets stuck in his throat and he has to cough to force it out. "*Oui*," he repeats. "*C'est d'accord*." And then in English: "Alright."

The boatswain laughs.

"Oh, you speak English! No problem, then!"

Above them, on board the ship, men are talking loudly while a muffled, metallic, grating movement echoes on the bridge.

"In one hour we leave," says Oskar. "High tide. Twenty passengers for Tangiers, and afterwards Dakar. Hot down there! Not like here or like my country, Norway! I have to show you to the captain."

Jacky waves goodbye to the company, gives Oskar a friendly dig in the ribs and walks silently away.

Alain looks at the other four with a sorrowful smile.

"Alright, well, this time . . ."

He takes Irène in his arms and they kiss cheeks noisily while trying to smile.

"I'll think about your drunken boat," he tells her. "But, I swear, I won't drink too much! I'll be a good boy! I mean, I'm already a deserter, so . . ."

"No, it's called a conscientious objector. And I don't really know what being good means these days."

Sara goes next, hiding her face in the young man's chest.

"We said we weren't going to cry," he reminds her.

She looks up at him, eyes shining, and shakes her head.

"I'm fine. Anyway, it's not like they were going to shoot you! You'll be back in five weeks, and you can pay us a little visit before you go off on your travels again! But I'll miss you, all the same."

She turns around quickly and stands next to Irène and the two of them remain with their backs to the boys, whispering to each other.

Daniel and Gilbert give him a bear hug and clap him on the back, then finally kiss cheeks noisily, to show that they're men, that their kisses are not the sly, quiet type that signify tenderness or love.

"It is a bit like a cousin going away," Gilbert explains.

"Or a brother," says Daniel.

Alain grabs the collar of his sheepskin coat and pulls him close. He talks into his ear. Their eyes shine with the same dark gleam.

"Be careful, O.K.? Don't be a hero. Get yourself a cushy job. Let those other wankers march into battle if they want to, but you need to come back in one piece. Understood?"

"Yeah, I know. Jesus, give me a break! You sound like Maurice. You're going to see the world and I'm going to see the war. I've already told you why I want to see it. But I'm no hero. That's stuff's just for the movies. I have no desire to snuff it over there. And this way, we'll have plenty to talk about. I want us to be able to tell each other what we've been up to the next time we're together. So don't worry. I'll be back. Just like you. O.K.?"

Alain nods. He smiles sadly.

"Just be careful. You're not only going to see the war, you're going to be smack in the middle of it."

"You need to go," Oskar says. "It's time now."

He walks away, past the side of the ship, head down, without turning around. Alain tears himself away. Takes a step back, holding his bags, and looks at the four of them.

"I . . ." he starts to say.

Then he goes. He runs behind the boatswain, arms tensed by the unbearable weight of all his belongings. The sailor stops and waits for him. Then Alain drops his bags and runs to Sara and takes her in his arms and lifts up her slight body and they kiss full on the mouth as they've never dared to before.

"I'll write to you," he says. "One day, we'll be together for good."

They gently push each other away and stare deeply into each other's eyes for – what? – three seconds. Then it's over. Alain joins

Oskar, who takes one of the bags and throws it over his back as if it weighed no more than a pillow.

They listen to their footsteps on the gangway, they see their friend's hand slide up the railing, but he doesn't lean over, not even once, and Daniel knows that he doesn't want to show his face twisted with sorrow, wet with tears.

"Shall we go?"

Sara has turned around, already near the warehouse. She waits impatiently, hands in pockets, tapping her foot. Irène joins her first and the two of them start walking, quickly and lightly, arm in arm. Daniel and Gilbert quicken their pace and go through the half-open gate just after the girls. They don't speak. They let the girls share their secrets while the four of them walk northward along the narrow street, past the fences that surround the port.

A little further on, just as a breeze hits them cold in the face, Irène and Sara burst out laughing then turn towards them:

"Don't you know?" Sara says. "I'm going to get married!"

All four of them laugh. They joke around, push each other, indifferent to the cold wind and the tough times. Then they fall silent and walk back towards their homes, north toward their neighbourhood, which is like a suburb, almost like an island in fact, surrounded by the river, the wet docks, the marshes, connected to the rest of the city by three swing bridges when there are no boats trapped between the locks trying to manoeuvre their way into dry dock. Few cars pass, and behind the fences are the train carriages, the trucks and the warehouses and the thousands of logs from Africa, all covered by the night like a tarpaulin. Nothing moves. A few suspended street lamps illuminate nothing but themselves. Their bulbs shine so weakly that the light never reaches the ground, remaining enclosed in a feeble halo. Here and there, in the forecastle of a cargo ship, a lit-up porthole pierces a patch of brilliance in the night.

Daniel tries to imagine Alain alone in his cabin, perhaps testing his mattress or putting a bag on the floor, and he feels a pang in his heart that makes him grimace in the darkness. He doesn't know what a true friend is. He doesn't know the difference between an *ami* and a *copain*. He should talk to Irène about this: she knows so much about words and their nuances. Friend, brother ... Sister ... Who is what? He watches Irène's chestnut hair bubbling over her scarf; it looks almost blonde in the darkness and he feels like holding her by the neck and pressing her close to him and ... Once again, he is seized by this desire that often comes to him when she moves close to him with those intimate, tender gestures, those bursts of sisterliness that she has sometimes, that childish teasing that he has always known in her, or at least since her parents welcomed him to their home and adopted him and then loved him like their own son and this girl looked at him for the first time with those wide laughing eyes, pulling softly on his ear.

She is his sister, obviously. And yet, not at all. Above all, she is the person he feels closest to in the whole world. Who senses every shiver within him. The one he let enter his secret by opening, for hours at a time, the gates to his sufferings and nightmares, and whispering it all into her ear. The whispers sometimes choked with sobs. That is how she knows about the shining eyes of the sparrows hopping on the rooftop in the cold, the tiny birds watching that little giant pressed against the chimney. That is why she has almost the same memories as him. She went up with him to the roof, when he told her about the day of the round-up, so much so that sometimes he surprises himself by remembering that she was next to him as he leaned against the chimney, under the grey and icy sky, surrounded by ruffled birds, waiting for someone to come and get him.

Irène.

He watches her walking and he loves the way she moves and this thought disturbs him, dizzying him like a child on a merry-go-round seeing the faces rush past without being able to make any of them out.

Especially when, just after the swing bridge, the girls start singing "Milord" at the tops of their voices and dancing badly and laughing and inviting them, Gilbert and him, a pair of clodhoppers who follow without saying a word, to dance with them.

They fall silent again as they get closer to home, passing the walls of the factories, listening in spite of themselves to the deafening roar of the steelworks, groaning like a man-eating monster.

When Irène and Daniel find themselves alone, they hold hands for a moment, as they have often done, since childhood.

"Does she really want to marry Alain, Sara?"

Irène giggles.

"She's mad. But I've been telling her that, about Alain, for a long time. The way he looks at her and all that."

"Oh, really? I didn't notice anything. And he never mentioned it."

She pinches his arm.

"You never notice anything like that. You probably wouldn't even notice if a girl snuck into your bed! That's because you don't look. Anyway, blokes don't talk about love, everyone knows that. All they can do is go on about their performance and laugh like idiots."

Daniel can think of nothing to say in reply to this. He registers the words, tries to understand them, files them away in his pocket wrapped in a handkerchief.

Lying in bed, he tries to fall asleep, hoping to dream of ships and vast horizons and swarming ports, all ablaze with sunlight. He forces his imagination, summoning memories from films, but the images constantly vanish or freeze and turn dark. He falls asleep, his heart in chaos, his mind heavy with confusion and fear.

In the middle of the night he wakes up touching his leg, which has just been torn off by an exploding grenade. He lies there panting, covered in sweat, still blinded by the sunlight that flooded his nightmare, one hand touching his knee, and he has the feeling that he never falls asleep again, until his alarm goes off and he opens his eyes, dazed with exhaustion and sadness.

IO

He wakes with a start because he felt something move near him or heard a groaning sound breathe into his ear and he lies immobile in the blackness, muscles stiff, heart racing, and he stares into this impenetrable darkness and notices that he is still alive, because he's in pain. He is on his back, the blankets pulled up to his chin by his two fists, afraid that they will fall off him or be torn away by someone. There is always a long terrified moment before he remembers where he is: a bedroom heated by the gas stove that he can hear now, humming in the background. A new bed with clean sheets, where he is alone. Around him, the city still sleeps. The city where he was born, grew up, lived, loved. The city that holds all his memories of *before*. Scraps of torn newspaper blown by the wind. The ruins of a party swept away by a tornado. Paper chains ripped to shreds, Chinese lanterns extinguished. And in the middle of all this chaos he wanders, sometimes thinking he can hear wafts of music, an accordion waltz, a confusion of happy voices.

The rhythmic jingling of the alarm clock. The distant rumble of a truck, on the cours de l'Yser. The muted trickling of gutters. As he does every morning, he finds these blind man's landmarks and, as every morning, he will later have the feeling that he is opening his eyes for the first time in a long time. He dares reach out next to him with his hand and finds only fresh sheets, so he rolls onto his side then stretches out on his belly and sighs with relief.

Sleep takes him again, scattered with visions. Dreamed recollections. The nightmare of memory. He moves inside these moments from the past, sometimes moaning and weeping.

Each morning, his unexpected dawn is ripped by the ringing of his alarm, at the other end of the room. He waits for it to stop before rising effortlessly.

He washes himself at the sink in a corner of the kitchen, inhaling the mixed scents of coffee and soap. He rubs his skin until it's red. He holds the flannel underwater then wrings it out then rubs again to rinse himself off then dries himself with a towel. He cannot see his whole body in the little mirror hung in front of him but he knows his body bears no traces except for the scar below his collarbone and that hole in his shoulder blade. No pain. His body is tall and lean and hard. Muscles, tendons, bones. His body is still young, at nearly fifty. He knows it, he feels it. He won't get old until that has been accomplished. He will keep this strength and vitality intact the way you keep a weapon in secret, oiling it regularly, checking its mechanism. And exercising with it too.

His face is all marks, traces, scars. Paths dug in the too-soft ground, trenches never filled after a lost war. An ancient, ageless cartography. Cuneiform writing that you think you can understand without knowing how to read it.

Coffee, barely sweetened. Buttered bread that he dips in his drink and chews, sometimes closing his eyes. He lets the burning liquid pour down the back of his throat, feels its heat spreading through his insides.

Each morning at this wooden table, its uneven legs wedged with cardboard, sitting on his creaking chair, he delights in this moment, both hands cradling the bowl and those little gulps that bring tears to his eyes. And, almost splitting in two, he sees the man he has become savouring what others rush through, what he himself, for a long time, took for granted, until one day he had to lift up the body of a comrade who had died in the night to pick up the scrap of bread he'd fallen asleep on.

Each morning in his mouth the taste and the scent of a silent reconquering.

In the hallway, already filled with the smells of bleach and soap

– Madame Mendez must have put her washtubs on the fire – he hears the sound of her radio, the indistinct chatter of a presenter then music and, fading into the distance behind him, the voice of Edith Piaf. The street is narrow, dirty, sticky with damp. The stinging odour of burned charcoal. He steps over the gutter where whitish, lukewarm water runs, steaming slightly in the cold air. Once he's on the main road, he quickens his pace, matching his footsteps to his calm breathing. He moves through the crowds at the Marché des Capucins, slaloming between the trolleys loaded with crates and boxes and the vans parked willy-nilly on the square and customers carrying large baskets or dawdling in front of stalls. The smells of meat, vegetables, fish, diesel. The shrill cries of the barrow boys and fishmongers, echoing in the covered market, the laughter of butchers coming out of a bar, aprons stained with blood and forearms bare, accompany him like so many auditory landmarks on this itinerary that he has been following for several months now. Next he walks down narrow streets below dark façades, then he enters the roar of cours Victor-Hugo, jammed with traffic, stinking of diesel oil, shouldering his way through the mass of pedestrians, all rushing like him, sometimes muttering a vain excuse.

He enters rue Bouquière, the pavements already clogged with parked vans being unloaded by lads in grey shirts. Bundles of clothes, lengths of cotton, wool, terylene, in solid colours or prints or tartans or polka dots or floral patterns: for soft furnishings, dressmaking. Wholesale and retail-wholesale. A shop every ten metres, each with its own specialities, its own customers.

The one where he works is a long corridor, three metres wide, the ceiling four metres high, the walls covered with shelves full of rolls of cloth, offcuts, clothes in packets of twenty: trousers, suits, jackets, waistcoats, shirts and overalls. Look all you want, but you won't find any bright colours. Everything here is grey, charcoal, brown, navy blue. Beige at a push, but it stands out a mile. Pinstripes are as whimsical as it gets. Houndstooth is an extravagance.

The boss, Monsieur Bessière, is standing behind a counter, examining a tweed offcut. He barely even glances up as he greets him with a sigh.

"Hello, André. No lack of work today. And plenty of headaches as usual."

He says more or less the same thing every day. Drowning in work. Looking exhausted as soon as he starts the day, tired-eyed and pasty-faced beneath his greying brush cut, his forehead glistening in the dreary neon light. With his impeccable white coat, he looks like a doctor or pharmacist on the verge of a nervous breakdown, no longer able to bear informing people that there is nothing more he can do for them and that they must prepare to die with a great deal of suffering. Next, in the same cavernous voice, he complains that business is bad, that people don't dress properly anymore. That is how he justifies the pathetic wages he pays. If he could afford to pay more, he would do so with all his heart, that goes without saying. But the competition is pitiless. The major stores. Look at America. The peril is at our gates, and soon it will swoop down on small businesses and tear them to pieces. He mopes around behind his till, a pencil tucked behind his ear. Some days you'd think he was about to slide the key under the door and go downstairs to hang himself in the cellar.

It's a shame. He should remind him about his house in Caudéran more often, with its big garden, and the three or four apartments in town that he owns, even if he does have occasional difficulties with tenants. That would do him the power of good, poor Monsieur Bessière.

"Hello, André. Your work is ready for you. Thank you for being early."

He says that sometimes. When he's in a good mood.

André. The man always feels a twinge when he hears people call him that. The spare name came to him spontaneously last year in Paris when the man who was forging his papers asked him for it, just after he'd taken his picture. Family name, first name. The forger had a stock of blank identity cards, picked up during the Liberation from the prefecture offices, taking advantage of the chaotic battles being fought on the streets and the desperate demand for certificates of resistance from coppers. He was a former Resistance fighter. Georges. He knew him only by his first name. Georges told him all this under the red lamp of his little darkroom while he soaked the photographic paper in the developing tank. His voice went hoarse as he described the vileness of French cops. After rounding up the Jews and hunting down the Resistance fighters on behalf of Marshal Pétain and the Gestapo, they suddenly felt all republican and hurried through the corridors of the prefecture building in shirtsleeves, a red, white and blue armband around a bicep, to offer their services to the very people they'd spent the last four years hunting and fighting. It was like a huge herd of calves stampeding in all directions, terrified by the arrival of cowboys and desperate to save their arses from being branded with hot iron. The most they ever did against the Germans was to fire their .30 pistols through the windows, without even aiming, as the tanks sped past on the other side of the Scine. "One month earlier, those bastards would only have set foot inside the building on rue Lauriston to smash our heads with truncheons. But . . . what can you do? History is stronger than men, so they say. And we wanted to believe it, back then."

André Vaillant. He liked the sound of that straight away. He tried to forget his real name, the label attached to his previous life, which every day he tried to tear off: Jean Delbos. And so André Vaillant, born 18 March 1911 in Courbevoie, came into existence. Afterwards, he and Georges went to grab something to eat and drink at a greasy spoon on rue de Charonne, and the forger told him about the fighting around Madrid, the fall of Barcelona, the desperate flight of his brigade, his comrades in tears. The death of a dream. It was war, down there in Spain. Heavy artillery, planes, tanks. He saw it all. Hideous death. Friends blown to pieces. Defeat, foreshadowed by terrible massacres. But he doesn't remember being afraid. Rather, a desire to get stuck in, to go and hunt down fascists everywhere he could find them, to flush them out of hiding and confront them head on, to fight the last battle at every moment.

Then came the clandestine struggle. The secret meetings. The preparation of ambushes. The stakeouts. The enemy everywhere. On a street corner, behind a window, in a dark corridor, crouched behind double doors. You search for him and he finds you. After that, blackness. Falling.

And so came terror, though you would never admit it to your friends. Terror that pins you in the middle of the street unable to take a single step or prevents you sleeping for a whole week, woken by a door banging shut in the street. Terror that tears to shreds your paper sleep, with nightmares where you hear them climbing the stairs and smashing down the door, where you see yourself tied to a chair being beaten and tortured, not knowing if you'll be lucky enough to die before you give them the three names you know because you can't take it anymore, because no-one can withstand those weapons, those refinements of brutality, the pleasure they take in it and pursue unwaveringly, perhaps hoping that you won't talk so it lasts longer and they can get their kicks . . . That, that was the true terror, the terror that reigned during the years of the Resistance.

André listened to him talking quietly, his voice husky with emotion, controlling the urges of his hands, which wanted to move around, perhaps to make sure they didn't say more than he wanted to, to make sure they didn't betray him. Like an armless Italian. His shoulders twitched but his fists remained balled to prevent the hands flying around. He had known a Jew in Turin who talked like that, with his shoulders, arms severed by exhaustion.

He liked Georges, this Resistance fighter still tormented by fear, who talked and talked in order to keep it quiet.

Yes, he said, that terror at the idea of falling into their hands because he knew what would happen if he did, that vertigo he felt before he entered a building or crossed the street for a meeting, the silence that always settled within you in that instant, so heavy and massive that it seemed to spread all around and to point you out in the eyes of everyone as the person responsible for that sudden deafness of the air, he had felt that so many times and still dreamed of it now. "Some nights I wake up on the Gestapo's chair, even though I never sat on it. I'm there in the place of friends whom we never saw again afterwards or whose screams were described to us or the state they were in when they were sent back to their cell, shit, sometimes I'm there and I'm scared that I'll talk, can you believe it? And I wake up and I don't know who I am anymore and sometimes I bawl my eyes out like a little kid! It was my one obsessive fear, of course, but nearly fifteen years have passed since then and it still haunts me! How is that possible?"

André did not reply, he just nodded and kept looking at Georges, wide-eyed.

"Why am I telling you all this? My wife is the only one who knows. And two or three comrades who are like brothers to me."

The former Resistance fighter looked at him more closely, pushed back in his seat and smiled.

"You're not saying anything, but I bet you must have seen some things too. I can tell from your face."

Prisoner. It came to him suddenly, like that, unthinkingly, an improvised destiny. He had been taken after the evacuation of Dunkirk and had found himself in a Stalag near Bremen. Three escape attempts, all failures. After the war he had worked in a cotton mill near Douai, but he'd been sacked after a strike, and so after that he'd done some, let's say, more serious stuff, a bit of sabotage, a bit of . . . he hesitated, yeah, you know, a bit of armed robbery, so anyway, he needed a change of scenery and a new name.

Armed robbery. *Brigandage*. André found the word curious and beautiful. Like an old weapon that could be used again.

He wasn't sure Georges had believed him. He nodded but his eyes seemed full of surprise and perhaps admiration for this story-telling talent. But he liked the fable, in any case, and that was probably all that mattered. "*Brigandage*?" he repeated, as if also savouring the word. "I do that too," he added with a smile. "We're on the same side."

So, yes, André. He thinks about the Resistance robber and feels a bit bad about the lie he had to tell him. He thinks about what he is leaving behind him, these successive lives, two, three of them. He read somewhere that American Indians believe they have the equivalent in lives of the three horses[12] they possess, and he knows that two have already died under him or have unseated him before running away – where, he doesn't know, perhaps to eternal prairies where those animals go, calm and happy. The third is walking beside him now. He holds its bridle and whispers to it. He has not yet mounted it; he's waiting until they know each other better. Soon. And then will come the time for the final attack. He needs to preserve his strength. To gather as much of it as possible despite, sometimes, his tiredness.

He sits at his work table, at the very back of the room, separated from the rest of the shop by a high wooden set of shelves sagging under rolls of cloth and packets of shirts. A little nook that some-times smells vaguely of saltpetre. There is a calendar hung on the wall, where he notes down deadlines, jobs he has to do. A colour photograph of the Piazza San Marco in Venice, which he cut out of a magazine.

She had told him one day, in early '40: "When the war is over, we'll go to Venice. We'll leave the kid with my mother and we'll go just the two of us. What do you think? I've seen pictures, it looks really pretty. And apparently you have to see it before you die." He must have evaded her question, as he always did in situations like that. Lied about his real intentions and his plans. He has lied a lot

12 A homage to the novel *Tre Cavalli*, by Erri De Luca.

throughout his life. Bluffed, as in a game of poker. Like when she asked him where he'd been when he came back late at night or early in the morning, stinking of tobacco and wine, and he lied, again, and she listened to his muddled explanations with a weary sigh. She would never see Venice. They would never have to leave her son with anyone. And now he has no-one to whom he can tell the truth.

He lights the lamp and sighs as he sees the cashbooks, the invoices, the delivery notes, the credit notes handwritten by the boss. He gets started. For four hours, he knows he will be able to make his brain work unrestrainedly on calculations and writing and that he will leave the shop with his mind free and light because it will have thought of nothing but figures and numbers, will have been occupied by mental exercises that he forces himself to do, as he used to, over there, for whole days and nights, to stop his grey cells freezing up and his body being trapped in ice.

The door opens behind him and the sound of the flush and the stench of shit follow in the wake of Raymond, the assistant, who taps him on the shoulder with a "Monsieur André". Raymond is a short, stocky man with thick eyebrows and a lantern jaw, neckless and ageless, with long arms capable of lifting huge loads under which he sometimes seems about to disappear. He is old Bessière's creature. His own personal monster. Maybe he tampered with him in his basement, patching him up with bits of other poor devils, like mad Dr Frankenstein. Bessière treats him with a lukewarm mixture of contempt and compassion. He punishes him whenever he's in a bad mood, yells at him if turnover is low and makes deductions from his wages that André does not enter into the accounts or the payslips. Raymond goes off to stand behind his counter, always in exactly the same place, eyes staring vaguely from his square, surly, inexpressive face. He hangs the blue ribbon of his tape measure around his neck, and he checks in a drawer that his chalk sticks are there and takes out two pairs of scissors that he tries out vigorously, making the clear hissing sound of steel rubbing steel.

The telephone rings, an early customer opens the door. The day begins.

André forgets himself in numbers, gets drunk on additions, empties his mind into columns of figures. Sometimes he looks up at the photograph of Venice and stares for a few seconds at a woman in a red dress walking past the basilica.

About quarter past one, he shakes hands with Raymond, waves to the old man who replies with a sigh and goes outside and spits in the gutter, his working day over. Every day that he comes here, he scrupulously follows this shopkeeper's routine, never deviating from it. The way you might climb a rock-face, following a marked path, without neglecting any pitons, without allowing your mind to drift. No sudden jolts, no slackening. Because below you, the ravine is bottomless.

After that, he has time. On cours Victor-Hugo he is almost blinded by the sun as it shoots a few rays of light between the clouds. The air is milder. It's supposed to rain all week, as it often does here in winter. So he looks up at the patches of pale blue sky, he lets himself be dazzled by the violent bursts of sunlight that fall on the wet street.

He enters the café Montaigne and sits on a bench, in a corner, not far from the counter. From there, he can see who enters or who arrives on the pavement, through the big windows. Pupils from the nearby secondary school are sitting a little way off, leaning against the windows and laughing, winding each other up, ties loosened, shirt collars unbuttoned. He hears them talking about Algeria, Guy Mollet, Soustelle, calling for Mendès ... There are five of them. They drink coffee, leaning forward to talk over breadcrumbs, the remains of their sandwiches. Then they lower their voices, one of them whispers, and in turn they stare at his dark eyes. Their faces grow more serious as their eyes meet his.

André decides to look away so as not to be taken for a snitch. At the other end of the café, four old mens are playing cards. They laugh loudly, their chips clicking softly when they throw them on the green baize. Right by the door, there is that very old lady dressed all in black, tiny, a little dog with a long face and bulging eyes sitting on her lap, a glass of beer on the table in front of her. He sees them every time he comes in here. Same seat, same position. The old lady and the dog look out through the window, their eyes seeming to follow the same passers-by, as if they were waiting for someone who was already very late. André wonders who. Someone who is not coming. Or who never came back. But who is not dead, oh no, because she was never informed of anything officially. She did not see his name on any list. She doesn't know. Perhaps prefers not to know. And it's true that you sometimes read in the papers about unexpected reunions. So why not?

Later, the old lady will stand up and her dog will jump to the floor, with a shake of its cylindrical body, and it will chew its leather leash and they will leave, disappearing slowly towards the cours Pasteur. Tomorrow. Surely tomorrow . . .

He has just been served a sandwich and a glass of red when the door opens and a man greets him with a movement of his chin and approaches, removing his hat. They shake hands. The man waves at the waiter then sits down with a sigh, unbuttoning his coat and then his waistcoat. He is quite tall, with a bladelike face and dark eyes. Hair greying at the temples. He looks around casually then changes his seat so he's positioned perpendicular to André, and immediately shoots a glance at the street. Inspecteur Mazeau.

"Shit, I thought I wouldn't be able to make it. We had a double homicide in Mériadeck. A whore who slit the throats of her pimp and a john. There was blood everywhere, she did a good job. One of them was almost decapitated . . . Problem is, she can't explain to us what weapon she used. We haven't found anything. No knife, no razor, no cleaver, nothing. Just that bitch, pissed out of her head, with two corpses, in a room that looked like an abattoir. It was the hotel manager who found her like that, about ten o'clock, as she hadn't checked out. We don't think he's hiding anything, he's a vice squad informer. He runs his hotel and we close our eyes to the drugs he deals occasionally in return for him being a good snitch. Although with that kind of weirdo, you never know when they're going to betray you. The girl could hardly have shanked them with her nail file, so we're wondering. Apart from standing there shivering in her blood-soaked nightdress, she's incapable of doing or saying anything. We don't think she could have acted alone, but we don't know anything for sure, and hardened prossies like that don't talk to cops."

He exhales. He looks like he's just been running, or at least walking fast.

André stares at his forehead, which is glistening slightly. A few drops of sweat at his temples. The waiter arrives, and the man orders a ham sandwich and a beer.

"I'm starving, after all that crap. I haven't had time to eat anything since breakfast."

The old lady leaves with her dog. She shuffles slowly away. The teenagers burst out laughing. They are sprawled on their table, shaking with hilarity, or thrown back in their chairs, guffawing. The belote players lay down their cards grandly. André sees all these scraps of lives like little islands in an ocean of chaos.

"You're not very chatty today."

The waiter returns with the cop's order. He attacks his sandwich, chewing noisily, swallowing with difficulty, washes it all down with a mouthful of beer and exhales, shaking his head.

"Ah, that's better!"

"So?"

Mazeau shoves in another mouthful while watching him with narrowed eyes. Maybe he's smiling, or maybe his face is just deformed by the contents of his big gob.

"So, I have news," he says, mouth still full.

André nibbles a bit of bread from his sandwich. His throat is tight. He can no longer see or hear anything around him. He waits for the other man, preoccupied with eating, to come to the point. Cops are like that. They like to show who's in control of the situation by playing on the nerves of the people they deal with. Enjoying their power.

"One of Darlac's relatives. Some sort of distant cousin. Emile Couchot. Married in '47 to Odette Bancel. They have a wine bar on place Nansouty. That Odette, she's like the sister of his wife Annette. She used to whore for the Krauts too. Danced at Tichadel, just like Darlac's wife. They lived together during the Occupation. Apparently they put on a lesbo show for a hand-picked audience, including the Krauts, who liked that sort of sophisticated stuff, as we know. In '44, when they sensed the wind changing, the two sisters gave up their Nazi orgies and tried to find a way to cover their arses. So they went over to the people who seemed to be in the safest position at the time, cos their analysis of the situation was not exactly exhaustive, namely cops and gangsters. Annette shacked up with Darlac, and the other one, Odette, put her hand down the pants of Couchot, who was making a small fortune with his cousin Darlac selling objects stolen from deported Jews and taking commissions on the sales of confiscated goods. He wasn't the only one and he wasn't as greedy as the lawyers in Bordeaux, who were really filling their pockets, but he got enough to buy his bar and a lakeside cottage for him and his missus. He looks like he's gone straight, but it wouldn't surprise us if he was still doing a bit of business on the side. Anyway, Darlac goes to see him occasionally. And Darlac is not the kind of man who goes to see people just to pass the time of day. And as for family, he couldn't give a crap . . ."

André says nothing. He is digesting the information that Mazeau has given him, mentally sketching a family tree around Darlac. There is something not quite right here.

"How old is Darlac's daughter? Fifteen, sixteen?"

Mazeau smiles, a sly look in his eyes.

"What do you conclude from that?"

"That she was born in '42 or '43. Before her mother met Darlac. That means she's not his daughter. That he accepted her afterwards. That maybe she's the result of her mother bedding a Jerry. And that you must know the truth, you cops."

Mazeau shrugs. He glances over André's shoulder.

"In any case, how would it help you to know that?"

"So I can understand. Know what kind of man he is, how he reacts, so I can know what I should do to really hurt him."

André looks in the cop's eyes, and Mazeau nods knowingly, with a fixed grin. He looks as if he has understood these words.

"Of course," he ventures.

André bites into his sandwich without taking his eyes off the cop, who lowers his, looks away, sips his beer. They don't say anything more, and the hum of the café around them prevents the silence becoming heavy. Then André leans towards him and points a finger at his chest.

"And what's in it for you? Why are you telling me all this? Who are you with? Who are you betraying?"

Mazeau looks saddened and shakes his head. He gazes at André like a beaten dog.

"I don't understand why you're so mistrustful. Shit, you're always like this. It's like you don't believe anything anyone tells you anymore. If I give you information, it's cos we've known each other a long time, cos I know who you are, where you're from. And also cos you had the *cojones* to kill Penot. And cos I didn't think you'd do it. So I'm giving you Couchot. Another one of Darlac's relatives. All these shits slipped through the net after the Liberation, and it doesn't bother me at all if a bloke like you bumps a few off. Anyway, I owe you that much."

"You don't owe me anything. Just cos we were friends doesn't..."

"*Were?*"

"Yeah, well, I mean... I don't really know where I stand anymore, or where we stand. I..."

"Forget it. We all fucked up. We all lost our honour in that shit heap. But you know perfectly well that if I could have . . ."

The policeman finishes his beer, staring down at the table.

André looks out through the bay windows. His face shows nothing. He lets the other man swallow his remorse with his beer; it will pass very quickly, with the first belch. Inspecteur principal Eugène Mazeau was always a penitent bastard. Gnawed at by doubt and by the old moral lessons learned by heart in church schools, but capable of ridding himself of questions of conscience the way you might chase away an overly curious wasp, and then instantly ready for new subterfuges and betrayals. Whether through chance or some dogged scruple, he became part of a group of republican cops in '43 who put together a Resistance network within the Bordeaux police force. Like a coin that has spun on its side for a long time, he finally fell – and landed right side up. Since then, he has been living in the shade of the patriotic laurels on the head of Commissaire Divisionnaire Laborde, the man who runs the city, the man who sees everything, even the slender profits eked from activities condemned by the law and conventional morality but to which the great Gaullist fraternity decorously closes its eyes.

Mazeau had not acted either – he had done nothing, said nothing. But it wasn't up to him. Too young, at the time. And besides, Darlac had promised. Darlac knew what was being prepared. He had sworn in front of Olga, in front of the kid, one evening, that he would warn them as soon as he knew when the round-up was supposed to take place. He had held the kid in his lap. He'd kissed his hair. André remembers all this as if it had happened yesterday. The way he smiled at her, eyes shining with the thought that the three of them would escape the quiet massacre being carried out in Poland that everyone was beginning to whisper about as a little hell capable of spreading across the whole of Europe.

Mazeau sits up, as if emerging from a dream or a stupor. He tries to get the waiter's attention.

"You want a coffee?"

A coffee. André nods. The cop should leave now. He can feel that impalpable mantle of silence and solitude descending on him. No more talking. No more listening. He just wants to go there now and prowl around that address, around that Couchot and his wine bar. See what might be possible. But Mazeau has started speaking again.

"Darlac is convinced that this is all some settling of scores between clans. He thinks this has-been, half-dead gangster – Bertrand Maurac, aka Crabos – is coming down on that shit Destang, who's an old acquaintance of Darlac, and that he sent one of his men to mess up Penot. He reckons that Crabos decided to eliminate Destang and his gang before he snuffs it so he can pay them all back for what happened during the Occupation. Penot was an auxiliary in the S.A.P.[13] – he sneaked in during the Liberation. Anyway . . . you know all that. So, to calm everyone down, Darlac and his henchmen took the Crabos to the station the other day and sent him down to Spain, where he'll meet up with a few of his friends who are managing his money. No-one wants a war here. Laborde – you know, the commissaire divisionnaire? – he promised the mayor he'd keep the peace. It's like the pact they made when they took the city after the war. This isn't Marseille. Everyone knows each other here, but we don't knock about together. We never needed gangsters to control the city. Those sons of bitches, the ones here in Bordeaux, they're not very bright, but they're not really dangerous either. As soon as they start swaggering around, all you have to do is bare your teeth at 'em and they fall into line straight away."

The cop says all this in a quiet voice, arms crossed on the table, leaning towards André. The waiter brings them their coffees so he falls silent, eyes glistening, panting slightly, maybe a bit proud of himself.

13 Section Atterrissage Parachutage – the parachute regiment of the French Resistance's "shadow army" in the Second World War.

André drains his cup in a single mouthful. The coffee is lukewarm, too sweet. Leaving the other man to do the same, he gets to his feet, opens his wallet and drops a banknote on the table.

"What are you doing? Are you leaving?"

"What do you think? I need to walk. I can't breathe in this place."

Mazeau looks around, as if looking for a source of heat or a broken fan.

"I'll call you," André says. "I do really need to get going."

As he walks past the cop, he puts a hand on his shoulder in a gesture of consolation, or excuse. He doesn't really know why he does it, in fact. He leaves the café and the air is cool on his neck so he tightens his scarf and walks quickly towards rue Sainte-Catherine, full of parked cars and groups of pedestrians who wind between the smoking bonnets in Indian file. He goes down to the Garonne and the wind brings tears to his eyes. Wiping them away with the back of his hand, he tries to shake off that feeling of suffocation by breathing through his mouth in time with his strides, like an athlete.

Close to rue des Menuts, he suddenly turns on his heel, colliding with an old man locked in a struggle with his dog's leash, and walks for about fifty metres. There's a break in traffic and he quickly crosses the road. Once he's on the other side, he looks back across the street to see if anyone is following him.

He goes home, turning around frequently, sometimes retracing his steps. He is not proud of these spy-film precautions, but after listening to Mazeau and scrutinising his false facial expressions and his lying hand movements, he is tormented by the conviction that he cannot trust this cop, or any other cops, that perhaps he can't trust anyone at all.

In the afternoon he tries to sleep but can only doze as his heart is racing. Then he picks up a notebook and begins writing. He writes for a long time. His thoughts are unordered, a mass of memories that come to him randomly, like big fish rising up from a dying pond and struggling, mouths agape, on its surface.

He waits for nightfall, which comes suddenly with the rain. For a moment, he listens to the soft sound from the gutters, the erratic ticking of the drips, and he stares out through the window at the vague glimmers spreading over the cobbles on the street. He absorbs this discreet confusion, detecting its nuances, its rhythms and melodies and syncopations. He has never been to a concert, he knows nothing about music, but he remembers that Hungarian, Gregor, the cellist, who at night in the camp would listen to every sound possible, even sounds he never thought he could hear, and would describe them in a whisper. "And that, can you hear it? A kapo walking through a puddle of mud. His footsteps are heavy and slow. He's drunk. And now someone scratching his balls. You can hear his fingernails rustling in the hair." Once he had heard a man's final breath. He spoke a word, a name perhaps, as he died. Afterwards they had listened to the silence that reached them from the place where the dead man lay, at the other end of the shelter, blowing on them like a soundless wind. And then they had discussed, in whispers, what he might have said. "I think I know who I would call out for," André had said, "if I had the strength. If I didn't die in my sleep." Once, an aeroplane had flown over, high in the sky. Gregor had located the rumbling note of the engines and had held it until the end of his gasping breath, gripping his sleeve, interrupted by a cough and by sobs. He died before he could hear the thunder of artillery fire moving closer and filling their nights while they waited, deaf to all the rest.

He shakes himself and stands up. Dresses, trembling, then leaves.

It's a cellar bar. There are dozens of others just like it in the city, selling cheap reds in bulk to blokes who come with their crates of empty bottles, as well as more expensive, elaborate vintages or wines from little-known chateaux passed around on the sly as if they were smuggling something shameful.

A man sits alone at a table, bellowing about a friend of his who won ten million on the lottery and died behind the wheel of the Mercedes he bought himself after dumping his wife, who would have preferred to spend the money on a trip to America.

"That's fate, that is, fuck's sake! There's nothing you can do about that! The bloke would rather have a new motor than his wife or America – what can you do? And it's the same for me!"

"Hardly surprising," says a big man leaning on the bar, a glass of red in hand, "given what your missus looks like! But if I were you, I'd change my car instead. It's easier!"

"I'd take my wife to Noo-York! She's never stopped talking about it since she saw Americans during the Liberation. Near Paris, she was. And on the way back – boom! – I'd get another wife and buy myself a Chambord! If you've got cash, they don't give a shit if you're ugly or your feet stink. All they see is the dough!"

The three other customers laugh and drink to madame's health, while the man shifts in his chair, the laughter dying in his throat.

André approaches the counter and Couchot moves towards him, still laughing, gesturing with his chin to ask what he wants. André hesitates. He glances at the bottles lined up behind the man, who stares at him.

"I dunno . . . A dessert wine."

"I'll do you a glass of Sainte-Croix-du-Mont. I've got some of that in the fridge. You'll see, it's not bad at all."

The glass is cold in his hands. Golden sparkles in the hollow made by his palms. He smells the wine and his mouth fills with saliva. Scents he doesn't recognise, a mingling of sweet aromas. He drinks a mouthful and it makes him feel better. He lifts his head and looks around at the little bistro, at the men laughing and ordering another round. Near the back, on the right-hand wall, he sees a door marked "It's through here" and he walks towards it, turning back to the landlord, who nods at him.

Dark corridor. He stands still for a moment as his eyes adjust and he sees a line of light under the outside door and his hand gropes for a light switch. A weak yellowish glow, splashed like dirty water over the leprous walls. He walks to the back, where a door opens onto a tiny courtyard. There he sees a narrow little bungalow, solid outer shutters closed against the few rays of light that penetrate the louvred shutters. Inside, a radio is singing. To his left, the toilet door, with a heart-shaped hole cut out of it. The bulb inside illuminates only the hole. Squares of newspaper are hung to the end of a metal wire. A water jug that might be empty: he doesn't know, doesn't look.

He goes back into the corridor and walks to the outside door. No bolt or anything. He wonders then if they close the door to the bar.

Back in the main room, the laughter and the ranting have ceased. He walks back to the counter and picks up his glass under the watchful eye of Couchot, who is smoking a Gitane. André gestures to his glass.

"Do you sell this? It's really good."

The landlord moves closer, fag hanging from his mouth, and looks at him, one eye blinking in the stinging smoke.

"Yeah, I sell it. You live in the quarter?"

"A bit further off. Cours de l'Yser. Been there two months."

"Are you Spanish?"

"Why do you ask?"

"Cos it's full of Spaniards over there."

"No. I came from Toulouse. I was there for my job though: I was born here."

"Loads of Dagos over there as well. And you don't have the accent."

"You don't seem to like them much?"

"I've got family in Toulouse. They know all about the Spanish there. As far as I'm concerned, they're lazy bastards. Came and invaded us cos of their war. Bloody Commies. And they're still coming cos they're starving in Spain, not that I give a shit. I do have some good Spanish customers though. Every Dago I know has a strong drinking arm."

André finishes his drink. He invents a smile and sticks it to his face.

"What's better, a strong drinking arm or a strong fighting arm?"

Couchot squints at him.

"That's not bad. I might use that. And what's your answer?"

"There's a good reason why God gave us two arms."

Couchot does not reply. He opens a trapdoor and goes down to the cellar. André hears the sharp clinking of glass. The landlord climbs back up, holding a bottle.

"How much do I owe you?"

"Four hundred and fifty."

"Plus the glass."

"Nah, it's on the house. Free taster."

Couchot wraps the bottle in newspaper. André pays with a five-hundred-franc bill and drops the change into his trouser pocket. He takes his leave, and exits at the same time as another man, unsteady on his feet. The man who told that story about the idiot who died in a Mercedes. He starts laughing, out on the pavement, alone, leaning against a car. André walks quickly away, almost running, acid at the back of his mouth.

He vomits in the gutter. The wine is now nothing more than bitter puke, burning his throat. Further on, blinded by tears, he throws the bottle into the darkness, relieved to hear it explode on the cobblestones.

II

The man is stretched out below the counter, the broken bottle sunk smack in the middle of his face, the neck emerging incongruously from the pulp of flesh, cap still screwed on. Bourbon. Darlac knows this brand. He tasted it once then spat it out straight away. He hates the pukey taste of those cheap Yank drinks. Same goes for whisky. Worse, in fact. He's heard people say it tastes like peat. Yeah, right. Stop drinking compost, you twat, and shut your mouth.

Blood everywhere. Throat cut open. One blow to make him bleed, the second to disfigure him. Darlac leans over the carnage. One eye remains, half open. As for the other . . . The commissaire gives up trying to list the nature of the wounds. The coroner can write all that, if he feels like it, and, more to the point, if anyone's interested. The dead man is Roger Chavignon, thirty-five, who would come here to get drunk from time to time until he started falling off his chair and trying to start fights with the other customers and the landlord had to throw him out. Monsieur, normally so quiet and peaceful, almost shy, was a nasty drunk. Maybe that was why he used to get arseholed? So people would notice him, listen to him. Who knows . . . He lives, or lived, with a wife and brood of kids on rue des Menuts, not far from here. Part-time warehouseman at the Capucins, where he would sometimes help out selling vegetables. The commissaire contemplates this cretin and the bottle that seems to be bursting from his brain like a sudden thought, and says to himself, well, that's one less loser on earth. He imagines the investigation showing that he used to beat his wife – and his kids, because blokes like this are very keen on reproducing – and that his wife put up with the fear and the bruises and that she'll be here soon, throwing herself sobbing on the body of her lord and master.

Some people, Darlac thinks, deserve the shit they're stuck in. They consent to live amid the misery that has been deliberately created for them. But as a cop, he is there to ensure that the mire does not overflow, that the poor don't start taking justice into their own hands, just in case it occurs to them to blame the people who are truly responsible for their sad fate. That is how the world works. If everyone knows their place, the herd will be kept in line.

The culprit is sitting at the back of the room, in handcuffs, between two uniforms. He cried earlier, wiping his eyes with his blood-soaked sleeves. He was caught by some customers as he was trying to scarper. They duly pinned him to the floor and smashed him over the head with a chair before disappearing so they wouldn't get into trouble. A little pimp who got two of his own cousins to work the streets. Jean-Pierre Lopez. He lives with his mum, who looks after his books, having raised the orphans – her brother's daughters – after their parents' death. She is paying herself back what she is owed . . . It's not cheap, two little tarts to feed and clothe, little ingrates who would have just legged it as soon as they turned eighteen without even a thank-you, as if they hadn't done everything they were supposed to do for them.

The chief would not have bothered coming here were it not for the fact that the bloke was found with a gun. A big one, professional. He hadn't used it in the bar, admittedly, but that was just because he'd been saving it for something more important. A loser like him, on a big case, it's delicious: it turns around and bends over like a randy poofter and it says Mass for you before it gets taken.

Darlac nicked the father two years ago, the dominant male of the herd, now doing a ten-year stretch in Toulouse for being an accessory to murder. An active accessory, of course, a fact that the court was only able to establish due to a crafty lawyer. Like father . . . We all know the rest of the phrase, even if Darlac does not hold much with these so-called common-sense aphoristic predestinations. He goes up to the prodigal son and sits down on the other side of the table.

"So, Lopez, you still don't want to tell us why you killed Roger? You know it'd be in your favour if you confessed. Judges like honesty. So do we, for that matter. Remember what happened to your father. Wanted to fool the world and ended up getting the maximum sentence."

Lopez shakes his head.

"No," he says. "It's nothing to do with you."

"Nothing to do with us? Are you sure? You slit a bloke's throat in a public place in front of six witnesses and now you're trying to be discreet about it? What's this about? Some chick? A whore? The others say he was asking for it, that he went at you suddenly even though he hadn't even finished his first bottle. You know this bar?"

The pimp stares down at his fingers.

"Alright. You can tell us all that later. You'll be going straight to jail anyway, and by the time you get out you'll be half dead and senile. Tell me: where did you get your gun?"

Lopez looks up at him, surprised.

"Gun?"

"Yeah, the pistol, if you prefer. An 11.43. Nice weapon."

"Oh, yeah. A friend lent it to me."

"Friend's name?"

"Can't say."

Darlac's hand is crushing the man's face before anyone even saw him move. The chair shakes, and the two uniform cops move prudently aside.

"Friend's name?"

Lopez starts to sob silently, his whole body trembling.

"Shit, I don't know! I met him in a bar, one evening. We had friends in common, acquaintances, so we got talking, just like that, and he offered to lend me a gun so I could do some shooting practice. That's all there is to it, I'm telling you."

Darlac grabs him by his shirt collar and shakes him. He wants to squeeze his throat between his hands now, on either side of his Adam's apple, and watch him turn blue.

"Don't push it, you little shit. Tell me where you got that gun."

He lets go. The pimp collapses into himself, his head bobbing, face sulky like a chastened kid's. He blubbers and sniffs. This pathetic clown is beginning to soften. What comes next should be a formality.

"This bloke called Raymond. He's often in the Escale, on the docks."

"And you go into the woods to shoot at trees, is that it?"

The man looks up surprised, wipes his cheeks with the back of his hand.

"Yeah, something like that, yeah . . . To know how it works."

Darlac pats his shoulder and grins wolfishly at him.

"You're a good lad, I knew it. You're a bit like your dad: not bad, just stupid. Except here, you killed a bloke. So you'd better be helpful, if you don't want to end up with your neck on the guillotine."

He stands up and signals a detective, Lefranc, who is listening to the bistro landlord giving him the lowdown on every customer he's ever had, whining all the while that he has never seen anything like this before, because this is a peaceful establishment that closes at eight sharp every evening after the last aperitif, Inspecteur sir, sometimes not even giving the players enough time to pick up their cards.

"Come on, we've heard enough. Let's take him to the station – he has some explaining to do. You warn the public prosecutor's office. I want to be able to keep him. I'll call the prosecutor myself later tonight."

Instantly, the cops get moving. Two stretcher-bearers arrive noisily, banging the stretcher into everything, and throw a khaki blanket over the dead man and the bottle in his face. Then they lift him up with a heave-ho, sending a kepi rolling along the floor. At the other end of the room, Lopez is dragged to his feet and taken outside.

"The boss wants to talk to you. And only you," says Lefranc.

Darlac sighs, glances at his watch and walks over to the landlord.

"What do you want?"

"You're not going to close me down, are you? This is a reputable establishment."

The commissaire smiles: shows his teeth.

"No, we're not going to close you down. You're serving the public, my good man. You're keeping the people occupied in wholesome activities; why would we wish to prevent you continuing to do so?"

He turns away in search of his hat, which he left on the coat rack earlier. He glances up at the empty room, at the disorder of tables and chairs.

"This is going to be good publicity for you, I bet you anything. The vultures will all turn up to see the crime scene. They'll drink to the health of the deceased. It'll be sweet. If I were you, I'd open straight away, as soon as you've mopped up the worst of the dead bloke's mess. They're going to want to see a few traces, you know. They'll all circle it, glass in hand, like redskins around a whipping post."

He leaves without listening to what the man says as he busies his hands with rinsing glasses, and outside he stares at the thirty or so bystanders who watch as the vans drive off. He hates their ugly mugs, avid for details, disappointed not to have seen anything, not even the dead man's feet, barely even a glimpse of the killer's lowered face surrounded by uniformed cops. They console themselves by watching Inspecteur Lefranc and another man in plain clothes smoking by their car and exchanging notes from their notebooks. One of the onlookers even brazenly listens in to their conversation.

"Look at them," says Darlac. "Bunch of bloody sheep."

The two cops glance indifferently at the bystanders then go back to their confab.

Darlac takes a few steps towards the crowd and removes his hat with a flourish.

"If any of you want to go in and clean up, the boss is hiring."

People look away. Two or three women leave. The two detectives laugh. Darlac wonders if they're laughing at him or at those scavengers grouped on the pavement across the street. He gets in the car and drives off at full throttle, looking in the rear-view mirror and seeing their stupefied faces turned towards him, and he doesn't slow down until he has rounded the corner of the street. For him, this city, with its trivial occupations, its deathly peace, is merely a hostile backdrop peopled by little action figures whom he would like to knock down or crash into just to feel the soft, muffled thud of their bodies hitting his car's bonnet and being thrown into the air, like a furious kid sweeping all his toy soldiers off the table with the back of his hand.

*

This is where he feels good, Albert Darlac, after all this shit, these pathetic cases, these degenerates murdering each other, all the blood, the lies, the legal procedures that have to be followed, as if these parasites actually mattered, I'd stick them up against a wall and we'd charge every fucking family for the bullets . . . He thinks this as he watches the wine flow into his glass and his heart pounds with rage and hatred, but he knows that in a moment everything inside him will grow calm, curtain drawn, shutters secured.

He picks up a candle and examines his wine in its flickering gleam. He rolls the ruby liquid around in the glass. He sniffs, ogles it again, then drinks. Next he swishes the nectar round his mouth so his mucous membranes can soak it up. Swallows slowly. Sighs.

Grunts with pleasure as he reads the label on the bottle again. Emile's Saint-Emilion is really something. He feels the aromas flowering at the back of his palate. Premier Grand Cru, 1947. Surprising. He smiles. A rare event. Or maybe not. Maybe it's a sardonic grimace, a bitter or contemptuous sneer. Even when he's at home, as on this Saturday evening, sitting at the table, waiting for madame to serve him. Even with his daughter Elise, he finds it difficult to smile. He has eyes only for her, soft, fascinated, worried. And hand gestures, caressing, light, that recently she has been ignoring more and more often, now that she's a teenager.

She sits across from him, at the other side of the table, face leaning down over her plate, eyes hidden behind long brown lashes. With the tines of her fork she traces parallel lines on the tablecloth then erases them by going across them as she tries to draw a grid.

"You look thoughtful," Darlac says, putting down his glass.

The girl looks up at him as though she has just noticed his presence. She shrugs one shoulder, twirling the silver fork in her fingers. She glances towards the kitchen, from where they can hear her mother taking something out of the oven.

"No, it's just that . . ."

"It's nearly ready! Start the pâté without me, I'll be there in a minute!"

The voice tries to sound cheerful and bright amid the clanking and banging of utensils. The model mother, the busy housewife.

Darlac grabs the dish and cuts some thick slices. Chicken liver and foie gras. A present from the butcher at the Grands-Hommes market whom he helped out of a sticky situation last year: a gambling debt rather insistently demanded by some loser, a dilettante pimp who was trying to be threatening. As he was a former rugby player, a craggy giant who was promising to turn his butcher's shop into an abattoir, the honourable barbecue artisan, who sold roasts to old biddies from the Chartrons, was afraid for his safety.

But that scrum half didn't know whom he was attacking. He

could never have guessed that Darlac and the man who deboned meat for old ladies had been in business together in '43: a few valuable pieces of furniture, a few gewgaws and paintings stolen from apartments after the round-ups; and a plot of land just after Mérignac, on the road to the airport, three hectares of cattle pasture that would end up as building land one day, confiscated with a stroke of a pen by a prefecture underling and certified by a notary.

That brute of an athlete was surprised one night in the arms of his hooker, stinking of cologne, his pockets full of cash, by a dozen cops. And a little packet of opium folded inside a sheet of newspaper to seal the deal, slipped in there secretly amid all the confusion by a detective sent by Darlac. The man looked so genuinely shocked by this that the cops almost began to wonder, to doubt his guilt. But then they concluded that this arsehole was just a very good actor, like a lot of the deadbeats they interrogated. Move over, Jean Gabin and Gérard Philipe. Every day at the station it's like the flicks but in real life, like being at the bloody theatre, crying and laughing over half-arsed scripts. Any old detective knows as much as Louis Jouvet in *Entrée des Artistes* and can take apart all the fake confidences, the true deceits, can unmask the bloodthirsty ingénues, hunt down the lies, fill the holes in memory, prompt the actors – forcefully if necessary – whenever they dry up.

And then he got uppity, the giant: he yelled that he knew some very important people, thanks to his rugby career. Men at the mayor's office, bigwigs, he knew them all, you bunch of twats; he told them this while the girl was dragged outside by the hair because she was screaming too loud. He refused to admit that it belonged to him, that opium. He never touched the stuff. They were trying to frame him, but it wouldn't work. He yelled, he denied, fiercely, then he lost his temper and went for the throat of a detective, trying to strangle him with his massive hands, presumably in an attempt to squeeze the truth up and out of his mouth. Instantly set upon with rifle butts, fists and boots, he finally let go of the cop, who had been starting to turn blue. There followed a violent scrum, eight against one. Even after he was handcuffed and dragged to his feet, he kept worsening his case with each movement he made, kicking out and elbowing them in spite of his cracked ribs, with each word he spat out, red with blood, from his dislocated jaw, and then he hurled abuse at the pigs, adding charge after charge to his night's misdemeanours along with the bruises and the broken noses. Verbal abuse and assault and battery against officers of the law, attempted murder of a police detective, added to possession of narcotics and procurement. The cops took turns reading him his rights and smacking him over the head to calm him down.

The commissaire remembers the account his special envoy had given him, having pinched a bit of opium from a secret stash in the Vice Squad office. He smiles as he spreads pâté on a slice of bread.

"I just can't stand it anymore," Elise mutters, without looking at him.

Darlac, who had been about to bite into his bread, puts it down and leans forward.

"What's the matter?"

She looks up at him with her beautiful green eyes, her gaze soft as silk, and Darlac shivers.

"Those detectives following me around everywhere—"

"Which ones? What have they done?"

"Nothing. I—"

"What do you mean, nothing? Explain yourself!"

The words come out louder than he intended. He flaps his hand around, as if to catch them or soften them.

"Tell me, if there's something wrong."

"They're always there, following me around. On foot, in cars . . . When I go out in the morning, they're there. When I come out of school, they're there."

"You think they're not discreet enough?"

"No, I just mean . . . Well, I know them, so I feel like they're all I can see. And then, the other day, Madeleine – you know, my friend? – she noticed something and asked me if we were being followed, and she showed me the tall one, what's his name . . . ?"

"Morlaas?"

"Yes. And I didn't dare tell her, even though she was scared and I didn't know how to reassure her. And then, after a while, we didn't see him anymore, and it was alright. It scares me too. I always have the feeling that that man is going to come back and strangle me."

Her eyes are filled with tears. She gently pats them away with her napkin.

Darlac is furious. He tries to imagine his men standing ten metres behind his daughter, about as discreet as clowns at a circus. Discretion was his absolute condition. So much for that . . . "*Ach!* French police!" the Krauts used to snigger whenever anything went wrong, and sometimes they had been right, those bastards, even if the *französisch Polizei* had served them with loyalty and zeal and a certain degree of efficiency. Just ask those Resistance members surprised to find themselves nicked by French cops . . . or ask the ones encouraged to talk in the basement of the prefecture by the persuasive methods of Poinsot and his master butchers. Some of them would have given up their parents just to make it stop, but they were never asked for that much, just a name, an address. It was like extracting a playing card from a tower patiently assembled by trembling fingers. He always defended that honour, Commissaire Darlac. The honour of a job well done. The French made a pretty good fist of disposing of their own communists and Jews and terrorists, most of the time. The Germans were there as cover. Tough shit for them if they didn't manage to win their war.

But right now their job is to protect and entrap, and those dickheads are apparently incapable of it, even if that nutcase surely wouldn't be stupid enough to attack again anyway. That man got Penot with a knife, in his hallway, and bled him dry. No-one saw or heard anything. Not a trace, not a single fingerprint. Like a ghost. It would have been easy to shoot Penot, anyone could have done it: just walk up to him, revolver in hand, as he's about to get in his car and blast the contents of his skull over the dashboard. Nice guaranteed visual effect, and it would give food for thought to all those hangers-on, those cowards and nobodies who crowd around the big shots. Or get him while he's slurping up a stew in his favourite bar, because monsieur was a regular there, and everyone knew it. There again, there'd be warm brains on his plate and grape juice coulis splattered everywhere. And the first one to move would be served more of the same. The police photographers would have a ball. They'd take three rolls just to capture the beauty of the image. That's how it ends in Marseille, and sometimes even here. The bar closes for a few days, and it's a little quiet after it reopens, but the customers come again, sometimes from a long way away, to visit the cursed place and taste its specialities.

But this man . . . he must be a very patient man. He watches, he prepares. He follows, he's there, and nobody sees him. Monsieur Everyman. A grey man in this grey city. Camouflaged. And unlike the hordes of perverted loonies and lazy murderers and impulsive cretins who fill up the newspaper columns, this one seems to have a brain and to know how to use it. Darlac feels flattered by the challenge. It lifts him up above the dumb beasts that surround him: cops, gangsters, whores, swindlers, pimps, each more gullible than the next; a bunch of filthy, hopeless little piglets fighting over the shitty paddling pool where they shuffle blindly. The commissaire can sense that this is a criminal worthy of his enmity, a different species, acting alone without a doubt, in pursuit of a goal, gripped by an obsession perhaps. Pitiless, contemptuous of money and material goods. Some sort of mad monk? Shining his bullets up like silverware before lodging one in your gut. A refined man, maybe an intellectual ripened by years in jail, embittered by his treatment at the hands of the screws. A man unafraid of death, perhaps someone with nothing left to lose? Not the kind of man who will let himself be taken alive.

So the commissaire muses, his thoughts drifting into fiction, as if in pursuit of Fantomas. Or Judex[14]. He doesn't really see the difference, but he senses that, between him and this man, it's personal: *"Tell your father I'm back and I'll be back again."* He hears Elise's voice again in his head, shaken by sobs, repeating those words that the man had breathed into her face. But where he had returned from is a mystery. As is when he will return again.

Darlac's hand moves across the table and touches his daughter's, which is cold and limp, before she withdraws it with a suddenness that she tries to control but that he feels.

"I'll tell them to be more discreet. They're oafs. But you know what that bloke said to you. We can't take any risks."

The girl nods. Dries her eyes.

Madame returns at that moment, humming. The beauty of Cadiz has eyes of velvet, but her song is ended by the silence that hangs heavily over the table.

"Elise? What's the matter?"

Darlac clicks his tongue to shut her up, without even looking at her, so she sits down, her face turning hard and expressionless with humiliation and anger. She is no longer looking at anything; her eyes roam over the cutlery, the plates, the slices of bread in the breadbasket, as if checking that all is where it should be.

"You know perfectly well why my men are following you. They're protecting you from that lunatic. Can't you understand that? You want him to attack you again? You want him to . . ."

Annette Darlac suddenly leans forward to reach the pâté. Her wax mask comes between her daughter and her husband and both watch as she sits back down again, taking no notice of them, too

14 Fantomas was a famous fictional French serial killer, masked and mysterious. Judex was similarly mysterious and powerful, but fought on the side of good, avenging evil.

busy serving herself with brusque movements, too stiff-backed when she sits on her chair to conceal the tension within her. The clinking of the silver cutlery takes the place of conversation. All three of them eat grudgingly, each picking at their food with the point of a knife, each deep in their own thoughts. The girl shoots fearful glances at her father, who looks at a painting on the wall behind her, a pastoral scene from the eighteenth century by a Burgundian master, according to an expert when he had the items he'd accumulated during the war valued. "*A pupil of Boucher. – If you say so. – Worth around three or four million. It's a magnificent work.*" Darlac decided to keep the *daub*, as he called it. He hates that shepherd and shepherdess, flirting with each other surrounded by chubby sheep, a dog asleep at their feet. He hates the simpering look on the girl's face, the way the boy looks like a queer, but at that price it goes nicely over the sideboard, just as the porcelain dinner service, which was part of the same haul, goes nicely on his table.

Madame stands up without a word and walks to the kitchen. Darlac looks at his daughter. She meets his gaze briefly then turns away.

The arrival of the lamb provides a diversion: he examines and sniffs it while a hand protected by a dishcloth folded in four puts the hot oven dish in front of him. He grabs a large knife and slices into the pink meat. A pan of sautéed Sarladaise potatoes is brought to the table. He feels fine then, Albert Darlac, carving slices from the lamb while greedily eyeing the gills of wild mushrooms mixed with the potatoes. He serves everyone quickly; the muttered thank-yous sound stiff and insincere but he doesn't care. His plate is heaped, juicy, aromatic, his glass filled with ruby nectar. Nothing else matters but this moment of plenitude, and the first mouthful lifts him away from the grasp of any contingencies: let the world die, it is in instants like this that he feels fully alive.

So they eat in a silence sparsely interspersed with questions murmured by the mother to her daughter and the softly spoken replies. Her school, her navy-blue skirt, the latest news on Constance, a friend who had an appendectomy the week before. And about school: is Sister Anne-Marie, the Latin teacher, as strict as ever? The conversation is intermittent, semi-clandestine, under the feigned indifference of Darlac's gaze, alert for any looks, hesitations, unusual intonations, anything that might betray a secret shared by the two women, or even a simple decision taken behind his back.

He has second and third helpings of the meat, spreads another slice of bread with pâté, but he does not have any cheese and decides to leave a little wine at the bottom of the bottle for tomorrow. He is getting organised. After the *gâteau à l'orange* that madame has made – as she always does on Friday nights – he leans back in his chair as they clear the table, while he waits for his coffee to arrive. His face relaxes a little bit, as the bitter crease that drags his mouth downward goes slack.

Just the kind of evening he likes. He's in his armchair, leafing through the newspaper; his daughter has gone to her room, and madame is humming as she washes the dishes. She's always humming. It goes back to her music-hall days, when she used to sing at the Alhambra while high-kicking onstage. She sings to herself the latest hits heard on the radio. At the moment, she is endlessly repeating "Je t'appartiens" by that Gilbert Bécaud, who makes women daydream in front of their sinks with his breathless crooner's voice; either that or Edith Piaf, who whines loudly about her life as a poor girl. He hates that noisy dwarf. Madame also adores the bawling of Luis Mariano or Marcel Merkès and Paulette Merval. The annoying couple, with their soppy yelping. She even rewards herself with matinées at the Grand-Théâtre on Sunday afternoons with her friend Suzy so she can listen to all those loudmouths in sequins. And that's without even mentioning the records she listens to during the day on the phonograph that her sister gave her last year. He refuses to listen to that thing. All he likes is Maurice Chevalier and Ray Ventura, the only singers to put him in a good mood. He pukes over all those imbeciles singing about love, all that romantic billing and cooing.

In bed, while he waits for madame to finish her ablutions, he tries to read an adventure novel, maybe a Western, but he doesn't understand it at all and finds himself turning the pages mechanically, mixing up characters and incidents, then tosses the book on the floor. Annette comes out of the bathroom and approaches the bed. She is wearing only the negligee that he bought for her last week. Darlac slips a hand under the sheets to touch his hardened member. He still feels the same desire for that body which has not aged, not put on weight, which is still almost youthful, with its slender curves. He still feels the same desire he felt for her that first day, when he saw her in '45 improvising a striptease for Yank soldiers in a bar on the docks, dancing on a table.

She no longer dances or sings. Well, only those stupid songs she hears on the radio.

She comes towards him without looking at him, because he has forbidden her to in such moments. She takes him in her mouth – God, he loves that – then as he's not satisfied, he slaps her then gets on top and penetrates her brutally. She barely struggles while he rapes her: a punch to the side of the head flattens her, face down. He pulls her hair and insults her, then lifts her face up to see the look on it. "Go ahead and blubber, you bitch!" he mutters, and grunts a flood of obscenities. He plunges harder, forcing himself deeper, so much that it hurts him, but he likes it anyway because he knows she's suffering more deeply, body and soul, with every thrust he inflicts on her.

When it's over, she cries.

Curled up in the foetal position, she turns her back on him. No sobs, not a sigh. He knows she's crying though, because as always in these moments he touches her face to wet his fingers in her tears.

"That's it, go on. Cry your eyes out, you stupid bitch. You owe me that."

Deep sleep. A black hole, peopled by the occasional movements of shadows that pursue him until morning.

Telephone. Downstairs. He lets it ring, five, six times. He knows she's awake but that she won't move. He knows it's for him. He gets up, can't find his slippers, goes out on the landing barefoot, walks downstairs. Grumbles. Yeah, yeah, I'm coming, shit.

"Yes, this is Darlac. What? When? Oh fuck . . . And them?"

He listens, running a hand through his short hair, down the back of his sweating neck. It's the senior inspecteur, Carrère, who apologises and then explains.

"I'm on my way."

Darlac says that breathlessly. He hangs up, head spinning. The night dances slowly around him.

He goes back up to the bedroom, turns on a lamp. He watches madame while he gets dressed in yesterday's clothes. He knows she's not asleep. He knows she's listening out for his movements, his breathing, the slightest clearing of his throat, but he won't tell her anything. He's not in the mood for a crying fit or a discussion. He is still stunned by what he's been told. The last thing he needs is a hysterical woman to deal with right now. He'd be capable of . . .

Once he's out in the street, he feels better and walks at a good pace to his car. The rain has stopped, but not the wind. Damp and lukewarm. A south-westerly. The city is deserted and glows dimly in the bleak shine of the ghostly street lights. He drives fast, never slowing at crossroads, crushing the steering wheel between his hands.

As soon as he gets out of the car, he smells it: the stench of fire and cheap wine in the back of his throat. Two or three officers salute him and he responds with a grunt, pushing past a few onlookers in dressing gowns. He steps over fire hoses, walks through puddles, dazzled by the flashing orange lights on the police and fire-brigade vehicles. Carrère is there, a cigarette in his mouth, and he turns towards him, wide-eyed with shock. He points to a smoking building, the windows smashed and gaping, the roof caved in. There are firemen in there, moving joists and tiles, and their lamps throw beams of light through the smoke still rising from the rubble. The canvas sign is hanging from its rods, dripping water.

"It all burned in an hour. Petrol and gas, according to the firemen. And people heard an explosion before they saw the flames. Two other bottles exploded during the fire, which didn't help. I called you cos I know you know the place. I've got two men in there looking, but in the dark, with all this rubble, I don't know what they're likely to find. We're waiting for a generator so we can get some light."

An officer in a chrome helmet walks up, salutes, shakes the cops' hands. He introduces himself: Lieutenant Bordes. There are trickles of sweat on his face, and a big black moustache.

"We're searching for any victims. The roof collapsed, probably because of the gas bottles exploding, and that set the rest off. Even the supporting walls got it. We found traces of petrol in what's left of the kitchen. The gas was on. It's arson."

He speaks in a gravelly voice, with a Béarnaise accent. Someone calls his name; he apologises, and goes back to his men in the ruins.

Darlac is still staring at what remains of the façade: part of a wall, two dark rectangles and a broken window frame. Carrère's voice drags him from his reverie and he shivers a bit.

"You O.K.? Not too shaken up? Are they relatives of yours? Arson . . . Christ! That's all we need."

Darlac does not reply. He walks towards the rubble, stopping in the burned-out doorway, his feet in a puddle. The air is saturated with the smell of wine and cork, mingled with the bitter stink of charred wood and rubber. He enters under what remains of the bar's low ceiling, the plaster fallen away to reveal the hollow bricks beneath. The firemen are working by torchlight, more or less. There are four of them clearing the ground, breathing heavily, groaning as they lift up a beam, a half-burned cupboard. They are throwing tiles behind them. The two detectives, a little way away from the ruins, look hesitantly around, pushing the rubble away with their feet, hands in the pockets of their raincoats. Darlac watches them, forcing himself not to yell at these two cretins who seem to imagine that the clues are going to jump up at them, playing for time while they wait to go back to the office so they can sit in the warm and type up the procedures. He can't see a thing, his eyes stung by the smoke that still floats in the air, rises up from the depths of this disaster. He ventures into a chaos of collapsed beams, and thinks he can see the stump of a chair. One of the sleuths spots him, and both salute him.

"Haven't found anything," one of them says.

"In your pockets, you mean? Is that it? You've got nothing in your pockets, and yet you've been searching through them for quite a while now?"

The detective does not understand. He hesitates.

"Oh, just fuck off, you morons."

"But..."

"Let the firemen do their jobs. They're busy working. Get your fat arses out of here."

The two cops turn quickly, tripping over the rubble, and walk away grumbling. He watches them brush dust off their raincoats, turn up their collars, light cigarettes as they walk towards their boss.

The firemen clear, lift, probe. They talk in low voices. One of them has climbed up into what remains of the upstairs, and Darlac can hear the floorboards creaking as he walks, plaster falling in pieces or crumbling into clouds of dust, and his colleagues, afraid that he might come down through the ceiling at any moment, shout up at him to watch out.

Darlac does not dare move. He has the impression that, if he takes even one step forward, he will step on a body. He is afraid of profaning this place where the night is condensing. But he ventures forward anyway, on tiptoes, stuff squeaking and cracking under his soles. He sees the zinc mass of the bar, a couple of metres away, but cannot get his bearings. To his right, the stone staircase is now just a flight of steps falling into darkness. He tries to catch his breath. He has the feeling he must have forgotten to breathe since he came in here. He hears a van manoeuvring behind him, a man yelling over the noise of the engine to guide the driver. Two spotlights mounted on the roof illuminate the scene. The shadows of the men, looming huge on those walls that are still standing, have round backs and move slowly like predators busy eating the corpse of a prey. Against the back wall, the first floor has collapsed in an inextricable pile of floorboards, beams and bricks. He can see a sideboard, leaning crookedly against a beam, its open doors vomiting pale linen. The foot of a bed, sticking out of a heap of stones.

He remembers the bombardments during the war. Those houses with their bowels exposed and the people you would see standing dazed in front of their ruins, amazed to be alive. And then there were those they found beneath it all: in their beds, crushed under a sink or a stove, depending on what they were doing at the moment the bomb crashed through the roof and exploded. Not always in one piece. Or, burned to a wall, traces of human beings, the macabre mark of a body that barely existed at all anymore. Sometimes people called them, him and his men, to record what had happened, particularly when thieves had been seen in the vicinity by the civil defence, just in case those arseholes tried to complete the work of the English–Canadian ammunition by quickly grabbing a wallet or a few family jewels.

He hears the firemen walking in glass, crushing shards of broken bottles under their boots. Then one of them yells "Stop!" and everyone freezes, goes silent, and the silence thrums only with the drone of engines.

"There's one!"

The others move forward. He hears Carrère asking to be let through, because for now this is his investigation. Darlac rushes over, heart trembling. He doesn't understand the emotion that has taken hold of him. Emile and his wife were distant relations, never close to him, just another couple of stooges. But the girl? What was her name again? Arlette. He doesn't know what's happening to him, getting so upset like a woman. That girl was nothing special. Just a pretty kid who got men like him hard. He could have had her for free, as often as he wanted. But he hasn't eaten that kind of pie for several years now. Lost his appetite, maybe.

He moves closer. The men, bent over a pile of burned debris with the legs of overturned tables and chairs sticking up out of it like bits of dead bodies, pant and groan with effort, speaking with their hands and eyes. In the lamplight he glimpses feet with black swollen toes, a bare ankle, the other one sticking out from a trouser leg. A man's feet. A rubber sole melted on the heel, like a huge black blood clot.

There's a cross beam lying on the corpse, so four of them strain to lift it up and throw it aside. After that, they clear away bricks and rubble and the man's body, revealing a woman's body, face down on the ground.

They are lying in a soup of sweat, wine and water, amid a clutter of smashed furniture, broken bottles, half-burned rags, plasterboard. They are covered now only by scraps of cloth nibbled by the fire. Their faces are unrecognisable, their flesh raw, blackened, grilled. Mouths gaping. Teeth bared, white and shining. The bloody mask of their final screams.

A fireman steps aside to puke. He's young. Maybe these are his first burn victims. It's true that there's that smell now. The men breathe heavily, wiping their mouths with the backs of their gloved hands.

Darlac gets out of there, feeling as if his heart has swollen to fill up his entire chest and is banging against his ribs like a giant fist, chewing up his stomach. He stands in front of the windowless façade and lights a cigarette, but throws it away after the first drag, feeling sick.

A yell. Like someone being strangled.

"Here! Another one!"

"I thought there were only two."

Carrère beckons him over from the doorway. Darlac, breathless and dizzy, tries to run on his stiff legs.

The girl's body is under a bed that they're lifting up, curled up like a foetus, covered in her coat. All he can see are her pale slender ankles.

"Asphyxiated," says the fire-brigade lieutenant. "Look. No burn marks. She must have hidden under the bed when the house caught fire."

Carrère scribbles something in a notebook, not looking at what he writes in this shifting darkness.

"Take off the coat, so I can see."

Silence. The face still hidden by her hands, black hair spilling all around. Carrère reaches out a hand, softly, slowly. He whispers, "Here, like this," like someone who's scared of hurting a child. The glow of a lamp flickers above.

The mouth is wide open, eyes half closed.

"She's a kid," says the lieutenant.

He takes off his helmet and wipes his forehead. Turns his face away, eyes staring into blackness.

"Don't touch anything else," says Carrère. "Wait for the photographer."

Darlac moves away, breathing fast, trying to calm the creature that is stirring inside him. He can't understand anything. How could they have known the kid was there? And surely they wouldn't have killed her with the others. And why such ferocity? Burning a building, and the people inside it? This isn't Sicily! They would have picked her up and taken her to the Crabos or the Parisian, the famous Robert. He goes through their faces the way he would with a witness, showing mugshots of dickheads for an identification. What about him? And this one? And the witness frowns, hesitates, asks to see one again. Yeah, maybe this one, but it was pretty dark. Darlac knows them all, the men he is mentally viewing now. He knows their voices, their mannerisms, their habits, their vices, from the venial to the truly vile, their breaths reeking of tobacco or alcohol or rotten teeth, the smell of their sweat and their feet, and the rest, for those who only ever wash their cheeks after they've shaved. He knows their warts and beauty spots by heart, the shapes of their eyebrows and their hair, the colours of their eyes, even to the subtlest shades, blues, greens, hazels, blacks, and all their baleful reflections. And this memorised police file gets him nowhere all. He sees himself surrounded by this ring of Bordeaux gangsters with their political affiliations, Gaullists and collaborators, henchmen and Wanted posters, all these faces spinning around him endlessly like war-painted Indians in one of those Westerns, dancing round a cowboy who you know is going to come to a sticky end.

And then it hits him in the pit of his stomach. *He* came here. Him. The other man, that ghost. He was here, in this very square. Yes, that's it. He went in through that door on the side of the bar. He hid in the courtyard. Or in the bog. He waited until the bar closed, until everything was quiet. Apparently this bloke has something against café owners. The man is a walking nightmare, circling around Darlac. He'd better not sleep anymore, if he doesn't want him to come. Or sleep with one eye open, so he can trap him and send him back to limbo.

Carrère comes over, slowly crossing the road, head down. He looks up at Darlac, revealing a drawn and frightened-looking face, eyes shining.

"Can you believe it?" he asks with a sigh.

"Believe what?"

"All this shit . . . There were two of them living there, and suddenly we find that kid. I mean, where the hell did she come from? You're related to them – do you know anything?"

"No, not a thing. I only see them about twice year, if that . . .

Anyway, calm down. What's up with you? You've seen dead bodies before, haven't you? What I want to know is who did this. There's no point snivelling over the victims. There's a bloke on the loose in this city who's just burned three people to death.

"All the same . . . what was she doing here, that girl? Her face isn't harmed. We could get a decent photo and publish it in the papers. And maybe the customers or the neighbours saw something, someone suspicious lurking around . . . Everyone knows each other round here, it's like a village."

He's talking to himself, eyes on the ground, rubbing his chin. The two detectives show up at a trot, as if they've just found the arsonist's business card in the ruins.

"What have you got?"

"Nothing. We just came to see if you still needed us."

Carrère stares at them, dumbstruck. He looks like a good bloke, this Carrère: a serious cop, intelligent, human, an eagle in a henhouse, a nugget of gold in a bucket of gravel, but now you can see him holding his breath to avoid screaming with rage at these two morons, keeping his fists balled deep in his pockets so he doesn't punch them in their stupid faces.

"Alright, you can go."

They don't move, so he leans over them, almost on tiptoes, holding his hand to his mouth like a loudhailer.

"Fuck off," he says equably. "Vanish."

They walk away without a word, without the slightest hesitation.

"Where did those two twats come from?" Darlac asks. "I've never seen them before."

"They were transferred last month: one from Nantes, the other from Paris. They must have done something dodgy, but I don't know what yet, cos I haven't had time to dig into it. They sent them to us cos Commissaire Verne says they won't do as much harm down here."

"Are you leading this investigation?"

"Dunno. We've got stuck with the findings, and we'll have to type up all the paperwork, but it might still slip through our fingers. Often does. Why? You want to investigate it for the families – or for yours, anyway?"

In a quick, brutal movement, Darlac grabs him by the back of his coat, then lets him go.

"Never say that. Fuck. Don't even go there, or you'll . . ."

Carrère smiles slyly. With the back of his hand, he dusts his jacket where Darlac grabbed him.

"I get it, Darlac. Everyone gets it, cos everyone knows you. Your friends, and now your family, are off limits. We know. But you better be careful all the same: you think you're safe in your fortress cos you've got the gangsters by the balls, but your castle's built on sand. And your cousin probably wasn't much better than you, so I couldn't care less if him and his wife got roasted alive. But I don't think that kid had anything to with them. I think there's something going on here, and either I or someone else is going to find out what it is. So maybe we'll talk about this later. Now go. *Adichats*, as they say where I'm from. I've got work to do."

He turns his back on Darlac and walks quickly across the square. He talks with two firemen, greets the photographer who's rewinding his film, then disappears behind a red lorry.

Darlac is stunned. That quiet, slender little man with his calm teacher's voice packs quite a punch, gently informing you that you're the class shit and you're going to fail your exams and there's nothing you can do about it. He checks his watch and sees it's nearly 5 a.m. Then, gradually, he gathers his wits, regains some lucidity. His senses put him back in contact with the darkness, the damp air, the cold wind that makes him shiver.

He decides to walk to his car. Runs, almost. It makes him look like a fugitive. Not a good idea. He has to pull himself together. So he turns around and stares back at where he's just come from, the square invaded by vehicles, an ambulance approaching, and little by little, very slowly, he distances himself from all this shit, contempt taking the place of fear that he might get sucked into it.

He opens the door and collapses on the seat of this silent car, its windows tinted with mud. He's sickened by the mere thought of going home and facing the questioning gaze and hostile pout of madame and the silent, swaying provocation of her hips. So he drives towards the Marché des Capucins to drink something hot or strong, and maybe eat something heavy and salted. He feels this desire in his gut. Violent. After that, he'll go to see Francis, his brother-in-arms, the toughest and most faithful of all, to put together a plan of action, a strategy, to try to eliminate this dangerous ghost, this invisible killer. Make the best of a shitty situation.

12

André puts down the newspaper and looks for something on his desk that he can grab to keep his hands busy. He finds a rubber and starts crushing and kneading it between his fingers then pulls it apart into tiny fragments, each of which he picks up and reduces to a soft pinkish dust that scatters over the pages of his accounts book. The kid was only fifteen or sixteen. She was found under the bed, in the ruins of the building that had housed a little wine bar. She had probably been hidden away in a first-floor bedroom, the window and door both bolted.

The newspaper lies in front of him, its pages open, and in the blur of his vacant gaze André sees an immense army there, ranged in perfectly straight rows, ready to invade the world and kill anything that moves. An infestation of insects governed by a perverse will. Each time his eyes stray back to the article, he sees again this armed quadrilateral, every word smashing him over the head with the butt of its rifle, pushing him back and stabbing him with a bayonet; each time, he is beaten by gloved fists and thrown to the ground where boots assail him. He is lynched by the fury of those words that he himself provoked and he has the feeling that these executioners lined up in columns are claiming him as one of them.

He feels submerged, drawn inch by inch towards the bottom, caught in a quagmire that is slowly sucking him down, and he looks around him at the grey décor, the shelves, the rolls of fabric piled up to the dirty ceiling, all this reassuring dreary sadness that is moving away from him. At the end of the counter, hunched over an order, old Bessière looks like a fading memory. He is seized by the desire to stretch out his hand and scream for help, beg some-one to drag him out of this quicksand, pull him onto dry land so he can get his breath back and climb far from the edge of the abyss.

But he can tell now that he no longer belongs to this world because everything seems to be darkening around him, losing its shape and colour. He has known it since the day he died, but the illusion in which he has been floating all these years vanishes again. He tries to concentrate on the photograph of Venice, but it no longer evokes anything: no face, no voice, no regret. Suddenly he has nothing. Past and future are gone. He tries to stand up, but dizziness grabs him and knocks him down. He falls to his knees, hanging on to the table, and the boss looks alarmed and asks him what's wrong, his voice sounding muffled, echoing as if inside a cathedral. He pulls himself to his feet and meets Raymond's fearful stare – jaw hanging, a pair of scissors immobile in his hand – then grabs his coat and walks to the exit amid a fog of voices and images blurred by his tears. He hears himself say, "I need to go out. I'll be back," and walks down the street, along the narrow pavement, obliged to step aside for people coming the other way, to meander between cars and delivery vans, under changeable skies that smell of rain and the rising tide.

He enters the first café he comes to, the warmth and noise of voices cradling him as if he's crashed into a padded wall, his head sinking into this paralysing softness.

Coffee with rum. Telephone.

The taste of the alcohol sickens him and the too-hot liquid burns his mouth.

"I would like to speak to Inspecteur Mazeau. Tell him it's André."

He waits. In the receiver he hears vague office sounds, voices calling. The world grows clear around him. Behind the bar, he can see the details on the wine-bottle labels, the glass gleaming under lamplight, the dimness of the mirror behind the shelves.

"Yes. Fuck, what have you done?"

Mazeau's voice low, embarrassed.

"I need to see you."

"Yeah, I need to see you too. I have one or two things to tell you, you fucking idiot. Couldn't you have waited a bit?"

"Waited for what? I can't wait because I don't have much time. I won't always have the strength for this. Maybe I don't have it now, anymore."

"You've really fucked this up, you know that? Be very careful. I'll see you tomorrow. Call me tonight."

"No. Today. You have to explain what happened. If not, I'll hand myself in. In one hour. I can't bear this anymore, I—"

"Alright, alright. Calm down. Tonight, at the Concorde, about eight o'clock. I can't before then."

A click in his ear. André hangs up too, pushes away the half-empty cup and pays and leaves without hearing the waiter calling him back so he can give him his change.

All day long he walks around town with his quick, almost athletic stride. All day long he tires out his body so he doesn't have to think about that kid he burned alive, so he can empty his mind of the haunting vision of her charred body, the hallucination filling his nostrils with that terrible stench. But other images come to him, all mixing together, the shapes he saw with comrades in a corner of the crematorium, like a huge insect with a rough, excoriated shell, which they had first not even realised was a pile of human bodies, perhaps refusing to accept that what remained there could once have been creatures of flesh and blood. He tries to fill his eyes with glimpsed faces, pretty women in elegant hats and coats in the cours de l'Intendance; he attempts to ward off the horror by stopping outside the shop windows on rue Sainte-Catherine with their bright lights and their elegant newness; women, as always, with painted lips and light-hearted smiles, and he thinks, maybe because he's crazy, that one of these angels will touch his finger and save him from hell by sending him to a world of silence and softness, but nothing happens, of course, so he wastes time in the labyrinth of streets in the old town and hears the sadness of the day pouring into gutters down dark back-alleys.

He hurries, covered in sweat, eyes full of tears, running without knowing how he came here, through empty streets he knew as a child and stops, panting, outside the house where he grew up, waiting for someone to come out. His heart stops when a kid emerges with a dog on a leash, his cap pulled down to his ears, and he sees himself again haring over the big, loose cobblestones or sitting and playing in the angle of a door frame. So he leaves this neighbourhood of dark houses, almost at a run, before anyone else comes out, and ends up on the quai des Chartrons, drowning in the din of traffic. He looks up at the ships' bows and chimneys and white forecastles lifted by the high tide under a remorseless sun that holds the clouds apart and makes the city's colours and puddles all shine.

Suddenly, as he starts walking again, they are all there, around him, staring at him, whispering, and he sees them, all those that his raw memory cannot stop bobbing to the surface like drowned bodies rising from the bottom of a pond.

They follow him relentlessly. Remember, remember, you haven't forgotten, have you? Their voices echo in his very footsteps, the dead and the living, and every street corner, every square, is a theatre of shadows and regrets where a vague pantomime plays, and he sees them both again crossing the place des Quinconces, holding hands, the little boy in short trousers and a sky-blue short-sleeved shirt, her in a mauve lace dress with a red belt. My God, he mutters, walking towards this mirage, knowing perfectly well that no magical being is listening to him and that no-one will turn to him and exclaim: "Look, Daniel, it's your papa!"

My son.

He thinks of Daniel, in that garage, the day he finally decided to approach him; Daniel who had not recognised him and yet who stared at him so intensely. And who thinks he's dead, or knows it. He sought the child's face in his young man's features, but did not manage to superimpose the two images. All day and all night afterwards, he trembled. How to tell him? *What* to tell him?

He thinks again about the light body he lifted up onto the roof. "Wait here. And whatever you do, don't move. Maurice will come to fetch you. Now hide!" He sees the eyes wide with fear, the tears welling there but not falling. He remembers the bang the bolt made when he shut the skylight.

Again he starts walking like a fugitive, occasionally looking behind him, and little by little his shadows leave him alone with his remorse and he trudges on under the changing sky, blinded by the light or hurrying back bent under vast rainclouds that force him to take shelter beneath shop awnings, in the murmur of conversations and the loud hammering of rain on canvas.

On this pavement, across from the Saint-André hospital, he had been happy, holding them both by the hand. He tries to recapture this sensation, remembers a Sunday – yes, it must have been a Sunday because that was the day he went with them to the house most often: the rest of the week he was slouched round card tables or lying in girls' beds – and that Sunday they were going for a ride on a merry-go-round or going to see a puppet show in the public gardens, and the boy was jumping around, talking constantly, amazed by everything, falling silent when they passed groups of laughing German soldiers, holding tight to his mother's legs. He wishes he had some real memories, the kind you can date and savour and relive by embellishing them, but all that remains in his mind are blue skies deepening between clouds heavy with rain, the babbling of a little boy, the beauty of a woman whose face he sometimes struggles to recall. He has lived through so much since then, and been so far from life, sunk to the edge of nothingness, that his memory is an archipelago where only a few jagged rocky islands show through the surface. Reefs where, in nightmares, he crashes and is torn to pieces.

He has come here for the second time since his return to the city. The first time, he fell to his knees between two cars to vomit, his head exploding with pain as if he'd been clubbed. Groggy.

Breathless. A man had come over from the other side of the street to help him, holding out his hand and asking if he should call for an ambulance. André had sat up and seen the worried face leaning down over him, but had let go of the hand that was holding him and had fallen against the side of a car. He'd asked to be left alone, said it would pass, had thanked the man. "Are you sure? I can call someone, you know. I can't leave you like this in the street."

So there were still men capable of helping someone who'd fallen to the ground even if they didn't know them, even if there was no-one around to see, moved only by a deep instinct. So that, too, must have survived?

Seeing him on his feet, and more or less steady, the man had walked away, sombre and unremarkable, and André had watched him disappear into the crowd of other passers-by before starting to walk, himself, on that same pavement.

It's the two-storey house, with its white-painted, peeling shutters, in this street: rue Desfourniel. There are the second-floor windows, with the attic where they stored junk, the ceiling so low you couldn't even stand up. With that skylight, invisible from the street, opening on the roof that sloped down over the little garden. The kid was well hidden, pressed tight against the chimney. With Olga, as they were led to the cars, he hadn't dared turn around, never mind look up. And then the convoy had started up and rounded the street corner and everything had disappeared.

André remains there, standing on the pavement, staring at the closed windows, the broken line of the rooftops against the pure blue sky. He feels as if he can no longer move from here, as if he were a prisoner of this place and the block of time in which he is now rooted, like those prehistoric monsters discovered in the frozen earth, intact but dead. He wishes he could summon the ghosts and walk with them back the way he came, venting all his wretched guilt to them. It would be enough to feel them close to him, vibrating gently as they know how to do, to walk towards the house and climb up the pale stone staircase to the apartment and push open the door, so he could perhaps hold him close again and start all over the way it was before the catastrophe, except this time he would stay with them and warn them and get them both out of there, my love, my little boy . . . He whispers these pathetic words and nothing happens, of course, only a breath of air that makes him shudder and quake. And anyway, he knows that the ghosts come when they want to, a little humming crowd or a solitary shadow; they were there earlier, urgent, distressed, absorbing all the air around him so he could hardly breathe, and now they are leaving him in his absolute solitude, trembling with cold, incapable of tearing himself from this street corner.

In the afternoon he goes into cafés and attempts several times to get drunk, but the cognacs he tries to swallow come back up, choking him, burning his throat, or he vomits the glasses of wine he's drunk as soon as he gets outside. It's been this way for a while: he can't drink alcohol anymore. A feeling of disgust takes hold of him and nausea grips his stomach, or his throat swells up and he suffocates and has to spit it out again. Doesn't matter how the drink smells in its glass, grand cru or cheap plonk, fine whisky or home-made hooch. The waiters watch him from behind their counters, sometimes laughing at this nobody who can't handle his booze, often suspicious or concerned because he could choke to death there or puke in the middle of the bar, teary-eyed, greenish-faced, staggering as if he were already pissed.

The smell of burned bodies, stuck at the back of his throat. He has the impression he can smell it on his clothes. As if he's wearing it. Or maybe it's even inside him, as if he himself stinks of the flesh from all those pyres.

Finally he manages to get a little bit drunk. In a bar close to the university, full of loud students angrily denouncing Algeria, he drinks three kirs, which add to what he's been able to hold down from the previous attempts. He feels the world grow softer around him, the floor more yielding beneath his feet. The yells and laughs of the young people become muffled and the air turns to cotton wool, and when he looks around him everything seems fresh and curious, distant and flat like a cinema screen. Hazy, interchangeable faces. Phoney beings.

By the time he gets out of there, night has fallen. He's shocked to realise he's spent nearly two hours sitting at that table and now has no idea what he was thinking about all that time, because it wasn't even about the young girl he killed. He starts walking quickly, to sober himself up, because this drunkenness is no help to him and it's drowning his brain in a mist that suddenly worries him. He walks for a while before arriving at the place de la République, where the café de la Concorde is located, the scene for his meeting with Mazeau. He is more than an hour early, so he walks past the bar twice, observes his surroundings – parked cars, motionless figures – and looks through the window at customers sitting at tables or standing at the counter. He senses a trap – a dragnet, as they call it in the papers. He thinks that the cop might well want to catch the arsonist of place Nansouty because it would be good for his promotion prospects. Because we are always betrayed, by ourselves as well as others.

So he turns, goes, comes back, stops at a bus shelter to observe any suspicious movements. He decides to intercept Mazeau before he goes in so they can talk while they're walking and he won't be cornered in the café. He feels fatigue rising through his legs, a burning venom mixed with the alcohol. He would like to go to bed. To sleep, perhaps.

André leans on the post of the bus shelter and closes his eyes but opens them almost instantly because he's afraid of nodding off while standing and falling to the ground, the way he does sometimes. He rubs his eyes like a sleepy kid and that's when he sees them: there are three of them, walking briskly up the street, almost running, shoulders hunched, faces hidden under hats. Mazeau is in the lead. It's started to drizzle so they keep their heads down and don't look around. Mazeau and another cop enter the Concorde while the third crosses the street and stands opposite the café, lighting a cigarette then melting into the darkness, leaning against the trunk of a plane tree. All André can see of him is the glow of his fag whenever he takes a drag. His heart speeds up, hurting him. His entire thoracic cage hardens with this pain and his breath shortens.

He forces his chest to swell, sucking big gulps of air through his mouth, using his fingertips to massage his painful ribs, passing one rain-slick hand over his face and the back of his neck.

He finds enough breath to start walking back up the street towards place Pey-Berland and his stiff legs obey him, more or less. He passes the walls of the courthouse, his hand brushing the rough stone. The street is empty, with cars parked along one side, the only light reflected from their wet bonnets. Little by little, he manages to walk more quickly, to breathe more easily. He sees the mayor's office ahead of him, the traffic on the square, and at that very moment the wind carries the smell of tobacco to his nostrils and he turns around to see a man throwing himself at André, yelling "Police! Don't move!" as a car door opens just in front of him.

The cop behind him tackles him round the waist, pressing his arms to his sides, but André succeeds in reaching the car door and slamming it shut with all his weight on the man who was coming out, and who now screams in pain because his leg is trapped in this suddenly locked jaw. Another man is getting out, on the driver's side, so André shoves himself backwards and the cop's head hits the wall with a thud and his arms loosen their grip, allowing André to elbow him blindly in the face. He feels something crack and then hears the cop slump to the ground with a moan. The man in the car is still yelling and his colleague, who is clumsy and overweight, steps onto the pavement and stands up tall, holding his arms out wide to block André, a whistle in his mouth. But he uses it only once – in a strident shriek – and then drops it, because without warning he is lying on the ground, being trampled by this silent man who has charged at him, foot first, as if he was going to simply climb over him. As he struggles, fumbling inside his jacket to find his pistol, he probably doesn't see the fugitive disappear around the corner of the street, nor does he hear his colleagues who have run out of the Concorde, alerted by his whistle, and now arrive on the scene at full pelt.

André hares down the street for about a hundred metres then, knackered, has to stop, and to hold on to the walls as he staggers on, his lungs crushed. He looks behind him and does not see anyone in pursuit. He imagines the cops consoling each other, licking their wounds. Spotting a bus coming towards a stop, he hops aboard and collapses in the first empty seat. He is drenched with sweat and rain, and his coat smells of wet wool mixed with the acrid stench of sweat. Other passengers stare, and in the rear-view mirror he catches the eye of the driver watching him. He undoes a few buttons of his overcoat, loosens his tie and opens his shirt collar so he can breathe more easily. He tries to work out where he is, and suddenly through the windscreen he sees the line of lanterns at either edge of the pont de Pierre. The windows on the side of the bus are wet with condensation and rain, and even after he wipes one with his sleeve, all he can see of the river is absolute darkness. Then he spots the street lights on avenue Thiers and a few neon lights glowing in cafés.

He gets off at the first stop, in place Stalingrad, and stays there in the wind watching the bus move away with the strange relief of a prisoner who's escaped a convoy. He would like to go back to his flat, because theoretically Mazeau doesn't know his address, because no-one knows it, or even his true identity. He thinks about his bed, about a coffee and a few biscuits, and that image makes his stomach growl. But he has to cross back over the bridge, go through the Saint-Michel quarter, and walk even further after that, and he doesn't have the energy for that, his whole body weighed down with a fatigue he has not felt in a long time and which, right now, he doesn't know how to overcome.

He decides to walk up the avenue and find a hotel. There are a few in this neighbourhood because the gare d'Orléans is close by, so he plunges through that dark gap, below the lanterns that swing in the cold mist and drizzle. He passes cafés full of people, their windows blurred with condensation, and sometimes a door opens, letting out a murmur of merriness and a warm whiff of cigarette smoke or fried food. Then he glimpses a sign lit up by a large bulb announcing the Hôtel Saint-Emilion and pushes the door open, holding onto it to prevent himself falling.

The man behind the reception desk with his grey, close-cropped hair sits up, tensing at the sight of André limping towards him. He even recoils slightly and shoots an anxious look at the front door, as if the night was about to spew other scary monsters into his entrance hall.

"What do you want?"

André stands at the counter. His head is spinning slightly, the floor moving. He forces himself to meet the eyes of the man who is staring contemptuously at him.

"A room. Got any left?"

"Might have. No bags?"

André takes out his wallet, pulls a 10,000-franc bill from it and slaps Bonaparte's face on the countertop.

"I can pay."

"I should bloody well hope so!"

The man takes the bill and rubs it between his fingers. Then he sighs.

"O.K.," he says, picking up the register and handing it to André. "Put your name here. As long as people can pay, I don't care about the rest."

André writes down the name of a man who died at Christmas

'44. He sees his wide open eyes again, his twisted mouth. The crumpled rag in his still-closed fist.

"Unusual name."

"Can't help that," says André, trying to smile.

The man slowly shakes his head, looking pensive, and puts the money in his cash drawer. André doesn't move. He looks at the plaque on the wall behind the man showing the prices for rooms: 4,000 on the street side, 5,000 on the courtyard side. The man follows his gaze and, sighing, hands him a 5,000-franc bill, then grabs a key from the rack on the wall.

"Room twelve. First floor. Shower and toilet at the end of the corridor. I changed the sheets this morning, and the towel. Don't be surprised if there's some noise around midnight – I have customers who arrive late."

The room overlooks the street. That crook with his sergeant-major's face must have taken his little slice: what he thinks is the price of his silence for keeping quiet about the arrival of a traveller without any bags and with a strange foreign name. The wallpaper is piss-yellow, or maybe beige. On the ceiling, a bulb radiates warm light under a fringed reddish lampshade. The bed creaks slightly when André sits on it. The mattress is soft and deep, slouched like some sly beast capable of effortlessly absorbing any body that lies on it and releasing it, partly digested, a few days later. Still on the bed, he takes off his coat and his jacket and rotates his shoulders, massages the back of his neck, stretches his back and finally gets to his feet. He turns on the sink tap and drinks a few big gulps of water, then stands breathless in front of the mirror, inspecting the greyish image of his dark-ringed eyes, his gaunt features.

He gives himself a bit of a wash with the sliver of soap lying on the edge of the sink. He tries to remove that feverish dampness from his skin, and the sick, acrid reek that rises from his body. Naked, he looks at his lanky frame, with its lean muscles and protruding bones. Relieved that he's still standing.

He gets dressed again and falls asleep straight away on the bedspread, the shutters open on the avenue, letting in the irregular rumble of traffic noise and the dim glimmers of light that prevent the darkness from suffocating him. He dreams of fire. Figures in flames at the other end of impassable corridors, women's screams behind locked doors that he cannot break down, burned bodies piled up in a garden, among whose charred faces he recognises Olga's.

He wakes up terrified in a blue darkness emitted by the window, amid the murmur of rain, and he sits up and stares around at the indistinct shapes in the room, with no idea where he is. Then the sound of a woman giggling through the dividing wall and the creak of floorboards reassure him a little and he falls back asleep, face sunk exhausted in his pillow. But, each time, the furnace lights up again with a roar of flames and Olga screams, her hair on fire, and he can't reach her, his arms severed by the terror of his nightmare.

Early in the morning, head heavy, he leaves the hotel without seeing anyone and crosses the bridge over the muddy river where a few dawn rays are twisting in the water. He walks, seeing nothing, across the city as it wakes to the metallic clatter of buses and lorries. He passes through the stink of their exhaust fumes.

Back near his apartment, on the cours de l'Yser, he starts the same game he played the day before, trying to spot men waiting to ambush him. He walks up and down in front of his street, he goes into a just-opened bar that smells of bleach and the sawdust that the owner is scattering over the tiles.

Coffee and croissant. Suddenly he feels so good that, for a minute, nothing seems very serious or dangerous. He savours this moment when his body no longer feels like a burden he must carry around, before he leaves and crosses the road, looking out for anyone roaming suspiciously through the neighbourhood.

He enters the dark corridor as if he were entering fire: barely breathing, muscles so tensed they're painful. They might already be here, hidden in any corner, ready to leap out with a yell, ramming the barrels of their guns under his chin. He practically runs to the staircase, recognising the same odours that he smells every morning, hearing the radio from Madame Mendez's flat, seeing the old, cracked, peeling greenish paint on the walls, and slipping upstairs like a thief in this sad, grey, reassuring quietness.

With relief, he opens the door to his apartment and stands in the middle of the room for a moment with the sensation that he has been away for so long that it pleases him to find every object in its usual place, the shapes unchanged, the smells of floor polish and clean laundry that strike him with a mixed feeling of newness and quickly rediscovered familiarity. Then he takes off his clothes, drops them on the chair and walks to the kitchen, where he starts warming some water in a large saucepan.

He soaps himself, shivering, and rubs his skin until it turns red, as always. The soap makes his eyes sting, but he likes its taste on his lips, its smell that finally overcomes the rank stench that guilt and fear coated him in the day before. Feet in a tub, he rinses himself, pouring some of the hot water over his body, and feels himself come back to life. He tells himself he will never leave this lair again, the only wretched place where he feels any kind of peace. For an instant he dreams of a recluse's life, living in a cave on a mountainside where the only things that matter are the sunrise and the sunset and the echoes of the past in a silence of furtive creatures and the wind in the trees. He thinks all this while rubbing his head dry, and when he removes his towel he jumps, almost tripping over the edge of the tub, because Mazeau is standing in the entrance to the kitchen, pistol in hand.

Instinctively, André hides his crotch and the cop smiles nastily at this modesty, then gestures with his gun.

"Drop the towel, you're not a fucking girl. I prefer you like that – powerless."

André rolls the towel into a ball and holds it tight to his stomach.

He can't do a thing. He can see no object, no kitchen utensil lying around that he might throw in his visitor's face. And anyway, what then? A bullet travels faster than a knife. Mazeau is no longer smiling. He pushes his hat brim back and leans against the door frame.

"Weren't we supposed to meet last night?"

Naked under his gaze like this, André feels the way he used to feel watched by kapos or S.S. guards. He wonders if he would have the strength or the courage to kill this man. He thinks very precisely about how he might disarm him as soon as he relaxes, once he feels so in control of the situation that he would lower his guard and not see the blow coming.

"I was scared," he says. "Too many cops."

"You messed up three detectives."

"I was scared. They were coming out all over the place. I didn't realise."

André makes himself look at the ground, pretend to be contrite. He lets his shoulders slump a bit. He can sense Mazeau on his guard. He knows how suspicious cops are of everyone and everything, knows he won't be able to fool him that easily. The cop stands up straighter, more solidly on his legs, and André guesses that he's tightened his grip on the butt of his gun.

"Didn't realise what?"

"That it would have been better to let them arrest me. It's all over for me now, I know that."

"Yes, you twat, it certainly is all over for you. You killed three people, including that kid. So come with me quietly and I'll take you to the station."

"I'll tell them everything. I'll say you were the one who gave me the address. You trapped me. You knew that girl was hiding there."

"I didn't know shit. You wanted some scum with connections to Darlac, and I gave them to you. The girl was another of his schemes. He must have picked her up I don't know where and he was hiding her there while he worked out what to do with her."

"I'll tell them everything and I'll take you down with me. Only difference is, I don't care. I've been living on borrowed time, ever since I got out. I'm already dead. You've got a wife, you've got kids."

Mazeau snorts with laughter. The pistol trembles in his hand. That is all André sees. Wonders if . . . Gives up the thought.

"Who'd believe you? I mean, who the hell are you? Everyone thinks you're dead – even you think that. You changed your identity, practically changed your face, and fifteen years later you come back to get revenge? Can you remember what kind of bloke you were, till '43? A gambler, a womaniser, a wheeler-dealer? You didn't bite the hand that fed you, back then, did you? Who would even listen to you whining about the concentration camps and everything you've been through and your pathetic vengeance? You think your old pal Darlac's going to let you strip him naked without saying anything? He'll get out the old police files, he'll embroider his memories, and you'll be nothing but some sad little loser come to settle a few scores. Anyway, no-one gives a toss about deportees anymore, haven't you noticed? All they care about is the Resistance and its heroes! And I was on the right side. So what do you think? People just want to forget all that shit, especially now their sons are being sent to Algeria to have their guts sliced open by the *ratons*. They've got bigger fish to fry than listening to the adulterous husband of some dead Jewish bird go on about his miserable life. Just think for a minute: you're fucked. You killed three people and you'll be lucky if you escape the guillotine."

He stops talking and rummages in his pocket, coming up with a wallet that he throws at André's feet.

"There you go, look at that, André Vaillant. Now I know what to call you. Come on. Get dressed and let's get out of here."

André does not move.

"We're not going anywhere. Or I'm not, anyway. Go ahead and shoot, if you want. You haven't understood anything."

Mazeau cocks his pistol and lowers his aim.

"I'm going to shoot you in the leg. I'll say you attacked me. Legitimate self-defence. I'll be lauded for my self-control, cos you'll only be injured. I'll take you to rue Castéja[15] and everyone will congratulate me. My colleagues, the chief super, I'll be promoted. And you'll have to limp to the Fort de Ha[16]. You've been there before, haven't you? I don't care if the law condemns you. I don't believe in all that crap. As far as I'm concerned, justice is a bullet in the head for any scum we catch, and that's all. And as you're already dead and as you don't care either, we're almost in agreement. So, you follow me, you end up dying, and I do pretty well out of it."

André nods. He takes one step forward and the cop aims the gun at him, arm stretched out tense, the knuckles of his fist turning white as he grips the butt tightly.

"I need to go to the wardrobe. Can I?"

Mazeau takes a few steps backwards.

"Slowly. Go very slowly."

André moves forward. He can feel the rough floorboards under his bare feet. He concentrates on that to fill his body again with sensations and strength. Mazeau is still pointing the gun at him, hand steady. He's two metres away from him, raincoat and jacket undone so his shoulders can move freely.

The outside door bangs and they hear the shouts of children in the corridor. Laughter, a stampede of feet on the staircase. Mazeau turns around, startled, and André sees the look on his face and uses his towel to knock away the cop's gun hand and throws himself at him and then the two of them go flying over the top of the armchair.

Mazeau hits the floor head first. For a few seconds he's stunned,

15 The central police station in Bordeaux was located in this street until recently.

16 Former medieval fortress, very close to Bordeaux's city hall, used as a prison from the middle of the nineteenth century until 1967. All that remains of it today are two towers within the walls of the National School for the Judiciary. During the Occupation, Jews arrested during round-ups were held there while awaiting deportation, as were many Resistance fighters.

groggy, eyes staring up at the ceiling. André grabs him by his shirt collar, sitting astride his chest, and with an effort lifts him up and smashes his head against the wooden floor to knock him out. He doesn't know if the cop has let go of his pistol; all he's thinking about is trying to make his gestures more efficient, but the man is heavy, hard to drag, so André kneels on his chest and the man struggles, trying to roll over sideways to knock him off, trying to knee him in the ribs. Mazeau's face is purple, the veins throbbing wickedly in his temples and his forehead because he can't breathe, and suddenly it becomes slippery in André's hands, slick with sweat, the bones hard-edged and angular, and he bangs it against the floorboards, thinking that tiles would be more effective, less flexible, but all the same he dreads hearing the soft crack of his skull and seeing a pool of blood spreading over the wood, because he has witnessed that before once in the camp, when a kapo killed a prisoner because he hadn't moved out of the way for him as he was leaving the building, and André remembers the sound of death behind that scrawny face and the instant clouding over of his eyes, and the shudders that ran through his whole body as it slumped against the bloodstained concrete post. And suddenly, at the very edge of his field of vision, to his left, he glimpses the pistol rising up and he smacks it with the back of his hand but the gun rises again like a snake so he grabs the cop by his ears and yanks and shoves to smash his head against the floor until he feels the body go soft underneath him and stop moving.

He picks up the pistol and gets to his feet. Catches his breath. Mazeau is breathing peacefully, as though asleep. André dresses in haste, keeping his eyes on the motionless policeman, keeping the gun to hand on a nearby shelf, just in case, but the cop remains still. André knows he's not dead, probably not even unconscious, maybe faking it to lower his vigilance. Viewed this way, lying on the floor, arms stretched out wide, he looks like someone who's collapsed with exhaustion and is now recovering. Or thinking.

Because André now leaps to the conclusion that should have come to him earlier, as soon as the cop first appeared in his flat: out in the street there are two cars full of cops waiting for a sign, or for a certain period of time to elapse, before they intervene. Almost certainly they have blocked both ends of the street. They will hurtle up the stairs, guns at the ready, and smash down the door and pin him to the floor and drag him outside like the body of a felled stag or boar, and throw their trophy in the back of a car. He runs over to the window, but of course he cannot see anything; obviously they are not going to be waiting outside the door, waving to him.

He grabs a suitcase and tosses a few old clothes inside it, along with his notebooks and pens. He goes into the kitchen to pick up his wallet, checks that he has everything he needs, not forgetting his chequebook. When he returns to the living room, he sees the cop moving slightly and doesn't know what to do because in a minute he might get up and yell at him or attack him. Gripped by uncertainty, he aims the pistol at the cop's head, but his hand trembles and the trigger seems to resist the pressure of his finger. He thinks he ought to tie him up and gag him – that's what they do in films – but maybe the policeman is just waiting for him to try that in order to go for his throat.

He gives Mazeau a quick kick in the face, prompting a muffled groan, then he kicks him again and again, screaming with rage, kicking with both feet at this body that no longer moves at all. After that he remains immobile for a few seconds in the middle of the room, letting his eyes wander from the unmade bed to the table where he writes down his memories every evening, from the window where the dawn light is coming in to the cracked ceiling still dark with the remnants of night.

He decides to leave his den and run down the stairs, the pistol held out in front of him, and he knows that, this time, he won't have to press very hard on the trigger to shoot down the first cop that bars his way. He goes flying out the door, breath held, as if by not breathing he might escape the attentions of the men lying in ambush. But he runs twenty or thirty steps, and reaches the corner of the cours de l'Yser, where he closes his eyes against the sun on the horizon. People walk past without seeing him, and the city opens up with a roar and he is swallowed by its huge, swarming mouth.

And then he is walking down streets he barely recognises, suitcase in hand, wandering lost, drifting towards the river by following the slope, the path of least resistance, bowed down by the noise, shaken by the din of traffic on the docks. Beyond the warehouses, the high tide lifts up the boats like dazzling white cathedrals in the bright sunlight, with slow-moving cranes bent solicitously over them. He walks, avoiding the eyes that he thinks are staring at him – the fugitive, the stowaway, the hunted ghost – and he constantly dreads the touch of a hand on his shoulder, the thought of an arm surging from the crowds massed around the bus shelters and knocking him to the ground, slamming his face into the tarmac, don't move, you piece of shit, we've got you now and we're not letting you go this time.

Outside the offices of the Transat ship company, he looks at colour photographs of big passenger–cargo ships going to Africa and he thinks that he could soon be arriving in a heat-battered port, roaming through the chaos of its commotion, lost, again, in a country that would not be the end of the world but a dead end where his poverty would pale into insignificance beside the others'. He imagines putting his suitcase down by a filthy counter where whites macerating in a bitter sauce of sweat and alcohol would let their hatred and their filth stew under the lazy blades of a gigantic fan. He sees himself in the dusty, shadeless streets riddled with exhausted figures, broken by their work, faces black and shining, poor devils, whining children, women bowed by their burdens; he sees himself in that world like a nail hammered into an eye.

He would like to dream up images of a river with luxuriant banks, the water rippling as canoes glide through it, listening to calls echoing in the air and distant voices answering them, but he cannot: the pictures shrivel up as soon as he thinks of them.

People say leaving is a kind of dying, without knowing anything about it. He knows it's true. But now that he has come back, he may as well die here, and for good this time. The destination is less uncertain.

He picks up his suitcase again, finding it surprisingly light, and retraces his footsteps. He walks quickly, as he likes to do, matching his breaths to his stride. He no longer hears the city, and sees only vague shadows that he passes in a continual hum.

Another hotel. Cours Pasteur. Standing behind its counter, the receptionist looks like Juliette Gréco. He fills out the register, pays for two nights in advance. The woman gives him his key, staring at him in surprise or with suspicion, and he meets her gaze: hazel irises and lids heavy with eyeshadow. She tells him there are towels in the wardrobe. As he walks away, he hears her hoarse voice again:

"It gets a bit noisy, around midnight, for an hour or so. Then it calms down again."

He turns and shrugs.

"I'm just telling you cos some of our customers complain."

He tries to smile.

"I never complain."

She nods, then picks up a magazine which she opens with a brusque gesture. And, as he moves off towards the staircase, she speaks again:

"The cops hardly ever come here."

"Why are you telling me that?"

"No reason. Just so you'll know."

"If they don't come here, that's because everything's fine, right? That's reassuring . . ."

His hovel of a room is painted pale blue and overlooks a narrow street where young people's voices echo, shouting and laughing. André drinks long mouthfuls of water from the tap. When he sits on the bed, he's surprised by the silence and the firmness of the mattress. Then he lies down and lets his fatigue settle over him.

Just as he is starting to nod off, he suddenly jumps to his feet and goes to the sink to splash water on his face. Then he slides his suitcase under the bed and takes the pistol from his pocket, wondering where to stash it. He opens the wardrobe, looks on top of it, then under it, for a place where he can put the gun, but nowhere looks safe so he gives it some more thought, passing the weapon from one hand to the other. Then he aims at his reflection in the dirty mirror over the sink and catches sight of his stiff, sinister figure in the darkness of this seedy room and sighs, finally slipping the pistol into an inside pocket of his coat.

When he goes past the reception desk, the woman does not look up from her magazine, but he knows she is watching him from under her dark brown fringe. He strides quickly, decisively down the street and pushes open the door of the bank with an energy that surprises Philippe, the cashier, who recognises him and smiles.

"Monsieur Vaillant, how are you? It's not payday, is it?"

Behind him, the secretary hammers away at her typewriter, copying columns of figures onto a stack of carbon papers. As usual, she does not greet him, remaining concentrated on her work.

"Monsieur Bessière sent me because he needs cash to pay a supplier who's been making his life a misery."

"Cash?"

The cashier adjusts his glasses as he looks at André.

"It happens, as you know, from time to time. It's the Duchêne company in Bègles. He wants to settle all his accounts with them because they're late with deliveries, they wrangle over offcuts and they don't supply the sizes we need. It's never-ending with them. So, earlier today, on the phone, Bessière got annoyed and decided he didn't want to deal with people like that anymore."

"Yes, I see, but—"

"If it's a problem, I can go back to the shop and tell him, and he can come himself. He's not going to like it though – you know what he's like..."

"No, no, it's just that ... How much do you need, I mean how much does he need?"

"Five hundred thousand."

The cashier nods without answering, then purses his lips.

"It's just that ... I'm not sure I have that amount here."

He walks to the back of the room and opens a large accounts book, his finger running down various columns of figures.

"Oh, we do. You're in luck. We had a deposit yesterday, and I can see that it's still here. Good, good..."

He has André fill out a form. Signature, stamp. Then he goes behind the cash register and opens a metal drawer with a little key that he wears around his neck. He puts the notes – denominations of five and ten thousand – on the countertop, snapping them between his fingers as he counts them.

André takes the money, carefully wrapped in a thick paper envelope. He says see you on payday and waves as he opens the door. Out on the pavement, he glances quickly around and, not seeing any cops on stakeout, starts walking towards the hotel, because now his only desire is to sleep, to abandon himself for a few hours somewhere the police won't know where to find him, giving Mazeau time to decide whether he should talk, whether he should admit that he played solo and lost.

13

Algeria appeared to them first as a discontinuous line of flickering glimmers at the level of the waterline in the already fading night. Hearing the shouts of those who saw it first, standing at the ship's bow, the others rushed over to see it too, shoving each other and standing on tiptoes, leaning on others' shoulders or jumping in the air in an attempt to glimpse the land that had been promised to them, even though they had never wanted or asked for anything. They were silent after that, blinking from the sea air that blew in their faces or because they were tired after hours of rough weather that had liquefied their legs and turned their stomachs and a night spent almost without sleep on this old tub, being thumped by waves, the air stinking of blocked bogs, piled up on top of each other on deckchairs or camp beds, dazed by seasickness, and sometimes spattered with vomit because a few people were unable to resist this sneaky, punchy eastern swell. So, pitching or rolling, guts or bowels, they didn't know the difference and often remained bent over the barrier trying to puke, a glaze of sweat covering their faces that were the same olive-green as their uniforms, sticking their fingers down their throats to puke, hitting themselves in the bellies to puke, puke, puke, and dying for an end to this shaking of their entire beings, from their brains to their bollocks, turned to jelly, endlessly stirred like a mass of treacle that they wanted to eject by any means necessary, like that half-wit, made crazy by nausea, who'd tried to open up his stomach with a knife to get rid of the guts he couldn't manage to vomit up. It had taken three of them to stop him disembowelling himself, and a caporal had knocked him out with a punch to the back of the neck to calm him down and then declared that he'd get a week in jail, the prick, for disobedience and attempted self-mutilation.

Daniel had managed to find a spot on the upper bridge, below the gangway, and, with Giovanni – a man from Lorraine he'd met at the training camp in Mulhouse – rolled up in their blankets, using their kit as a pillow, they had managed to grab three or four hours' sleep amid the deafening roar of machines and the worrying vibrations that shook the ship's frame every so often. When they heard the others shouting, they sat up and contemplated the string of lights stretched out before them, the two of them open-mouthed, their blankets sliding off their shoulders, as if they had witnessed a miracle.

"This is where the Athenians landed," says Giovanni. "What a shit heap..."

Daniel does not reply. He watches the sea as it emerges from blackness, transforming by turns into steel and bronze, and the sky as it pales then blazes amid a flock of purple clouds massed in the distance that he imagines are guarding the Strait of Gibraltar. The Pillars of Hercules, as they say in those sword-and-sandals films. He takes the frame from his chest pocket, unfolds it and captures this dawn in a long panoramic that he cuts as soon as the ship's bow slices through the surface of the water and points towards the coast, a line that grows thicker with every passing moment.

"Is it better, if you look at it like that?" Giovanni asks.

"I dunno. It's the same thing, but different. I don't know how to explain it."

"Yeah, it's the same shit, but without the stink..."

"I think it's a better way of seeing things. You isolate what you want to see from the rest and that makes you see it better."

Giovanni reaches out for the steel rectangle.

"Show me."

He makes a darkroom with his two hands and puts his eye to it, grimacing as he blinks. He walks around with the frame, smiles, then stops.

"That's funny . . . you're right. I love the flicks, but I'd never thought of making my own wherever I am."

He gives the frame back to Daniel, who folds it and slips it in his pocket.

"Why didn't you ask for a deferment, since you're a student? All this shit would've been over by the time you were done."

Giovanni is still staring at the horizon, where Algeria moves closer. He nods and smiles sadly.

"I'll tell you one day. Not today. *Sois sage, ô ma Douleur, et tiens-toi plus tranquille ...*"[17]

"Who's that?"

"Baudelaire. I'll lend it to you."

They fall silent. Four other men have joined them and are yelling, leaning against the handrail and going into raptures about what they can see. They wonder aloud if there'll be dark-skinned whores to fuck, and one of them mimes a wank, crotch thrust forward, in the direction of the coast.

"Just wait till you see my big gun in action. I brought plenty of fucking ammo too!"

They laugh and slap their thighs.

"And even if you miss the target, it doesn't matter!"

"It's war, innit? We're not going to be scared of a little *trou de balle*."[18]

They fall about laughing, collapsing into each other's arms. Pass around a flask of hooch, looking about to make sure there are no officers who might see them. They cough and choke, gasping that fuck it's strong but really good.

"Want some, mate? My dad makes it, from plums."

A small, dark-haired boy is waving the flask under Giovanni's nose. He grabs it and turns to Daniel.

"What shall we drink to?"

17 The first line of Baudelaire's poem "Recueillement". Translated into English as "Meditation" by Robert Lowell, this first line reads: "Calm down, my Sorrow, we must move with care."

18 *Trou de balle* can mean both "bullet hole" and "arsehole".

"Who cares? Drink to whatever you want."

"To the French army, then, and its glorious soldiers!"

He downs a mouthful and passes the flask to Daniel.

"To our dead, in the past and the future."

The other lads stare at him in the silence that has suddenly fallen. The small, dark-haired boy gets his flask back, puts the cork in it and drops it in a pocket of his khaki trousers.

"Why'd you say that?"

"It's war, isn't it? You said it yourself. People always die in wars."

"Shut your mouth," says one of the others, with a ginger crew cut. "It'll all be over in six months, and we'll go home. The colonel in our training camp said that, and he knows what he's on about. He was in Indo and he couldn't wait to get here to give these *ratons* what they deserve. What the fuck did he say that for, about the dead?"

He is furious. He waves his cap at Daniel.

"You twat! You'll be dead before me!"

Daniel stares him down. What can he say to that? And what if it's true? Exasperated, the boy gives him the finger and turns around, pushing his mates out of the way so he can lean on the handrail. Daniel picks up his bag and hoists it onto his back. For a few seconds, gasping and unsteady, he wonders if he'll be able to walk a single step with this weight crushing his shoulders, riveting him to the metal gangway. He hears the boy whispering insults and curses that are suddenly lost in the flurry of an unknown language. Giovanni comes level with him and leads him away by the arm. The lads make jokes about them. Queers. Why don't you go somewhere quiet so you can have each other? Fucking arse bandits.

They join the crowd of squaddies on the bridge. The smell of tobacco, sweat, dirty feet. Even the sea wind cannot dissipate this festering reek. They'll be there in an hour. The N.C.O.s bellow. A platoon stands near the railings, about fifty men in combat gear, wearing helmets, rifles on shoulders, bags at their feet. Daniel watches, surprised. A caporal explains that it's for the news. First they film the men who look most like soldiers, to show people we're not here to mess around. Afterwards, they show the dickheads who smile at the camera, happy to be there, who've come full of enthusiasm to crush the rebellion and protect the population. Always the same routine. Daniel glances at the stripes on the man's chest, suspicious of this over-chatty officer, wondering if he's trying to spot the troublemakers, the rebels, the reds.

"Where you from?" the caporal asks.

"Bordeaux."

"I've got an uncle in Bordeaux. He works in the shipyards, at the Chantiers de la Gironde. He's a boilermaker."

Daniel looks away. His eyes search for Giovanni and find him giving a cigarette and a light to a *chasseur alpin*[19], who protects the flame with his huge beret.

"I joined as an N.C.O., cos you get paid more. It's for my mother, who's alone with my little sister. To help them. I'm not like some of those bastards though. You don't have to call me 'sir'."

Daniel stares at him. He looks normal, likeable, blinking and shivering in the wind, digging his hands into his pockets and looking sheepish like any old squaddie.

"What about you? Where are you from?"

"Limoges. Well, near there. My parents are farmers. My mother's on her own though, she has to do everything. There's a neighbour who helps her out sometimes, but he's getting old."

"Didn't you try to get an exemption?"

"What do you think? They need fresh blood. They couldn't give a toss about my mother."

"I've got a friend who—"

"Good for him. I hope he makes the most of it. His family are probably even deeper in the shit than us. I reckon in the army they think that if you've got a bit of land and a few cows, you must

19 The *chasseurs alpins* are the elite mountain infantry of the French army.

be fine. They've got no fucking idea what farming is, those lazy bastards."

Whistles and shouts. Men moving, gathering. The caporal shakes his hand, crushing Daniel's fingers in a vice-like grip hardened by calluses.

"I've got to go and pick up my men. One thing's for sure – it's not going to be a fucking picnic, wherever they put you. Apart from a few pen-pushers in signals or equipment, and even then it can get rough, from what I've heard. Watch yourselves, you and your mate."

He walks away into the jostling khaki crowd, reaching on tiptoes to see where he's going.

The day has lightened, the clouds scattering to reveal a wide pale sky where seagulls hover and caw, their cries audible even over the hubbub of men's voices all piled up on the bridge, pressing against the handrails to stare at the flat, dark sea. The city rises up slowly in front of them, white, absorbing all the light and all their gazes, and Algeria begins for the men with this dazzling chaos under an unbearably blue sky.

Off the boat, the docks still seem to move under their feet and some of them get seasick again. They wait outside a warehouse, beneath a creaking crane whose movements they eye anxiously as it lifts half-tracks and armoured cars and jeeps off a cargo ship guarded by gendarmes. There are maybe two hundred of them, vaguely bunched into platoons, sitting on crates or lying on the concrete, smoking and talking in whispers because of the N.C.O.s prowling around them like glaring, barking dogs. But above all because the tumult of the sea and the other men is no longer there to cover their voices, so all the bravado and the jokes and the yobbish poses, all that bullshit they shared on board the ship like some final fuck-you to the army and its discipline, all that ceased as soon as the first men began walking down the gangway, awaited on the docks by stony-faced officers in sunglasses, pistols at the waist, and by a line of canvas-topped G.M.C. trucks, the drivers sitting with their feet on the dashboards, smoking or asleep.

"Well, this is it now," says a tall, lanky blond lad with milk-white skin.

Daniel looks up and sees him standing, hands on hips, in full sunlight, nodding sorrowfully. He said the words to himself and he is looking around him at the activity of the port, the passing trucks, the Arab dockers slaving away under the hot sun, some of them in turbans, and yelling in their language and laughing as they rotate a cargo of crates at the end of a chain so it can be unloaded properly. Their skin is almost black. Their faded shirts are haloed with sweat.

Daniel too watches the men working, his mind empty, because there is nothing else to do. He lights an American cigarette and tastes the copper flavour in his mouth as he takes his first drag. He has smoked so much that he feels as if he is constantly chewing cardboard. The lukewarm water in his flask, which he drank a little earlier, changed nothing. The taste of aluminium replaced the taste of copper for a moment as he swallowed, and that was all. He smokes and looks at his watch. That's all he does. Three hours have passed since they got off the ship. In that time, they've seen convoys leave and waited for the dozen or so trucks that will take them to a barracks where they'll be given their combat equipment and their weapons. A capitaine goes to find out what's happening. They see him drive away on a jeep, and some of them moan a bit, so the sergents bark at them to shut their gobs and wait, and they do, all of them, reduced to this exhausted obedience.

Giovanni and Daniel can't think of anything else to say to each other. They're in a daze, one sitting, the other stretched out, his back propped up against their bags, crammed into any scrap of shade they can find with all the others. The sun slowly hunts them down, its harsh unyielding glare and steady progress across the sky the sole proof that time has not stopped. They wipe their foreheads, their necks with a large perfumed handkerchief that a woman's hand slipped inside their suitcase so long ago, or so it seems. They roll up their sleeves. Flasks are passed around. A siren howls in the distance. Daniel notices only the silence seeping through amid the agitation of the port. The dockers have disappeared and he can no longer see any of the gendarmes who had been supervising the unloading of the armoured cars. The cranes are immobile. Even the seabirds have shut their beaks. There are three of them sitting on the roof of the warehouse, smoothing their wing feathers. How many hours have passed? He feels as if he has woken from a nap that's destroyed his perception of time. He begins to understand what their first enemies will be: sunlight and time. And this is only March. He tries to imagine what it will be like in summer, under the real heatwave.

The capitaine will return on his jeep at the head of a convoy of trucks. They will have to climb on board, with N.C.O.s ranting at them, yelling insults. Suddenly, it will be the most urgent thing in the world to get this bunch of lily-livered pansies, these queers, these fairies to leave this dock where finally a bit of shade is starting to spread beneath the warehouse.

All they will see of Algiers is roads vanishing from the back of the truck, glimpsed cafés with packed terraces, and every one of them will be filled with the same desire for a glass of anything as long as it's cold, with ice cubes floating in it. They will leave behind them this life full of colours and noise and dust and crowds and cars and kids and carts pulled by bald donkeys led by men frowning in the too-bright sunlight. Daniel will lean out to get a better view, like they all will, curious, and too tired to be worried, and from the overheated shade of the covered truck where they will all be sitting, it will seem to him that this country consists only of light and that it can only be seen through a dazzling glare.

They will enter a camp, surrounded by a cloud of dust and exhaust fumes, and they'll jump from the trucks in the orange rays of sunset and be led towards a sort of bunker where they will have to wait again for a supplies officer who will get his underlings to distribute uniforms that stink of mothballs, telling them, yes, for fuck's sake, of course it's the right size, I've done this before you know. Not that it'll make any fucking difference when you're yomping through the desert or you've got *fells*[20] on your arse, it's not a fucking fashion parade you know, they shoot you no matter how elegant you look, these men couldn't care less if they put holes in a perfectly fitting uniform or a potato sack cos they know there's meat inside either way. So the supply officer's underlings shove piles of khaki clothes at the queuing newbies, go on, you're done, don't piss around, get out of here, there's people waiting you know. On the other hand, the adjutant is more careful about the shoes he gives them, saying yes it matters cos your feet'll swell up if they don't fit, here you either walk properly or you die, got it, you bunch of pricks? And get your arses in gear cos we've got to have our soup tonight, fucksake, and now follow the sergent to the armoury to get the rest of your stuff.

Rifles shouldered, carrying their kit, helmets hanging from their wrists like women's handbags, they will hold their uniform rolled up under their arms and will drag themselves over to a huge tent and drop their equipment on a camp bed before escaping to the shelter used as a canteen, hurry up, chop-chop, curfew at twenty-one hours, we leave tomorrow at six, so go to sleep and no wanking, you can think about your girlfriends another time.

Around midnight, they will be torn from a fragile sleep by gunfire, shouts, orders, and through gaps in the canvas tent they will glimpse the cold gleam of flares. The sergent will tell them to stay in bed while he walks to the doorway of the tent, sub-machine gun in hand, to see what's going on. They will hear brief bursts of fire, closer, more muffled, it's the watchtower machine guns firing back, the sarge will say, returning to his bed.

20 Slang term for Algerian armed rebels.

"Is it often like this?" a voice will ask in the blackness.

The men will all be wide awake, eyes bulging in the dark, and they will all shrink into the canvas of their beds, as if to avoid the trajectory of a stray bullet, already crushed, already pinned down by what they do not yet dare call fear. They will see the incandescent end of the sergent's cigarette glow and the smell of Virginia tobacco will spread through the air above them and he will cough before saying in a hoarse voice:

"Every time a new load of squaddies arrives. The only people who say there's no war here are those fucking politicians. Welcome to Algeria, lads. Sleep well."

He will end this speech with a little rattling laugh and they will hear him take two or three more drags on his cigarette then, almost immediately, start snoring, like a peaceful beast.

14

Two weeks. Two weeks, ten hours a day, they've been working on this, him and his men. Couchot's customers, acquaintances, relatives, friends and enemies have been interrogated, hassled, searched. Nothing. Watertight alibis, non-existent motives, rock-solid integrity. Innocent angels stunned by the questions the nasty cops ask them, gobsmacked imbeciles who barely even understand what they're being asked and above all why they are being bothered about all this. At worst, law-abiding bastards completely unconnected with this case.

Like that Robert, that little pimp, a complete unknown until now, who put the kid to work in an attic with various paedos before selling her to the Crabos. Upon enquiry, it turned out his real name was Gaston Daumas, a crook from the Porte de Pantin who took refuge in Bordeaux after a settling of scores – three blokes dead on the carpet, and he was very nearly the fourth. Their colleagues over there seemed pretty pleased to know that he was far away, saying they hoped the warm, humid south-western climate might soften him up and do him good. They were reassured to know where he was, just in case, but they had nothing to hang on him, no really awkward questions to put to him.

He coughed up the truth about little Arlette without any difficulty. Yes, he put her to work at the Crabos' request, because he owed him a few favours. No, he didn't know where she was, but he knew which gang had picked her up, and old Crabos had sent him word from Spain not to move, to keep a low profile because this whole thing had nothing to do with him. This must be someone settling old scores, lancing old boils, burning the contents of skips where unburied corpses lay rotting.

Darlac slapped him around a bit, but soon gave up: this queer could take a beating, and he was obviously scared to death. He must have double-crossed a big shot in Pigalle to have hitmen after him like that. One day they would find him filled with bullets from a .45 and they wouldn't put much into effort into identifying the killer: the Paris boys would pick up the cold meat. The world was so much more peaceful when everyone just minded their own business.

They didn't even get anything from little Arlette's parents. They'd had to wait for the father to sober up a bit before they could interrogate him, waiting in that filthy kitchen of his, between a table still covered with plates where last night's dinner had gone cold and a sink filled with dirty crockery; they'd had to wait for him to drink a bottle of water and make himself puke in the scullery that they probably used as a toilet, before he stated, sitting ramrod straight in his chair so he wouldn't fall off, his skin greyish-green, that he didn't even remember when his daughter – a nice kid who was always very kind to everyone, and who had done well at school – had left the family home. When he was asked why he hadn't told the police about her running away, he had mumbled that he'd expected her to come home of her own accord, seeing as she was better off here than outside. The two detectives grew weary of listening to his stammered drunkard's answers and watching his shifty eyes. They stood up suddenly from their rickety chairs so they wouldn't start beating him up and warned him that it would be better for his personal safety if he didn't tell porkies or forget anything.

The mother, dishevelled, her eyes red and swollen, stared in terror at the policemen, leaving most of the talking to her husband who could answer their questions better because he knew more about that kind of thing. Her daughter used to help her a lot around the house, cleaning and looking after the little ones. A real little woman, she was, serious and all that, could easily have been a schoolteacher. And she moaned because now she had to bring up the four that were left on her own, one of them a little nipper only a year old who screamed like a stuck piglet in a cot at the foot of his parents' bed. "We do sometimes wonder if it's normal that he bawls like that all the time. My husband says maybe he needs some injections to calm him down." They couldn't get any more out of this defeated woman who mourned her eldest daughter, burned alive, between whining about the poverty that oozed from the walls, soiling everything in this hovel and making the children sick and mean.

Faced with such misery, the cops retreated and informed the social workers because of that nipper in his cot, with his bulging eyes and his skinny limbs shaking, and because of a little girl they saw hiding behind a door, wearing nothing but a pair of shorts and an undershirt in this icy hellhole, her arms covered with nasty bruises, an imbecilic smile on her cracked lips.

So this is what is running through Commissaire Darlac's sorrowful mind as he walks towards the church of Saint-Pierre under a grey sky, through the damp air that sticks to the city between rainstorms. For a few days now he's been imagining himself as a policeman in Nice or Marseille. He'd be like a fox in a henhouse there, without having to be a two-faced bastard and salute commissaire divisionnaires and kowtow to capitaines, in those cities where the sky is blue and the air so corrupt that no-one even thinks of holding their nose. But he would have to make new connections, new contacts, prove himself all over again, and that would require too much effort and, above all, too much time. And as now he's at an age when time seems to speed by, this thought calms his Mediterranean fever and he glares up at the threatening sky and draws his head in, dreading the coming rainstorm more than some divine judgement that he doesn't give a shit about.

Here in Bordeaux, he knows everyone. In a way, he's one of the princes of this little kingdom that appears so peaceful. As if to prove this idea, he pushes open the glass door of one of his baronies, "CHEZ PIERROT", and breathes a sigh of relief as he spies Francis at the back of the bar, sitting at a table in front of a cast-iron stew pot, digging out spoonfuls of meat and sauce. There are about ten customers in there eating lunch. Local shopkeepers, travelling salesmen, grey-suited pen-pushers. Some of them are alone, others talk very quietly. Whispered conversations and the clink of cutlery and crockery.

Sitting at the table with Francis is a young blonde woman who the commissaire would think pretty were it not for the make-up plastered all over her face and the false lashes that make her blue eyes look devoid of all expression. She wipes up the sauce from the bottom of her plate with a hunk of bread and finishes her glass of water. The two men nod at each other, and the cop sits down with a sigh, taking off his raincoat and unbuttoning his jacket. The girl does not react at all, does not even look up at the man who's just sat down. A waiter brings her a large cup of coffee in which she drops three lumps of sugar and begins to stir slowly, eyes lowered, apparently absorbed by what she is doing.

"Have you eaten?"

Darlac shakes his head.

"Roger! Bring a plate for my friend! We'll share it. Nothing fancy!"

Darlac watches as a glass of wine is poured for him, then drinks it in big gulps as if it were water. He turns around to look at the entrance.

"You expecting someone?"

"No. It's just that these days I don't like having my back to the door."

Francis clicks his fingers under the girl's nose. She bats her long eyelashes, holding her cup pressed to her lips.

"Didn't you hear what he said?"

The girl looks blank, then turns to Darlac as if she has only just noticed him.

"Go and drink your coffee somewhere else and leave us alone. We've got stuff to talk about. Afterwards, go to my flat and wait for me, and don't move. Understood?"

The girl gets up without a word, eyes lowered, taking her coffee with her, and sways over to the bar where she hops onto a stool. Darlac sits in the still-warm chair she has just vacated and watches her go, sizing up the flawless body perched on high heels.

"Who's that one? Where'd you find her? Is she mute or just stupid?"

Francis laughs.

"Oh, she talks. More often than she should. But we had a little talk this morning, so she's not giving me any shit today. I call her Alison. I give them American names nowadays – the johns prefer that. I'm sick of bloody Ginettes and Lucettes anyway. Those are names you'd give a cow! This girl does rich blokes. Dirty weekends, secret getaways. I rent her a studio flat in the cours de l'Intendance. It costs quite a bit, but those tossers love it. They think it's chic going to see whores in a swanky neighbourhood. And the place is always packed. And on Saturdays and Sundays, monsieur goes on a business trip and I'm the one who cleans up. Sometimes they take her to Arcachon or the Basque coast, and that costs them a packet. I started it six months ago – I don't remember if I already mentioned it to you – but anyway it's working so well that I'm planning to get another one to meet the demand. That's the future, that is. You don't need a whole herd of girls on the street with their tits in the air or leaning on the counter in crappy bars. And you get to choose the clients. You don't have to put up with cocksuckers, or weirdos with their little perversions, or loonies who beat the girls up or tightarses who don't want to pay so you have to convince them afterwards. All that shit causes aggravation over not very much and sometimes, even here, your colleagues don't like it much when the pigsty gets out of hand . . . And I haven't even mentioned all the top brass we get . . . Two or three members of parliament, bosses galore, honest shopkeepers . . . Word of mouth, discretion assured, and impeccable service given by top-quality birds . . . those are the three keystones of my business! Just like in Paris! And those suckers are queuing up for it!"

He bursts out laughing, pleased with himself, and pours more wine into his glass. Darlac cannot help smiling as he serves himself with beef stew.

"Anyway, I'm keeping the client list warm for you. It's always useful to have these bastards by the balls."

Darlac nods. He sniffs his plate then boldly spears a chunk of meat.

"Not too bad, is it?" says Francis.

The commissaire nods, drinks some wine, wipes his mouth.

"Alright," he says. "You didn't get me here to talk about food, did you? What have you got for me? Cos we've found fuck-all."

"Were you expecting me to give you a name and address?"

Darlac sighs.

"Spit it out."

"No-one's been able to tell me anything about the bloke who did it. We've talked to dozens of men – and the girls too, cos sometimes they get weirdo clients who tell them stuff . . . but nothing at all. And no-one can see why any fucker would even want to stab Penot or burn Couchot and his missus. You want to know what I think? Look closer to home. This is someone who's lashing out at people who are close to you, or who used to be, like Penot. And he had a go at your daughter too. He's prowling around you – you know he is. And I wouldn't be surprised if we found out there were cops feeding him information. You know, the types who just adore you and would like to pin a lead Liberation medal really deep in your chest or plant the Grand Cross of the Legion of Honour at your graveside . . . What about your commissaire divisionnaire, Laborde? He'd push you down the stairs given half a chance, wouldn't he?"

"Leave cops out of this. I'll take care of my business."

"It's not just your business though, if they're talking about it in town."

"Laborde's been talking? To who? When?"

Francis leans back in his seat, looking sharp in his waistcoat and his English-made pinstripe shirt, and smiles sardonically.

"Stop messing around," says Darlac. "That doesn't work on me. Just say what you have to say – let's get it over with."

Francis pushes his plate aside and crosses his arms on the table, suddenly looking serious.

"You know Lucien Lavaud? Lulu le Veau, as his friends know him?"

Darlac shakes his head. He has sat forward too and is leaning across the table. He can feel pins and needles under his skin.

"Fat bloke. Soft and fat, and slow since he got out of the nick three years ago. He used to rob post offices. Bit of a crackpot, used to do all kinds of shit. He put on weight in prison, and he must have been softened up by the raving queers you get in that place. Apparently now he's acting as a fence, but I don't know much about that ... Anyway, I heard the other day, in a bar at Barrière de Bègles, that he was going on about the man you're looking for. He said the cops were not close to collaring anyone cos this man was cunning and he had personal reasons for doing what he was doing, and that he wasn't even close to being finished. He also said he got all this from someone who knows the details of the investigation."

"One of ours?"

"What do you think? I'm just telling you what I heard. Now, bear in mind that this bloke is a bit of a crank. He drinks, and he talks a lot of shit. Michou knew him in prison. Said no-one would go near him. He used to sit on his own at meals most of the time."

"And a clown like that is a fence? Why would anyone trust him?"

"No idea. He's not in my network, and I don't want him to be. If there are blokes stupid enough to work with him, that's their funeral. Should be easy enough to get your hands on them anyway ..."

"What does he fence, this loony?"

"Not sure. Gold jewellery, furniture, curtain rods ... how should I know? He must be in cahoots with one or two gangs of layabouts who break into houses."

"Where will I find him?"

"Barrière de Bègles, in one of those bars. Or rue Son-Tay – his bird runs a bistro there, apparently."

Darlac stands up.

"Let's go. Hurry up."

Francis drinks a mouthful of wine then lays his knife and fork across his plate.

"I haven't had dessert yet. And don't worry, that clown's not going anywhere. Sit down and have some lemon tart."

But Darlac, his raincoat already over his arm, doesn't move, so Francis signals to the waiter to bring him his next course.

"Or you can go on your own. I need to eat in peace."

The waiter brings him a slice of tart and a cup of coffee. Francis gestures at the chair that Darlac had been sitting in.

"A coffee?"

The commissaire nods reluctantly and sits down with a sigh.

"You're going to end up fat too, you know. Like that other twat."

"Maybe. But my pockets are full and my balls are warm. He's sitting on an anthill with a stick of dynamite up his arse. That changes everything, in my opinion."

Francis deliberately takes his time, nibbling at his tart and sipping his coffee as Darlac watches furiously, smoking in silence. One by one, the other customers have left and now the café owner is alone behind the bar, tidying up. Darlac seethes. He lights another cigarette and sucks his coffee down to the half-melted sugar at the bottom of the cup. He looks at his watch: nearly two. He feels himself turning bad: violent and venomous. It overcomes him sometimes, this desire to hurt someone, to make them suffer. Of course, Francis is not the type who would just let him do it. He is even capable of inflicting great pain on others, and taking great pleasure in the act. But anyway. Darlac feels this black mood seeping through his veins, inch by inch. He is convinced that he has finally found the first line of inquiry likely to lead him to the man he's searching for.

Suddenly, Francis stands up.

"O.K., I'm ready when you are."

A dark bar near the boulevard, almost deserted at this time of day. A wino at the counter is talking to the owner, a small fat man with a moustache, who is reading the newspaper behind his till and occasionally muttering a sort of vague echo to the slurred monologue.

"We're looking for Lulu," says Francis.

The owner keeps his eyes on his paper.

"Who? Lulu?"

"Yeah. Lulu le Veau."

Finally the man looks up at him. With a sneer.

"Le Veau? This isn't a butcher's, you know. You've come to the wrong place, pal."

The drunkard, slumped over his glass of white wine, squeals with laughter, then chokes and coughs and spits on the ground, bent double, then rinses his throat by downing the rest of his wine.

"Police," says Darlac, showing his card. "His name is Lucien Lavaud. We know he's a regular here, so answer our questions or I'll close your filthy little dive."

The wino staggers away to sit at a table. Chair legs squeak on the tiles.

"You should have said so straight away," says the bar owner, folding his newspaper. "If it's the police who are asking, that's different. Anyway, it'll take my mind off the news, which is not very good. Can I serve you something? On the house."

Darlac and Francis both refuse with the same hand gesture. The owner leans on the counter and looks around, as if someone might be eavesdropping.

"I haven't seen hide nor hair of him this week. Usually he comes here to eat lunch on Tuesdays and Fridays, but I haven't seen him since last Friday. He'd normally be here today. But don't worry, sometimes he vanishes then comes back looking like a fool and buys a round."

"We're not worried," says the commissaire. "You know where he crashes?"

"How should I know that? Somewhere near the train station, that's all I can tell you. You should know that, shouldn't you? You're the police. This man spent five years in prison and you don't know where he is? If only my brother had been that lucky, during the Occupation: he'd still be alive!"

"Went to jail, did he, your brother? Should we get our violins out?"

"No. Just Buchenwald. Died there in early '45. Arrested by French cops. Hey, maybe it was you!"

The man has raised his voice a bit. He has rolled up his newspaper and is waving it at Darlac like a truncheon. The commissaire turns his back on him and signals to Francis to follow him over to the exit. As he is about to leave, hand on the door handle, he turns back to the bar.

"It's better for your brother that he died over there. Otherwise, he'd look like that," he says, gesturing with his chin at the wino. "They weren't made for the weak, those Kraut camps. But just so you know, I didn't arrest him. I didn't go after that sort. I left them to others who knew how to deal with them."

He leaves, paying no attention to the gobsmacked look on the man's face and the gaping mouth – a dark, toothless hole – of the drunkard who lifts his head and stares at the closed door, the greyish light of day reflected in his swollen-lidded, tear-filled eyes.

They drive, each lost in the spiky thorn bushes of his own thoughts, their faces like identical lead-grey skies. Through the windows they stare out at the city submerged in drizzle. The glistening cobblestones rumble beneath the wheels. In ten minutes they reach the bar on rue Son-Tay where Le Veau is a regular.

They spot him as soon as they enter: he's at the back, facing the street, and he's reading the racing pages in the paper, cigarette balanced between his lips. A large, round man with short-cropped hair. He's in shirtsleeves, a jacquard waistcoat straining over his protuberant belly. Darlac notices four old men playing cards in a corner, by the window. A woman smokes an American cigarette while she goes through her cash drawer. She says hello to them, one eye half closed. They do not respond, walking straight over to Le Veau's table and sitting down. The man sits upright, back stiff against his seat.

"Can't you sit somewhere else? What do you want?"

"To talk," says Darlac.

He takes out his card again, and Francis does the same. The man sees only the red, white and blue, having no time to decipher their names.

"Inspecteur Pricipal Germain," says Darlac. "And this is Inspecteur Gauthier."

Le Veau sighs, glancing helplessly at the barmaid, who has not missed a word of this.

"And would you gentlemen like something to drink? Because this establishment is for paying customers. You can't just come here and polish the chairs with your arse."

"Police," Francis says, without turning round. "Mind your own fucking business."

The old men have stopped playing cards and are furtively watching this unfold.

Le Veau tries to sigh, perhaps as a way of staying calm.

"I don't understand," he says. "What's going on?"

"The other day, when you were drunk, you were giving your two pence worth about the arson at place Nansouty, and you seemed to know a lot about the bloke who did it. I would like you to tell me where you got this precious information. Just tell us the truth and we'll be on our way. No-one will be any the wiser, and we'll leave you in peace."

"Is that all?"

Le Veau sighs again. He wipes his forehead with the back of his hand. Darlac is gripping the edge of the table as if he's about to lift it up and throw it across the bar.

"Well, you know," says Le Veau unctuously, "it was a detective who told me, and I imagine you know as much as he does. So that's why I don't really understand what you . . ."

Darlac smiles. It's such a rare occurrence that Francis frowns, watching it happen, noticing his hands turn white as they grip the table edge more tightly.

"This is a very serious case, so we're double-checking every-thing," says the commissaire. "We're corroborating every witness statement."

"It was Inspecteur Mazeau. I know him a bit. I . . . Let's just say I have an arrangement with him, and he trusts me."

"Eugène Mazeau?"

"Yeah, that's the one. You know him?"

"Of course! We work in the same department. He's a good cop. It's typical of him to have a valuable bloke like you as a contact. So, what did he tell you about this arsonist?"

Le Veau tenses, taken by surprise.

"You should know that already, shouldn't you? I thought he worked for you?"

"I told you: we're double-checking everything. I've decided to start again from scratch, so I'm going over every statement, and you're one of our most important witnesses."

The man puts his hands flat on the table, sitting up straight as if he's about to impart a military secret.

"He told me this man would never be caught. Or not alive, anyway. And that he wouldn't stop until he'd finished what he'd set out to do. You know, mission accomplished, as they say. To be honest, it seemed like Mazeau knew the bloke – he seemed so sure about him."

"Really?"

Le Veau waves his chubby hand in front of him.

"Yeah, well . . . That's the impression I got. But you know what he's like, Inspecteur Mazeau: he likes to talk, and he tends to exaggerate a bit. Sometimes he even kids around, so I take what he says with a pinch of salt . . ."

"Very wise," says Darlac, suddenly standing up. "Anyway, you've earned some brownie points. You seem like a serious bloke to me; someone we can count on. And, you know, I'm not the sort of bloke who goes around doling out compliments. Thank you."

He holds out his hand to Le Veau, who takes it weakly, a shadow of hesitation in the gesture, then shakes it while staring at the strange expression on the cop's face, which is twisted into a weird rictus grin.

"I might need you again. Where's the best place to find you?"

"Oh, I don't go far these days. I give Simone here a hand, make a bit of grub for the regulars."

Francis is also on his feet, and he now walks up to the bar, where Simone is nervously smoking, close to the telephone.

"You see? There was no need to get all worked up, was there? Words are one thing, but it's the thought that counts, don't you think?"

"Hark at you, a cop philosopher!" The woman grimaces. "Please don't forget to open the door on your way out, by the way. I would hate to see it smack you in the face."

They go to their car and jump quickly inside to escape the rain.

"So?" says Francis.

Darlac does not reply. He stares through the window at the grey sky and the rain-drowned city.

"So . . ." he says after a while. "So Jeff and you are going to take care of this Veau. Do what you want to him – escalopes, blanquette, I don't care. But I don't want to see him again. Do it tonight. Before he has a chance to speak to Mazeau. Just make sure there are no witnesses. You spoke to his missus, so she'd be able to identify your ugly mug without any problem."

"I know a cabin in the woods near Biscarosse where no-one would disturb us. Who's this Mazeau?"

"He began his career in '37, when I was made inspecteur principal. He joined the department, and I was sort of responsible for training him. He's a fixer with an eye for a good scheme. The kind of smooth talker who could sell second-hand shoes to a man with no legs."

"That could be useful, putting one over on people, when you're a cop."

"He's small-time though. Anyone with half a brain can see him coming a mile off. He looks like the sort of priest who has it off with choirboys. During the war, he chose the right side at the right time. He always manages to hedge his bets. And he's a waste of space as a cop: he wouldn't be able to find his dick in his underpants if you told him it had gone missing. But he knows which arses to lick. Anyway ... One thing's for sure: he has nothing to do with the arson investigation. Which means that he really does know something through his other informers. Which means that he knows who this fucker is. Mazeau is one of Laborde's men though, and that is a problem. It means we're walking on eggshells. We'll have to tread carefully here, for a change."

"Maybe it's the other cops on the case who've been talking and he's just repeating what he's heard."

"No. The men don't think like that. They don't pose those sorts of questions about this bloke's determination or the mission that he's on. No ... They're up to their necks in this investigation, saddled with all these witnesses who've seen and heard nothing ... They're all floundering in that shit heap. As for me, I just play dumb whenever the link with me comes up. With Couchot, they asked me why someone would attack one of my cousins, after what happened to Elise. My daughter is under protection, even if I don't think he'll attack her again. That was more of a warning shot. And we're going to look into every person I know or I used to know in the past. When I've found his motives, I'll have found my man. Maybe I'll even find him before I find his motives. And if that happens, you can bet your arse I won't waste any time trying to understand them."

They go back to the city centre and Darlac picks up his car and drives home, choking on a rage that won't let go of him, making his heart race. Often, during the journey, he touches the bulge in his jacket made by the pistol that he wears all the time now, whose weight he likes to feel on his shoulder. And often he has to fight the desire to take it out and point it at the faces of the people around him, those grey imbeciles shoving past each other along the pavements, poking each other in the eyes with their umbrellas, waiting impatiently in bus shelters. He wants to wave his gun about and open fire on two or three nobodies, committing an act of power and terror so his enemy – who is, he imagines, following him around like a ghost – will have to come out into the open and face him, man to man. Of course, he quickly dismisses these Western-style visions; he knows perfectly well that you don't hunt shadows with a gun. Above all, he knows that the one he is searching for – the one that is following him – will not vanish in broad daylight.

15

They take off their bags and drop them on the floor and lie on their beds, the sub-machine gun on their chest or the rifle by their pillow, and for a few moments the only sound is their breathing and their sighs, amid the buzzing of flies and the creaking of beds, in the darkness of the shelter where no-one thinks to close the door on the white light that has been burning their eyes and tanning their hide for the past three weeks.

Daniel, eyes closed, listens to this exhausted stirring. He lets his body grow heavy and the canvas of the bed becomes stretched almost to breaking point by the weight of all this fatigue. On his skin, he can feel the mixture of sweat and dust drying, turning his face into a marble mask, earth-coloured, like the faces of the dead they found on their second patrol in the ruins of a tiny village, two peasants with their throats cut, on whom the killers had let loose a dog. All the newbies had puked and the others had had to breathe through their mouths, scarves covering their noses, so as not to retch at the stink, because whatever they might say, laughing with a beer the next evening, they fall asleep just as often to this vision of rotting corpses and black blood as they do in the company of the girl who writes to them from time to time. Daniel remembers how they'd all had to retreat because the wasps were attacking them after being disturbed in their feast by a caporal who'd been ordered to find papers on the bodies or any other clue that would enable them to be identified, and they had waved their hands around for a moment to get the wasps off them while the lieutenant called H.Q. to report the discovery of the bodies and find out what he was supposed to do.

He tries to rid his mind of this image of cadavers, but it surges back constantly to his memory like a rubber ball thrown against a wall that bounces crazily and returns, flashing bizarrely like those electric pool balls you see in cafés. He opens his eyes and stares at the whitewashed ceiling, a blind and silent screen. With his fingertips, he touches his rifle and the scope and keeps his hand on the warm metal as he watches the others lying on their beds like him, and his mind is empty. All he thinks about is the shower he's going to take, the smell of the soap, the feel of a clean shirt on his shoulders. He thinks about these trivial things, these tiny details, these fleeting sensations, shutting himself away with them as if he were hiding in a secret, impregnable fortress.

He sees the sergent sitting immobile, body leaned forward, boonie hat in hand, shoulders lifted up by his slow, deep breathing. Occasionally he shakes his head. There are beads of sweat scattered over his shaved skull, running down the back of his neck, making it glisten, trickling down over his chin. Even he seems to be feeling it now, that battle-hardened bull, lean and tough, who tells everyone that he left behind his fat and his fatigue in Indochina, sucked out by the mosquitoes and the leeches, washed away by the monsoon and the buckets of lukewarm water that they would pour over their heads, night and day, over there, as if that shitty place might, by turning them to liquid, absorb them alive into the mud in which they sank sometimes up to their thighs, flooded by their own dysentery.

Even he was affected, this man who, after ten days of yomping and shooting exercises, had wanted to punish the newbies by making them do night patrols followed by the search of a wadi, where all they managed to do was scare a flock of sheep whose shepherd was nowhere to be seen, disoriented and senseless, perhaps returned to the savage state of those sheep, like them too, pretty soon, dragging their feet and stumbling through gravel, who might become a sort of nomadic horde at the edge of exhaustion, looking to massacre something.

Even him, the sergent, who they had all wanted, at various times, to push into the ravine below the cliff edge that crumbled beneath their feet, the stones rattling endlessly into the precipice more than a hundred metres beneath them. They had advanced, almost crouching on the hillside, hanging on to tufts of vegetation that would tear out in their hands at the slightest misstep. He went first, practically running, and then, two hundred metres further on, on stable terrain, leaning on a rock, he had cocked his sub-machine gun and looked at the peak on the other side of the valley, repeating that no-one would go to search for any cretin who fell into the abyss because there was no point knackering themselves dragging a pile of smashed-up bones back to the camp.

Daniel stares at him, that son of a bitch – Castel, he's called – sitting at the foot of his bed, slouched forward, letting the sweat run off him without moving, as if he was praying . . . and who knows, maybe this man is one of those soldier monks, on a crusade in this land of infidels and unbelievers. Maybe, in the privacy of his digs, he beats himself with a belt to expiate some mortal sin . . . It was Giovanni who talked about that the other evening. Mortifications, they're called. Loads of mystic loonies do it all over the world, sometimes in processions, to redeem men's transgressions. So here, in the war – the supreme transgression – he can flay his skin to bits, this stupid sergent, all alone in his room, he can whip his back until the bones show, and he's not there yet. And if that makes him pleased with himself, I can add some salt, rub it in his wounds, just to see him twist and scream and ask about his whore of a mother.

In the evenings, they go to the meeting hall to have a few beers, about thirty of them: all those who are not on duty or doing fatigue duties or ill or already too drunk. The radio plays songs – Charles Trenet or Gilbert Bécaud – that no-one really listens to because they're drowned out by the yelling of the tarot card players when one of them succeeds in keeping *le petit* until the end or because someone else still had a trump that no-one had counted, so there's lots of shouting over at the card table and a flat cloud of cigarette smoke that floats around the dented lampshades hanging from the ceiling. You could almost believe you were in a gambling den somewhere, were it not for the crêpe-paper garlands stretched across the room as if it were a youth club party. A capitaine who occupied this old abandoned farm for the first time after an attack in '56 had managed to get tables and chairs, a bar and some lampshades from an officers' mess in Oran. He had knocked out the briquette walls that divided the hutches where the farm workers used to sleep. And so, since then, there had been more than a hundred square metres of space that the men took turns cleaning, maintaining and supplying with various forms of fuel.

Daniel watched a game of volleyball for a minute, and then, when it began to grow dark – the mountainsides turning black under the golden sky – he got a beer and went to sit at a table where Giovanni and Jean-André, the platoon's machine-gunner, are having an intense discussion in low voices. They sit across from each other, leaning forward, almost lying on the table, tense, fists balled around beer cans, hissing into each other's faces.

"We're not the criminals. It's the *fellouzes*[21]. Didn't you see what they did to some other *bicots* the other day? And all of our lot with their bollocks shoved in their mouths and their eyes gouged out? Why do they need to do that, eh? And we're the criminals?"

"What about us French though? What good have we done since we got here? The colonists exploit them, and we come and make war on them because they're rebelling. We set fire to villages, we torture them, we bomb them. We're just as guilty of massacres as they are."

"Oh, stop. You haven't seen anything. I've been in this shit heap for a year now. The things I could tell you ... You talk like a Commie, and you act like a know-it-all cos you went to college. So shut your

21 Slang term for *fellaghas*, another word for the armed Algerian nationalists.

fucking mouth. We'll talk about it when you've seen a mate of yours die next to you. You piss me off."

Jean-André gets up, knocking his chair over behind him. He stands there, covered in sweat, his crumpled shirt open over his skinny chest. He drinks a mouthful of beer and points at Giovanni, waving his can around.

"You know fuck-all, you stupid twat. It's just theories, all that. You won't be such a smart-arse one of these days."

People at other tables turn towards them, but in the chaos of chattering voices and songs bellowed out by the radio, no-one bothers to find out what they are arguing about.

"What's up with the wop? Shooting his mouth off, is he? Got his knickers in a twist? Maybe his mama's too busy whoring to cook him spaghetti?"

The man who yelled this is one of the card-players. He turns away from Giovanni and grins grotesquely at his mates, who burst out laughing. His name is Marius Declerck, he's from Roubaix, and is generally considered a decent lad, a bit slow on the uptake, whom it's not a good idea to tease after he's downed seven or eight pints of lager in an evening, which happens pretty often.

Giovanni is on his feet. Daniel tells him, "Forget it, he's a prick," holding him back by his arm. The man's shoulders are visibly shaking with laughter, but the conversations have gone quiet and the blokes at his table suddenly stare at their cards with extreme concentration, as if they were playing high-stakes poker.

"Say that again?"

The man stands up too. Tall, broad-shouldered, with thick, short arms. He stares down at Giovanni, a nasty smile on his face, and in his hand an empty bottle.

Not that Giovanni cares. He'll sink his teeth in the bloke's throat and not let go. He's seen little mutts hanging like that from the necks of massive mastiffs, having to be knocked out before their fangs can be extracted from the big dog's flesh.

"What I'm saying is that you're hardly even French and you're screwing up the morale of the lads. But that's wops for you. They fuck everything up. Just look at the mess they've made of their own country – nothing works at all. Even the Krauts couldn't count on them. So, I'm saying, you should go home to your spaghetti-eating mates and leave us French to do what needs to be done here."

Giovanni walks up to him, grabbing a chair on his way. Around him, men silently get to their feet. Some of them leave their beer on the table, others take it with them, swallowing a mouthful on the fly as if to make the sensation more intense. Someone has turned off the radio.

"Stop it, lads. If an N.C.O. arrives, you'll be for it."

"Shut your face. Let them settle it like men."

And with perfect timing, Vrignon, the lieutenant, makes his entrance with a caporal.

"I'd rather not know what you're up to, but you'd better stop this shit now. Understood?"

Everyone sits down. Chairs scrape the floor. Radio switched back on. *"J'attendrais toujours ton retour..."* [22] The vibrato is drowned out by static, but no-one cares: it soothes the tense atmosphere.

The giant has gone back to his card game. Giovanni is trembling. Daniel asks him if he's alright, but he remains silent, his gaze sunk into the wood of the table like a knife. Then he stands up and walks over to Declerck. The other players stop what they're doing, look up at Giovanni, wide-eyed. One of them pushes his chair back a little.

Giovanni is leaning in close, speaking almost into his ear. At the other end of the room, the lieutenant, leaning on the bar, cranes his neck towards them. Declerck remains immobile, eyes staring vacantly, cards in his hand.

"You'd better watch yourself, mate. I'll get you, sooner or later. There have been plenty of others, ever since I was a kid, blokes

22 "J'attendrai' was a popular French song recorded by Rina Ketty in 1938. The quoted lyric means "I will always wait for your return'.

bigger and tougher than you, who've regretted spouting that kind of shit to me. Got it, *Komrad*? Maybe you find German easier to understand, eh?"

"Go fuck yourself," says Hercules. "If you want to try it, you'd better make sure I'm asleep. Now piss off. You're lucky the lieutenant's here."

Giovanni puts his hand on Declerck's shoulder, and instantly feels a shudder of repulsion that runs through the man's entire body.

"I love you too."

He walks away and sits down next to Daniel. He's smiling.

"What did you say to him?"

"Nothing."

He's still smiling – with his eyes as well as his mouth – and he gives Daniel a mysterious look. He picks up his bottle and lifts it towards him.

"Cheers, mate. *Vive la sociale*[23]."

They clink bottle and can together. The beer is already lukewarm, but they don't care. Two other men walk up to them. Two Parisians. Olivier and Gérard. They join the toast.

"You've got balls, Zacco. He'd have snapped you in half. That Marius is a complete nutter when he's pissed. They had to transfer him here cos he lost his temper in Kabylie and almost kicked a bloke to death."

"How do you know that?"

"From that caporal – the little one, you know? Carlin. He's a good bloke. We were on guard duty the other night, and he told me."

"Well, nutcases always have a great time during wars," says Giovanni. "Allowed to carry a gun and use it, allowed to kill ... there are loads of blokes who wallow in that like pigs in shit."

"What can we do about it?" asks Gérard. "Maybe human beings are just bastards who don't care about each other."

"Not all of them though," says Giovanni.

23 A toast to the 1905 French law separating church and state.

The four of them fall silent as if by tacit agreement and stare vacantly around this room where the soldiers kill time, necks shaved, clothes dishevelled, sweating too much beer, with their faces like kids or halfwits.

"Yeah," says Daniel. "Maybe not all of them, but quite a lot. Anyway, I'm going for a walk. I've had enough of all these wankers."

He stands up and walks out into the courtyard, bottle in hand, and as soon as the door to the meeting hall shuts behind him the roar of chatter and laughter is scattered by the cold wind that roams the mountain and snaps the flag high up on its pole. He walks past the watchtower, stuck in the middle of the camp, and gives the password just to annoy the man on duty, half-asleep on his machine gun, and who replies by telling him to fuck off, you stupid twat. Daniel moves away and the sentry continues reeling off his string of insults, voice muffled by the sandbag barrier. He's a Breton who had to leave his father and his uncle on their boat in Audierne to come over here and arse around. Le Goff, he's called – Yvon to his friends – and he says he misses everything, the sea, the wind, the rain, and tells anyone who'll listen that one day soon he's going to get the hell out of this dump, screw the F.L.N. and the *katibas*[24] and the general staff, this place has fuck-all to do with him, let them all die here, all he wants is to be on the boat and to catch fish and to surf waves as big as houses and to dive into the hollows where it's almost black as night and that's all. He says all this during marches, when they're having a rest, and the men around him stare tiredly at the sun-bleached sky, the bare hills, the scrawny bushes, the paths traced by centuries of wear that they are now the only ones to use, their supplies clattering over the bumps, and they struggle to imagine that the sea can suddenly make night fall between two mountains of water under an overcast sky. Giovanni once started reciting a Victor Hugo poem.

24 The F.L.N. is the Algerian National Liberation Front. *Katiba* is the Arab word for a battalion or company of rebel soldiers.

"L'homme est en mer. Depuis l'enfance matelot,
Il livre au hasard sombre une rude bataille.
Pluie ou bourrasque, il faut qu'il sorte, il faut qu'il aille . . ."[25]

The men were astounded that anyone could know all those words by heart, and that anyone would think of saying them here, under a live oak, arms wrapped round knees, backs soaked with sweat under their bags. The Breton had listened silently, eyes lowered, then he had thanked Giovanni. He'd said, fuck, that was good. Victor Hugo must have been through some serious storms to talk like that."

Daniel dives into darkness, skirting the main farm building where the lieutenant and the N.C.O.s are quartered, and he walks through an abandoned garden where a few rosebushes are flowering, grown wild because no-one has the time to prune them. He can feel in his stiff muscles the ground slowly rising and he comes to a low wall topped with barbed wire that protects this spur of greenery perched high up, about thirty metres above a little canyon.

No moon. Only a few stars shining and vanishing in the misty sky. Only the night so dark that you wonder how so much sunlight can beat down on this earth. Near him is an old wrought-iron garden bench that someone left here and that wobbles when you sit on it.

But nothing moves when he leans against the back.

"What are you doing here?"

He jumps to his feet and stumbles over a rock, and a hand grabs the shoulder of his shirt. It's Castel, the sergent.

"Sit down, it's alright."

His face is illuminated by the flame of a lighter. He hands him a packet of cigarettes.

"Can we smoke here?"

"It's fine. We're protected by the rocks. Anyway, you really think

25 "Man is at sea. A sailor since childhood, / He's been battling hard against dark chance. / In rain or squalls he must go out, he must leave . . ."

they'd send a sniper to hide out in the middle of the night, just to take out two blokes having a fag?"

Daniel picks out a cigarette. Castel lights it.

"So?" the sergent asks.

"You scared me."

Daniel takes a drag. Virginia tobacco. Sweet.

"I didn't scare you. I surprised you. It's not the same thing. That's not fear. You don't know what fear is."

Thick, drawling voice. Daniel can hear him blow smoke through his nostrils.

"How can you say that? You don't know me."

"Yes, I do. I know you better than you think. I've seen you suffering for three weeks now . . . I know things about you that you don't know yourself."

"What are you, a wizard or something? Can you read people's minds?"

"No. Your faces. And your feet. The way you walk, the way you look around. The way you hold your weapons and the way you shoot. I've seen so many men die that I know how to look at those who are alive."

"You must be a philosopher."

Daniel feels Castel's fingers tighten around his neck and his vision fills with red stars. This man is going to crush his throat.

"Don't get smart with me. I can kill you just like that if I want."

He forces Daniel to bend over then suddenly lets go of him. Daniel leaps backwards. All he can see of the man on the bench is a vague mass.

"Sit down, you dick. Of course I'm not going to kill you. There are *fellouzes* for that. And your own stupidity, when things start heating up."

A brief, mirthless laugh.

"And no, I'm not a philosopher. Too much brawn and not enough brains, I guess . . . I'm just a soldier, the type of bloke that always gets sent to be made into mincemeat so philosophers can continue pontificating without having to get off their fat arses. Just like in the Middle Ages – there are those who pray and those who fight."

"Don't you ever pray?"

"Pray to who? Do you know anyone?"

They can hear the sound of the wind in the small valley below them. Castel lights another cigarette. He scrapes his feet on the ground, as if annoyed.

"There's nothing and there's no-one, and that's all there is to it. Life and death. Afterwards, we're just carrion – like those two Arabs we found the other day. Remember how they stank, those two piles of shit? There's that, and then there's nothing. And we're all the same. Vietnamese, French, *fells* . . . You swell up, you stink, you ooze, and that's it."

He stands up. The bench lists to the side. Daniel sees the sergent's silhouette above him.

"Come on. I'm going to wash my face and crash out. Five, tomorrow morning. There's going to be movement in the sector, and we have to find those sons of bitches. You'll see what I meant about fear, cos it's not going to be an easy ride like you've had up to now. We're setting up an ambush. With a bit of luck, we'll put them out of action completely. Shit, yeah. We're going to hammer them."

He walks away, dragging his feet through the pebbles, mumbling incoherently. Daniel wonders what time it is. Not ten yet, because the curfew bell hasn't rung.

He thinks over what Castel said about fear. He thinks about how cold it was that day, and of the day that rose so slowly that he prayed to a god – any god – for a little sunlight to finally arrive. In the first rays of dawn he saw birds, all ruffled up, hopping about on the roof tiles close to him, watching this little giant through their minuscule eyes, and he smiled as he threw them a few crumbs of the bread that his mother had left him in a paper bag. He talked to them, and it seemed to him that they listened, that they left and then came back to see if he was still there. He had prayed to them, several times, asking them go and see where his mummy and daddy were and to bring them back to him, and to tell them that he was cold and needed to pee. He had muttered these silly requests to himself and waited for the genie to appear from the chimney. He had hoped his wishes would come true as soon as he had uttered his last words, as happened in the stories his mother told him at bedtimes. But nothing happened, of course. He remembers eating the bit of bread and the saucisson that his father had given him. He remembers the strong, thick taste of garlic. He has never been able to eat it again since.

That evening, as night fell, the skylight had opened and he had seen the face of that man, a beret on his head, his features weirdly shadowed by the corridor light, as if he were wearing a scary mask. He had shivered and moaned at this apparition, before recognising Maurice and climbing towards him, stunned by fear and numb with cold.

Fear. The fear that had gripped him when he heard those footsteps and yells on the staircase. His mother's fear, when she began to moan and weep. She took him in her arms and held him tight against her and covered him with kisses, her black hair in his mouth and nose, her tears wetting his face. My sweet little boy. My love. The fear of the hammering on the door, so close to where he stood. *"Police! Open up!"*

We'll come back. Wait for us. Stay close to the chimney. Be very careful. Be good. I love you. Mummy and I love you very much, O.K.? Be very careful. Wait like a good boy. His father closed the skylight. His father. Who had come back to the house a week earlier, after being gone for days, as he often was. He reappeared sometimes, his hands full of money and ration coupons. Smiling, joking. Singing all the time. And Mummy would start singing along. She was always waiting for him. He would see her staring through the window at the street.

He tries to remember his father's face. He remembers his singing, the songs he bellowed at the top of his voice. But his face is a total blank.

Daddy had held him tight, kissed his hair, then closed the skylight.

Doors had banged shut in the street, people had yelled. Sometimes the cops blew whistles. After that, there had been an immense silence.

"Daniel?"

He shivers. For half a second he doesn't know where – or when – that voice is coming from. So far from here. The memories cling to him. Unable to hold on, he had peed on the tiles. It had run down to the gutter.

"Yeah. I'm here."

Giovanni. Walking carefully, breathing hard.

"Fuck, I think I've had too much to drink. The Parisians had a great time. They're good blokes."

He sits down. The bench pitches slightly, then stabilises. Daniel swallows his desire to weep.

"What are you doing here in the dark on your own?"

"Nothing. Just thinking."

"Not a good idea."

"I talked to Castel. He was drunk. He told me we're going to ambush them tomorrow morning."

Giovanni exhales.

"Well, it was bound to happen. Shit. We're fucked now."

"He says there have been *fells* spotted in the area."

They fall silent. The night is turning cold. Daniel rubs his hands together. He asks Giovanni:

"Are you scared?"

"Yeah, I'm scared. All the time. I feel like everything's threatening me. And I'm not just scared of dying here."

"What else?"

Giovanni sighs. Shifts on the bench and makes it lean sideways again.

"I don't know yet. If we get out of here in one piece, I don't know what kind of state we'll be in. Have you seen the others? The ones who've been here for a few months? Have you heard them?"

"We're going to war tomorrow, Zacco."

"They're going to war. I'm not going to shoot at Algerian Resistance fighters."

"Oh, really? So you're just going to walk towards them, smiling and holding up your Party membership card so they'll shoot in the air cos you're on the side of the goodies? Have you seen this place? As you said, have you seen the reaction of the others when you try to talk to them, when you try to make them understand? Did you hear that twat earlier tonight insulting you? For fuck's sake – they're the people too, you know! They're the ones we have to deal with. Anyway, how are we going to get out of this mess if we're getting shot at, if the blokes next to us are injured, or worse? Are we going to start yelling, 'Ceasefire, comrades! Peace in Algeria!'?"

"So what will you do when you see someone's face in close-up through your scope? You won't be shooting a film, you know. You're the best shot in the platoon, mate. You never miss at two hundred metres, but those are cardboard targets or tins of corned beef. When it's a *fell*, a real man of flesh and blood, you'd better not miss then cos Castel and the lieutenant will know that you've done it on purpose."

They fall silent again. As they can't see each other, on this moonless night, and as the jebel is silent, they are only voices and breathing, motionless in the cold air that moves around them now, leaving its icy hands on their necks.

"Shit, I don't know," says Giovanni, after a while. "I've drunk too much. I'm not used to it. I feel lost."

The wind makes the dry leaves tremble in the tree above them. They lift their eyes to this invisible shivering.

"C'était un temps déraisonnable
On avait mis les morts à table
On faisait des châteaux de sable
On prenait les loups pour des chiens
Tout changeait de pôle et d'épaule
La pièce était-elle ou non drôle
Moi si j'y tenais mal mon rôle
C'était de n'y comprendre rien.[26]

That's Aragon. I don't know what else to tell you."

"I'm sick of your bloody poetry."

"I know. But it's the only way I know how to think."

Giovanni gets up and sighs and stands for a moment, smoking. He blows smoke out softly after each drag. He swears very quietly then crushes his fag butt under his shoe.

"I'm going to try to get some sleep. See you tomorrow."

Daniel listens as he walks away, stumbling over the stones. Poetry. As if this was the right time, the right place. He thinks about Irène and how she loved to recite it all the time too. They'd be a perfect pair, those two pinkos: they could recite poetry while selling *L'Humanité*[27]. It would be cute as hell. Irène and Giovanni. What am I talking about? Irène. Irène.

He realises he is saying her name out loud. And the wind brings him a scent of thyme and dust, and tickles his shoulders. He shakes out the shiver like a dog.

Night all around them. A deep, chasm-like silence surrounds the headlights of the GMC trucks, the roar of the engines and the noise

26 From Louis Aragon's poem, "Est-ce ainsi que les hommes vivent?" ("Is This How Men Live?"). These lines can be translated as: "It was an unreasonable time | We had put the dead on the table | We saw wolves as dogs | Everything changed pole and shoulder | Was the play funny or not? | If I didn't play my role well | That's because I didn't understand it at all."
27 The Communist Party newspaper in France, at the time.

of men's voices, like the mouth of a monster hesitating to swallow a toxic prey. Not a star in the sky; nothing but the fathomless blackness of the universe high above the commotion of the platoon as it gets ready to set off. At ground level, the dust is already rising, visible in the vehicles' luminous beams, drying their mouths already dehydrated from bad sleep and too much booze. Men help each other to climb aboard trucks and sit on benches that kill their backs, even though they haven't started moving yet. They're closely packed, so their rifles are held between their legs, loaded, safeties on. In front of each soldier is his bag, with his helmet on top. Bareheaded, they feel the cold only when they climb on board the trucks, so some of them rummage in their pockets to find their caps and warm their shaved scalps.

There are forty trucks on the road, doing maybe fifty kilometres per hour, and the men are shaken around, their spines rolling against the seat back, and they are thrown into each other as the trucks jolt and lurch over ruts and cracks in the ground. They all yell at the drivers to slow down, banging with their boots and their rifle butts, but nothing happens. They call them sons of bitches and the drivers tell them where they can stick it and after a few miles they simply curl up in the foetal position, arms crossed over their knees, arses crushed and backs singing with pain, the soldiers already ground down before the mission has even begun.

About ten kilometres from their quarters is a mountain pass where weapons are transported on the backs of men or mules, where groups of *fellaghas* come at night to seek provisions from the hamlets located on the edge of the forbidden zone. They will continue over the peaks to seize control of the north side. The south will be taken by Capitaine Laurent's platoon.

Lieutenant Vrignon, looking wan in the feeble light of dawn, told them all this straight out, standing legs apart on the path they must take later, indifferent to the icy wind that sweeps the spur where the trucks stopped. The men stood leaning against the vehicles, seeking any protection they could find from the Algerian blizzard, and they all noticed Sergent Castel's approving nod, his respectful mimicry when the lieutenant mentioned the name and rank of Capitaine Laurent.

Above them, the stars went out. While Vrignon continued his long-winded speech, not even flinching in the cold, they drew their heads into their shoulders, pulled their large cotton scarves even tighter over their chins, and their bodies trembled, the muscles petrified, as they stamped their feet.

When the sergent ordered them to start marching, Daniel felt almost happy, lifting the bag that must have weighed at least twenty kilos onto his back and helping Giovanni with his, because they had given him two satchels full of magazines for the machine gun. They walked quite quickly for an hour, the cold from the stones seeping up their legs, the sun rising behind them, pursuing their huge, deformed shadows.

There are about forty of them. They say nothing and most of the time they stare at the path they walk or at the feet of the man in front. Earlier, Daniel saw the cliffs where they are headed blaze brightly in the golden light of dawn. Picked out by the slanting light, even the stones were illuminated, like embers breathed on by the wind. Now, in a white dazzle, he can feel sweat seeping from every pore, streaming over his skin and then drying up like a wadi lost in the sand. He can taste its saltiness on his lips, can feel his eyes burning. He tries to soothe this by rubbing his eyelids with the back of his hand, the way children do when they are sleepy.

When the path descends into a wide basin where thick grass and a few green bushes shine in the sunlight, they take the chance to light cigarettes, pass each other packets of tobacco or lighters and talk among themselves for the first time in two hours, though what they say can be summarised in twenty words, including swear words, plus a few insults offered without conviction, without conse-quence. Their column of whispers and muffled laughs stretches over more than a hundred metres as they tread close-cut turf sprinkled with blue flowers. Then they all hear the same thing at the same moment: men speaking Arabic. And they all see, on the ridge line at the other side of the green crater, the silhouettes of two goats. In a single movement they crouch down, fingers tight to triggers. The sergent sends a caporal to scout the land to the left with ten light infantrymen who leave their bags in order to move more quickly. They run along the side of the basin, and the only sound is their footsteps, muffled by the firm green ground. Two scouts move slip behind an embankment, while the rest continue their progress on the slope, all of them bent double.

The goats line up in growing numbers on the ridge. They do not move, slowly chewing as they stare at the soldiers. Daniel has often seen this sort of backlit line-up at the cinema, when Apache horsemen mass at the summit of a hill before attacking a procession of carriages or a platoon of cavalry. He takes his Garand[28] rifle from its holster, pulls out the scope and puts his eye to it.

Giovanni puts a hand on his arm.

"What are you doing?"

"Nothing. Just looking."

"And what do you see?"

"Those fucking goats."

A metallic shudder runs through the column of men. Everyone on the alert. The inaudible jingling of slings as they shoulder their rifles. The intensified pressure around rifle butts, pistol grips, triggers.

Just ahead, two men are walking, hands on their heads, surrounded by the herd, which is beginning to descend towards the bottom of the basin. An old man and a tall, skinny kid, as far as Daniel can tell by looking at them through his rifle scope. Each carries a stick, and a satchel. The two scouts arrive behind them and smash them to the ground with the butts of their guns, holding

28 American-made rifle, equipped with a scope, sometimes used by snipers during the Algerian war.

them flat on the ground with a foot on their necks. They are surrounded. Their satchels are emptied out, the contents kicked away or crushed beneath a boot heel. The goats scatter, bleating, taking advantage of the situation to cavort in the grass and finding between the clumps of little bulrushes pockets of water lapping and hissing beneath their hoofs.

The lieutenant sends Daniel and Giovanni westward as lookouts. He yells at the rest to remain high up, except for three whom he tells to set up a machine gun at the top of the slope that the path follows. Next he sits on a rock and picks up the radio receiver, back turned to the troops in order to speak, as if he were making a private call.

Daniel and Giovanni climb up on top of a big rock that overlooks the green hollow. From here, they can see the entire valley that the platoon climbed through, a frozen swell of hills and ridges. The sky is slowly whitening and the light beats down on their eyelids as they scan the few bushes growing stubbornly and randomly in places. But the bushes are too far apart, too scattered to hide a group of *fells* or an imminent attack. Daniel enjoys imagining the figures of animals or men that he hunts down with his binoculars, evading the capricious traps of light and shadows. Behind him, he hears Castel interrogating the two shepherds in his hoarse drawl, so he turns around and sees the two poor devils on their knees, hands still on their heads. He looks up to see all those soldiers in a circle around them, guns vaguely aimed at them, or shouldered as they smoke cigarettes and drink water from their flasks. Then Castel starts screaming. He smacks the old man on the top of his head, not very hard, though Daniel hears the sharp sound it makes and the man curls into a ball, then kneels up again, protecting his face with his hands.

"When did they go past?" the sergent yells. "You must have seen them!"

The man shakes his head, waves his hands. He says he didn't see anyone, that he went out this morning with his goats and his son. Have pity, he says, and other things in his language, in his choked voice. The boy asks the sergent to leave them in peace, but a kick sends him sprawling onto his side and he immediately gets back on his knees, swaying slightly and keeping his head lowered, his lips moving although nothing can be heard of the prayer – or curse – that he is uttering.

"Look!" Castel tells the old man. "Look at this, you scum!"

He takes out his pistol, releases the safety and presses the barrel to the boy's temple.

Giovanni grabs Daniel's sleeve.

"Talk, or I'll blow his head off! Talk, you son of a bitch! It'll be one less rebel anyway, cos they'll come here to take your little bastard!"

The old man says again that he doesn't know anything, hasn't seen anything, that he only came here to feed and water his herd, please, please, leave us alone. The boy trembles and shakes and moans, his eyes crazed with terror.

Giovanni is on his feet. His fist tightens around the cocking lever of his rifle.

"Don't say anything. Don't move," Daniel whispers. "Leave them. They'll calm down."

"They're not going to kill that man – they can't!" Giovanni chokes.

The sergent makes a sign to a soldier. The man primes his submachine gun and aims a burst of gunfire at the herd of goats. He does it gladly. Maybe half the magazine is used. The goats leap in all directions or collapse to the ground or limp away then roll down the slope, bleating like children, like old women, and to hear them, you'd think it was a group of people being massacred. Two drag their bodies around with their front legs, and three are lying on their sides, their bodies jerking. The others try to climb the sides of the grassy crater, but the men are kicking them back down, shouting and laughing, then the crippled goats crawl along the ground, braying, and the soldiers laugh even louder. Lieutenant Vrignon, who turned around when he heard the gunfire, watches without understanding. He hangs up his telephone, picks up his sub-machine gun and runs towards the sergent and the two Arabs, who are now holding their heads and crying, and his feet get stuck in ruts and he stumbles sometimes against large tufts of thick grass.

He squats next to the two men and forces them to look at him by lifting up their chins with the barrel of his gun, and he too barks into their faces and hits them with the back of his hand while Castel holds them by the hair.

The interrogation lasts another five minutes. Castel and two soldiers strip the boy naked and force him to stand up, hands on his head, and the two soldiers tease his penis with the points of their daggers, telling him even a bitch in heat wouldn't want that soft piece of meat. They throw the old man by his hair at his goats and the soldier who did that rubs his hands, grimacing and whining with disgust because a lock of hair is stuck between his fingers, white and bushy and dry as tow, stuck there with sweat.

A few men laugh. Others pretend to look away.

Then the lieutenant whistles as if calling a dog and the men turn to look at him and respond to his signal by reforming the column on the path.

The two shepherds are sitting down, their faces in their hands. The boy has hastily dressed again, shivering as he pulls his old rags tight around him. The remaining goats have come back and are nibbling or sniffing or pushing at them with their muzzles, while bleating.

Daniel comes down from the spur where they had gone to keep a lookout, and behind him he hears Giovanni whispering insults and threats at the officers, the army, this whole fucking war.

"And we let them do it . . . Jesus, can you believe it? They could have killed those two men and what would we have said?"

Daniel does not reply. He doesn't know what to say. He concentrates on putting his rifle back in its slipcover, then lights a fag and offers one to Giovanni.

"I don't know what we could do. Maybe nothing. Because this is a war and we don't have any freedom left. We're not even ourselves anymore."

"Of course we are! Shit, what do you think? Look around! We're just the same as before, with the same ideas, the same reactions, aren't we?"

Daniel meets his eyes: huge, shining and very dark. He would like to be able to think like Giovanni. He'd like to be able to think, full stop.

"I don't know. Shit, I don't know anything anymore."

His friend tosses away his cigarette, loads up his bag, gets tangled up in the straps of his rifle. He looks as though he is about to throw everything to the ground, but Daniel helps him lift up his kit. Around them, the men are blowing and sighing as they hoist up their loads. None of them watches the old man and his son picking up the contents of their bags. A bit of bread, some dates, a few crumbs of cheese. In the transparent air, under a sky of a deep, dense blue, the light picks out each detail like the point of a scalpel. Perhaps no-one can look at that without pain.

They start walking again and the heat silences them and exhaustion rises through their legs, making their footsteps heavy and slow. The path climbs gently, incessantly, subjecting them inch by insidious inch to its rule.

A few hours later, they have a break in the shade of a copse of live oaks and eat their corned beef from the tin, and slices of saucisson with rubbery bread. They drink sparingly from their flasks of water and click their tongues, perhaps to rid their mouths of the briny or metallic taste. The sergent is the only one who remains on his feet, the sling of his sub-machine gun across his chest, the weapon behind his back. He says sitting down makes you weak, and he goes from group to group asking everyone if they are alright, advising them to save their water because there's none around in this country of sand and dust; it's like a precious metal, hidden in the depths of the earth. Not like in Indo, he adds, where two days in the humidity made you mouldy like an old bit of bread and where you could fill your flask just by holding it to the end of a giant leaf for five minutes.

Men offer him slices of saucisson and squares of chocolate and he refuses scornfully, content to pick and swallow handfuls of nuts and grains from his pocket. It's said that no-one has ever seen him eat anything more substantial than that during any march or patrol. That he's never thirsty; that a single gulp of water is enough for him, where a squaddie will down his entire flask; that he runs smoothly on very little because all he carries around with him is the bare minimum: muscles and nerves, basic weaponry, plus a grenade that he keeps on him so that, if the *fells* ever get him, he will blow himself up – him and the idiot who walks over in triumph, thinking he's caught a prisoner. It's also said that he brings in bottles of gin by military courier and that he cuts it with lemonade to give it some flavour and that he gets drunk alone in his hovel, a former pigsty whose first human occupants, in '56, cleaned it with a flame-thrower before whitewashing it. Those who have been inside talk about a canvas bed, a table and chair, a washbowl perched on a three-legged stool in front of a mirror and a single wooden shelf. Weapons hung on hooks on the wall. And nothing else. Oh . . . yes. Photos of Chinks with those fucking gently sloping hats. And landscapes with yet more Chinks or Gooks, who can tell, slaving away, bent double over the waters of a paddy field.

That is what they say about Sergent Castel. Behind his back, and at quite a distance.

No-one really hears the clicks that echo above them. Castel drops to the ground, the lieutenant yells, "Down! Down!" and Daniel sees Declerck, thrown forward as if kicked, fall head first in the dust then twist his torso, holding his throat to stop the blood from pissing everywhere, but it pours between his writhing fingers, and the giant of the north struggles, groaning, kicking out and rolling over, as if trying to fight off an invisible enemy. Giovanni crawls over to him and uses his dirty scarf to compress his ripped throat, telling him it'll be alright, don't worry, we just need to press down on this to make it stop.

Above them, there is a buzzing and the leaves of the trees are torn off and rain down on the men like confetti. The trees wail as their branches are eaten away. Daniel looks around him at the men pinned to the ground, on the verge of burying themselves like insects in the sand in order to avoid the bullets that seek them out but ricochet from rocks or land in the soil, creating little clouds of dust. Giovanni is still lying next to Declerck, one hand pressed to his neck, the blood-soaked scarf in his hand, but the wounded man no longer moves, lying on his back with his eyes and mouth wide open, his fingers tensed and buried in the earth.

The gunfire ceases suddenly. Heads are lifted. Vrignon, the lieutenant, adjusts his hat and goes over to Castel. The two of them gather up the men, tacking quickly, backs bent, between the abandoned bags and guns. A few look away from the sight of Declerck's corpse, while others can't stop staring at it. Stupefied. All that blood. They've probably never seen so much. A piglet can be bled, squealing, into a bucket, but a man's blood pours out like red water from a burst pipe, spreading over the dry earth, already absorbed into it, now nothing more than a dark stain. They are pale, jaws slack or tensed, faces shining with a sweat that has not been caused only by the heat.

The lieutenant crouches down, and those who were still standing imitate him, gripping their weapons with sweat-slick fingers. He stares at them without a word, meeting every gaze, wide-eyed or defeated. He is probably waiting for his breathing to slow before he can speak.

Castel is lying on his belly in the undergrowth, looking through binoculars at the side of the hill.

"They've got a machine gun," says the lieutenant. "They're containing us here, waiting for us to leave; that's why they're aiming high and shooting in short bursts. It's possible they've got another position a bit further on so they can catch us from both sides. Evidently they don't have a mortar, otherwise we'd all be dead, and we're not going to wait till one arrives, if it happens to be on its way. Alright, so we've lost one. They got him by pure chance. It could have been any of us, O.K.? I don't want to lose anyone else. What I want is for us to get out of here without any injuries. And we're not going to let those sons of bitches get away with it – we're going to kill a few of them, so at least Declerck won't have died for nothing. Understood? So stop crawling around like cockroaches and start acting like soldiers again."

The men mutter and nod, slowly getting up. Giovanni puts his blood-covered hands in the dust and wipes them on his trousers. Daniel meets his vacant gaze that then looks away, eyes lost in the deathly pallor of his face.

The sergent gets to his feet. They all stare at him in terror, instinctively cringing.

"Lieutenant, let me reconnoitre. We should be able to find that machine gun. I think I know where they were shooting from."

Vrignon looks up at him, glances around at the men sitting in the shade and shakes his head. Aggrieved or resigned.

"O.K. I'll call the battalion to let them know."

"Two men with me to see where they are," says Castel. "You can cover us from here. Short bursts – save the ammunition. We don't know how long we'll have to stay here. Pauly and Normand. Delbos, you take your Garand. Those blokes up there are not made of cardboard – you need a bull's-eye. Got it? Leave your bags. Just take your gun and some grenades. Come on, let's get moving!"

When he hears his name, Daniel shivers and stands up at the

same time as the other two, slowly, then removes the rifle from its slipcover and takes three magazines. As soon as he leaves the shade, the sun beats down on his shoulders, trying to force him to the ground. Daniel follows Castel, who climbs up through the thicket of trees, emerging from their cover to throw himself behind a rock. The four of them find themselves on their knees and the covering fire starts up. The hillside shakes, with clouds of dust, shards of rock, fragments of branches and leaves sent flying by the impact of the bullets.

They start climbing again on all fours, hidden by the thick, dry underbrush that rustles as they move through it and scratches at their faces and arms. Daniel is just behind Castel, who goes quickly, but he finds himself sliding over the stones as they roll beneath his shoes, as if he was running on a carpet of marbles. He's short of breath and the burning he can feel in his legs seems to be radiating from his very bones, cooking his muscles from inside. He can hear the two others, Pauly and Normand, panting behind him. They too skid and slip, and swear in whispers.

The gunshots come more sporadically. The platoon's machine gun must have been placed in a good position, because they can hear it more loudly now. Above them, the *fells* fire at random but they seem invisible. Nothing moves apart from the scraps of foliage torn from the trees by bullets and the puffs of dust raised by their impact. It looks as if the hill itself is answering back to the shots.

A volley of bullets hisses past over their heads and Daniel hears Pauly yell and fall heavily and groan, "I'm hit! Shit, lads, they got me, those fuckers!", so he goes back and crouches next to the wounded man while Normand fires his sub-machine gun in every direction, staring at the bead, as if the *fellaghas* might appear from anywhere to finish them off.

"Where does it hurt? Fuck, I can't see anything!"

Pauly pants and moans. His eyes roll back in terror.

"My back," he manages to say. "At the top."

Daniel pulls him towards him so he can turn him onto his side, and that is when he sees the slash in the battledress jacket and beneath that the bloodstained undershirt and beneath that a smear of blood, like a sort of burn. He touches the skin around it, feeling only the bulge of a rib.

"It's nothing. Just a scratch. It's bleeding a bit, but that's all."

"Bollocks to that! I get hit by a bullet and you give me that shit!"

Daniel feels himself pushed aside and falls on his arse. Castel is already leaning over Pauly.

"Show me. What have you got?"

He makes him lie face down and examines the wound.

"This is nothing, you prick. Another centimetre and it would have hit your spine, but you've got nothing worse than a cracked rib, so stop fucking whining. Stay here and don't move. We'll pick you up on our way back. And shut your mouth, you understand? Normand, take his magazines and let's go. Their machine gun's over there, in that thicket. We're going to take it out."

He leaves, with Daniel and Normand following. Bent double, noses to the ground, sucking up dust. The sergent lies down behind a mound of earth. He passes Daniel his binoculars.

"Look over there. That pointed tree higher up. Below that. You see the barrel sticking out? The leaves move sometimes too. Wait until they fire again."

Not two hundred metres away. Dense undergrowth below live oaks and junipers. Daniel can see nothing but the leaves shining brightly in the sun, motionless. Nothing moves or even shivers.

"You don't see anything?"

The sergent is whispering into his ear. Daniel props himself up on his elbows, holds his breath. He sees the smoke before he hears the crackle of gunfire.

Now he can make out a few centimetres of the barrel and part of the tripod. He wonders how he didn't notice it earlier. He doesn't have enough saliva to speak: his dry mouth, lined with dust, emits only a sort of choking noise. He thinks about his two flasks of water, waiting for him down below, in the shade. Looking for the shooter, he notices the slightest tremble in the rough, stiff foliage that rarely moves in the breeze. His forearms tremble. His back and his shoulders are burning, and the collar of his jacket scratches the back of his neck, which is covered in sweat. He searches the depths of the thicket for a lighter mark, a bit of skin, a circle of light sliding over a face.

Suddenly he distinguishes the shape of a face, unmoving, above the firing axis of the machine gun.

Rifle. Adjust the scope. He's lost his target: his field of vision is trembling too much.

"Here. Take a drink, and afterwards blow his head off."

He does not remember ever having swallowed anything better than this lukewarm, dirty water. He manages to say thanks and returns to a firing position, moves slightly to the side, finds a better support.

The man is still there, in the shadow of the undergrowth, immobile at his machine gun. He can see him better now. Face leaning forward, eyes lowered perhaps, as if he's praying. He is surprised by the power of this image. This profile framed by an emerald and black blur, sparkling in the sunlight. Depth and contrast.

Daniel centres him in the eyepiece, lifts it a little to compensate for the fall of the trajectory and holds his breath again. For ten or fifteen seconds he can feel nothing but a drop of sweat tickling his skin as it runs from his temple down to his cheek. And in the scope he sees the man lying flat and with his other eye the dark green thicket where he lies shining in the blazing sun.

Deafened by the detonation. His shoulder absorbs the shock. In the scope he can no longer see anything, then he finds the mouth of the machine gun again, searches for the figure of the gunner.

Castel scans the bushes with his binoculars.

"I saw something move. You got him."

He picks up the walkie-talkie and speaks to the lieutenant.

"We got him. Move now before they replace him. I'm going to check it out."

Daniel continues staring at the undergrowth. He cannot take his eyes off the place where he saw that immobile face. Perhaps he was already dead, he thinks, and at the same time he half expects him to reappear. The sergent tugs at his sleeve.

"Come on, let's go. Stay three metres below me." Then, to Normand, he orders: "You – find some shelter for Pauly."

"You're not going to wait for the others?"

"What others? They're coming, the others. Don't worry. Our orders are to comb the ground. There are choppers coming."

They run in zigzags through a dense thicket of low bushes that cling to the canvas of their trousers as they go, hundreds of skeletal fingers trying to hold them back. The sun is ahead of them, laying a burning hand on their chests, licking their faces like a furnace. Lower down, the platoon has split into three groups and is climbing towards them. Daniel is distracted by the clinking of his straps as he runs. He does not feel anything, neither fatigue nor fear. He has probably just killed a man and he is running towards his corpse without thinking about anything. Least of all death.

"Look up there!" the sergent shouts. "Look at those cunts running away!"

Daniel notices bushes shaking in all directions near the ridge line. Castel empties a magazine at this movement while yelling insults at the retreating rebels. He kneels down to reload his submachine gun.

"Come over here," he says. "Let's see what you got."

They enter the undergrowth, training their guns all around in the hot darkness that surrounds them and Daniel sees the man's body, lying on its side. The top of his jacket is soaked with blood. Daniel slowly approaches to see where he hit him. He has no cheek or jaw left. Something twisted and bloody is hanging from his face.

"Watch it," Castel whispers. "They might have booby-trapped it."

Daniel turns towards him, incredulous.

"With a grenade underneath. Pin out, just the lever supported. You move the body and it blows your head off. I'll go. Follow me."

Castel straddles the man, crouching down and slowly passing his hand under his legs, under his torso. Just as he stands up to say something, the gunner makes a rattling noise and his legs move. Castel jumps backwards, catching hold of a branch and swearing.

"Fuck, he's not dead!"

Daniel starts to tremble. He points his gun at the wounded man's head, but he feels as if his arms are incapable of any movement except for this trembling that runs from his shoulders to his hands.

The sergent grabs the man's shirt and lifts him up, leaning his back against a tree trunk. The man half opens his eyes, moves his head slightly. The torn-away part of his face drips blood. He groans, tries to speak.

Daniel moves closer.

"Will he make it?"

Castel looks up at him, surprised, then shrugs.

"No. Impossible. Have you seen him? It took off half his face."

"You can repair that kind of thing though, can't you?"

"Yeah, right. I'll call the surgeon and we'll book him a nice room in a hospital, with a pretty nurse to wank him off. Give me a fucking break! He's going to die, simple as. One of our men got killed back there, for fuck's sake. What more do you need? What if it turns out this bloke shot him? You're not going to pin a medal to his rotting corpse, are you? This is war, lad, you don't seem to have figured that out yet. We didn't do all this just so he could pull through. He doesn't even know he's dead already. He's trying to speak. Maybe cos he can't shut his mouth anymore."

Castel laughs silently at his own witticism. Then he says nothing and stares at the man, who is breathing feebly, head leaning to the side, eyes half closed. They hear the tramping of the patrol moving closer and the voice of the lieutenant asking: "So? Where are we?"

The sergent loads his sub-machine gun and fires three bullets into the man on the ground. His body jumps at each impact and rolls over onto its side. Daniel would like to scream in this racket and then in the silence that follows, but his throat remains knotted, rough as rope.

"Any other stupid ideas you want to share? You started the work, I finished it. Don't tell me you only shot at him earlier to scare him off, right? Don't tell me you practise shooting every day to impress the birds at the fair when you've gone back to your miserable home-town. No-one forced you to do that. You were really happy when the lieutenant gave you the Garand, and you looked after it the way you look after your own balls. So? I'm not interested in your fucking moods. You understand?"

A caporal arrives, along with a dozen men, all out of breath, while the others continue climbing the slope. He glances casually at the corpse then leans over the machine gun to examine it.

"Russki-made," says the sergent. "Serious shit. This thing never jams and it's accurate. The Vietnamese nailed us easily with those. But they knew how to fight, not like these *fellouze* bastards."

The men push the corpse with their feet or with the barrels of their guns like a bunch of monkeys who don't understand what death is. Some of them hiss insults then stand around, without moving, perhaps taking advantage of the shade.

"It was Delbos who got him," says the sergent. "He'll pay for his round when we get back."

The others congratulate him. Pat him on the back, tell him well done for avenging Declerck.

"You see? In war we're all the same, when it comes down to it . . . Yesterday you almost got into a scrap with him, and today you shoot the son of a bitch who killed him."

The man who says this, his face close to Daniel's, eyes staring into his eyes, is called Dumas, or Duprat – Daniel can't remember. He stinks of sweat and rotten teeth, and his eyes appear by turns battered and wide open, which Daniel thinks gives him the twisted, unpredictable look of a dangerous madman, so he wrestles free from his grip and promises everyone a drink, and the mere idea that cold liquid might fill his mouth and flow down his throat suddenly feels like a daydream, confusing his mind so completely that he has to walk out into the sunlight to rid himself of it. He wipes the sweat and dust from his face and looks up at the summit of the hill, where the men are traipsing, and above it the sky is so blue it looks hard, like the bottom of a plate that has just come out of a kiln.

He joins the others as they travel across the ridge line, looking out for Giovanni without finding him. One of the Parisians, Gérard, tells him that the lieutenant ordered Giovanni and another soldier to stay behind with Declerck's body, and to look after the bags too, because they were just carrying out a quick reconnaissance mission before going back. The ambush mission was cancelled. Choppers cancelled too, so no combing of the area. Apparently there was going to be a big operation in the coming days.

"So I heard you got the shooter?"

"Yeah, I got him. I didn't kill him, but I got him."

The Parisian doesn't understand.

"He was still alive when we got there. A bit of a mess, but alive. It was Castel who finished him off."

"He did that?"

"I started, he finished."

"Fuck. But all the same . . ."

Daniel stops to light a cigarette, letting the column leave him behind, and as he starts walking again he tries to put his mind back in working order. Eyes to the ground, he does not notice the red-soiled valley that stretches out below him to the east, studded with rocky outcrops like teeth in the mouth of a monster. He tries to recollect the face of the man he shot, but the memory fades as soon as the image forms in his mind and he is left with only the vision of the corpse on the ground and the men prodding it with their boots.

For two hours they patrol the other side of the hill and find nothing, vainly scanning the horizon from various high points and searching bushes, but all that ever emerges is the odd snake, which they crush with the butt of a rifle. And when the lieutenant yells at them to be quiet, the silence covers them like a veil, heavy and oppressive, and they find themselves alone, guns hanging from their hands in this empty land where even the southerly wind seems to have fled.

In the trucks, on the way back to their quarters, they say nothing, worn out, heat-dazed, suffocated by the exhaust fumes from the vehicle jolting along in front of them, black smoke pouring from its arsehole in an endless flood of diarrhoea, wheels raising tons of dust. They protect themselves by wrapping their large scarves around their faces, which makes them look like Tuaregs or the Mujahideen, as if this war were forcing them to resemble their enemy.

Night falls almost as soon as they enter the command post. They jump heavily from the trucks, then drag themselves over to their quarters, shaking the dust from their clothes with exaggerated exclamations.

Daniel looks everywhere for Giovanni, finally finding him in the shack that serves as an infirmary, helping to wash Declerck's bare-chested corpse, which lies, imposingly, on a trestle table. It seems to Daniel that, at this moment, the dead man occupies all the space in the room, making it hard for anyone to move around him. The corpse is supposed to be taken to town by jeep tomorrow morning. It will need an escort – half-track and all that crap – because the thirty-kilometre trip there is infamously hairy. The nurse speaks to him without looking up from what he's doing, softly wiping the ragged edges of the bullet's exit wound with a cloth.

"Before he starts stinking," the man explains. "In this heat."

Daniel seeks out Giovanni's eyes, but his friend remains focused on his task, holding a bowl full of brownish, muddy water with blood clots floating in it. So he watches Giovanni taking care of the corpse, the same man he wanted to kill just yesterday, removing his dirty shirt, delicately cleaning his white, marbled skin with a flannel, smoothing back his dust-grey hair. He watches this dead man, whose ignorant hatred had seemed to drive him through life, this brute whose family could say, as they mourned, that he was shot in the back by those Arab dogs when he wasn't hurting anyone. His view of this pale, muscular body is strangely superimposed on the image of the scrawny, copper-skinned machine-gunner he shot that afternoon, and he feels as if he has walked on one of those landmines they're always warning you about, that explodes only when you remove your foot from it to take the next step. And he thinks the only way of escaping it is to jump as far ahead as possible. To end up in pieces rather than dying on the spot.

16

Mazeau has not shown up in the department for the last week. Rumour is that he caught it while he was arresting someone, that he had to stop by the Saint-André hospital to check that, apart from the two broken ribs and the dislocated jaw, he was fine. His men don't know who did that to him. He went in there solo. An informer, apparently, whom he tried catching with his team one evening, and then met face to face the next day. A big, tough man who knocked three detectives to the ground outside the prison. A giant, some say. Think about it: he scattered cops like pins in a bowling alley. Unafraid of anything or anyone. And there's no way they can shoot the bastard, because they need him to talk. There are a few theories about the fugitive's identity – they know a few massive bad men who hang around in the area – but after double-checking, it turns out these crackpots all have iron-clad alibis.

Darlac wanted to know what scent that joker had picked up. He ferreted about, buying drinks for the pimps in the Vice Squad who kept checking their tie knots in the bar mirrors every five minutes or eyeing the time on their gold-plated watches or just smiling slyly at him as if to say: "What are you after, mate? We don't know anything, unlike you. The kid who burned, we didn't know her, and we left Crabos in peace cos he wasn't bothering anyone." He soft-soaped novice detectives, buying them a coffee to get them to talk, handing them the sugar bowl, offering them his cigarettes, but those morons didn't know anything either, *nada*, fuck-all, they just stared at him surprised and suspicious, their eyes shining in the flame of the lighter held by the commissaire, and the worst thing was that it was true: they really didn't know anything, didn't understand anything, like kids in a nursery school, like fucking honest cops.

He hung around the other departments, listening patiently to the songs they sang him; he detected false notes, let them hum their old refrains. He has a musical ear. He almost wanted to applaud this choir of voices, all sworn to sing the same tune, cross my heart and hope to die . . .

Commissaire Divisionnaire Laborde grabbed hold of him in a corridor to ask him what his problem was with Mazeau, what possible connection the detective might have to the arson investigation.

Darlac hesitated. He looked at the slicked-back hair, the English tie, the impeccable suit with its black silk pocket handkerchief, the blue eyes behind elegant round gold-framed glasses; he weighed up the physiognomy of this cerebral politico, searching for the honest man that everyone talked about but finding only a wily schemer, and decided to raise the stakes. Laborde would be the best cover possible if things turned sour.

"I'm trying to find Mazeau before this bloke gets to him. He's a dangerous man. We really need to give him some protection."

Laborde blinked behind his intellectual's specs.

"Protect him? You'd give him about as much protection as the blade of a guillotine! Do you think I'm stupid, or what? Who's supposed to have threatened him? He never said anything about that to me."

"I was tipped off. The bloke he's looking for is some loon he was in business with. He's going round telling everyone that he wants Mazeau dead."

"And who told you this?"

"Le Veau. Mazeau told him he wanted to find this bloke before the bloke found him. I'm going to help him."

"Le Veau? Lucien Lavaud?"

Laborde burst out laughing, there in the middle of the corridor. The hilarity shook his entire body, obliging him to hold on to the wall, to take off his specs so he could wipe the tears from his eyes.

"Jesus, Darlac, not him! Not to me! Le Veau is a small-time

crook! He cleans glasses in a café for his fat missus! How could you believe such a pathetic clown? Anyway, the idea that you are Mazeau's white knight is completely ludicrous. Tell me a proper fairy tale instead – at least they're a bit more believable!"

Darlac did have a good story to tell him – about a knight accused of treachery who beheads an evil duke and shits on his grave – but he preferred to shrug it off and beat a retreat. In a way, just by talking to him about it, he had implicated the commissaire division-naire in the plan he had in his head. So, Sleeping Beauty or Little Red Riding-Hood, he was prepared to spend sleepless nights getting it ready. He was going to set the wolves on him. He couldn't wait to hear their teeth tearing into Laborde's arse cheeks.

"Think what you like," he said. "You'll see who's right about this case."

He heard Laborde cackling sarcastically, then walked off past the curious stares of the uncomprehending guards with a shrug. He put his hand to the pistol under his armpit, nestled safely in its shoulder holster. A shiver ran down his spine. It was a shiver of pleasure.

Mazeau lives practically in the countryside, in Mérignac, in a house surrounded by meadows where cattle and horses graze, enclosed by hedges and copses of oaks, less than a kilometre from the place de l'Eglise, on the road to the airfield and the American base. It is a single-storey stone house, built at the beginning of the century, perhaps the former residence of a lawyer or a doctor. Tall trees all around it. The sound of birdsong. A dirt driveway bordered with fruit trees leads to the house. A hint of spring shows soft and green in the budding trees. Mazeau lives there with his wife, a former court clerk who quit her job to bring up their three children. Today is Tuesday; the children are at school. Darlac saw the youngest two leave earlier. The oldest is at school in Bordeaux and won't be back until late that evening.

Better that the children should not be there.

It is half past nine. Darlac leaves his car outside the gate and walks down the driveway, rutted in places, the grooves filled with water. The earth sticks to his shoes, making a sound like a wet mouth. When a French window opens onto the terrace and Mazeau appears, in a burgundy dressing gown, head bandaged like a walking mummy, Darlac stops dead and suddenly finds himself wondering what to do with his hands: shove them in his pockets to show his resolution, or leave them hanging, signifying his peaceful intentions. In the end, he keeps his hands out of his pockets and waves vaguely in greeting. He takes a few steps further, then stops again.

All he can see of Mazeau are his dark eyes trained unblinkingly on him. For the rest, with the yards of bandages that cover his face, it could almost be anyone.

"What the fuck are you doing here? I've heard you're looking for me?"

He says this as best he can given his blocked jaw, which makes him sound like a congenital idiot.

"You're not hard to find. We need to have a quiet talk."

Mazeau does not move or speak, mouth half open. Then he sighs noisily.

"Well, you may as well come in."

Huge living room, chairs and sofa upholstered in midnight blue velvet. Inlaid coffee table. Rugs – Persian probably – stretched out over waxed dark oak floorboards that creaking softly with every footstep. An immense fireplace, with enough space to roast a sheep and to seat the shepherd and his dog. The smell of polish and cold ashes.

Darlac stands motionless for a few seconds, contemplating this opulent interior and trying to work out where the pathetic breathless bloke who is closing the French window fits into it.

"Nice place you've got here."

"I'll ask Mariette to bring us some coffee."

Mazeau opens a glass door and asks for coffee, explaining that he has a visitor. A high-pitched, surprised voice replies enthusiastically.

Darlac feels oppressed by the peacefulness of the place. By the silence, barely broken by the swing of an unseen pendulum. But he is pleased to have brought trouble and disturbance to this affluent calm.

"Sit down," says Mazeau. "I've got an appointment at the hospital, so I don't have much time. So . . . what do you want?"

Darlac sits facing the windows, through which he can see a clump of daffodils swaying in the wind. He observes Mazeau's battered head against the light, seeing only his pupils sparkling below the swollen, bluish arch of his eyebrows, amid a setting of bandages and sticking plasters.

"The bloke you know. The one you told Le Veau about. The one you tried to nick the other night and who smashed your face up the other morning when you went to see him on your own."

"Are you joking?"

"Me? Never. You can't even imagine how serious I am. That bloke cut Penot's throat. He attacked my daughter. He burned down the bar belonging to Couchot, a cousin of mine, along with that kid who was staying there. Three dead, as you know. He's got something against me, he beat the shit out of you, he took your gun . . . that's enough, don't you think? You know him; I want him. I talked to Laborde about this yesterday. I'm putting my cards on the table here. We can work together on this case, like we used to in the good old days."

"Laborde called me. He had a feeling you'd come, but he didn't think it'd be this soon. As for the good old days, as you call them, I thought you wanted to forget them?"

"We haven't got all day to rake over the past. And you're not in a fit state to argue with me anyway. Look at you . . ."

The door opens to reveal a tray carried by a rather tall and pretty brunette. She reminds Darlac a little bit of Martine Carol.[29] She says hello, eyes lowered, then places a silver coffee pot and two porcelain cups in front of her husband. Slender figure, nice legs. She fills the cups, and asks Darlac if he's a colleague of Eugène's.

"Yes," Darlac replies. "I came to ask him for a few tips on an important case. That's why I'm disturbing you so early this morning."

"You should have called. You could have eaten breakfast with us!"

Mazeau shifts uneasily in his chair. He has tensed up, stiffened, but soon the pain forces him to relax, and he softly massages his ribs through his wool dressing gown.

"No. I would have disturbed you even more if I'd done that. It's very kind of you though. I'm just dropping by quickly cos some things need to be talked about discreetly, man to man."

Darlac smiles as he picks up the cup by its handle, holding it with his thumb and index finger, pinkie in the air. The woman has nice teeth, and very sweet eyes. Confusedly, he hates Mazeau even more. This house, this wife. All this charm and harmony.

Then his heart speeds up. He's the only one who's seen the two men running outside on the soaked driveway. He swallows a hot mouthful of coffee while Mazeau stirs his sugar. No sound but the light clinking of spoon against china. He jumps at the ring of the doorbell. The coffee trembles in his cup, and he drains it, scalding his oesophagus. The Mazeaus glance at each other, surprised. Madame goes out to answer the door. The two men watch her exit the living room, hear her footsteps in the hallway, jump up in unison as they hear her scream. She walks backwards into the room, banging into the glass door. The panes shake. A man in a balaclava is lifting the woman's chin with the double barrel of his shotgun. He continues moving forward, driving her towards the fireplace. She moans and pants, her huge eyes expressing pure terror. The man exhales noisily. A heavy build, back curved around his gun. Jeff.

29 French film actress, considered the Gallic version of Marilyn Monroe.

They had agreed it would be someone else. A certain Gunther, a former legionnaire, tough and reliable, with ice in his veins. Jeff has his finger on the trigger. Darlac has always told him to prop his finger against the trigger guard. But that nutcase never listens. He does whatever pops into his moronic head. He has always enjoyed caressing imminent death with his finger, feeling the resistance of the springs in the mechanism.

Another man enters, just behind. Also in a balaclava. Revolver in hand. Large calibre. A .45. Darlac sees the round heads of the bullets in the chambers aimed at them. Hammer cocked.

"Calm down," he says. "What do you want?"

Francis' eyes meet his for a second then gaze vacantly towards the back of the room.

Mazeau takes a step towards his wife. The man intercepts, holding his weapon about thirty centimetres from the detective's head.

"Move another fucking inch and you're dead, you cunt."

"Let her go. She has nothing to do with all this."

"All this what? Do you know why we're here?"

"No. But I know it has nothing to do with my wife. Leave her in peace."

Francis nods at Jeff.

"Strip off!" the fat man orders the woman. "Now!"

Mazeau starts shouting. He'll get them for this, he'll track them down. They'll have every cop in the country on their trail. He tells them again to leave his wife alone. He groans with pain and holds his jaw and bends forward over his aching ribs. He asks them what they want.

"Same thing as you, dickhead. The man who burned Couchot. That kid was ours and now she's dead. The culprit will have to pay for that."

Mazeau turns to Darlac. He shakes his head. His bandages have come undone, exposing his black, swollen forehead.

"What is this shit? Did they follow you?"

Darlac pulls a face that says he hasn't a clue.

"I'm an inspecteur principal and this is Commissaire Darlac," says Mazeau. "You're making a very big mistake by attacking us. But, please, leave my wife out of this."

"You're the one making a mistake by not answering. Tell us what we want to know and we'll get out of here without touching your missus."

Mazeau looks questioningly at Darlac. The commissaire nods and blinks, encouraging him to talk.

Mariette Mazeau starts screaming again because Jeff has grabbed the collar of her dress and is yanking it, tearing the poppers open so that her bare shoulder and bra strap are already visible. And his shotgun is still trained on her, his finger on the trigger.

"Calm down!" Darlac shouts. "She's going to do it right now. Fucking hell, Mazeau, just tell them so we can get this over with!"

The shot makes them all duck. Shards of stone fly across the room and fall spattering onto the floorboards. The air is thick with plaster dust and for a few seconds nothing can be seen but their frozen silhouettes. The woman has collapsed on the floor and is screaming, holding her arm as blood pours from it, forming a long puddle next to her. Below her elbow, there is nothing but scraps of cloth and flesh.

Jeff has taken a step back without letting go of his rifle, as if to get a better view, and he's repeating "Fuck, fuck, what is this shit?" as he watches the woman, who gradually sinks down and turns onto her side, moaning and mumbling incoherently, choked by pain or shock.

To start with, Francis lowered his gun, but when Mazeau starts towards his wife, he shoves the revolver's barrel against his temple, his hand trembling and his eyes distraught as he keeps staring over at the woman stretched out on the floor. He does not see Darlac take his out his pistol and casually shoot a bullet into Jeff's chest. The fat man recoils with the impact, his back hitting the wall where he remains standing for two or three seconds, shotgun in hand, his eyes rolling in disbelief, then collapses, knocking over a pedestal table as he falls.

Mazeau touches his crotch. Then lifts his hand to his face and looks at it and sniffs it. He tenses, hopping from one foot to the other. The smell of shit hits his nostrils instantly and the detective falls to his knees and then flat on his belly. Darlac goes over to the woman, who is inanimate, soaked with blood. Breathing weakly. Almost no pulse. Her torn-off arm is still bleeding so he pulls off his tie and knots it around the end of the stump and under her shoulder, then wipes his blood-covered hands on her dress. He stands up, in a daze. He sees the telephone at the other end of the room and walks hesitantly towards it, his head numb and spinning, as if he was drunk.

"I'm going to call for an ambulance. Take care of him."

"What? What did you say? " Mazeau groans.

Darlac notices that he is half deaf, as they all must be after those two detonations in an enclosed space. Francis does not move. He has uncocked the hammer of his revolver and holds the gun with his arm dangling, staring down at Mazeau who moves slowly in his shit, moaning softly. Darlac repeats his order, this time with an added gesture. Francis sighs, then hits Mazeau on the back of his head with the butt of his gun and the detective falls back heavily onto the carpet and stops moving.

Darlac explains to the man on the switchboard that there's been a serious accident: severed arm, massive bleeding, weak pulse. Tourniquet in place. He tells him to fucking hurry up, yelling into the receiver, and the switchboard operator tells him to calm down, assures him that a vehicle will be sent immediately.

Darlac returns to the carnage. Feels a stab to the heart when he sees the massive body of Jeff slumped at the foot of the wall beneath a streak of blood that still glistens in the golden light of the lamps.

"Go get your car," he tells Francis, who remains motionless. "Move, for fuck's sake. Not your first, is it?"

Francis too stares at the fat man's corpse.

"Jesus, why did you . . . ?"

"Because he was dangerous. Uncontrollable. He was a shit magnet."

"You had no right. All that cos he went for that bitch?"

"Shut your mouth, Francis. Go get the car. We have to get out of here before the ambulance and the gendarmes arrive."

Francis decides to holster his gun and leave, slamming the door behind him.

Darlac approaches the woman, who is lying on her side, and pushes aside her hair, which is stuck to her face, to get a better look.

"It'll be O.K.," he says softly. "The ambulance is on its way."

He takes a cushion from the sofa and slides it under her head. She moans and her panicked eyes open wide, just off the floor, trying to see something, to work out where she is perhaps, then they close again as she breathes a plaintive sigh. At the sound of the car engine, Darlac stands up and forces himself to shake off the feeling of numbness that has overcome him. Francis enters and stands immobile, nodding mechanically.

"Take Jeff," says Darlac. "We can't leave him behind."

"Shouldn't have shot him then, should you? Why did you do that?"

Darlac sighs then bends down and tries lifting the body up by the armpits. He barely manages to raise the torso from the floor.

"Why are you just fucking standing there?"

Francis grabs the legs. They drag the corpse, banging into furniture, its dead weight tugging at the rugs, which buckle into waves and folds that trip them up. The dead man's head falls against Darlac's forearm and his half-closed eyes make him look like a fat, lazy king nodding off. In the doorway they put him down for a few seconds to catch their breath and calm the crazed pounding of their hearts, then they start again towards the car, groaning with the effort.

It takes them several long minutes to hoist the stiff into the boot of the car. They hear a siren in the distance, getting closer then further away, so they jog back into the house, each grab Mazeau by one of his arms and take him outside and shove him on the back seat.

"Start the engine. I'll be back in a minute," says Darlac.

He goes back into the house and uses his handkerchief to wipe the telephone receiver and the cup from which he drank, then decides to throw it against the wall, where it smashes. He glances at the woman. She doesn't look like she's bleeding anymore, so he moves over to see if, by any chance . . . No, she's still breathing, feebly, face pale and skin shining with sweat.

Back by the cars, he decides they should go to that cabin in Biscarosse where they've already taken care of Le Veau. Francis goes first. Darlac, driving away from the house, stares into the rearview mirror, on the lookout for the arriving ambulance. He thinks again about Martine Carol and that woman lying almost dead by to the fireplace. He doesn't know why, but this vision haunts him as he drives down a straight, dismal road, bordered with green pines under a grey sky.

It's a rubber-tappers' cabin at the end of a sand path packed down by rain and the passage of tractors. The smell of pine resin and mushrooms. The westerly wind blows humid through the treetops, making the trunks bend and sway slightly. Darlac and Francis barely even glance at this vertical melancholy, their eyes blank through the holes in their grey wool balaclavas. They take Mazeau out of the car and have to carry him inside the shack because he is now nothing more than an inert body, moaning and stinking. They put him on a chair but he collapses and falls and lies on the floor weeping softly.

"Just tell me who set fire to Couchot's place," says Francis.

"We'll let you live. You can look after your wife. Think about her."

The cop lifts himself up on his elbows, trying to meet the eyes of the two men standing above him. His eyes are full of tears, his broken nose full of snot.

"Why do you want to know that? What are you playing at, Darlac? You're with them, aren't you, you bastard?"

"No, they're with me. Now answer the question."

Francis takes out his revolver and presses it against Mazeau's right knee.

"Answer, or I'll blow your kneecap off. After that, I'll do the other one. You won't be able to get upstairs any more, in your wheel-chair."

He cocks the revolver. Mazeau coughs, chokes.

"You're going to shoot me anyway."

"No, we're not. You talk and afterwards you keep your mouth shut and everything will be fine."

"And my wife? She—"

Francis pulls the trigger. Mazeau screams and grabs his knee with both hands, rolling on the ground.

Darlac shakes his head to soothe his throbbing eardrums. He sighs. He looks through the open door at the pine trees that surround them, straight and dark, and briefly imagines a host of dead sentries. He can no longer hear the wind in the treetops. Only Mazeau's plaintive voice, saying something that hits him between the eyes with the weight of an iron bar.

"He's called Jean Delbos."

Darlac crouches down behind the cop, who is lying on his side.

"Delbos?"

"Yes. He wants you dead – you and everyone close to you. It was him who got Penot."

"That pathetic little ... I thought he died in the camps. Apparently, he's back."

Darlac stands up, staggering slightly, his vision blurred by dizziness. He signals to Francis that the interview is over, then goes to the doorway.

"What do we do with him?" Francis asks. "Shall I finish him off?"

Darlac meets his wide-eyed stare. He smells the mixture of sweat and gunpowder on his skin.

"Given the situation . . ." Francis adds.

Mazeau is crying, curled up on the ground. Francis presses the barrel of his gun under the man's left shoulder blade and fires. The cop's body seems to unfold upon impact, and then go slack. They stare at him in silence for a moment in the smell of gunpowder and wet earth.

"We can't leave him here," Darlac mutters. "And we need to get rid of the fat bloke. I don't want their bodies to be found."

Francis sighs and shakes his head.

"Shit, do you realise what you've done?"

"Of course I realise. I told you not to bring Jeff. Not for this kind of work. His nerves weren't up to it. All you had to do was scare them, and it ends up as a fucking massacre. So now we clean up, and cover ourselves."

"Alright . . . What's done is done, anyway. I know a place, not far from here. A sort of ditch. I'll throw some quicklime in. I've got everything I need in the cabin."

Darlac leans against the wall and slaps himself two or three times, bringing a bit of colour back to his cheeks. He tries to smile at Francis, but can't. His face contorts, almost as if some searing pain were twisting his innards.

"Who's this Delbos?"

"A bunch of memories. And a ton of shit to come if we don't find the fucker immediately."

They leave again, both driving at fifty kilometres per hour on the empty road. Two kilometres down the road, they find a more or less passable path where the cars jolt and shake over ruts. The ditch that Francis mentioned is a space where the earth has collapsed under an uprooted pine tree. At least three metres deep. They strip the corpses of their papers, rings and watches, and drag them over to the hole, then shove them both in.

"I'll come back tomorrow with the lime," says Francis.

He rubs his hands, shakes the sand off his trouser legs and puts the collection of papers, rings and watches in his pocket.

Darlac stares into the hole without saying anything. The two bodies are slumped, sprawled over each other with that indecency dead bodies have when you throw them on top of each other like that.

He takes the A-10 back to Bordeaux. Twice he nearly falls asleep, dragged from his torpor by the vibrations and the swaying of the car as it drifts into the verge, and he stops at a roadside café, in a car park packed with trucks, and staggers like a drunkard into a room where the hubbub of conversations and laughter dies instantly, making him hesitate in the doorway. He approaches the counter and leans on it, and that is when he sees his hands covered with blood, his shirtsleeves marked with brownish stains, and he hurriedly thrusts them in his pockets as a fat bald man walks over and asks him if he's here to eat. He's not hungry, hasn't even thought about food, but says yes because he doesn't know what else to say, so the man gestures to a table set for two, over there, in a corner near the window. The man mentions that the *plat du jour* is lentils with sausages, and Darlac says yes, that'll be fine, and asks where the toilets are.

Under an open fanlight that lets in the damp air, he uses a bar of soap to wash his bloody hands and scrapes out the brown paste that is encrusted under his fingernails, then rolls up his sleeves to hide his sin beneath his jacket. He splashes his face with cold water and drinks big mouthfuls from the tap, and wipes himself with a wet, filthy hand towel. In the mirror he sees a haggard face with dark rings around the eyes. He pinches his cheeks, trying to bring the colour back again, but the little pink marks quickly fade.

Sitting down at the table, he pours himself a glass of red and swallows it in big gulps. The plonk stirs up stomach acids, making him grimace. The waiter brings him a terrine of pâté, a plate of lentils topped with two huge sausages and a basket of bread. He stares at this assemblage of food and wonders what he's doing there with all these loudmouths who will down a bottle of red and then get back on the road, steering their twenty-ton trucks towards Bordeaux or Spain. He doesn't know what he should do, holding his knife and fork in the air without any memory of having picked them up; he doesn't know what to think either; is not even sure he's able to think about anything right now. He can feel two men to his left staring at him, so he decides to dig into the pâté. He starts eating and his mouth waters and suddenly he feels hungry.

He eats it all, in the end. Cleans his plate. The oven-baked apple is delicious, with the sugar caramelised on top. The restaurant has gradually emptied and now there are no more than a dozen men, talking more quietly, laughing and toasting each other and having one more for the road. He watches them on the sly, noting their clumsy gestures, their red faces, their glistening foreheads. He feels like a cop again, spying on these men who don't even see him, and once again feels the contempt that always raises him above the common herd as he watches them, and suddenly he feels better and his mind starts to gauge and assess and plan the coming days.

Outside, perked up by his lunch, he savours the coldness of the air and the deep grey of the clouds that mass in the west, pushed by a bitter wind. So he doesn't think anymore about Jean Delbos, fucking Jean come back to Bordeaux to make him pay, and as he starts his car he feels almost happy to finally know his target, or his prey – he hesitates over the words as he turns on to the road behind a lumbering truck – target or prey? Both, probably. It'll be easier like that.

Approaching Bordeaux, he thinks about that woman, as beautiful as Martine Carol, whom they abandoned in front of the fireplace with her arm torn off, and he tries to remember the soft feel of her hair when he lifted up the back of her neck earlier to wedge a cushion under her head and a desire for kisses tickles his lips.

17

When André paid him in cash for three months rent in advance, the landlord, whose name is Ferrand, simply nodded and slipped the money into one trouser pocket, while taking the keys to the room from his other pocket. "Make yourself at home," he said. "And feel free to call me if you need anything." He lives practically opposite, barely twenty metres away, alone with his mentally ill daughter, Arlette, who can be heard laughing and crying and groaning in the mornings, when the windows are open. Screaming too, sometimes, as if terrified or tortured. The pigeons and all the other birds that hang around on the rooftops fly away. When that happens, the house-keeper quickly closes the window and the scream is suddenly muffled, its faded sound echoing in the street, a ghost dissolved into air.

A bedroom three metres by four, and a sort of living room that's not much bigger. But clean. Walls, ceilings, floorboards. It has all been renovated, repainted, sanded, polished. A small kitchen has been put together in a little back room: gas stove, cupboard, stone sink. The sole luxury: a little water heater. As soon as the landlord closed the door, André washed in hot water, shivering all the same in his little nook, under that fanlight jammed shut, with the filthy glass through which only the bleakest, dimmest light penetrates, even in the middle of the day.

It's on rue Surson, a hundred metres from the Quai de Bacalan. Near the river though, the view is only of the railings around the port and the brown concrete of the warehouses. Whole blocks of houses in the area belong to major wine merchants. Acres of storehouses and bottle-filling factories. Trucks shuttle the product to the docks, from where the stuff leaves to be poured down rich people's throats all over the world.

Often, in the mornings, the entire neighbourhood stinks of cheap wine. Today is one of those mornings. André goes out under a clear sky amid a racket of sparrows swooping from the rooftops and rolling in the gutters. A little bit of spring, already in a panic. His fingertips caress the butt of the pistol. He never goes anywhere without it now. There are eight cartridges in the clip. Enough to give him the chance to flee, to believe that it is still possible to emerge from this.

He walks quickly through the cool air, passing a fence intended to hide the ruins of two or three houses destroyed in the bombing raid of 17 May '43. The neighbourhood is full of these sudden gaps lighting up a narrow street as if some wild urban planner had wanted to create a square. But what you can see after all these years is the plumbing clinging to what remains of a bathroom, walls with faded paint jobs, drab tiling, a whole private interior world exposed to the four winds, a dreary patchwork the only decoration. A flayed part of the city's back, the skin turned back, left hanging in the impossibility of a scar. He rushes on, hands in the pockets of his reefer jacket, then enters a bar on the cours du Médoc where he has already been twice before since moving to this area. There are four or five workmen leaning on the counter, satchels over their shoulders, drinking coffee and chatting with the owner. They reply mechanically to André's hello but speak only sporadically after-wards, maybe because they slept badly or because they're already tired. He picks up the newspaper and flicks through it as he often does, and when he sees the photograph and reads the headline, it seems that everything else fades into darkness and silence around him.

POLICE HAVE "PROBABLY IDENTIFIED" THE PLACE NANSOUTY ARSONIST
Our readers will remember the criminal fire that burned down a wine bar in place Nansouty on the

night of 24–25 February, causing the deaths of three
people. Bordeaux police, after a meticulous investi-
gation, have identified a suspect, whom they are
actively seeking: his name is André Vaillant, but he
was born in Bordeaux, on 16 November 1916, under
the name of Jean Delbos. Until a few weeks ago, when
he disappeared, he was working as an accountant
at a fabric wholesaler on rue Bouquière. Considered
missing after being deported, the suspect must have
returned to Bordeaux a few months ago. The motives
for his acts are currently being investigated. Anyone
who may be able to provide information on this indi-
vidual (see photograph) is invited to contact local
law enforcement authorities.

André examines the blurred face, smiling, squinting in the sun, and
recognises it instantly without being able to recall precisely where
or when this photo was taken. But he knows it was in another life, in
a world that has now disappeared. Even though the trees that are
visible behind him have probably grown, even though the same soft
breeze still rises with the onset of ebb tide in the Arcachon bay. He
knows that, if he went back there, he would find that same diapha-
nous morning light above the horizon, as if the day was welling up
from the gleaming silt at low tide or from the flat sea of high tide.

He wishes the image would come to life, so he could see Olga
pass by and smile at the lens or pull a face at him. Maybe she would
be wearing that mauve dress with golden polka dots that suited
her so well when she was suntanned, after walking on the beach or
lying in the sand to read a romance novel. Then he would see other
figures, probably recognise faces from that time when they would
spend Sundays, from May onward, in that little shack near the port
in Andernos that Abel had bought at a knockdown price from some
sucker who owed him money and who, months later, was found

hanging from a tree in the forest: ruined, knackered, abandoned by his wife and his daughters and the women he had kept for years.

When they could, they would arrive late in the afternoon on a Saturday, by bus, and Abel would come to fetch them in his car, smiling behind his sunglasses and his thick moustache. They would go to buy oysters, enormous sea bream that they'd grill, or crabs if they'd decided to make a fish soup. Olga insisted on bringing white wine and Abel told her every time that there was no need, that he had crates of the stuff in stock and three or four ready in the fridge.

Abel was a big spender, a gambler, a thief, a charmer, a fraud. A handsome chap, as women and cops say. You could give him your shirt and he'd cut the sleeves off and sell it back to you, persuading you that it was too hot for sleeves, and you'd have thanked him as you paid him cash on the nail. He could sniff out a sucker just by looking at him, before he even spoke a word. In the street, he could spot a prey by the way he walked, by the way he held his hands in his pockets, the way he crossed the road. Afterwards, when he'd got his hooks in them, he would work subtly for his prize, using reason, persuasion, analysis. He was capable of making a profit from all those stupid, naïve, greedy people, who always turned nasty whenever they felt their actions protected or permitted by the law or by anyone in authority, even the lowliest minion. He knew all the places to find ordinary cowardice, unconfessed baseness, buried secrets. He would tap into cash stashed in various places, not all of it entirely above board. Sometimes he'd open a cupboard where a skeleton was drying, dispossessed of its hoard by heirs in a rush or a particularly corrupt notary. He would find treasure troves hidden on lost islands surrounded by oceans of lies or little, shark-filled pools of disgrace.

He was a benefactor, Abel: an anarchist banker, a sort of godless inquisitor of the petit-bourgeois; he would pass the question on to his clients, he always said, before passing them on to the cash register. And how he revelled in this quest for salubriousness. Over aperitifs he would describe swindles that would not have fooled a five-year-old but which somehow entrapped respected fathers willing to dispossess ancestors and children in order to make some quick cash on the side. How these would-be schemers would throw away their money in the hapless and greedy pursuit of wealth.

He'd been in prison twice, the first time in '34, but he'd come out more determined than ever to wring out the savings from complacent crooks who slept close to their nest-eggs, gun under the pillow. He'd learned to play poker while he was behind bars, had even come close to having his face rearranged because he'd cleaned out a gang boss who considered himself invincible, and that had seemed to him an honest way of earning money, a way of adding to his day-to-day business. That was how André had met him, at a poker table; they'd spent a whole night observing each other, cards in hand, eyes half closed in the drifting cigarette smoke, neither of them winning or losing. In the morning, with a taste of copper in their mouth and a searing migraine, making them walk slowly, they had eaten breakfast at the Capucins among tough men and loud-mouths, butchers and truck drivers fuelling up on *rillettes* and red wine.

To begin with, Olga had hated this man who stole away her husband at night, was almost jealous of him, but he brought her flowers and cakes, spoke well, was not only charming but ridiculously kind. And it wasn't every night. André knew how to find opportunities elsewhere. She let herself be won over, and anyway she knew that, with him, André would be good, and though he would come home early in the morning, he would at least come home, stinking of tobacco, with a baguette and warm croissants. Abel was there when Daniel was born; he'd held the baby in his hands first in fact, because André, weeping with joy, his body trembling, did not even have enough strength to wipe the tears from his cheeks.

She was always happy to go to those Sundays by the Arcachon

bay, letting herself be lifted up by the muscular arms of that affable con artist who would cover her with kisses without any ulterior motive, even if one day he said to André – who would sometimes go to bed with drunken slappers after wild parties in backrooms – that he should be careful not to mistreat a rare pearl like Olga because she would end up in the arms of a man who did respect her. That had troubled André for a few days, and he had suddenly become attentive, considerate and sincere, before once more being possessed by his demons, lured by the voices of sirens, and he had forgotten his friend's warning.

She liked walking alone, early in the morning, by the waterside or in the forest, not going back until about eleven so she could make lunch while she waited for the men to return from fishing. She prepared the food with Jacqueline, aka Violette, a former whore from Marseille who was chatty, volcanic, beautiful and coarse as a rough diamond, sparkling in strange and unexpected ways, who had run away after being fucked by different men on moored boats for two days solid, a punishment enforced by her pimp. Violette had arrived, staggering, covered in blood and cum, at the apartment of a distant cousin, who was herself with a client and who had introduced her to Abel. Everything was arranged between the two of them, just like that. He took her home with him, gave her a room, brought in a doctor who'd been struck off – a gentle, silent abortionist – who had healed her and rid her of the vile goo that had been growing inside her, the residue of one of those forty or fifty men who'd screwed her in a wardroom stinking of rust and sweat.

Often surprise visitors rolled up in cars: card players, little misfits trying to act tough, a girl on their arm, a bottle of fizz in their hand, men that Abel or André had met one night or in obscure places on some kind of sleazy business. A wild, noisy bunch of shady men in fedoras and funny men in straw boaters full of ripe gossip, drunken pimps come to make coffee for their current favourite and take her out for a break, poor little slut.

When there were too many people, when there weren't enough seats for all the wild beasts, wily coyotes and timid strays, Olga would go for a walk and sit down on the beach in the sun, skirt pulled up to brown her legs, and on Sunday evenings André would delight in all the subtle shades of her suntanned skin and she would let him find the parts that the sun had not been able to reach because he always knew how to make her feel hot even in deep shade.

Darlac dropped by, several times. They were all his prey, but he came without dog or rifle and reassured them all that he was not a hunter of small game. He knew everyone, and everyone knew where they stood with this young detective with his eye on the jackpot, always there, with his colleagues in the daytime and alone at night, around the card tables or in the bars, drinking with the whores or their pimps, watching the top burglars and the armed robbers that were pointed out to him. He saw everything, but knew when to close his eyes, and people said he was corrupt because he had big needs, would swagger brazenly, living it up with all the girls who fell for his handsome mug and his cop card, happy as a wolf in a sheepfold. He played them off against each other, breaking up alliances, controlling the puppets, pulling the strings, tying slipknots in them, always several moves ahead. This mastery of the underworld enabled him to solve big cases that put him at the head of the race for promotion: senior inspecteur principal, commissaire . . . The future was bright, and commissaire divisionnaires were slapping him on the back.

André and Darlac liked each other. Who knows why? Maybe because of Olga who, without ever trying, attracted the cop's insistent gaze, his tender solicitude. And above all because Darlac knew how to make himself useful and then indispensable when André had a few run-ins with a gang of armed robbers on the Basque coast and when some of Darlac's colleagues, who should have minded their own fucking business, tried to have André arrested for abuse of trust and passive procurement. Darlac had saved his skin, but now had a firm grip on his balls.

He comes out of the bar feeling groggy and disoriented, then begins walking down the street, staring vaguely at the ground. All he sees are feet and legs, shapeless forms. Like a drunkard lost in a whirl of memories.

He reaches place Gambetta, the air full of noise, and it takes him a few seconds, standing still in the middle of this rushing crowd, to shake off the fog of the past where the faces of Olga and Abel still float, blinding him with their smiles. His own face, blurred and ghostlike, is in the newspaper and he would like to become invisible, a real ghost, instead of wandering, flesh and blood, amid all these dangerous eyes.

He catches a bus and is buffeted about for a quarter of an hour, hanging onto a hand strap, until he gets off outside the station. He hurries over to rue Furtado, passing the garage on the opposite pavement, then stops and stands for a moment in front of the shop window of a baker's, watching left and right for anything suspicious. There's that young bloke smoking a cigarette outside, leaning against the signboard. The apprentice. André examines the cars, squinting through the reflections on the windows to distinguish figures inside.

Because he feels sure that Darlac is already on his scent, now he's identified him. The commissaire knows everything he needs to know about him: he knows the people he and Olga hung out with before the war, their night friends as well as their day friends, the people she knew when she worked at the factory, the women especially; those people André met sometimes, feeling uncomfortable in the middle of their discussions, their talk of unions and the Spanish Civil War, their anger at the fascists and the bosses who should all be lined up against the wall. He sensed their mistrust, perhaps even their contempt of him, like those superstitious people who are afraid of night birds.

He knows that Darlac will stop at nothing to make them talk, even if they don't say anything; he will hassle them, terrorise them, send in his henchmen. André's heart races at this thought. And then there's Daniel. Darlac only saw him three or four times – the kid could hardly walk – but one time he brought him a red and yellow wooden horse that Daniel started pulling behind him, laughing at the sharp ringing sound that the little bell around its neck made. Yet another ruse to make Olga smile, make her notice him.

Darlac. His partner in crime. His party wingman. In those days, with Abel, the revels began at midnight and went on till dawn.

André decides to cross the road. He grips the pistol inside his pocket. He will shoot the first cop who tries to bar his way.

The apprentice crushes his cigarette butt under his shoe and nods a greeting. He tells him the boss is inside, at the back. André goes in, sees the man leaning over an engine that roars as he adjusts the carburettor. Deafening noise. Suffocating clouds of smoke. Then the engine slows down and begins purring.

André struggles to breathe. He puts it down to the exhaust fumes that fill the air.

Mesplet turns around and stares at him without showing any surprise. He lights a cigarette then holds it tight between his lips, cycs half closed because of the smoke.

"I told you not to come here again."

"I've come to get my bike."

"After more than three months? We almost chucked it. But as we'd had to fix practically the whole thing, it seemed like a waste. I decided to sell it in the end. It's going to cost you a packet, I'm warning you now."

"I can pay."

Mesplet bursts out laughing.

"Oh yeah, that's true. You could always pay. You just take cash out of your pockets and everything's fine, your problems go away."

André tries to think what to say in reply. The lack of oxygen makes his brain work slowly. He forces himself to breathe.

"I'm tired. Just give me the bike and I'll go."

He says this in a single breath. Mesplet is about to respond, but changes his mind and shakes his head. He stares intensely at André as if reading the signs of a lie in the wrinkles on his face.

"Follow me."

The bike is on its stand. It glistens in the dark corner where it waits for him between two piles of old tyres.

"The kid had fun dolling it up. He was the one who fixed it. I helped a bit."

"How much do I owe you?"

"Thirty thousand."

André takes the notes from his wallet and counts them.

Mesplet shoves them in the chest pocket of his overalls.

The bike is heavy. André struggles to manoeuvre it between the tightly parked cars. Going past Norbert, he hands him a thousand-franc note. "For the bike," he says. The boy reads the note as if it were a telegram and watches the man walk away, bent over his machine. He carefully folds the note, squeezes it into his pocket and taps it as if to keep it warm. Then he holds the bike while André puts on his leather helmet.

"Where's Daniel?" he asks.

"He's in Algeria, Daniel."

While he rides carefully through town, clumsy and mistrustful, he thinks about Daniel, a soldier in that Algerian shit heap, and his body trembles so hard that he worries he might fall off the bike.

He parks it about fifty metres from where Darlac lives and pretends to mess with the engine while stealthily observing the house. It is nearly eleven o'clock and he knows that Darlac's wife, Annette, will leave in five or ten minutes, carrying a big shopping bag, as she does every Tuesday and Thursday, and get in her 4C.V. Up to now, it's been impossible to follow her. He remembered this motorbike, an old wreck he'd bought from Raymond, the assistant, purely as an excuse for going to the garage, to begin with. He just wants to know where this woman goes, so regularly, always at the same time.

For three weeks he's been spending his mornings in a bistro at the corner of the street. He sits at the window with his notebook and a detective novel and he reads or writes or pretends to read or write, scrawling a succession of incoherent words while staring constantly at the cop's house. On the third day the owner asked him if he was a writer or what, and André replied that he was writing his memoirs, the war and all that, and that he needed to see people in order for it to come back to him. The owner shot a surprised glance at the four or five blokes who sat there, regulars for the most part, slumped in their chairs or leaning on the counter, barely even speaking to each other after the usual greetings had been exchanged. They were alone now in front of their glass of red or white or even rum, ordering the next one with an assured, almost peremptory hand gesture, perhaps enjoying the respect that was their due, a sozzled mirage, a momentary mumbling dignity. He then explained, in a quiet voice, as if to excuse them, that they were all poor sods who'd got stuck up shit creek, not really bothering anyone, sometimes a bit simple or a bit mad, sad as stray dogs. "You know what it's like," he'd added, without malice, and André had looked in his eyes and seen a glimmer of humanity there that he'd liked, and he'd replied, "Yes, I know a bit about that", and the man had smiled and nodded and sighed.

Since then, when he enters the café, the owner smiles in greeting and brings him his coffee and shakes his hand, and they exchange sincere how-are-yous and listen to the other's answer. Like an odd little island, this dark and melancholy bar where this man, like a shipwreck survivor, holds out his hand to help anyone washed here by the ocean. André writes about him in his notebook. He writes that there are still men on this earth, that he has just met another one.

He is crouched next to the bike and he has no idea what he is

271

going to do. He follows, observes, gets close. He watches them live. The daughter, who gives the slip, more or less whenever she feels like it, to the cretin whose job it is to protect her, and runs off to the parc Bordelais to meet a young man whom she kisses on the mouth, draped around his neck, her body pressed against his while his hands explore the insides of her sweater. The supposed great cop thinks he controls the whole city, but when he's away his mice play.

André has the impression that he has cast his net around the cop in this way, and that he is, little by little, tightening it. He suspects that Darlac can feel this constant gaze upon him, can sense this shadow behind him without being able to evade it, and that sometimes, perhaps, he unknowingly pushes away the imperceptible touch of the spider web that is closing around him with the back of his hand.

Above all, he knows he is deluding himself. *The eye was in the tomb and fixed on Cain*[30]. He remembers this verse, probably learned at school. But he knows that he is not the eye of God. A man had once told him, before dying, hanging on to him and shivering, that God, whom he couldn't help believing in, was a blind and deaf chaos.

Annette Darlac leaves the house, slamming the door behind her, and walks quickly away, tall, straight-backed, somewhat stiff, dressed in a long black coat, a few blonde hairs escaping her mauve headscarf. She is carrying only her handbag, and her free arm brushes the side of her coat as it swings. The car is parked about thirty metres away. André waits for it to start before straddling his bike. She turns onto the boulevard, quiet at this time of day, and he lets two other cars come between them so she won't spot him. She is the superintendent's wife. It was Darlac, a long time ago, who explained to André the rules of tailing someone. All those cops' tricks and stratagems, those convoluted methods. He feels invisible

30 The last line of Victor Hugo's poem "Conscience".

behind his goggles, under his helmet. He can feel the machine's vibrations beneath him, running smooth as clockwork.

She turns left, onto Route du Médoc. The city gradually disappears, giving way to fields, copses, hedges. The road goes through pastureland, perched on an embankment. They could be anywhere. He falls further behind, because there is so little traffic on the road. Blanquefort is a large village, between marshland and woods. He crosses through its empty streets. A rural path, a low house with white shutters. He sees Annette Darlac get out of her car then push open the gate. Her blonde hair floats in the wind, her scarf now around her shoulders.

André drives past the house, stopping a bit further on at the entrance to a forest path. From here, he can see anyone who enters or leaves. A gust blows through the trees and he lifts the collar of his reefer jacket. The sky is changeable. The woods still smell of winter, of mushrooms. The scent of rain and humus. The house is small and surrounded by tall oak trees. He is dying to go inside, to surprise the woman. See her turn her frightened face towards him. And then what? The commissaire is a cuckold? He suddenly imagines himself shouldering open the door and finding a seedy bedroom farce. He no longer knows what to do. He should wait a bit longer. He has been waiting for so long that another day or another few weeks are nothing, and one day he will know what to do with the extra time that has been granted to him. Perhaps waiting itself can become a way of life. Believing that you know what you're waiting for in order to forget what is waiting for you.

It lasts almost two hours. He has time to smoke five cigarettes, to piss, to walk over to a clearing where two squirrels are screeching. Three cars pass, and birds sing loudly at times: he tries to make them out between branches dressed in their finest spring green. The sun shines down on him, so he leans against a tree, eyes closed, and savours this gentle warmth. Two hours. But for years now he has not been able to understand how time passes. Or even *if* it still passes. He wonders if something, all around him, has wound down to a halt. As if all that remains of his watch face is a second hand circling back endlessly to its starting point. Days giving way to nights. The nights always blind, the days always so grey.

The woman gets into her car, makes a U-turn and leaves. André feels his heart speed up and pushes the motorbike to the front of the house, leaning it against the low garden wall. He opens the rusty iron gate, he walks on a dirt path between two rows of neatly pruned rose bushes. A blue door, flanked by two windows covered by white net curtains. He lifts the knocker, then wonders whether he shouldn't enter unannounced, to catch whoever it is unawares. He puts his hand on the door handle, but finally changes his mind and bangs the knocker against the door, the noise of it making him jump.

Light footsteps approach. The pistol in his pocket, in his hand, does not reassure him. He stares at the door and wonders what gaze will meet his, or flee from it. A little old woman with clear, hard blue eyes and white hair held in a sort of grey headdress holds the door ajar and stares at him, then glances suspiciously behind him. She stands upright, her chin raised.

"What do you want?"

Deep, husky voice. André recognises the German accent. The old woman is dressed in black. Long skirt, sweater. The white lace collar of a blouse around her neck.

"Let me in."

The old woman tries to shut the door, but André blocks it then pushes it back. She retreats, standing in the middle of an anteroom with blue wallpaper and a tile floor that gleams dimly with cold light. He closes the door behind him. Doesn't know what to say. He doesn't understand what Darlac's wife was doing here, in this old Kraut's house.

"You're German?"

The woman shakes her head.

"No. Alsatian."

They all say that. There are hundreds of them hidden away all over France, claiming to be Alsatian.

"Why did she come here, that woman?"

The old woman's hands move in front of her face. She doesn't understand. She pretends not to understand. In the camp, you could be shot on the spot if you didn't understand German.

The pistol in his pocket. He touches the trigger, closes his hand around the butt.

"What's your name?"

He's yelling at her, is about to stick the pistol under her chin, but somewhere in the house he hears what sounds like a chair leg scraping against floorboards, so André holds the gun and pushes the woman in front of him across a hallway that leads to a room with an open door, a flood of golden light pouring through the gap. The woman says something in German and André tells her to shut up and shoves the barrel of his gun into her back to make her walk faster. He wants to scream at her in her own language the orders he used to obey, shivering, cringing, because each enraged bark might be followed by a gunshot that he wouldn't have time to hear. Not a sound comes from this room filled with sunlight. He grabs the woman's neck and holds her tight against him, the pistol to her temple, and enters the room, a large bedroom where he immediately sees a dark shape against the light: a man in a wheel-chair.

He turns towards André, revealing his bilious face, armless shoulder, his stump of a leg. The entire right side of his body has been destroyed. In the reconstructed eye socket, a motionless blue eye does not even pretend to resemble anything other than a grotesque marble that you half expect to see roll onto the floor. His cheek is merely a fold of racked flesh, a hole that could have been filled with meat if you yanked hard and sewed it shut with butcher's twine. The temple is a blue-skinned eardrum pulled taut over the artery that can be seen pulsing just beneath. A few locks of hair have grown back in the crater of his trepanned skull.

And it's alive. Suddenly realising this, André shivers and feels his throat tighten, his chest block. He hardly dares breathe.

There is another part of this man that lives. A hand lying on the armrest of his wheelchair, a foot inside a slipper, half of a vigorous body, slender and elegant in a garnet-coloured smoking jacket. His half-face is fine-featured and long, with a single green-grey eye and a well-formed half-mouth stretched to distortion by its other side.

André has seen bodies torn open before, blown up and dismembered. Pieces of men, skulls smashed and scattered in the mud. He has seen the living already dead, and dead men who seemed only to be about to catch their breath, who stared at you imploringly. He has probably seen human bodies in every state possible during the war. In the vile slaughterers' backyard, at the edges of ditches, on mounds of human carcasses, tangles of grimaces, piled-up nightmares. In the smoke above the shelters. In those days he turned in on himself inside an impregnable refuge, an underground hiding place, the key to which he always feared losing. So his heart no longer trembled when he was confronted with horror, perhaps because it lacked the strength. But in this instant, standing in front of this living half-man, he feels every inch of his skin shudder painfully. The eye watches him, from under the pulsing eyelid.

"What do you want? Who are you?"

Faint German accent. Clear diction. André is surprised that words can emerge intact from that mangled mouth. He doesn't know what to say. Realises he's still holding his pistol. The man gestures at the weapon with his chin.

"Are you going to kill me? Don't do it in front of my mother then."

The old woman is sitting on the bed, hands clasped between her thighs, and she looks at her son's broken face and her gaze caresses his devastated features as if, by sheer force of will, she could veil it in a tulle mask or even remodel it into human form.

André tries to think what to say. Or he could simply leave. Abandon this man and his mother to their Calvary.

"Why did she come here, earlier?"

He already knows the answer. He remembers what Mazeau told him about Annette Darlac and the Krauts. He remembers that the young Darlac girl is not the cop's daughter. The man lowers his head. He is in profile now, showing a handsome, thoughtful face.

"That's my secret. I am her secret."

The old woman says something in German to which he replies with an irritated hand gesture.

"And now, leave. I don't know why you came here and I don't care. Or kill me, if that will make you feel better for whatever reason. It doesn't matter: I am dead now anyway."

"Only half dead."

The man sits up and stares at André just as he rolls up his sleeve and shows the numbers tattooed on his forearm. The woman gets to her feet and walks backwards to the head of the bed, eyes wide and mouth hanging.

"I'm dead too," says André.

The man nods. Then smiles with his half-mouth.

"Well, no-one will get out alive, right?"

"You're Elise Darlac's father. Annette slept with you during the Occupation. Darlac adopted the kid when the war ended."

"You know things. How does that help you?"

The man suddenly stiffens. His face twists into a grimace and he moans. The mother takes a step towards him and then changes her mind. He exhales heavily, several times, as if to expel the pain from his body.

"Amputated limbs have phantom pains. Did you know that? I can still feel the chilblains from Stalingrad. I left parts of myself over there, but they hurt as if they've regrown."

A smile stretches over the left side of his face while the rest remains pulp, unmoved. Afterwards, he closes his eyes and calms down and his mother sits back on the bed. Outside, the sun is setting and shadows are invading the room, climbing from under the furniture and darkening the ceiling. The silence is so deep and so sudden that André can hear the blood buzzing and beating in his ears. It feels as if the world beyond has died, or as if they now exist in a pocket of time and space torn free from the rest of the universe.

André leaves the room to extricate himself from this whirlwind that has sucked him up. He takes a few steps down the hallway and then turns around, and it seems to him that there is no longer anything in the room: that Nazi officer and his elderly mother existed only in a dream from which he's just woken. But then he hears the wooden floor creak, a dry cough, and he knows there really is something in there.

Out in the garden, he wonders if they are watching him walk away, through the curtains. He feels as if he has visited ghosts and, were it not for the fact that he held the insubstantial body of the old woman against him, that he felt her resist when he pushed her forward, he would now expect to see them pass through the walls and accompany him. And that is why he does not turn around and he hurries to leave this place, dazed and unsteady.

18

Martine Carol is dead. Darlac is holding a photograph of Mariette Mazeau, one of those smooth, soft-focus portraits that people can get taken in one of the studios on rue Sainte-Catherine or on the rours de l'Intendance and that make them look better. Subdued lighting, a hazy glow. But Darlac knows that this face had no need of such artifice. He knew it ten days ago, the moment that woman appeared bearing cups and a coffee pot on a silver tray, her mere presence erasing the room's *nouveau riche* bad taste. Straight away, he thought of the actress who would sway into the jaws of the trap, as in a film. So he repeats it to himself like a newspaper head-line or a radio announcement: Martine Carol is dead.

And I saw you die. I think I knew as soon as you entered the room that it was all going to end badly. I saw the bullet that would tear off your arm as it left the shotgun. And the terror in your eyes as your blood poured out, your arm in tatters. In the palm of my hand I held your warm, slender neck. And I shot the stupid bastard who did that to you, shot him like a dog.

He relives every second of that morning. He sees Jeff again, collapsed at the foot of the wall, his eyes just as round and empty dead as they were when he was alive. He enjoys this image. Relief and pleasure.

I killed him for you.

At her bedside, behind the screen in this main hall of the Saint-André hospital, he waited whole evenings for her to open her eyes again, he wiped her burning forehead with a handkerchief soaked in eau de cologne, he spoke to her in a whisper, come on, stay with us, don't worry . . . But the woman didn't move, her wan face on the pillow like a wax mask. Only her chest rose, as she breathed too fast, her breaths sometimes convulsed with what sounded like sobs. The doctors thought she would make it. She had lost a lot of blood, but they'd given her a transfusion in time. The heart was what worried them: less robust than they would have expected for a woman of thirty-five.

Yesterday she opened her eyes, stared fearfully at Darlac, and closed them again to let a few tears fall, murmuring indistinctly. That night her heart stopped beating.

He contemplates the photograph placed on his desk amid a disorder of reports, notes, other photos. He hears nothing of the morning bustle, banging doors, bursts of laughter and angry shouts, the obsessive rattling of typewriter keys. All those stupid fucking cops running around and barking at each other. This photograph does him good. He likes to think that there is, in the chaos of this world, a person worthy of affection and tenderness. That face, like a sacrificed saint's, would, if she'd been allowed to live, have been capable of redeeming men's sins.

Commissaire Darlac hears himself rationalising. He knows exactly what his two-penny mysticism and his teenage virgin's adoration is worth. He is past the age of wanking over photographs of stars or naked sluts then hiding them under his coat again to keep them safe from teachers and priests. And anyway, he's seen too much in his life. Done too much. He is immune to any kind of giddiness. His heart will never skip a single beat. But he surrenders simply to the beauty of that face, to the memory of that body, to the whole of that being who appeared just before the massacre.

Earlier, when the telephone rang and the nurse announced the woman's death, he sat down heavily and took out her photo from the folder devoted to the disappearance of Inspecteur Mazeau and he merely examined it, full of sadness. It is so long since he has felt sad that he can't even remember the last time. He abandoned himself to this delicious weakness. Perhaps to forget that he arrived early this morning in order to be able to work in peace and quiet and to put an end to that sleepless night with his wife, as wide awake as he was, curled up in a ball, fists tensed on the edge of the sheet pulled up to her neck. He had tried touching her so he could tire himself out a little bit, hoping it would help him sleep, but her legs were so cold, her feet so icy, that he felt as if he were pawing a corpse. He spent hours in the dark alongside this inert body, barely even able to hear her breathe. About five, he got up, driven from his bed by nausea and a migraine.

So, the office. Its smell of stale tobacco, sweat and dust. He avoided his night-shift colleagues so he wouldn't have to hear the usual litany of fights on the docks between drunken sailors, whores picked up for disturbance of the peace, car thieves caught with their hands in the glovebox, tramps slashed with knives, all those drop-outs and losers brought in by the police vans, this nightly routine where the scum is skimmed off the deep black water the way a head of foam is removed from a pint of lager, to make sure it doesn't over-flow. All this shit, typed up in triplicate. Typos, blurred carbons, wrongly followed procedures. The lingering stench of unwashed bodies, vomit.

He puts the photograph in a drawer, then stands up and walks over to the window. Clear blue sky. The sun readying itself to spring above the rooftops. Cigarette. First of the day. His head spins a little, but the taste of tobacco, and the smell of the smoke hovering around him, disperses the daydream that lulled him for a few moments.

Martine Carol is dead, but the Mazeaus were attacked by a former deportee, Jean Delbos, back in Bordeaux to wreak his revenge. Unmasked by Inspecteur Mazeau, he had violently attacked him before stealing his service revolver. Inspecteur Mazeau has disappeared, probably taken from his home during the attack that left his wife dead. Darlac thinks over the details and digressions of this fabrication: yes, it holds water. The dickhead journalists all bought it. He feels like a cat that has jumped from a tenth-floor window and has landed on the back of a stunned dog. A survivor. All-powerful. Even Commissaire Divisionnaire Laborde seemed convinced: he has decided to throw the kitchen sink at this case. A cop killer must not get away with it, he said.

Since the previous day, half a dozen detectives have been following up old leads, delving back into the past. The war and the Occupation are likely to confuse things, cover the tracks. Thank God. Darlac would prefer to avoid his own past being investigated. It is riddled with old footpaths known only to him. He opens a folder and takes out the photograph of a young man, which he procured from the prefecture's identity-card department: it is Daniel Delbos, son of Jean and Olga Delbos, born 18 March 1939, officially adopted by Maurice and Roselyne Jouvet on 10 November 1946. Parents dead after being deported. Currently in Algeria with the 85th infantry regiment.

He remembers having held that little bastard in his arms, two or three times. Having taken him sweets. Given him a toy, maybe. It has to be said that Olga was so pretty, and so alone, some nights . . . But a bit Jewish, a bit ginger . . . Secretary in a factory where she hung around with communists. Bordenave, a detective in secret services, had warned Darlac in late '40: you should watch yourself with Delbos and his wife. They're not the kind of people you need to be seen with right now. With him, Jean, it was maybe alright: he was a clown, a small-time gambler, we could pick him up whenever we wanted and control him. But with her, you need to beware: her parents were Hungarian Jews, living in Paris with the grandparents. And on top of that, she was a communist – or as near as makes no difference. This was the war – surely he'd noticed. And we were occupied. Did he grasp what that meant? The Yids and reds were for it, without a doubt. He should distance himself from that lot pronto. And it was better that he, Bordenave, was the one to tell him, rather than the riff-raff that was taking over now – and he wasn't only talking about the Krauts. "Stay on the right side and nothing will happen to you," he had added.

Darlac took this warning to heart. In any case, Olga was too contemptuous of him for her to be of any use to him: she wouldn't say anything, reveal anything, even inadvertently, because she considered him a mortal enemy of her and her husband and a danger to her life and her son's life. And he didn't give a shit about politics. Pétain was an old fool, the Jews were a filthy race, the Commies dangerous cretins and the Krauts inarguably the victors who must now be taken into consideration. Full stop. He simply had to get used to that fact and not get his fingers caught in any doors. What he was gradually coming to realise was this: there were positions to be filled and there was money to be made. Play his cards right, and it could all fall his way without him even having to ask. He just had to seize his chance when it came. To be there: right place, right time. Not difficult, when you're a cop. So not only had he held the big stick, but he'd used it when he'd had to, hitting and hurting, dealing body blows and cracking heads without any reluctance at all. Ruthless and respected, he'd soon imposed his authority on his classroom of enemies. This was war. They could hate him all they liked. He would teach those little fucks.

And now he has the feeling that the war has started again.

At this moment, he is driving north towards the docks, jolting over the cobblestones, stuck behind slothful trucks, their engines roaring as they rev up, only to move fifty metres and then get stopped by the press of traffic again. He hardly looks beyond the fences surrounding the dock area where men and machines are busy working. All that unionised work disgusts him, those lazy-arse whiners, those pinko protesters, they sicken him. And ports have always made him anxious. Those murky zones where cities start to drown, where fog hovers, those places of exchange and transit, all those strangers arriving, all those people and goods leaving for God knows where. Ports are places of disorder and upheaval, with their unwritten laws laid down by crooks who are never caught. Once he had to run an investigation here: a stake-out lasting three nights. And he felt as if he were in enemy territory, sensing the hostility of each object, fearing the threat of the slightest shadow, hating the night itself, deeper than in town, and its silence, always broken suddenly by a peal of laughter or metallic screech. An unstable silence, just like the water and its ever-shifting reflections. Even the boats worried him, steeped in that deep blackness with their illuminated portholes, behind which he imagined foreign faces, concentrated on some plot, some deal, some stiff that needed to disappear.

He leaves this uncertain space behind him and crosses the swing bridge. Muffled thunder of wheels. Francis is waiting for him on the corner of rue de New York, opposite the police station, smoking with his elbow out the open car window. He extricates himself with difficulty from the driver's seat and nods at Darlac, then the two of them walk rapidly towards number thirty-five without saying anything.

"Roselyne Jouvet?"

The woman who opens the door stares back at them with her dark, surprised eyes. Then the lines in her face tense as she appears to understand, even before they show her their police I.D..

For a moment she holds the door half open, probably blocking it with her foot.

"What do you want?"

Putting his card back in his pocket, Darlac holds open his jacket so she gets a good look at the Colt .45 in its shoulder holster. He sees the look in her eyes when she notices it.

"To talk to you. Isn't your husband there?"

"He's working."

"What about your daughter? Irène, isn't it?"

The woman visibly shivers. She stares at the two men, her gaze lingering on Francis, who is rummaging around in the pocket of his raincoat. The sound of keys.

Darlac steps into the doorway.

"Can we come in? Unless . . ."

She opens the door wide and precedes them through a narrow hallway that leads to the kitchen. Water is boiling in a washtub on the hob. The smell of soap is sharp and acrid. Francis sneezes. The woman leans on the sink and watches the two of them standing on the other side of the table, hats on heads, eyes ferreting around in the shadows. Their presence seems to fill the room, to suck all the air out of it.

Darlac already knows that this will be difficult. He senses her tension, hostility, suspicion. She's seen cops here before, without a doubt. He knows that the husband nearly got taken in '43. He knows that Poinsot had planned to take care of her, but had not had time. He should check that, when he gets the chance. She's probably seen nervous detectives here before, one of them pistol in hand, sitting a child on his knees, stroking its temple with the barrel of his gun while his colleague carries out a body search.

"Did you know Olga and Jean Delbos?"

"They're dead. Leave them in peace."

"You didn't answer my question."

Darlac nods at Francis, who goes out into the hallway and starts opening doors and cupboards and drawers.

"Answer me and we'll be on our way."

"Of course I knew them. You already know that, or why would you ask? We took in their son, Daniel, and adopted him. So?"

"Do you read the newspaper?"

"Not every day."

They hear Francis tipping out the contents of a drawer. The rough jingling of coat hangers on a rod.

"Well, guess what . . . Jean Delbos is not dead. He's come back, and we're looking for him."

Roselyne puts a hand to her mouth and closes her eyes for a few seconds. When she opens them again, they are filled with tears that do not fall.

"I was closer to Olga. She was like a sister to me. None of this has anything to do with you."

"Oh, but it does . . ."

Darlac pulls a chair out and sits down with a sigh. He takes off his hat and looks up at the woman, who has not moved. She appears paralysed, breathing through her mouth, her chest rising and falling rapidly as she tries to control her emotions. At the back of the house they hear Francis whistling as he empties cupboards and wardrobes.

"Jean Delbos is accused of six murders. Including those of a policeman and his wife. That makes him one of the most wanted criminals in the country. Starting to get the picture now?"

Roselyne does not react. She wipes her palms on her apron, hands flat, as if she was smoothing down the fabric.

"Sooner or later, he's going to come here to see you, to see his son. Always happens with men like this. When they feel hunted, even the most cunning of them, they go to their old lairs, like animals, where they can pick up their own scent again. That day, when he comes back, I want you to tell me. Find a phone and call us. You'll figure out a way to arrange another meeting. Invite him in, just like the good old days. And we'll be there."

Roselyne stands up and grabs two dish towels then picks up the washtub by its handles and moves it from the hob to a steel plate. The shrieking of metal. Francis enters the kitchen and leans on the door frame, watching her do this.

"And you seriously think we'll do what you say? You think he'll fall into your trap?"

"Seriously, yes. I have never been more serious in my life."

"Get out of here. I have nothing to do with all this. It's in the past. Just do your job and leave me in peace."

She leans back against the sideboard, arms crossed over her chest. Darlac gets up and stands in front of her.

"Did you hear that?" he asks Francis, without taking his eyes off Roselyne. "She brings up a murderer's son and she claims it's all in the past! I don't think she's really aware of how much shit she's in. So listen: your adopted son – what's his name again? – oh yes: Daniel. He's in Algeria at the moment. That's good. He's doing his duty for his country, no problem there. Except that he was brought up by communists so he's probably one himself, and blokes like that can never be trusted in a war. He's probably just as worthless as his father. You should know that there are disciplinary battalions in the army, and he could find himself in one of those next week if you don't make an effort. And those units, they're in the thick of it, you know what I mean? On the front line. All it would take is a phone call and –" he snaps his fingers – "national security . . . the general staff will take care of him. The army has plenty of ways to fuck up a young soldier's life. So it's up to you: if you don't help me, I can make you pay. And your . . . adopted son will pay too. He'll come back to you in a box cos, you know, a brave lad like that, he'll be the first to attack the enemy lines. You beginning to get the picture?"

Now the tears are rolling down Roselyne's face. She tells them to leave but they don't move. Hands in pockets, they watch as she wipes her cheeks with a large handkerchief then covers her face with it and tries to suppress her sobs. Finally they leave without another word, closing the door softly behind them. Out on the pavement, Darlac shrugs and says it'll probably do no good, but at least it puts those sorts of people back in their place, makes them respect him. He adds that he enjoys this kind of thing. Nailing them to the floor alive and watching the fuckers struggle. "Strategic terror," he says proudly.

Francis nods but does not reply. He hasn't talked much since Jeff died. Darlac is no longer sure he can really count on Francis to have his back for him. And he's not at all sure that it's in his interest to have to keep one eye on this trusty mutt that is currently walking with its ears down, growling faintly. He thinks strategically. He knows it is safer to face ten enemies than to rely on an ally you can no longer trust. At least with the enemies, you know what you're up against.

They agree to meet the next day. Darlac looks into Francis' eyes: clear, blue, straightforward, but almost hard and icy, even if their colour is more suggestive of azure skies, mild April days. Francis gets into his car after glancing vaguely over at the pavement on the other side of the road: no-one there, the cobbles sloping down towards the gutter.

Back at home, Darlac hears the radio on full blast. He doesn't even bother trying to work out who's singing in his home. He goes to switch it off before taking the time to remove his hat. Madame appears at the kitchen door. Sweater sleeves rolled up, blue apron. She wipes her red eyes with the back of her hand, which holds a knife. The smell of garlic and onion.

"Do you really need to wail like that? You deaf or what?"

She turns her back on him and immediately he hears her humming something as she opens a cupboard. He undresses, feeling the usual dull, bitter throb of anger that stabs through him whenever he walks in his own door. He puts his pistol in a drawer of the sideboard and locks it with a key. For some time now, he's stopped removing the magazine. He always leaves a bullet loaded in the chamber. Fuck safety recommendations. The only safety recommendation he believes in is to be in a position to open fire first, or at least to be able to retaliate effectively and shoot your enemy. Whether you survive or not. But he feels sure that he has a better chance of getting out alive, even if he's badly wounded, if he kills the other bloke. He is certain that death always chooses the one who is least determined to escape him because he doesn't know him, the one who has never yet seen that darkening, the sudden grey light of an eclipse, the instantaneous chill in the air that announces death is about to strike.

He opens his bar – an old writing desk with inlaid ivory and ebony doors and drawers, picked up a long time ago at a storage unit piled high with wonders – and he hesitates between two bottles: Cinzano or cognac? Cognac. He needs to feel it burn. He pours it into a balloon glass and downs a large mouthful that makes him gasp and brings tears to his eyes. He exhales. Christ, he needed that: the devastating wave of alcohol flooding through his whole body. He walks over to the living-room area and sniffs the drink, the way he knows it should be done. He has seen bigwigs from Paris do it, even a minister once, holding the glass like an expert, rolling this liquid gold around the sides. But all he can smell is alcohol fumes. He doesn't care about the rest. The Kraut officers had the same habit in the common rooms of the prefecture, but some of them just gulped it down like schnapps while others went into raptures with members of the cabinet. He takes another drink and now he feels the heat rising up inside him giving him strength. Suddenly he is sure of himself again, belligerent and panting like a fierce dog.

He hears the floorboards creak above him, so he finishes his drink and exhales again, shaking his head to rid himself of the sudden dizziness, and he climbs the stairs, holding onto the banister until his head stops spinning. Standing outside Elise's door, he puts his ear to the wood. But he hears nothing so he knocks, twice, and abruptly enters. The girl, leaning over her notebooks, illuminated by a reading lamp, with a textbook open in front of her, slowly lifts her head to him and gives a tired smile. She blinks, eyes shining. Her legs are stretched out under the desk and her shoeless feet move in navy-blue tights, and Darlac doesn't know if it's the light and the shadows it paints on her face, in her eyes, but suddenly she looks like a young woman, smiling in her white, open-necked blouse, her blonde hair spilling over a cheek. He walks closer and his heart beats faster. That's normal, he thinks: it's the alcohol, the fatigue. But, standing very close to the girl, he is embarrassed by what he feels, and he leans down to kiss her as he always does and she moves her lips towards him and he feels them touch his cheek.

The desire to plunge his hand down the cleavage of her blouse and to feel the roundness of a breast inside his palm is so powerful that he brusquely moves aside, his throat knotted, watched by the girl who looks amazed and asks him if he's alright. Yes, he replies breathlessly, yes, he's fine, just a bit of dizziness, it'll pass, and when she stands up and moves close to him and touches her fingers to his burning, sweat-soaked neck, he grabs her hand so tightly that she cries out in pain and he says, no, I told you, I'm fine, leave me alone, so Elise steps back, holding her arm, you hurt me, what's the . . . ?

He leaves the room, practically bent double over his throbbing erection, a rutting beast escaping now to the bathroom where he frees this tension at the first contact with his fingers, groaning, his face twisted in the mirror, grumbling obscenities at the girl he imagines pressed against him.

Afterwards, he looks in the mirror at his pale face glistening with sweat, the deep lines an arrow of disgust and contempt. He shakes his head, trying to rid himself of that bad dream, but succeeds only in giving himself a migraine that feels as if it will smash open his skull. Acid rises up the back of his throat and he has to close his eyes and hold on to the edge of the sink, just above the streak of his semen stuck to the earthenware.

So he splashes water over all of this – his face, his heavy-lidded eyes, the milk-white flob purged from his body – and leaves the bathroom, feeling groggy, before returning downstairs. In the kitchen, he sees his wife from behind, immobile, arms hanging, in front of the gas cooker, the black seams of her stockings running up under her skirt towards that perfect arse where he will pour out his rage later, and he can't understand what she's doing there, head high, body frozen, knife in hand.

19

Daniel folds Irène's letter and pushes it to the bottom of his trouser pocket, his heart swollen because, behind the words, he could hear her voice, her inflexions, even her laugh, and for five minutes he wasn't in this shit heap anymore, he was torn away from this war and taken close to her. She said she'd received a postcard from Alain in Copenhagen, where it was snowing. He's fine, he's happy, he's learning to speak English. He sends his greetings, his friendship. She also talks about other friends, about university and boring professors, about lecture halls with their oppressive silence, about poetry, which she is discovering with passion: *not those quotes you learn at school, but real poetry, I know you don't care, but where you are at the moment I think it would be a good way of escaping what you must be experiencing, although you don't say much about it* . . .

He does not really see how poetry could change anything here: could it relieve the heat, make the rain fall, bring the dead back to life? What words, what meanings? Peace on earth and goodwill to all men? The kind of crap that preachers spout on Sundays in church? What twat of a writer would be capable of saying anything powerful enough to jam the infernal machine that he feels roaring around him, even if it's idling at the moment? Words melt before iron and fire. Not long ago Maurice told him about Jaurès: even he had not been able to do anything, in '14, for all his great speeches and fine words. No-one can ever speak louder than the mouth of a cannon. So . . . poets, with their poetic ways . . . He would like to understand what Irène is saying with her poetry. He would like to agree with her, speak like her. Maybe one day. He closes his eyes. Drifts into a daydream. He hears her voice whispering lines of verse to him, her lips to his ear. For a few seconds he is no longer in

Algeria. The quarters, its dust, the shouts of young men at play, the blazing sun, the exhaustion, the boredom, even the war and its weapons all vanish. Perhaps that is what Irène's poetry can offer? The possibility of escaping from time, of no longer feeling weighed down by the world.

He should talk to Giovanni about this. He believes in words too. He'd like her letter. It'd be a good excuse to talk to him again, a way of approaching him, of finding something else to talk about other than the shit through which they're wading. Since the ambush and the deaths of Declerck and the *fellagha*, his friend has been avoiding him. He barely even says hello, dodges all discussions. Daniel would like to talk to him about what happened because it would help him to see clearly through this fog that surrounds him, dense, heavy and suffocating, to try to understand what he felt when he held that man in the centre of his scope. He would like to be able to find a few words to describe that perfect instant he experienced, that luminous clarity, to try to express the power that surged through him when he pulled the trigger, like an electric punch followed by a sort of K.O.

He'd also like to tell him about the dream that he's had every night since: after firing, he rushes towards his target but his cotton-wool legs are incapable of carrying him and they give way beneath him, and when he suddenly finds himself in front of the bush there is no longer any dead man there nor any machine gun, not even the faintest trace of blood, so he feels relieved and wakes up and, for just a moment, liberated of this weight, he persuades himself that he has not killed anyone and everything goes back the way it was before, calm and clean, until reality descends on him with its filthy arse, pushing him down into the canvas pallet of his camp bed. He shivers and sees again that angular face, the copper skin, the man's fixed profile and then the torn flesh of his wound, the debris of bones and teeth, the body jolting as the sergent fires three more bullets into it. He sees again the others prodding the corpse with the toes of their boots, their first contact with the enemy, proof that he exists beyond the stories told by officers and old soldiers. And then sleep is suspended above him, in the blackness, like a cloud hovering over a dry land, from which no rain will fall.

At university, we created a committee for peace in Algeria and loads of students come to the meeting, sometimes just to talk crap, saying we should let those bougnoules *fight it out among themselves instead of sending French boys to be killed there, you know the kind of thing . . . There are also discussions about independence: there are those who say we should negotiate with the F.L.N. to keep Algeria but in better conditions, with equal rights, but me and my friends, you know, Philippe and Régine, we're for independence straight away because colonialism has done too much damage, not just in Algeria but everywhere. We have arguments sometimes and we don't speak to each other for three days and then we make up, but I think they'll end up agreeing with us because there's really no other solution.*

He would like to talk to them, those students in their comfy chairs, but he doesn't know what he would tell them: the heat, the thirst, the blisters on his feet, the fear, the dust, the filth, the insomnia, the stupidity, the alcohol, the solitude and the tears and the smiles when the post arrives, depending what their letters say . . . The war? He has been here two months and he hasn't seen any of what he imagined he would see, but is war imaginable? He has never heard heavy artillery fire, and he still hasn't seen fighter planes screaming past over hills. They barely even got to see six banana choppers[31] flying over a ridge last week before they disappeared almost immediately afterwards. No combat. Stinking corpses one day in a ruined farm, and the ambush last week. That big twat Declerck lying face down in the sand, and the torn-off face of that *fell* next to his machine gun.

31 The H-21, a tandem rotor American helicopter known as the "Workhorse", was widely used during the Algerian War (and later in Vietnam) for the transport of troops and medical evacuations. Its characteristic curved shape earned it the nickname of the "Flying Banana".

Apart from that, days and days to fill. Time planned out by the officers in little boxes that absolutely have to be filled out. Preparing meals. Cleaning and unblocking toilets. Emptying bins. Pouring diesel oil on rubbish and setting it on fire. Going out on patrol. Practising shooting. Cleaning weapons. Changing the oil in the trucks and half-tracks. Changing a tyre on a jeep. Going out in search of water. Writing letters home. Playing cards. Reading letters from home. Getting smashed.

Mum has looked preoccupied for the last two or three days, I don't know why. When I ask her what's up with her she says it's nothing, that she's worried about you. But I can tell there's more to it than that. Last night, when I came home, they were talking, her and Dad, and then they suddenly went silent. They looked embarrassed. Are you telling each other secrets? I asked, and Dad laughed: Yep, big secrets, too big for a kid like you, he replied and Mum laughed too, but I know them too well not to tell that there's something else going on. Whatever you do though, don't mention any of this when you write to them, because they'll have a go at me for worrying you. But I'm telling you because I have to tell someone, and there is only you.

There is only you. She'd underlined that phrase. What did she mean? She tells everything, all her moods and emotions, to Sara, who's like a sister to her. And then there's that friend she knew in secondary school, Régine, whom she tells everything to as well. Friends for life, until death. When they were kids, they talked all the time, him and Irène. They had their secret cabin, in a corner of a box room at the back of the courtyard, where Daniel would some-times cry on her shoulder because he couldn't remember his parents' faces anymore and she would rock him, even though she was smaller than he was, understanding without knowing.

There is only you. He repeats these words to himself, sitting on a crate in the narrow shade of a shelter, watching the others play ball in the dust.

Irène.

The lads jump and shout on either side of the net hung between two posts then suddenly yell at each other, arguing over whether the ball went over the line of stones around the court, and in those moments they stop moving, panting, faces grey with dust and striped sweat, while the traces of the disputed point are examined by the most determined of them, pacing the invisible line like surveyors, complaining and swearing, all of them, that they are sure, then laughing and promising that next time they will appoint a referee.

Sometimes the sentry in his watchtower intervenes, claiming he has a better view from where he sits, like a tennis umpire, he says, and the players all laugh and tell him to fuck off and keep his eyes on the slopes of the valley that you're supposed to watch when you're up there, baking under the wavy canvas roof, leaning back against sandbags with only the machine gun and three flasks of lukewarm water for company.

Sometimes Sergent Castel joins the game. He just walks onto the court, ignoring the team that is standing there, and he points to one man and says, "Alright, you, fuck off, I'm replacing you," and he starts playing without a word, without a gasp, without showing any effort at all, his knife-like face utterly impassive. Of course, when he's there the others don't yell as much. They complain quietly, concentrate on playing better because the sergent's like a bloody volleyball champion: he never misses a shot, making vicious winners from impossible angles, sending over unreturnable serves. The men furtively ogle his lean, slender muscles, moving beneath his skin like a nest of snakes, and the long scar that runs across his chest and up to the base of his neck. A fragment of mortar shell in Indo, a huge stroke of luck: right next to him, another piece, a kilogram of metal sent hurtling at three hundred kilometres an hour by the gods of war, took off half of a caporal's head, a clean cut, almost anatomical. He told them this the other night in the meeting hall, pissed out of his head, dressed only in a pair of shorts, an undershirt and a belt with a sheathed dagger hung from it. A few blokes found it hard to believe that such wounds could really exist, new squaddies, virgins to the horror. The sergent stared at them gravely, his eyelids heavy with alcohol blinking over his clear eyes, then he smiled sadly before downing a can of lager without breathing and retreating to his lair to put his drunken body to bed. He walked mechanically towards the exit, kicking out of the way any chairs and tables that happened to lie in his path, and for the minute that followed his departure no-one said anything until a man from Dunkirk, known as Jeanjean, said: "Once, in the factory, I saw a bloke cut in two by a steel sheet."

The conversations had begun again, because true horrors were seen only in war, as a few of them knew. Sure, men might get crushed in a work accident, or suffocated, or ground into mincemeat, or split in half, leaving a finger or an arm or a leg inside a machine, and sure, it was the same blood that poured out. But it was as if it didn't count somehow: dying for a boss was less significant than dying for your homeland, less chic. And they went on talking until lights out, about flesh and bones and blood and men's sufferings, and they had all been drinking, the ones who talked, arms waving expressively, and the ones who listened, nodding or rolling their eyes. Daniel had moved from one group to the next, dazed, sickened, until he had found Giovanni, who had bought him a beer, the first they had shared since their row. But they barely said a word, too drunk, too distraught, lacking the strength to break the silence between them, a silence as dense and substantial as the *fell* Daniel had shot. "I don't understand anything anymore," was all Daniel said. Giovanni had nodded his assent then theatrically clinked his bottle against Daniel's before downing the contents. "Me neither," he said before turning away and going to bed.

The days pass like that. They keep busy. From time to time the N.C.O.s take groups of about twenty men on a march around the camp. They do some shooting practice, simulate combat situations. The men apply themselves, do what they're told. They aim straight, crawl, run, climb and jump. Clumsy, wobbly, exhausted. Castel often tells them they're dead, but they don't care, lying on the gravel and trying to get their breath back. Sometimes they apologise.

"Sorry, sergeant, I didn't see him . . . I screwed up."

"Yeah, right," he replies. "You can apologise to the *fell* who shoots you in the face. I'm not sure they really appreciate French politeness anymore, but it's worth a go, I guess. You hopeless prick."

Occasionally a few of them act like soldiers and are rewarded with a pat on the back from the sergent on the way back to the camp, while the others sweat under their helmets, panting and limping, shirts stuck to their skin, cursing the stones that their leaden feet keep tripping over, holding empty flasks over their open mouths in the hope that a final drop will fall.

Daniel can't help loving all this. He isn't afraid. He always tries to find the right reaction, the appropriate movement, the quickest way. He suppresses the vibrations of the machine gun in his closed fists and grits his teeth as he makes sure that his bursts of gunfire are brief and well-aimed, not ricocheting randomly from stones or tearing apart bushes like the long, spluttering, wayward farts of bullets that the others make, leaving them with lungs and magazines empty, almost relieved. He is able to hold off his fatigue until he gets back to quarters. During the training exercises he feels full of energy, lifted high above the others, and he knows this is the best he's ever felt.

Now and then, Castel will pat him on the shoulder without saying anything, or stare at him and nod. Never a word of encouragement. Never does he pick out Daniel as an example to the others. Only this silent complicity between them. Oh, except for one day, when they got back to the camp: "That was good, but when the day comes, you'll have to hold it all together. You ain't seen nothing yet."

But today the sergent remains invisible, keeping to his digs the way he often does whcn nothing's happening. It's said that he can sit for hours on the ground, legs crossed, hands on his knees and eyes closed, with his weapons ranged around him. Sometimes when the men knock on his door and get no reply, they open up and go inside and find him like that, then make their excuses and leave, and tell the lieutenant what they saw. He always advises them to leave the sergent the fuck alone.

This evening, everyone stands around the flagpole, with the flag hanging motionless in the air, as tomorrow's missions are announced. The sergent stands at the back, hatless, unmoving, thumbs wedged in his belt, impassive behind his dark glasses. They have to find water because the level of water has dropped again. They'll pick up a water truck in town, as a safeguard against the coming heat of summer. He asks the N.C.O.'s to choose the men who will be in the convoy. A jeep and a half-track with seven men. The lieutenant announces that he will be on the mission because he has to see the colonel. The sergent will stay here to hold the fort. Dismissed.

Daniel is chosen. So is Giovanni. A trip to town. Already they are dreaming of a pastis and a bowl of olives. Some of the lads complain: they're scared shitless, talking about ambushes and mines. Others are happy to go: they want to see girls walk past in the street, and they're planning on a trip to the brothel – they have the address and the price list: it's pretty cheap if you fuck a native. But Carlin, the caporal, remains inflexible. Meet tomorrow at 5 a.m.

They go off to eat boiled potatoes and sardines in oil. Two or three saucissons and a few terrines of pâté that came in the post are gobbled down. And, mouths full of charcuterie, the men go on, as they always do, about how much they miss home. Fuck, what wouldn't they give for a glass of red, a bowl of their grandmother's hotpot, a dozen oysters with a glass of white ... The lads sigh as they tell each other stories of feasts they've eaten and secret recipes.

They drool and sigh again and push back their empty plates.

Daniel can't sleep. He tosses and turns on his pallet in the relentless heat. Irène. Everywhere he sees her face, her smile, her sulks. Her body. He sees her as she's leaving the bathroom, rushing through the hallway, her nightgown half undone or her slip revealing the tops of her thighs. He hasn't looked at her for a long time, but right now she is all he can see.

Irène.

20

He has not seen Abel for nearly twenty years. Abel Mayou, a notorious fraud, two spells in prison, the last time in late '40 for having extorted funds from the mother-in-law of a deputy mayor in Bordeaux. Five years. He spent the Occupation in the fortress of Ha, sharing his cell with Jews and Resistance fighters. They'd tried to use him as a spy, getting those arseholes to talk, but it was no good. Not even the prospect of being freed, not even money could get him to cooperate. He wasn't interested. So he did his five years and he got out in '45, having lost quite a bit of weight, quite a lot of hair and some of his pride too. Maybe he had T.B. He certainly had no cash, and he was thin as a rake. Apparently he wasn't such a poseur anymore when his whore, la Violette, picked him up outside the prison.

Darlac had been relieved when Abel was locked up. Given what was happening – all these opportunities opening up for profiting from the shit heap of war – he felt happier knowing Abel was safely at a distance. He would undoubtedly have stuck his nose in wherever he smelt something fishy, and the cunning bastard would have taken a malign pleasure in thwarting some of Darlac's most lucrative schemes. He would never have worked with the Krauts. Too rebellious, too disobedient. He hated the wealthy and the powerful too much for that. A first-rate con man he might have been, but he claimed to have moral principles, and was happy to talk about them during those Sundays by the waterfront, while laughing at the rich suckers he'd swindled. He was no Robin Hood either; he kept it all for himself: fine wines, cars, women, that house on the bay . . . The losers he invited to that place in the shade of the pines would guzzle down all his food, slurp *grands crus* like they were the usual gut-rot they drank in their local bars, spread foie gras on toast like it was sandwich paste, then unbutton their jackets to let their swollen bellies hang out, leaning back in their chairs or lying sated in the grass, a hat balanced over their eyes.

Abel was too crafty to piss them off by forcing them to show some gastronomic respect or by trying to teach them about the finer things in life. They would have reacted badly to any lectures about taste or their lack of it, especially in front of their wives, whom they often brought along with them to get them out of the house, as they said. Those oafs, those losers were his eyes and ears in the city and all over its suburbs. He gave them free rein at his table in return for premium information or useful gossip. Once he'd got them drunk on Médoc or Pomerol, they wouldn't stop talking. And Abel pampered them, letting them burp and fart to their hearts' content, listening attentively to all their secrets, their slanders and lies, solemnly swearing not to breathe a word.

Darlac turned up sometimes, invited by Abel, whom he'd met in the chief's office and had then met up with again because each of them had quickly seen how the relationship could prove profitable. The thugs didn't talk quite so freely with Darlac there, but the presence of a corrupt cop reassured them: it was good to have that kind of connection when your business was as risky as theirs. That was where he first met Jean Delbos. That was how they became friends.

Friends. The word comes to his mind and he pushes it away and tries to defend himself, but he cannot help remembering that, for at least four years, they had seen a lot of each other, sharing evenings, girls, losses and winnings at cards, pale early mornings and hangovers. And sometimes a few confidences, when Delbos would tell him about his life, his wife Olga, her parents (Hungarian Jews who arrived in France in '21), her friends (communists who dreamed of enrolling in the International Brigades in Spain), people with whom he seemed ill at ease, this poor, untrustworthy accountant living buttoned up tight in the straitjacket of his daily life, this night bird who could not imagine life without the daylight of his wife.

No-one in the force has heard anything about Abel Mayou since he got out of prison. Done his time and gone straight, everyone says. None of the city's gangsters even seem to know who Darlac means when he mentions him. The old-timers remember him as a con man from the pre-war years, but that's all: maybe he's dead, they say, or maybe pissed off elsewhere.

Darlac shakes these thoughts from his head, refusing to consider them more deeply. He gets out of the car and is drenched by a downpour as he walks along the pavement to the house, ducking his head as he waits for the door to be opened.

Darlac has trouble recognising the man who stands in the doorway and whose eyes flicker from side to side, trying to spot any other cops hidden behind him. Thin, bald, dark-eyed and hollow-cheeked. A sick man. Darlac does not like sick people. He mistrusts their weakness or their pig-headedness, when they start whining about their fate or philosophising about the unshakable principles they hide behind as a form of dignity in their last-chance saloon.

"Well, well. Commissaire Darlac. And you came here alone, no cavalry? You're taking risks."

"Let me in. It's pissing down out here."

Abel moves out of the way to let the cop into his entrance hall and leads him to a dim living room, lit only by a French window with rain streaming down.

"How are you?" Darlac asks.

"As you can see. Did you come here to ask about my health?"

"I'm looking for Jean. Jean Delbos."

"Jean is dead. Olga too. End of story."

"He's not though. And you know it. Olga, sure – she died in the camps. But he came back. He's calling himself André Vaillant."

"Vaillant? Doesn't sound like him."

"He's killed six people. Don't you read the paper?"

"Not every day. Anyway, who cares? For me he's dead, even if he did come back. Even if he came here, he'd still just be a fucking ghost. And I don't let ghosts into my home."

Darlac pulls a chair from under the table and sits down. He unbuttons his raincoat and his jacket, revealing the butt of his gun in its holster. He sees Abel notice it. Sees him smile, blink contemptuously.

"You didn't always feel like that about him. At least not when you were trying to screw his wife."

Abel sits down and leans his elbow on the table.

"I should smash your fucking face in. I should skin you alive for what you just said. But I'm tired. Anyway, I don't attack pricks with guns cos they don't know how to defend themselves like men."

He coughs, catches his breath, takes a handkerchief from his pocket and spits phlegm into it. Seeing his face turn red, Darlac wonders how long he's got left. He thinks about that other walking corpse, Crabos, and wonders what's become of him, down in Spain. If the cancer finally killed him off, catching him off guard one day, like a vicious bull in a corrida.

Hand trembling, Abel points to the door. His handkerchief is rolled in a ball inside his palm.

"Fuck off. You stink. You make me want to puke. Other people die and you're the one that smells like a rotting carcass."

Darlac does not move. He just nods at this insult, eyes to the ground, and waits for the moment to pass. Abel has another brief coughing fit, and puts a hand to his chest as if this might help him breathe more easily. Just then Darlac hears the door open, someone exhaling, an umbrella being closed. A woman's voice. Soft and muffled.

"It's me. Everything O.K.?"

Almost immediately a head appears in the frame of the door. The woman is wearing a red scarf, which she unties as she stares at Darlac. She is tall and thin, almost too thin. Darlac looks for her breasts, but can't see much under the sweater she wears. Short hair. Long, handsome face. Huge dark eyes. Little or no make-up. She looks like a portrait of the Madonna stuck on top of a pile of bones. Darlac doesn't like feeling anything hard under his fingers. He likes the soft sweetness of flesh. She stares at him indifferently, as if he were just some door-to-door salesman, flogging Hoovers or fridges. He stares back.

"It's Commissaire Darlac," says Abel. "I must have mentioned him to you."

The woman continues looking at Darlac, then runs a hand through her hair and moves out of sight.

"Oh, yes. I remember. Darlac. He wasn't commissaire before though, was he?"

He can hear her take her shoes off, hang her raincoat on the hat stand in the hallway. When she comes into the room, her feet shuffling along the floor in a pair of old slippers, shopping bag in hand, she goes first to Abel and strokes his face, then nods at Darlac before going through to the kitchen.

"Who's that? Your skivvy?"

"Shall I put salt in his coffee or is he leaving now?" the woman asks from the kitchen.

"This is Violette. The woman I live with. Now, fuck off."

"Violette who? Does she have a surname or did you just pick her from the ground one snowy night?"

Violette comes out of the kitchen, rummaging through her handbag, then tosses her identity card at him.

"Marini, Violette Giuletta. Born in Nice, third of November, 1916. Parents' names: Angelo and Anna Marini."

Darlac puts the document on his knee, then gets to his feet, letting the card fall to the floor.

"A wop whore. Just what you needed. I hope she knows how to clean a toilet and cook spaghetti, cos you don't look in a fit state to enjoy her other skills. Tell Delbos—"

Abel stands up and moves towards him, grabbing the lapels of his raincoat.

"I told you, Delbos is dead to me, even if he's alive. He never deserved a woman like Olga; he was just the kind of little shit that cops like you like having up their sleeve. I don't know what the two of you got up to together and I don't want to know. If he's killed people, then catch him and leave us the fuck alone. Got it?"

Breathing hard, he lets go of Darlac. Then coughs and sits down.

The commissaire stands motionless in front of them, staring at each one in turn, grinning at the woman's tense, hostile expression. Then he turns his back on them and leaves without a word. Outside, under a low grey sky that is still spitting rain, he thinks about the passing of time, how it distances people from each other, like rafts drifting downriver, wrecked, rudderless ships that have survived terrible storms. And he, Albert Darlac, is navigating through this inland sea like some big, scary carnivore – a shark or a killer whale: he doesn't really know the difference, and doesn't care either – capable of diving through fathomless abysses or of floating close to the surface, on the scent of blood.

Behind the wheel of his car, he lights a cigarette and lowers the window to feel the wet air on his face and to let these stupid thoughts be blown away. Fuck it: don't think, don't weaken. Just keep going. Act. Fuck them all.

21

The convoy leaves just before dawn. Inside the half-track, Daniel looks up at the haze of stars that floats above them, and Baltard – a lad from Normandy, sitting behind the .50-calibre machine gun and stroking its handles – laughingly asks him how many there were.

"If you count them all, I'll buy you a whore this afternoon!"

Bernier, the caporal, chuckles as he gets into the vehicle, and Giovanni shakes his head, staring at his shoes.

The road is mostly flat, so the men only have the dust to worry about. Dawn rises sudden and clear, as it often does here. The landscape appears almost painfully stark, bristling with sharp rocky ridges, reddish scree, chasms still filled with the blue, transparent night. The men are packed close together, sleepy, dazed by the screech of the caterpillar tracks, their faces invisible in the shadows of their helmets. The machine-gunner must have fallen asleep for a little bit: Daniel sees his skinny body jolted around in the turret, as the wheels bounced over ruts. There is a part of the journey where the valley steepens and narrows, the walls rising sharply to either side, scattered with puny bushes, where the road slows down in bends with no visibility. The drivers leave fifty metres between vehicles here, because if there is going to be an ambush, this is where it will be. And the men hold their weapons and scan the rocky slopes, watching the unsettling shapes made by the shadows of boulders. The machine-gunners turn their barrels towards the rockslides on the valley sides where nothing moves but the cold wind that rises with the sun. After half an hour, the soldiers go back to dozing like tortoises, the gun barrels are lowered, and the column rumbles forward again, lifting tons of ochre dust, in a suffocating cloud of thick, black exhaust fumes.

They don't see a soul on the road, apart from a gendarme road-block where a bus is being searched. Its passengers – women, children and old people, all of them Arabs – are herded by the road-side, hands on heads, the machine gun on the cops' armoured car trained on them. Suitcases, bundles, baskets, all have been thrown to the ground and emptied out. Clothes and utensils are mixed up in the dust. Daniel turns his head back to get a better view of these humiliated people, and is surprised, once again, that not one of them moves or protests, and it seems to him that he can see, despite the growing distance, the forty or so pairs of dark eyes unblinkingly following every movement made by the gendarmes, shining with a mixture of fear and hatred.

He elbows Giovanni. He hisses into his ear, over the roar of the vehicle as it crunched over the rutted tarmac.

"Did you see that?"

"What?"

"The search. Those people."

"That's war, comrade. Haven't you noticed? Some people even get killed."

"For fuck's sake! I get it, alright?"

"No, it's not alright. I'm going to get out of here."

"What do you mean?"

"I'll show you later. In town."

In the paved streets, the air becomes clear again and they stare, surprised, at the trees bordering the avenues, the passers-by on the pavements, the white façades of buildings. They take off their helmets and put their guns at their feet and stare up at the obvious tranquillity around them. They say hello to the kids dressed in rags who wave their hands and yell at them in Arabic.

"They're calling us sons of bitches," says Giovanni.

"Why do you say that?" asks Bernier. "Speak Arabic, do you?"

"Because it's true. And it's what I'd do if I were them."

"Careful with that big mouth of yours, Zacco. This isn't a fucking communist rally."

"Oh yeah? And what are you going to do about it, with your little stripes? Throw me in prison? Fine – at least I'll be out of this shithole."

"Shut your fucking mouth. We've got something better than jail for pricks like you. That'd be too easy, wanking in the shade while the rest of us get our balls cut off. There are special battalions where you'll go out hunting *fells* every day, and where you'll have to roast their bollocks with electric shocks until the fuckers sing the 'Marseillaise'. And you'll have to obey orders if you don't want to be in the front line all the time, at the head of the patrol, ready to take the first *crouille* bullet that comes flying through the air. Prison? That's too fucking good for the likes of you, mate! You're like those *ratons* in their underground dens, and you deserve the same fate as them!"

The caporal yells and spits all this in his face. He is standing up, pointing the barrel of his sub-machine gun at Giovanni like a threatening finger. Daniel pushes away the gun and tells him to calm down, to sit down, but the caporal turns on him, grabbing him by the collar of his uniform.

"What's up with you, eh? Scared I'll hurt your girlfriend?"

"We're here, ladies!" shouts Baltard the machine-gunner. "The colonel can help you finish your argument."

The caporal sits down and spits on the ground, cursing through gritted teeth. Then he stops speaking because the convoy enters the camp where the regiment's H.Q. is housed, a former colonial infantry barracks of which only the façade and one wing remain, the rest knocked down so it could be extended. Barbed-wire fences now protect a vast area filled with shelters, tents and warehouses, parked trucks and armoured vehicles and men, with roads and roundabouts traced in white-painted stones, with billboard signs covered in acronyms and numbers.

Daniel has been here before, but he is still amazed at how calm this place is, with its criss-crossing paths and its rows of off-white or khaki prefabs, some squaddies hanging around in their undershirts, hands in pockets and fags in mouths, while others climb into trucks, guns and kit on their backs. At a crossroads marked with pebbles, a clown in a helmet screams and gesticulates in an attempt to control traffic. Water truck that side, escort this side, and don't give us any shit. Behind their windscreens, men give him the finger and advise him to keep a closer eye on his whore of a sister. They park the armoured vehicles and the lieutenant's jeep by the side of a tank parked arse-backwards outside a two-storey building that gleams with a fresh coat of paint, white with green shutters. They switch off the engines and in the silence that follows they hear the clatter of typewriters and they sit there for a moment, guns in hand, listening to this peaceful, mechanical murmur. Then Baltard, whose protective goggles make him look like a giant insect, mentions the slender fingers of the typists and wonders if he could just go and say hi to them to find out what else they can do with their hands. They laugh quietly, staring through the open windows at the fans that beat at the warm air, but they cannot see a single pretty face or shapely body. The only sound is that incessant, bitter rattle, like a tiny army of invisible machine-gunners shooting at them.

A jeep arrives at full throttle, skidding in the gravel as it comes to a sudden halt, and an adjutant, cap on backwards, yells at them without getting out to go and leave their weapons with the duty sergent, over there, at the other side of the courtyard. After that, they will have three hours in town before going back to their god-forsaken little hellhole. Seeing the lieutenant, he stiffens in his seat and instantly salutes before driving off at top speed again, the jeep swallowed by the cloud of dust its wheels stir up.

On their way out, one of the orderlies gets to his feet behind his sandbags and recommends a few places to them: a café where you can drink cheaply on a terrace, and a well-kept brothel where the girls are clean and young and do anything you want. "Have a good time!" he yells, grabbing his crotch and sitting down on a canvas folding chair in front of his machine gun. There are seven or eight of them there, hesitating on the pavement, already rummaging through their pockets for cash, but the noon sun oppresses them, threatening to melt them if they stay in the same place much longer, so they start walking towards a long, straight avenue lined with plane trees and filled with shade, and cross a blindingly white square – a monument to the war dead stuck like a greyish-green shipwreck at its centre – their feet stamping through the transparent fire that flickers in a haze over the ground.

They have spread out under the trees, suddenly intimidated by the girls they pass, who ignore them, sometimes shaking their beautiful hair as if to rid themselves of the men's insistent stares. Daniel and Giovanni hang around in the streets for a while, stopping in front of shop windows and staring covetously inside. They buy half a kilo of strawberries, which they eat straight from the bag, like sweets. Then they sit at a table on the shady terrace of a cheap café – *Chez Perez: snacks all day* – where some old men play dominoes and drink pastis in a corner. The owner comes over immediately and, seeing them in their frayed uniforms and their dusty boots, asks them if it's not too tough out there, in the jebel, and he shakes their hands and thanks them for what they are doing for this magnificent country of Algeria, the most beautiful province of France, a treasure that we won't let the Arabs take off us. He says the Arabs, or the Muslims, never *ratons* or *crouilles* or *bougnoles*. He says that, without France, they would still all be living in mud huts with their goats because that's their nature, that indolence. It's not that they're bad people, though of course there are some bad'uns at the moment, with those groups of brigands – yes, he uses that word – those F.L.N. savages who are enlisted by force and who must be exterminated, but mostly they're just lazy: if you don't tell them to work, and tell them how to do it, they do nothing, and you have to yell at them or they don't listen. Anyway, you only have to see the way they fight, treacherously and lazily, sitting or lying in the undergrowth so you can't see them. And say what you want, but the climate doesn't explain everything. I'm telling you, it's like a kid who's been naughty: give them a good thrashing whenever they break the rules, as many times as it takes, and they'll stop doing it and everything will be better.

He pours out all this in a confidential tone, never once raising his voice, calm and certain in his observations and solutions, and the two friends let him talk, nodding their approval from time to time, watching women pass out of the corner of their eyes.

"Anyway, enough of all that. What would you lads like to eat? Some of my special *brochettes*?"

They wouldn't say no. And two pastis and a carafe of water, with plenty of ice. The man hurries back into the obscure depths of the bar.

"And that's why we're here," says Giovanni. "For these stupid fucking whites. We should blow his bar up, that prick."

Daniel does not reply. He lets the sounds of the street wash over him. The shouting and laughter, the roar of engines, the horns honking. The din of a city. He never realised he would miss it one day. Life is here, he thinks, in all its raucous confusion. Women pass, walking briskly, heels clicking on the pavement. Their light dresses dance around their legs in time with the swing of their bare arms. Tanned skin. High heels. It seems to him that he has never seen so many women. He says this to Giovanni and his friend laughs.

"That's because you don't look. There are women everywhere, all the time. Your Irène is not the only one, you know!"

"Why do you say that?"

Giovanni snorts, then squints enigmatically at Daniel.

"Because I know what you don't know yourself yet, apparently!"

The owner brings them two plates, each with three glistening *brochettes* surrounded by grilled tomatoes. Then he places before them a carafe of water dripping with condensation and two glasses of pastis.

"Drinks are on the house," he announces.

They grab the drinks and sip them, eyes closed, with sighs of pleasure. Oh fuck, that's good, they murmur. They drink and eat, not saying anything else, and they lick their fingers and fill their glasses with iced water, then lean back in their seats, hands cradling their full bellies, smiling with mute happiness.

Giovanni sits up, looks at his watch.

"Come on, we need to get going. I have to introduce you to someone. A nice bloke."

He is already on his feet. Daniel gets up too and they take the money from their pockets to pay. As they walk away, the owner wishes them good luck and shouts that he's fully behind them, behind the army. They walk fast, Daniel behind Giovanni, who is almost running, explaining that they only have an hour and a half before they have to return to the barracks.

Suddenly, turning a corner, they enter another city. Empty streets, faded façades, broken pavements, scrawny dogs sniffing dry gutters. They hear a newborn crying behind closed shutters. They hear the sound of metal on metal, and Daniel catches a glimpse of a man at the end of an alley straightening the bumper of a 202 with a sledgehammer. "Not long now," says Giovanni. Gradually the streets become narrower and shadier, and the air is filled with strong smells coming from shops behind metal shutters. The silence grows as oppressive as the heat. Ghostly voices echo in the dimness. Daniel listens closely, scans the shadows, glimpsing fragments of poverty. Giovanni turns to him:

"You've never been here, I take it? Welcome to Algeria. Don't worry, it had the same effect on me. When you come from a European city, it's a shock. You can see why they want to get rid of us, can't you? It's like some fat bloke sitting on your chest. First you

312

feel like you're suffocating, you think you're going to die, then you try to get him off you by any means necessary."

"Where are we going?"

"To a friend's place. Well . . . a bloke whose address I was given, and who might be able to help me get out of here. I met him last month, when I came here with the lieutenant, you remember, that time when we were on leave almost the whole day?"

"Are you serious? You're really going to desert?"

"I'm not going to fight against these people. We would do the same if we were in their place. We *did* the same, during the Resistance. You of all people should understand that."

Always that bite in his heart. Daniel tries to think how to reply.

"They'll sentence you to death."

"They already have. We've all been sentenced to death. Only difference is we don't know if or when we'll be executed. It's a slaughterhouse, and it's time for us lambs to scarper. It could be you, me, anyone in a uniform. Death strikes at random – you don't know why, or who will get hit. Well, except for all those fucking colonists and those jumped-up whites who think they can make themselves at home in someone else's country. Anyway, if they want to sentence me, they'll have to catch me first. I kind of think they've got bigger fish to fry."

A barrow creaks towards them, a man bent double between the two handles, with a whole mess of objects piled on top of the platform: chairs, crates of vegetables, cloth bundles and a cat lying stretched out, indifferent to the barrow's vibrations, unmoving, perhaps dead. The street is so narrow that they have to stand in a doorway to let this swaying load pass. The man pushing the barrow is tiny and old, not an ounce of fat on him, his arms wiry and his fists wrapped round with rope that is tied to the wooden handles. He does not look up at them. He spits in front of his feet as he passes them. Daniel watches him move slowly away, limping because one leg is shorter than the other, even more wobbly than his barrow.

Giovanni grabs Daniel's sleeve. Breaks into a jog. "Nearly there."

They turn right outside a carpenter's workshop. The smell of wood. A few planks leaning against a wall, some pale shavings on the floor. A green door, a narrow two-storey house. It looks like a little tower, stuck there. They knock three times and a woman opens the door almost instantly. Her round face is tattooed with blue dotted lines, her eyes agleam in the darkness are ringed with mascara. She wears a richly brocaded scarf on her head. Seeing the two uniforms, she instinctively takes a step back and half closes the door.

"What do you want?"

"I'm Giovanni. I've come to see Robert. I came last month. Giovanni the soldier. Delsart sent me."

The door closes. Giovanni gives Daniel a reassuring smile then hides his embarrassment by staring up at the building's façade. Silence. A bird singing somewhere trills excitedly in the leaden air.

"Come in, please," says the woman, opening the door again.

She bats her eyelids, her gaze golden.

As they enter the gloomy hallway, she glances around at the street outside. In front of them, the figure of a short, sturdy man appears against the light of a doorway.

"Who's that?" he asks without moving.

Giovanni puts a hand on Daniel's shoulder.

"A *copain*. An *ami*, I should say. You can trust him."

Still the man doesn't move. They stare at each other in this hallway, shadow to shadow. The woman stands behind the soldiers, hands concealed in the folds of her dress.

"It's alright, Chadia. You can come. It'll be O.K."

The woman squeezes between Daniel and the wall. She gives something to the man that they can't see. Then they guess what it is when he holds the object against his thigh. A revolver.

"Move forward," says the man. "We'll sit in here."

They follow him to a tiled patio filled with greenery and flowers. It is like being at the bottom of a well, with a breath of coolness and the sounds of water, invisible.

"We have to be back in an hour," says Giovanni.

The man puts the revolver in his pocket and sits on a wicker chair, inviting his guests to take two leather pouffes.

"It's nothing against you," the man tells Daniel. "But there are security instructions I have to follow, and I don't really want this house to attract notice because there are too many soldiers coming to it. It's my father's house. They don't know the address. Well . . . not yet. It would be impossible in my house; they have already been there three times. Anyway, what's done is done . . . My name is Robert Autin. That's not a secret. I'm a maths teacher at the secondary school; everyone knows me in this city. But you have not been here, and you do not know who I am. Understood? Never breathe a word of this. To anyone. Can you understand that? You have to realise that a different aspect of the war is being fought here, and in other places, far from the military operations."

Deep, curt voice. Robert stares unblinkingly at Daniel, eyes wide, and Daniel does not move, holds his gaze, heart racing, breath short, and he nods and whispers, "Yes, monsieur." Robert lights an American cigarette and hands them the packet. They smoke in silence for a moment, then Robert stands up.

"I'm going to get us something to drink. So, have you made your decision?"

"Yes," says Giovanni. "As soon as possible."

"They're not keen on deserters, you know."

He disappears behind a door carved in dark wood. Silence falls again.

"Who's not keen?" Daniel asks.

"The Party. They say we should stay in our units and undermine the officers, try to change the minds of our fellow conscripts, because they're workers, farmers, and we should always stand side

315

by side with the people. And deserting is always connected with cowardice, so it's supposedly frowned upon. But I don't care about all that. I feel like a coward here anyway. I'm scared of the *fells*, scared of the other squaddies, I'm even scared of myself. I don't know my own mind anymore. They might convince me to do anything. That's what they want. Don't forget what they said during training: 'When you've seen your friends get their throats cut, and their balls stuffed in their mouths, you'll know why you're fighting in Algeria.' You remember all their speeches, their propaganda? The photos they showed us of ambushes, corpses? You remember the things the others said? I've seen enough, I've heard enough. I'd rather hide in a rat-infested hole until the war is over than take part in this shit. This has fuck-all to do with me. And I don't understand . . ."

Robert returns, carrying a tray: three little ornamented glasses, a teapot, a carafe of water.

They fill the glasses with water. A dull heat falls on their shoulders from the square of milky sky hanging above them. Daniel can feel his shirt glued to his back with sweat.

"So, how is Delsart?" Robert asks. "Still laid up?"

"Yeah, he can't get out of bed now, because of his gammy leg."

Giovanni turns to Daniel.

"Delsart is my uncle, you know: my mother's brother. He got a bullet in his leg in '47 during the miners' strike. He's the leader of the local branch of the Party."

"I knew him when I was a primary school teacher near Lens," Robert Autin explains. "Are you in the Party too?"

"I'm not. My sister's in the Young Communists. And the Communist Students, I think. And my parents are, but they don't go to many meetings."

Giovanni and Autin say nothing, both looking at him with the same smile of fake indulgence, or perhaps pity.

"Well, anyway," he adds, "I agree with what it stands for."

Autin nods, then nimbly serves tea, the spout floating high

above the glasses, making a gurgling sound as they are filled.

"Delsart's fine," says Giovanni abruptly. "I got a letter from him last week. He can't say much – you never know who might read it. He's continuing to fight against the war though, back there. Aragon went to Lille the other day apparently; my uncle got a book signed for me. Can you believe it? He wouldn't tell me what Aragon wrote. He'd told him that I was here, in Algeria:

Everything changed pole and shoulder
Was the play funny or not?
If I didn't play my role well
That's because I didn't understand it at all."

"What are you on about?"

"It's Aragon. From *The Unfinished Novel*. That describes what I'm feeling, more or less."

Autin seems to digest the lines of verse, his glass hot in his hand. He sets it down suddenly.

"Well . . . That's very nice, but you won't be reading his inscription tomorrow, you know. It could take a long time – it all depends on the network. Ideally, you wouldn't come back from your first leave. That way, you wouldn't have to cross the whole of Algeria and risk getting arrested. I'll see what I can do about fake I.D., but it's not a sure thing. Everyone's suspicious these days. The A.L.N. lot don't even trust each other. We'll try to get you a fake leave. By the time they check it out – if they even bother – you'll be in Paris. That's not really what it's for, but never mind. You call here. If I don't answer, Chadia will tell you about the meeting, your contact, and all that. You must follow instructions. No more than ten minutes in the meeting place. You go back again the next day, same time. You can stay the night at the Hôtel de Constantine, on rue de la Victoire. Ask for Achille, and say I sent you. And don't hang around in the streets after eight at night. Got it?"

Above them, suddenly, the cries of swifts scratch the silence. Daniel looks up, heart pounding, mouth dry. He sees them trace their crazy geometry on the small patch of sky. Giovanni looks at his watch and stands up.

"We have to go."

Autin leads them back to the door, glances both ways into the street, then pushes them outside. He wishes them good luck and the bolt snaps in place immediately afterwards. They practically run through the streets, which are gradually filling with children and women. Old men sit outside their front doors smoking, and the sweet smell of tobacco sometimes accompanies the two soldiers for a few paces. Daniel feels dozens of eyes staring at him, hears discreet laughter and words he does not understand. Algeria. They sprint, heads down. It's gone four, and they're due to leave at half past. In the European part of the city, they melt into the crowds wandering past shop windows as the shopkeepers lift up the metal shutters, they pass café terraces filled with customers, overhear the hum of conversations.

They find the others waiting in the shade, near the vehicles. The drivers, who have not had any time off, sit further off, talking to a mechanic with greasy hands, his uniform stained with engine oil in a sort of customised camouflage. Baltard and Bernier, the caporal, are still joking about their visit to the brothel. They say they were thrown out in the end because they kept wanting more and more, dicks still hard as rocks. They could have screwed every *fatma*[32] in the whorehouse. They were ready to spend all their savings just to see if their cocks could hold out long enough for them to try them all. They make gestures as they speak, and it looks as if they're getting their hard-ons mixed up with machine guns. "You should have come with us," they tell Daniel, "instead of going off with him like a pair of poofters." Daniel says nothing. Some others, listening to all this, start to sulk: they got lost in the Arab part of the city and never found the bordello they'd been recommended.

"Fucking hell," says Meyran, an old man, only six months from

32 Slang French term for an Arab woman.

the end of his service. "So we finally sat down on this terrace and started boozing, so we could cool off our nuts. I feel like I've got a metal helmet on now and I'm shooting jizz all over my insides! And Peyrou, he's had so many beers that he has to stop every fifty metres so he can piss. He's like a dog, spraying it on lamp posts. He'd better leave his dick hanging out his pants on the way back, just in case! He could flood a wadi, that fucker! Ah, I bet that fucking whorehouse doesn't even exist! It was this Polish bloke from the Foreign Legion who gave me the address when I was in Ghrib, last January, on my way back from a mission. I bet that bastard was just having a laugh."

"How is that even fucking possible?" the caporal asks.

Everyone laughs. Meyran leans back against a jeep and grips the bridge of his nose between a finger and thumb.

"Oh, fuck," he says. "I'm going to crash out in the back of the truck. I hope I don't shit myself!"

His two mates nod their agreement so slowly it looks as if their skulls are filled with molten lead. The lieutenant crosses the court-yard and they all stand a little taller, smoothing the creases in their uniforms, pinching their cheeks to sober themselves up.

They climb into the vehicles more slowly than they did this morning, holding their kit bags, their weapons, and leaning on them as they sit down, bending over and collapsing, dazed, practically falling asleep already, and Daniel and Giovanni grit their teeth and smile as the yellowing sky moves past above them, filled with the screams of swifts flying through the hot air.

22

I watched Bordeaux grow larger through the iron girders of the railway bridge and my heart sped up. Crouching darkly by the Garonne under its pinkish scab of roofs. A bitter sob got stuck in my throat when I saw the perfect line of black façades, the watery gap of place de la Bourse, the dark trenches of streets sinking into the city. The river, still muddy, made motionless by high tide under the grey sky, looked like a monstrous dirt road. And the port. The boats moored along the docks, near the warehouses, bristling with masts, below cranes that leaned over or stood up straight like flick-knives. I watched all this with my face stuck to the glass like a curious kid, desperate to guess what he'll see next.

A woman sitting opposite me watched me, surprised, and when our eyes met she gave me a brief smile, perhaps amused by the stupefied, dazed expression on my face and the ghostly pallor of my skin, because I felt as if all the blood had suddenly drained from my body, leaving me empty and frozen on that leatherette seat.

The train braked and I felt the force pushing against my back. The screech of steel made the people on the platform turn away. One kid put his hands over his ears and his mother leaned towards him, laughing. The people around me stood up and began picking up their things from the luggage racks. They got in each other's way, muttered apologies. I helped the woman who had smiled at me to get down her enormous suitcase and I wondered how someone so frail could lug such a massive weight around. When I put it down, she lifted up the bag without any apparent effort and breathed a quick thank-you before leaving the carriage. I waited until I was alone to grab the large sailor bag that a friend had given me in Paris. Inside I had crammed everything I owned: some clothes, three books, my notebooks and a brand-new toilet bag that I'd bought just before leaving. I had left the key to my apartment on rue Beccaria with a neighbour, Gaston – a sad, sweet old man who lived alone with two cats and a few memories – and a month's rent in cash on the kitchen table. He had promised me he would take care of everything. I had given him my radio, along with about a hundred detective novels that lined the wobbly bookshelves in the entrance hall. He said he would read them and think about me, because he thought I looked a bit like those men you sometimes see in those kinds of stories about gangsters and cops.

He held me in his thin arms and then I left. I walked to the station so I could see and feel Paris around me once again, probably for the last time, and I stopped on the pont d'Austerlitz in spite of the north wind blowing over the Seine that whistled in my ears. I looked out at the two banks, the Ile Saint-Louis and the two arms of the river, and I went over the map in my head, working out the places where my friends lived, the places I had been happy, almost despite myself, when I'd had to start living again. I let the faces stream past. The smiles. The voices, mingling. Hélène. Suzanne. A woman came over from the other end of the bridge, tall and slender, and the wind blew her dress and her badly buttoned raincoat around her.

I fled towards the station before she could start dancing.

"Me? I dance."

As soon as the train set off, I closed my eyes. I did not want to watch this city disappear behind me, sucked inexorably backwards by our speed. I listened to the wheels hammering against the rails, more and more quickly. I let myself be rocked by the abrupt jolts as we went over the points, and I imagined the landscape of roads, the greyness of the ballast and iron, the handcars stopped against the bumpers, the rusting, abandoned freight cars at the end of a siding.

Once, when we were first getting to know each other, Suzanne had arranged to meet me on a bridge above the railway tracks of the gare du Nord, without telling me why. And, as it was very close to a dance where we were headed, I had not asked. She arrived carrying a bouquet of flowers and we watched the trains go past, and I'd started messing around, mooing like a cow, so she put her hand on my arm to make me shut up and then told me that her father, a railway worker, used to take her on his train sometimes, before the war, when he was coming here. He was arrested in '43. Died during a Gestapo interrogation. Then she stopped talking, and we stayed there for a while, shoulder to shoulder, not saying anything, watching the converging lines of the rails shining in the sun, all that grey or reddish gravel where nothing grew, and I found it all so horribly sad. "You might have come to terms with all that and be able to laugh about it, but not me," she said softly. Then she threw her bouquet on the empty flatbed of a slowly moving freight car and we went, hand in hand, to meet our friends.

"We left from the gare de l'Est," I told her after a moment. "And I haven't come to terms with anything."

I walked more quickly, leaving her behind me. I walked around Paris for two hours, in tears. I don't know how I ended up on the pont au Change, dripping with sweat, my teeth chattering. She and I never talked about that again, afterwards.

When I looked through the window again, I saw a whole host of houses and shacks, gardens with drooping fences and listing huts, meagre hovels with crooked chimneys blowing threads of black smoke into the air, and further off the broken line of factory roofs. It was April, and everywhere this grey misery was disguised and brightened by pale green bushes and hedges.

Paris did not want to let me go; it clung to my legs, it pulled at my arms. Familiar, friendly voices whispered inside my head: "We're still there and we'll live for a long time. Don't leave us – you'll forget us!" But I forgot nothing, forgot no-one. That was my torture, perhaps my punishment. My life was behind me, overcrowded with shadows I had abandoned, always fleeing, eluding, out of indecisiveness and cowardice. For the first time, I was consciously moving towards something; I had made a choice; I had a plan that I would see through to the end, an objective that I would destroy once I had achieved it. So perhaps the tormented shadows that pursued me would melt away, sated or appeased. Or I would have to disappear in order to see them again, though I did not believe in heaven or any kind of redemption. I did not believe in anything that might console me.

I tried to sleep, to read. Most of the time I watched the landscape rush past, flat and colourless beneath rainy skies. The cities horrified me, impenetrable and ugly. Hostile. Slouching beasts digesting their ration of human flesh. I wondered if Bordeaux would inspire me with the same fear, if my memories would be enough to guide me through its labyrinth.

I lifted my bag onto my shoulder and it seemed heavier than before. Locomotives snorted under the high steel framework, and trains braked with metallic shrieks. I walked towards the exit amid the small silent herd of hurrying travellers, weaving between reunited families and lovers, kissing and holding hands. Outside, I stopped under the glass roof to look around and sniff the air. The sky was heavy with charcoal-grey rainclouds, patches of deep blue showing through in between. Westerly wind. Gusts of lukewarm rain. I braced myself and began to walk blindly through the streets.

I didn't sleep that night. I had found a reasonably well-kept hotel near the place de la Victoire. The ground-floor room was tiny and its window looked out onto a narrow courtyard sunk in permanent darkness. I went to bed straight away, fully dressed, and lay there in the blackness listening to the rumble of pipes, the sly creaking of doors opening and closing very softly, as if people were sneaking around. It wasn't late; I could have gone for a walk up rue Sainte-Catherine, sharing the pavements with the crowd that was still undoubtedly meandering past the shop windows; I could have had a drink in the place de la Comédie, wandered over to the docks, but I felt a fugitive's fear and didn't even dare go out for a snack in the café across the road. I felt sure that everyone would recognise me, that all eyes would turn to me as towards an intruder, an outcast. Like in those stories where an ill-fated son or a disgraced husband, whom everyone thought dead, returns to the village years later and feels the eyes of everyone he used to know planted in him like pins.

But who would know me now? Who would remember me? And anyway, so many of us had been sent over there to die that no-one would pay any attention to this belated homecoming. People's memories were already haunted by too many ghosts: who would believe in a revenant?

I devised strategies. I imagined all the sufferings I could inflict on Albert Darlac. I could kidnap him – how, I didn't know yet – and take him to a remote place where I could torture him for a long time before letting him die of hunger and thirst, tied to a tree, or nailed to a table. Where I could stare into his terror-crazed eyes before abandoning him there. I could simply shoot him in the middle of the street or in his car. Blow his head off with a shotgun after approaching him and saying, "Hello, remember me? And remember Olga too?" My mind spun with images of horror. Blood, flesh and brains. Screams and supplications.

But other images became mixed up with the ones I was inventing. I had seen everything it was possible to do to a human being. I had seen the executioners at work. That tranquil hatred, as natural as breathing.

I was not tranquil at all, and sometimes even breathing was hard.

Around six in the morning, I went out. I would have liked to feel out of place, surprised. But all I saw were the same pavements cluttered with rubbish bins, the same blackish cobblestones, barely even gleaming in the feeble glow of the street lights. This city has always been so sad. My footsteps led me to the Marché des Capucins, already swarming with people at that hour, the air filled with cries and complaints. Nothing had changed. The same smells, the same voices. I went into a café where I often used to go with Abel before the war to eat something before we went home, and I ordered breakfast from the owner: still the same man, tall and broad-shouldered, but fatter and older now, though still lively and supple like a boxer, his eyes alert, watching over the waiter, looking out for new faces amid the crush of regulars. As he brought me my meal, he smiled at me, and I responded with a nod and a smile of my own, and I thought in that moment that he had recognised me. But no: he asked me to pay straight away, and he joked around with a man at the other end of the room while he waited for me to find the right change. Then he turned his back on me without another word.

It was daylight outside by the time I left. I walked the streets like a foreigner in a city that I knew by heart and that towered over me, silent and grey and indifferent. Everywhere I went I was assailed with visions, memories, voices. I thought I would gradually go mad, that in the end I would talk only to the dead or to the shadows that accompanied me, but I continued wandering the streets and courtyards, looking into eyes that didn't see me, glimpsing figures that seemed familiar to me. The places I had lived, the bars I'd haunted for nights on end, where I'd wasted all that time . . . they were all there, almost unchanged, and my memory was now just a constant buzzing. It built into a migraine, and I entered a café at random, practically collapsing onto a seat and ordering a mineral water.

It was nearly noon. A shiver ran right through my body. I felt as if I was drowning in myself. So I did what people usually do when they're drowning: I struggled for air.

There was a telephone directory next to the phone, on the counter. I opened it and halfway down a page found Abel's number. I hadn't dared call him from Paris. I had always been afraid to hear his voice – or worse, to hear nothing at the other end of the line but an oppressive silence filled with bitterness and reproach.

"Jean" was all he said, after I called him. His voice sounded breath-less and distant, half lost in static crackle. "Of course, come."

He lived in a bungalow in the Saint-Augustin quarter. I heard a limping footstep coming towards the door and then a small, pale, thin man, eyes sunk deep in their sockets, his few grey hairs slicked back-wards, was staring at me from the doorway. I must have looked stupid or frightened, standing there in front of that tottering figure, that absent gaze, because he said to me, "Hard to recognise each other, isn't it? But I know where you've been and you already know where I'm going."

He invited me into the hallway and said, "At the end, on the right." I heard his felt slippers shuffling over the tiled floor. I entered a living room that gave on to a jardin de curé [33] where the sun was enlivening a few spring colours. He asked me if I wanted anything to drink and, without waiting for a response, he disappeared into what must have been the kitchen and came back holding a bottle of white and two glasses.

"Sauternes, 1933. I opened it last night."

He poured the wine and finally looked at me. He smiled and I tried to see the face I remembered in his drawn features, the skin so tight to his protruding bones that it looked in danger of tearing.

"What should we drink to?"

"Your health?" I suggested.

He shrugged.

"Christ, no. Too bitter. To your return . . ."

"What's the matter with you?"

"Cancer," he said, tapping his chest. I'm falling to pieces in here. But don't worry about me . . ."

We drank in silence, glancing at each other over our glasses. Abel clicked his tongue.

"Not bad, is it?"

I nodded. I didn't care about his wine. We could hear birds chirping through the half-open French window. I stared at Abel, eaten alive by disease, and I still couldn't remember his full face, his lively eyes, the vivacity of his gestures. Then he leaned towards me and looked straight in my eyes and the hardness of that stare was painful.

"And Olga?"

I thought my heart was going to explode. I sucked in a mouthful of air and breathed "No".

He sat back in his chair and turned his face towards the light that was flooding the garden. He wiped his eyes with the back of his hand. He told me he would have preferred it if I hadn't come back. Especially just to tell him that.

"You thought I was dead . . . That both of us were dead, didn't you?"

33 An enclosed garden combining vegetables, fruit and herbs with flowers, traditionally grown for decorating the church altar.

He put his glass down, poured himself more wine.

"It's not the same thing. Sometimes it's better not to know. But since you're here . . ."

So I told him. Olga had fallen ill in Drancy. A nasty cough that tore at her throat. A fever that wouldn't abate. Then three days on the train. We held each other close and talked like we'd never talked before. I felt as if I were recapturing all those years that I had evaded, fled from. The years when I had cheated on her. She said we were going to make it, now that we had been able to talk about all that. That we would find Daniel again, grown older, and that life would start again. We remained locked in an embrace. She let herself fall against me, exhausted. I could feel the sick heat of her body on mine, the fever that made her tremble and shake. And still our sleepless words, her mouth on my neck, my lips in her hair. The small space I managed to clear for her so she could sit down and sleep for a while. And the arrival at the camp, the S.S. selection process. Her tired eyes that spent a long time looking for me, without finding me.

Out of breath, I stopped talking. Birds were singing in the garden. That carefree life took me by surprise. I felt as if I had just been cured of deafness, as if I had emerged from a glass cage. Abel stared at me with his dark eyes that shone from the depths of his face. He coughed, and spat into a handkerchief. Tears ran down his cheeks while he tried to catch his breath. He asked me why I had waited so long to come back. He said, "And Daniel?" He spoke aloud all those questions that had been lacerating my mind for years, questions to which I had no answers. Perhaps that was what they call the moment of truth.

"How could I? I didn't do anything for them. Wasn't even capable of protecting them. Darlac had promised that he'd warn me; he knew there was going to be another round-up. And I believed him. And I kept playing cards and running after women as if everything was fine. Olga and my son would sleep in their clothes for fear of being arrested in the middle of the night and I would get angry with them when I got home and saw that. Unbelievable, isn't it?"

327

"*So you think time will just wipe away your sins? Why exactly did you come back?*"

"*I knew you'd say that.*"

I was about to continue, but he lifted his hand to silence me.

"*What I had to say to you, I told you back then. About Olga, about the kid. You know perfectly well what I thought of you: you were just a womaniser, a gambler. An insignificant little shit. I told you that, didn't I? You weren't very happy about it, usually. You'd get all angry and red-faced. Or you'd swear that you were going to turn over a new leaf. And you were so full of yourself, the cock of the walk, so proud of your supposed friendship with Darlac. I used to meet him in Andernos, just to keep him at a distance from my business: he knew what I did, and I knew what he was: a cunt of a cop with no morals at all. But I wasn't worth the bother for him, even if he got me later on. And you believed that he would protect you. And you fell for his cop bullshit cos he wiped out your gambling debts by busting anyone who you owed money? I warned you about that too, didn't I? And when the wind changed, and he went over to the other side, I told you to be careful, didn't I? For Olga and the kid . . . I wasn't much better, but I could see beauty in other people . . . and I don't just mean a pretty face, I mean whatever was precious inside them. Whatever was priceless. I used to rip off twats and bastards: I could spot them a mile off, remember. But I could recognise good people like that too. And Olga was undoubtedly one of the best people I ever knew. And I hated you for treating her the way you did, with your whores and all the worthless tarts you used to fuck on the sly. I should have beaten the shit out of you.*"

He stopped, almost panting. Spots of colour had appeared on his grey cheeks. His hands were trembling with rage.

I stood up. It was a knockout. I had no reply for any of that.

"*And then you come back to tell me that Olga's dead . . . It's the living you should embrace. You live with your dead, with all the people you saw die in Poland . . . But what's the point? The dead never come back. Ghosts are only good for books or films.*"

"I live with whoever I can. I didn't come back to whine or to hear you lecture me. You don't know what I feel, you don't know what I went through over there. You can't know. I came back for Darlac. It's all I've been thinking about for months."

He laughed so hard he started to choke, and was overcome by another coughing fit.

"What do you want? To kill him? Put a bullet in his head? What would that change? There are dozens of cops in Bordeaux who slipped through the net. They caught Poinsot and some of those bastards who worked for him, but the others? And that's without even mentioning the prefects and their underlings, all those common or garden shits who served the Krauts. Darlac's commissaire now. He rules half the city. Untouchable. If you want to be a righter of wrongs, you're going to need weapons and ammo."

"I'm not a righter of wrongs. I couldn't care less about justice. I want Darlac."

"What about your son? You know you have a son?"

I didn't know if I was still his father. I didn't even feel I had the right to talk about him. For him, I was dead, and it was undoubtedly better that way.

"I wouldn't even dare approach him."

Abel struggled to his feet. His legs wobbled slightly and he faced me and stared into my eyes. He said there was no point discussing any of this. He told me he'd done what he had to do: he'd helped Maurice get the little boy down off the roof, as soon as the neighbours had been able to warn him. He drove the car, armed just in case. Afterwards he'd taken him to Maurice and Roselyne's house. I'd only ever met them four or five times. The way they lived their lives was so different to mine. Olga and Roselyne worked together at the factory; they were friends, they thought the same way. They didn't like me either. I think they were making an effort for Olga, who probably hoped I would change, that I would become like them. Abel gave me their address, in Bacalan, over that way, beyond the wet dock, then he walked over to the door. When he

329

opened it, he offered me his hand. I went to shake it. It was bone-dry and extremely hot. I noticed that his forehead was glistening with sweat. I walked down the two steps to the pavement and turned back to face him. He was leaning against the door frame, staring vacantly towards the end of the street.

"About Darlac," he said, "I know a cop who's worked with him for a long time. Maybe you remember him? You must have seen him occasionally back then; he was always hanging around Darlac, looking conspiratorial. He's a bastard, but not as bad as the others cos he chose the right side during the Occupation. He's got scores to settle with Darlac. Detective Mazeau, he's called. Ask to speak to him, and tell him I sent you. He owes me. I don't know what he'll be able to do, but at least he can fill you in. It's up to you what happens after that. And now, forget me."

Mazeau. I found it hard to remember what he looked like. And then it came back to me. A tall man with pale eyes and chestnut hair, fearful-looking, shifty, who would straighten up whenever he was around his boss, Darlac.

I started to thank Abel, but he had already closed the door. I stood there for a while, unsure what to do, my mind empty, dazed by the sunlight that poured down on the street. I had probably never felt so alone in my life. Even my ghosts, as Abel called them, had left me. I knew they weren't far away, were still watching me, but I could no longer feel them pressed around me, whispering. So I started walking, driven onward by a sort of dizziness that threatened with every step to send me hurtling to the ground.

23

It never rains but it pours. Commissaire Darlac thinks about this pearl of popular wisdom – not the kind of wisdom he's ever given much of a toss about. But all night, after being woken by madame's gentle snoring, he has been absorbed by meditations over the validity of clichés. This is about as philosophical as he ever gets. Tonight he surprises himself by carefully weighing up the meaning of each word, contemplating abstractions, and this makes him feel as if he is rising above the mundane. It also gives him a gnawing migraine that makes his head heavy and sometimes splits it with searing pain, forcing him to close his eyes and ball his fists with the urge to kill someone.

So Jean Delbos is back, as an avenging angel. Back from the dead. So the ghost that had seemed to be stalking him a few weeks ago is real. And if he doesn't do something, Darlac knows that sooner or later the spectre will appear one night at the foot of his bed pointing a gun at him, or holding a petrol can in one hand and a match in the other. The superintendent understands why, of course. But if every person he'd betrayed came back to demand justice, there'd be a queue snaking out to the pavement. And if the dead joined in too . . . well, then he'd just have to find a way to kill them all a second time.

On top of that, Francis has been unresponsive for the past week. Not answering his phone. Not at home. No trace of him in the places he usually hangs out with his whores. No-one knows anything – not the fences he does business with, not the girls who work for him down on the docks or in the centre of town. The clowns propping up the bars don't know either. Darlac gave one of them – René Tauzin, aka the Cyclops – a good going-over because he seemed to be hiding something, but it got him nowhere. He threatened to gouge out his other eye, to nick him for pimping and drug-dealing, because that pathetic wretch dabbles in powders and exotic herbs that he palms off on the girls and on a handful of rich bastards who picked up the habit in the colonies. But . . . nothing.

One who's come back, the other who's disappeared. Darlac doesn't know if he should be looking for a link in all this coming and going. All he knows is that you solve your problems one after another. Or eliminate them.

For now, stunned by the rhythmic throbbing of every painful artery in his brain, he is resting against the side of a front-wheel drive, smiling as he watches Mesplet, the owner of this garage with its stink of oil and petrol, its chaos of cars and spare parts and tyres stacked in teetering piles ready to collapse on any careless visitor. He hates this dark, grimy disorder almost as much as he hates the impassive man who stands in front of him, arms crossed, leaning on the door of a Renault Juvaquatre, this man who has been lying to him for the past ten minutes.

"So you maintain that Delbos has not been here? That he hasn't tried to get in touch with his son?"

"I already told you."

"You hung around with him in '43, you gave his son a job, and you expect me to swallow that?"

"Swallow what you want, I don't care. Me and Maurice and Roselyne, we were friends with Olga, not him, cos of the union and all that. The factory brings people together, you know. Well, no, obviously you don't know . . . But Jean wasn't one of us. He was a great bloke to have a laugh with, but he didn't take anything seriously, apart from his little business deals. He never even took his wife seriously, or his kid, later on. We liked him well enough, but we didn't really know him. We couldn't understand what Olga saw in him. Well, I mean, he was a good-looking chap of course . . . elegant and all that . . . Always cheerful, in a good mood. And apparently he was really good to her . . . That's what she used to say all the time anyway. Everyone knew he was cheating on her all over the place. Even she must have guessed. In fact, I reckon she knew, but she put up with it. We couldn't understand that. We thought that if Olga loved him that much, he couldn't be completely bad, but that's not enough to make him a friend. Anyway, my point is that he wouldn't be likely to come here for help."

"You realise that if I manage to prove that you've been protecting a criminal, I can get you locked up for ten years? You do realise that?"

Mesplet shrugs. He grabs a long screwdriver and bends over the Renault's engine. Darlac hears him swearing through gritted teeth, grunting with the strain.

The cop turns to Norbert, who is putting a bumper back on a Dauphine.

"What about your apprentice? Doesn't he have anything to tell me?"

Crouched in front of the car, the boy doesn't blink, but Darlac can tell that he has stopped moving, that he's waiting, not daring to turn around. The boss stands up, red-faced and breathless.

"Fuck off out of here. We have nothing to say to you. All that is in the past. Everyone thought Jean Delbos had died in the camps, and maybe it was better that way. Go look for him somewhere else."

Ignoring this, Darlac moves closer to Norbert. He picks up a hammer from the bonnet and bangs it hard against the metal, and the kid, as if knocked backwards by the noise, falls on his arse, dropping the bumper, and looks up, frightened, at the cop. Darlac hits the car again, twice. The steel shell caves in under the blows, and the entire car shakes, and he holds the hammer high in the air, ready to smash up something or someone. Claude takes a step forward, then stops. He tightens his grip on the screwdriver and his chest rises, probably trying to suck more air into his lungs, but he doesn't move.

"So, lad? Nothing to tell me? You want me to hit you in the face with this thing?"

The boy tries to see his boss, and finally gets to his feet. Shifty-eyed, fearful.

"Name and address?"

The cop writes it in his notebook.

"And you didn't see anything either, I suppose? You don't know anything?"

"No, I . . . The boss, he doesn't tell me anything. He's the one that talks to the customers. I don't know anything."

Darlac sniggers. He makes a sort of squealing noise that screws up his face and throws the hammer across the garage. Then he walks to the door, open wide on the street, and turns around:

"Alright! You know, I like it when people treat me like a fucking idiot. It makes me angry, and anger makes me sharper, it gives me energy. Understand? That's the way I am. Basically, I like it when people resist, at the beginning. Eh? Like the Resistance, Claude. Ring a bell? You know all about resistance, don't you? But what exactly can you resist? Like the bonnet of some old rust bucket – hit it with a hammer, and it starts to cave after the second blow. Hit it five times and the whole thing's smashed to pieces. Beyond repair! You twats will be hearing from me. And you're going to pay – you and all the others who are covering for this piece of shit. So long, and good luck. You'll fucking need it!"

His voice echoes under the iron framework and the two mechanics stand motionless, watching him walk towards his car, parked haphazardly on the kerb.

Behind the wheel, Darlac moans or wheezes or laughs. Even he can't tell what the sounds are as they come out of his mouth: the screeches and rumbles of an animal, cries of pure rage, as if it's about to smash open its own head because it's just been plunged into a vat of boiling water. So he winds down the windows, violently yanking at the handles, and waits at the end of the street behind a post van, and when it moves off he heads towards the station and charges into a crowd of nobodies carrying luggage and they yell and whine because he drove over their suitcases and he tells them to go fuck themselves. He screams at them to shut their traps, dickheads, bitches, fucking queers. He leaves behind him a wake of indignant cries and insults and as he turns into the cours de la Marne he sees a constable, looking dazed, eyes wide under the visor of his cap, thinking, should I?, lifting the whistle to his mouth, and then deciding to turn a blind eye because, after all, no-one got killed.

Darlac does not go home – he doesn't feel like meeting those dark blue eyes – so he calls her and says he's working, she says O.K., which means she couldn't care less, that it would be all the same to her if he was killed by a maniac wielding a kitchen knife, wading through the blood of his entire family. He hangs up, hissing insults, but it doesn't make him feel any better. Nothing can console him now for the glass wall that separates them: you betrayed me and we're both going to die, but you first.

He hangs around a few bars, sees a few ugly mugs that he knows, one of whom is on a *département* blacklist, and ends up eating some tepid, overcooked food, washed down with cheap wine, at the counter of a bar near the Saint-Pierre church and asking the owner if he's taking the piss, treating his customers to this kind of slop. When the man gets on his high horse, Darlac tells him who he is, what he is, and reminds him that his bar was shut for six months in '55 because six or seven of his waitresses were on the game and there were two pimps propping up his bar, one in the mornings, the other in the afternoons. Sure, but that's ancient history, the owner says. He's not involved in anything like that anymore; he learned his lesson the hard way, back then. Darlac knows that Crabos got back into the business on the sly, between two cancers, and dealt some drugs too, as a way of paying off his debts more quickly. The commissaire says that, if he gets a sniff of even the slightest thing wrong in this place, he'll order the team from Hygiene to come down and inspect him, and those weirdos always find something wrong when they want to, enough to justify disinfecting the whole hovel with flamethrowers, from the cellar to the roof. The owner stammers that there was a mistake in the kitchen – worse, that they were negligent – and the chef will hear about it, of that you can be sure, and then insists on offering him a coffee. Darlac leaves him to his percolator and walks out into the damp night.

An idea has been running through his head for a while now, so he decides to go and see what he can do about it. He thinks about that apprentice again, that little crankshaft wanker, who's either two-faced or chickenshit, he can't tell which. Probably both. The kind of man that can't withstand pain very long, so you can make him pass out or sell his own grandmother without too much effort. He's seen a few like that in his time, and they're easy to spot, these men who have a raw nerve somewhere or an open wound, so all you have to do is twist it a little or rub a bit of salt in it, and their will is instantly broken, every principle they've ever had instantly betrayed. On the docks he turns south, towards the station and then Bègles. He drives through the hesitant suburban night, scattered small islands of light under attack from obscure depths, and soon he is lost amid empty streets where the shadow of a cat sometimes slips by and vanishes.

At last he finds the place on his map, under the gleam of his torch. A cul-de-sac at the end of this street, a dead end in the labyrinth where he will find an infuriated Minotaur. A one-storey house with closed shutters, dark as a cave.

Darlac is about to lift the door knocker when he hears a woman screaming from inside, furniture banging against walls, and then a man yelling. He listens to this racket for a while, trying to picture the scene, not that it's difficult: a flurry of punches, some shoving, insults. The woman is probably lying on the floor, given the shrillness of her cries, perhaps protecting herself from the man's boots.

He bangs on the door so hard that a sudden and absolute silence falls inside the house. Nothing moves. All Darlac can hear above the moan of the wind is the tapping of an electricity cable or maybe a loose gutter. He knocks again. Four times. "Who the fuck's bothering us now?" the man yells from inside the house.

Darlac takes out his card as the bloke opens the door.

"Police."

He climbs the two front steps, pushes the door open all the way as the man takes a step back and enters the hallway without paying him any more attention.

"Hey! Hey!" the man complains. "Where do you think you're going like that?"

"I came to see your son, Norbert. Is he here?"

"Who are you?"

"Commissaire Darlac. You want to see my card again?"

Darlac keeps walking, but the man grabs him by the shoulder and forces him to turn around. He's a big bloke, slightly taller than Darlac, and he smells of wine. His waxy face gleams with sweated-out booze.

"You can't just barge into my house like that, you cop bastard! Get the fuck out of here now!"

A long-haired woman, eyes swollen from crying, leans against a door frame. She wears only a slip, with one strap torn off, so she has to constantly pull up her neckline in order to conceal her breast. She pats a blood-soaked handkerchief against her mouth and nose and watches the two men. Her arms are covered in bruises.

Darlac feels the man's hand tense on the shoulder of his jacket.

"Let go of me, and I'll explain."

"Fuck that. Get out of here."

The man lets him go though, all the same, and Darlac takes advantage of this fact to grab his pistol. The man recoils.

"Jesus," he says. "I didn't do anything."

Darlac moves closer to him and slams the gun barrel into the bridge of his nose, then smashes him over the skull with the butt. The man falls to his knees and Darlac hits him again, splitting his ear by using the pistol as a hammer. The man groans, his face streaming with blood which drips slowly onto the floor.

"Alright," says Darlac, leaning over him. "Now shut your stupid mouth and let me do my job. I'm not your fucking wife who you can beat like a dog whenever you've had a drink. Try that with me and I'll smash your fucking face in until your brain runs out your nose. Do you understand me, dickhead?"

Darlac stands up straight and turns to the woman.

"Is your son here?"

She doesn't have time to respond. Norbert appears behind her, holding a shawl that he drapes around her shoulders before pushing her gently into the kitchen. He looks indifferently at his father, who is moaning weakly on the ground. With a little nod, he takes a cigarette from his pocket and lights it, then starts smoking, never taking his eyes off the man on the floor. Darlac instantly grasps the rock-hard hatred lodged in this kid's heart.

"You know why I'm here?"

"For that bloke . . . the one you're looking for."

"Exactly. You know who it is?"

"I do now. You said it earlier. It's Daniel's father."

"That's right. His father, who came back from the camps in '45 and who, instead of coming here to find his son, stayed up in Paris to have a good time. He's wanted for several murders. You think that's normal, a father acting like that?"

Norbert looks down at his own father again.

"No," he says. "Daniel talks about him sometimes, but he says he doesn't remember much about him. Says he wouldn't even recognise him."

"Of course not. From what I know of this bloke, Jean Delbos, he was a gambler and a womaniser. Didn't give a shit about his wife and kid. So how could Daniel have any memory of him?"

Norbert nods his agreement.

"Why did you come here?"

Darlac leads him aside. They enter a small living room. The chairs are lying on the floor; Darlac picks them up and arranges them around the table.

"If this bloke, Jean Delbos – your mate's father – comes to see your boss, for whatever reason, call me. Here. My office number is on this card. My men will know where to find me if I'm not there when you call. Help me, and I'll help you."

"You'll help me? To do what?"

"Your father. That bastard lying on the floor out there. I'll file charges against him and you'll be rid of him for a long time. And you and your mother won't be afraid anymore. You understand? I was sickened by what I saw tonight. But it has to be quid pro quo. I'll have him called in tomorrow. Your mother will have to come in to press charges. It'll scare the shit out of him. He won't be so tough then. What do you think?"

"Sounds good to me."

Darlac holds out his hand, but Norbert seems to hesitate.

"There's a bloke who brought a motorbike in to be repaired. A Norton. I don't know if it's him. But the boss yelled at him and threw him out, twice. Anyway, maybe it isn't him. I'm just saying . . ."

Darlac conceals his triumph. It was so easy.

"Don't worry, lad. It probably isn't him. But keep your eyes peeled, and I'll keep my promise."

He holds out his hand again, as warmly as he can, and shakes the boy's, which is weak and cold, and he crushes it a bit, just so the kid knows who's in charge, so he knows that he could get hurt.

24

Same way back. And still the same dusty heat, even in the shady parts of the valleys. They drive more slowly as the two water trucks are full to the brim of water, which must already be hot and will probably taste of dirt and rust. Baltard is slumped over the machine gun, perhaps asleep, indifferent to the jolting movements of the caterpillar tracks. The path, which is beginning to meander now, is still paved but with occasional ruts that shake the men's bodies as they look around them, seeing nothing through the cloud of dust but the parched slopes of the hills on either side.

Daniel fights against sleep, his mind numbed by confused thoughts: a long daydream in which he imagines his first leave, his arrival in Bordeaux, the hugs and kisses, Irène's body held tight against his. In odd moments he regrets not having gone with the others to see the Arab whores, so he could ease this painful impatience, purge the brutality he senses within himself and keep only his purest desire for her. But he senses, he knows, that nothing is ever entirely pure, that part of it is always an exchange of bodily fluids, of odours, of grunts and moans, that love does not consist only of staring deep into each other's eyes and touching your fingertips together. He knows all this and he knows nothing, his knowledge restricted – as with all virgins of his age and gender – to what he's heard others say and what he's seen in magazines like the ones that used to circulate the barrack room during training. Reduced to tossing off as he tries to imagine what it will be like when he's the one doing those things and she's wriggling about and moaning. Virgin. To hear them talk, you'd think there weren't any in the platoon; listening to some of them, you have to wonder if they've *ever* been virgins. The lads talk about practically nothing else in the evenings, slouched over the tables in the mess hall, taking turns to recount their experiences, their heroic adventures, their greatest fucks, their most intensive bombardments. Licking, teasing, pumping, screwing, banging. Daniel listens to all this and feels as if he is hearing about work at a building site. It's all heavy lifting, all diggers and bulldozers. And it's not exactly a holiday for the girls either: they go from horse riding to active gynaecology, not forgetting the contortionist poses in the back seats of cars or in a corner of a factory changing room. Anonymous wombs, faceless pussies, cunts, cracks, holes, chasms, gash . . . Apparently there are even special things, but the man who's saying this suddenly stops mid-sentence, claiming that he really shouldn't talk about it like that, and the others push him for details – come on, fuck, you've said either too much or not enough – but no, the bloke suddenly acts all shy, blinking fast and looking down, no, lads, sorry, I prefer to keep that to myself.

Ooh, la-di-da, you big fucking wuss! I bet you finish yourself off with your hand, don't you?

Daniel laughs, daydreams, gets hard, listening to all of this. Wonders sometimes how it's even possible. True or imagined, these stories do everyone good. What they're talking about is life. Everyday, peacetime life. A local dance in a village hall. A girl, a paso doble or two, going out to smoke a fag in the summer night, slipping your hand under a corsage . . . Their eyes shine, and not only with lust. There are breathless silences after each lewd epic, and dreamy eyes that betray a tenderness that men never talk about to each other. Eyes lit up by the distant sweetness of civilian life, so much more beautiful seen from here, in these shitty quarters where they waste their best years in fear, hoping only that they won't be the next one to take a bullet, to step on a mine and leave their legs behind, to get their bollocks sliced off by *fellouzes* . . . All the shit they have to go through every day at home, the routine, the slow, gloomy weeks spent waiting for Saturday or for payday, are nothing, seen from here. They cling to the hips of girls they've screwed – or haven't

– like sailors clinging to lifebelts after a shipwreck in the middle of a storm-tossed ocean.

Amid the roar of the caterpillars and the rumble of the engines, they hardly even hear the explosion. But they see it straight away, above them: a cloud of black smoke rising through the air like a huge balloon before dissolving.

Daniel is thrown backwards with the others by the sudden braking, and for two or three seconds they are all entangled. Enough time to understand what's happening. Someone yells, "Mine! Mine!" and Daniel is surprised to hear the voice so clearly, then he realises that the engine has stopped. The half-track's front doors bang open and they hear men running, shouting, "Quick, quick, fuck's sake, come on!" He grabs his rifle and jumps out of the vehicle and the others follow him and there, crouched behind it, none of them understand, to start with, the meaning of that hammering on the metal body. Then, seeing the sparks on the road and realising that they're being shot at, they split in two to move forward, behind the water truck, and that's when they finally make out the sound of the gunshots, up there on the hillside to their left, on the shady slope scattered with bushes and boulders.

"Where are those cunts?" Baltard yells, behind the half-track's machine gun.

"Over there," says the caporal, with a vague wave. "They've got a machine gun. I just hope they don't have a mortar."

Baltard loads the gun then fires a few short bursts blindly, screaming insults at the enemy, and they see the bullets hit the hillside, producing little mushroom clouds of dust. The men hunch their shoulders round their heads. Daniel feels every gunshot like an unsuspected artery that is suddenly beating so hard it's about to burst.

"There! Under the trees! You can see the puffs of smoke! No, lower!"

The machine gun's bullets spray the top of the bush and vanish into the ground.

"Ammo! Give me ammo!"

"Go and open the crate for him," says the caporal to Giovanni. "You know where it is?"

Giovanni runs. Daniel follows him and leans on the bonnet of the armoured car to fire two cartridges at a rock where he saw something move. He hears Giovanni fire his sub-machine gun before climbing onto the platform. Peyrou and Meyran are lying on their bellies under the truck and firing their rifles pretty much at random. The machine gun rattles then stops then rattles again. Giovanni yells at the crate where the cartridge belts are stored. Between each burst of gunfire, they can hear the *fells* shouting from their hiding places.

"The lieutenant's been hit! Someone get him out of here!"

Daniel fires two shots, runs, gets down behind an embankment ploughed with bullet holes, and fires again. The jeep is thirty metres away, lying across the road, its front right side buckled over. He hears the machine gun hammering away behind him, and the smaller, almost pathetic shots of the M.A.S.-49s. When he gets there, he finds Ferrier, the driver, covered in sweat and blood, kneeling next to the lieutenant, behind the jeep. To start with, he does not understand what has happened. Then he sees the lieutenant's right trouser leg torn up, soaked with blood, and his face bone-white, big eyes full of tears staring up at him, mouth frozen in a terrified grimace. Daniel cannot see the lieutenant's foot. There is nothing left of the trouser leg but a few red tatters and for a few seconds he forgets to breathe because he can't get his head around the reality of the scene. He is about to ask what's happened to the rest of his leg, but a volley of bullets drums against the jeep, ricocheting loudly off the tarmac, so he throws himself to the ground and sees Charlin, who was the jeep's machine-gunner, lying sideways on the ground, gazing calmly at him, his head askew inside his helmet, with a deep blue gash in the middle of his forehead, as narrow and neat as if it had been chiselled.

"The radio?"

"Don't know," Ferrier pants. "Behind. Fuck, he's going to croak!"

Daniel jumps to the back of the lopsided jeep, the bonnet raised and twisted, the sheet steel puckered into sharp slats like razor blades. The windscreen is smashed and its frame bent. He crawls behind the machine gun, which swivels when his head bangs against its handle, and he shrinks behind the seats, pressing his body as low as possible when a burst of bullets hums past above his head. The lads fire back at the sparks of gunfire they see up on the hill, about a hundred metres away. He grabs the strap of the radio, wraps it around his wrist and gets out of there. But the radio is heavier than he expected and he is dragged back by its deadweight, unable to simply step across the jeep's platform to get back to safety. He throws his rifle on the ground, picks up the machine with both hands, groaning with the effort, and feels first a burning on his shoulder then a throb of pain deep in the flesh.

He falls face down on the ground and the radio crushes his wounded shoulder, and for a few seconds he doesn't move, mouth open, dust coating his tongue, trying to breathe, hoping that some strength will return to him. When he lifts his head again he can no longer hear – through the rumbling that pounds in his brain – the .50 on the half-track firing. Everything else has fallen silent, even the crackling of rifles and sub-machine guns. When he glances across the spare tyre at the hill where the attack came from, it seems to him that no sound has ever emerged from that rocky slope other than the silence of the wind. The caporal stands up and yells, "Cease fire!" and Baltard turns around, both hands still on the handles, eyes crazed, and stares at them all disbelievingly as they cautiously get to their feet, as if surprised to find them alive.

"They've pulled back, the bastards," says the caporal, scanning the hillside. "Peyrou, Meyran and Péret, go and see what's there. If we've wounded one of them, we can fry his balls to make him talk. Baltard, cover them, and don't fuck around."

He runs to the jeep and asks Daniel if he's alright: yeah, well, it's bleeding, it's in the muscle, a cut, like a knife wound. He goes over to the lieutenant, still being cradled by Ferrier as if he's a sick kid or a woman. Around this scruffy, bloody Pieta, propped up against a wheel, are scattered a sub-machine gun, two magazines, cartridge cases and blood, spreading in a corolla inside a rut in the path just in front of the two men.

Ferrier does not react when the caporal approaches and then crouches down. He examines the damaged leg, the cloth of the trousers stained not only with blood but with purplish-black diarrhoea.

"He can't stay there. Help me carry him."

The caporal takes one of the lieutenant's arms and drags him towards him, and Ferrier lets his hands drop to his thighs and watches the corpse move away from him and then tip over so suddenly that Bernier staggers under the weight and shouts "For fuck's sake, are you going to help me or what? We've got to lie him down somewhere!" So the soldier stands up and picks up the lieutenant's one remaining leg, turning his eyes away and breathing heavily with a sort of whine, as the two of them struggle to pick up the dead man properly without inflicting any further damage on his body.

Daniel turns to them helplessly, one hand pressed to the top of his arm to stop the blood spraying out, and he follows them to the water truck to where they half drag, half carry the lieutenant and gently lie him down. Then they stand for a few seconds contemplating the earth-coloured face with its badly closed eyes.

"O.K., what about the radio?" the caporal asks suddenly. "Does it work?"

He jogs towards the jeep and tips his helmet back when he gets there. He lifts up the radio set and puts it on the driver's seat. The men watch him fiddling with the buttons, then he starts speaking into the handset.

"Can you hear anything?" Ferrier asks.

Daniel shrugs. "What do you expect to hear?"

What they hear is water trickling and spurting onto the ground from the truck, which has been hit by bullets in several places. They go over there to wash their hands and faces and to fill their mouths and spit it out, and end up drinking it, shoving their heads under the jets and shaking themselves like dogs.

The three men who were sent up the slope return, almost at a run, out of breath, and they say, gesturing vaguely at the hillside, that there's a stiff up there, practically cut in two, it's so disgusting that Peyrou puked up all his beers and the other two nearly did the same. They console themselves by saying that it avenges the lieutenant – two *fells* for the price of one – and they should go back into town and drive around with him tied to the radiator grill of the half-track to show the locals that they'd had a good hunt. They force themselves to laugh, their faces pale and twisted, and they pull up their belts and wave their guns around, full of bravado, and then they do what the others are doing with the water, splashing it all over themselves, and soon their camouflage jackets are sticking to their skin and they bare their chests before seeing the lieutenant's body and suddenly falling silent.

At the moment when the caporal goes back to the jeep to call for help on the radio, they hear Baltard, still sitting behind his machine gun, yell, "Shit, lads! Quick!" Daniel rushes over.

Giovanni.

In spite of his wound, Daniel climbs onto the back of the half-track and finds his friend curled up in a ball, hands pressed to his stomach, with blood pooling beneath him.

"Hey, comrade! How are you?"

He forces a smile, puts a hand on his shoulder. Giovanni turns towards him, his face calm but streaming with sweat and tears.

"It hurts," he whispers. "The bastards."

Daniel tries to catch his gaze, which drifts vaguely between

346

blinks. He squeezes his shoulder more firmly and shakes him gently as if he's trying to wake him.

"We're going to get you out of here. You'll see. The caporal's calling for help. We just need to wait a bit."

Peyrou brings over a flask. Daniel trickles some water over Giovanni's face, and Giovanni opens his mouth and catches some on his tongue.

"Stomach wound," says Meyran. "He shouldn't drink."

The two of them lift Giovanni up and remove his shirt, then roll the rags up under his head to make him more comfortable. There are two holes above his navel, and blackish blood is slowly leaking from them. Sometimes he moans and they can see waves of pain trembling under his skin. Péret carries over a box marked with a red cross.

"I don't know what's in it," he says. "I found it under the seat, in the truck."

Meyran unpacks bandages, rolls of sticking plaster, a tourniquet. He opens a packet of compresses and soaks a few in alcohol.

"Watch out, this is going to burn. Hold tight."

He presses the compress onto the wound and Giovanni cries out and kicks, his boots thudding against the metal platform. With Daniel, they make a bandage to cover the wound. They are kneeling in the blood, which is starting to congeal in a brownish paste. They're still wearing their helmets, so sweat pours down their faces as they lean over their friend and trickles from their chins as if someone has just tipped a bowl full of water over their heads.

After that, Daniel cleans the wound in his shoulder, a deep cut that is pissing blood, and Meyran helps him bandage it tightly to staunch the flow.

"Does it hurt?"

He shakes his head, glancing down at Giovanni whose eyes are staring hazily into space.

"Where did you find the *fell*?"

"I'll come with you," says Péret, strapping his sub-machine gun to his shoulder. "It's up there, under the tree. I'll warn you though, it's not a pretty sight."

They climb up the hill, about a hundred metres. Tiny lizards scurry away from their footsteps, swishing the dry grass. Daniel turns back to look at the halted convoy. From there, it resembles a line of toys abandoned by some forgetful kid. The men come and go around the vehicles, like action figures in a game.

"Look. There he is, the son of a bitch."

At first all Daniel can see is a pair of feet in rubber boots, a trouser leg hitched up to reveal dark skin with black hairs. Then the body appears, with a line of red pulp across the belly, with grey patches on the surface. He moves closer to get a better view and tries to understand these shreds that lie in the hollow of an impossible crater in the man's abdomen. The hairs on Daniel's head stand up, so he takes off his helmet and rubs his hand over his skull, feeling a shiver of static under his fingers that starts running over his entire body.

"It was the .50 that got him," says Péret. "Fucking brutal, isn't it?"

Daniel crouches down and tries to search the corpse. He shoves his hands in trouser pockets damp with blood, finds a pack of tobacco and throws it away.

"What are you looking for? Can't you smell the shit? Come on, we don't want to hang about next to this thing."

Nothing in the other pockets. Daniel stands up again and searches the lines on the dead man's face – eyes half closed, lips curled back – for a hint of the life he once lived: the trace of a smile or a sparkle in his eye. And he wonders how old this man was. Eighteen? Twenty? But the dead man's face is just a pale, twisted mask; he is nothing now but an assemblage of meat and guts already starting to rot, brother or close cousin to the few corpses he has already seen in Algeria, petrified and grimacing. All dead men look

348

alike in war. Not like in the films, where they often appear well-rested, with just a spot or two of blood on their shirt or at the corner of their lips when it was really tough or cruel, so that you were almost relieved for them. And there's always some idiot there to say that kind of thing or to tear straight into the jungle to avenge his comrade's death against the elusive Japs or the Krauts solidly entrenched behind concrete walls or armoured cars. It has been a long time since he looked at the world through his foldable frame. These days, he is far more likely to stare through the scope of his rifle at the iridescent reflections cast by moving foliage, at targets, jam jars, the face of the *fell* behind his machine gun, concentrating on his own line of sight during the final seconds of his life.

Since Daniel doesn't move, Péret becomes impatient. He starts kicking stones, raising little clouds of dust.

"Shit, come on, let's go. Are you praying for him or what?"

Daniel wishes he could feel something. Hatred or disgust. Horror or contempt for this disembowelled *fellagha* who, just ten minutes earlier, had been trying to kill them. Down there in the valley, there's a dead lieutenant whose two kids will never see him again. And Charlin with a shard of steel in his head, a calm, silent, shy man who lived alone with his parents on their farm. And there's Giovanni, with two bullets in his belly, who would tear out his own guts if he could to be rid of the pain that is slowly killing him. He looks at this devastated body and sees nothing human in it. Only a carcass that is no longer even an enemy, that is no longer anything at all. Like roadkill.

They go back down and rejoin the others, who are paddling in the water that continues to pour from the truck. Daniel climbs in the half-track and kneels down next to Giovanni, who looks like he's asleep, mouth open and panting. His face is slick with sweat. The bandage is already saturated with blood and all around the wound the skin is marbled with evil-looking bruises. He whispers to him: it'll be alright. The chopper will be here soon.

The caporal is there, slumped on the metal bench. He keeps his eyes closed, head thrown back.

"So?"

"So what?"

"The stiff. Was it pretty?"

Daniel shrugs. "One less to worry about."

They can hear the others chatting further off. A door bangs shut. The caporal takes out a packet of Gitanes and hands it to Daniel. They smoke for a moment without saying anything.

"I can stay, if you like," says Daniel.

"Nah, it's alright. I should be there."

Daniel grabs a filthy rag and soaks it with water, pouring the contents of his flask over it. But it's warm, and it stinks of engine oil.

"It pisses me off, after how I insulted him earlier. I can't just leave him!"

Meyran is the first to hear it. He starts yelling, "Chopper's here!" and the men, who were all sitting in their vehicles, stunned by the silence whistling in their deafened eardrums, jump to the ground and scan the horizon. As soon as they see the Banana start to curve over the ridge, they begin waving their arms and shouting, until their voices are drowned out by the din of the rotors and the rising dust forces them to close their mouths and to squint, and to crouch down, instinctively, as if the blades might take their heads off.

Daniel stands up and waves too, then he bends over Giovanni to tell him, "Hear that? Straight to the hospital, then you're going home! They'll take that thing out of your belly in no time – it's just like an appendectomy!"

His friend smiles sadly and grips his hand. He tries to say something but the words get stuck in his mouth as his face is creased with pain. He squeezes Daniel's hand even tighter, then manages to stammer, "I've got nearly two red holes in the right side!" He closes his eyes, and Daniel frowns at him: "What did you say?"

Men in civvies emerge from the helicopter carrying doctor's bags. Daniel calls them over. "Quick!" he shouts.

Giovanni tries to lie on his side so he can curl up in pain. He moans, and Daniel jumps off the half-track to try and drag the stretcher-bearers over. But they are already running, and they yell through the noise and the dust, "Calm down, for fuck's sake, we're coming! It'll be O.K."

25

Three knocks at the door. Hard, fast, imperative. The police, André thinks. That's how cops knock, impatiently, and he imagines them out there on the landing, guns at the ready, listening for his footsteps. He goes to the window and sees nothing in the street: no vans or suspicious cars, no lookouts. Just in case, he asks who it is, and hears the voice of his landlord: "It's just me, Monsieur Ferrand."

The man enters as soon as he opens the door, without greeting him, without meeting his eye. He hands him the newspaper.

"This is about you, I think."

He taps a short news story on the front page with his index finger.

CRIMINAL ON A MOTORBIKE

André Vaillant, real name Jean Delbos, suspected of six murders committed in Bordeaux and the surrounding region, including those of Inspecteur Eugène Mazeau and his wife, drives a motorcycle, probably a Norton. The police, who are actively searching for this armed and dangerous individual, made this information public yesterday, in the hope that it will lead them to the suspect. Jean Delbos is about forty years old, and 180 cm tall, with a slim build. Anyone able to provide the police with useful information can call the central station or dial 17 .[34]

André looks up at Ferrand, who is watching him, hands in his pockets. He folds the newspaper and hands it back to him.

"So?"

"So I thought you should know."

34 The French equivalent of 999 at the time.

The man turns away, takes a few steps. Then he throws his newspaper on the table, near a notebook filled with small sloping handwriting.

"What are you writing?"

"Nothing . . . A detective novel."

The man laughs silently.

"You should have plenty of material . . . Can I read it? I love that, those noir thrillers. Especially written by a murderer."

André comes over to close the notebook and put it away in a drawer.

"Why did you kill those people?"

"I didn't kill the cop or his wife. The others, I . . ."

André falls silent. He stares at the man, who is motionless, impassive, hesitating over what he should do, strangely attracted, perhaps, by this killer who is front-page news. André knows he could take the pistol from under his pillow, get rid of the landlord to give himself time to flee. He could throw a sucker punch, knock him out. But this man just stands there, doing nothing, apparently waiting, and looking almost embarrassed, or maybe sad.

"It would take too long to explain, about the others."

"You were in the camps, is that right? They mentioned it in the paper before. Where were you?"

"In Poland. Auschwitz."

"That was for Jews, wasn't it? They sent the Jews to Poland. They sent my son to Mauthausen. He was in the Resistance. He was eighteen."

"Did he—?"

"No," Ferrand answers hastily, as if trying to prevent the word being spoken. "Almost. When he came back he weighed only six stone. And he wasn't short. And he'd put some weight back on by then. He was sick. No-one seemed to know what was wrong with him. Even the doctor was afraid to come. Me and his mother, we just watched over him, hoping he wouldn't die. There wasn't much else we could do. He's a fitter at Moto-Bloch now. What about you?"

"What about me?"

"Did you lose someone?"

"My wife and my son."

The man stares at him, shakes his head and sighs. He is about to say something, but André speaks first.

"There's nothing to say. I'm going to leave."

"I wouldn't inform on you. I'm not like that. You must have had your reasons, for killing those people. You're not one of those murderers who kill people for fun or to rob them. Not like all those Nazis and militiamen. You're not like them. I know that, cos I'm not scared of you. I can look you in the eyes, like that, no worries. And I can tell you one thing: someone informed on my son and his friends, in late '43. I've got his name and address, and if it were just down to what I wanted, I would . . ."

He stops talking and walks to the window. There is sunlight in the street now, shining on the façades on the other side of the road, and he stares at this light with surprise."

"If it wasn't for Arlette . . . I'm bringing her up on my own, now my wife is dead."

He turns to André and speaks in a firmer voice.

"You can stay here, you know. I've told you I won't go to the cops."

André examines the man's face, trying to decipher the lines for signs of falsehood, to tear away his smile to reveal a wolf's leer. Impossible to know. He feels plagued by contradictory signals.

"It'll cause you trouble, if I stay. It's better if I go. Thanks for everything. For your silence."

"I guess you don't trust anyone anymore?"

"I don't know. It's nothing against you . . ."

Ferrand sighs, picks up his newspaper and walks to the door.

"I'll leave you to pack. Just put the key on the table. I'll come and get it later."

354

He closes the door softly behind him and André listens to the sound of his footsteps fade as he walks downstairs. And then that crushing silence again. There are noises outside – the distant rumble of trucks on the docks, the cooing of a pigeon – but here, in this room, the silence deepens and devours him. Like a bomb crater. Or a ditch. He remembers the ditch where he died. Remembers the corpse on top of him, heavy and cold.

With his large bag on his back, he drives the motorbike over to the docks and abandons it near a bar that opens early in the afternoon and closes late at night, a bar frequented by sailors and women he can see perched on bar stools, wearing too much make-up, sometimes turning to stare at passers-by through the window, with expressions of sadness or contempt. He hopes the bike will be stolen within a few hours and that this will make the police's work a bit more complicated.

He walks along the docks for a long time, squinting in the slanting spring sunlight, then he takes a bus and walks a bit further, thinking about Darlac who is searching for him, who will tear the city apart in order to find him. André wonders if he still has the strength and the willpower to destroy this man, wonders if the mixture of hatred and grief that has fuelled his acts up to now might be slowly thickening into a glue that will paralyse him.

He has to knock twice before the door is opened. A woman's face appears in the narrow gap. Short salt-and-pepper hair. Large dark eyes, elongated by eyeliner. André says hello, but she doesn't reply, just stares at him in surprise or curiosity.

"Is Abel there?"

"Jean?"

The woman's face comes to life, with a sad smile.

"Abel told me you came round. I'm glad to see you."

Violette. André doesn't know what to say. He tries to return her smile, to find some appropriate words, but nothing comes to his mind.

"Come in. Don't stay out there."

In the darkness of the hallway, she smiles at him again.

"How are you?"

She whispers, and her voice is immediately absorbed by the silence.

"O.K., I guess. I didn't recognise you."

"Have I aged that much?"

"No . . . Maybe it's the short hair. But it's definitely you."

"Well, that's a relief."

She spots the large sailor bag on his back.

"Put that down. You're not leaving straight away, are you?"

After he has balanced the bag against the wall, the two of them stand there looking at each other in embarrassed silence for a few seconds.

"Abel's not doing too well, you know. The doctor's given him two months at the most. He's resting, in there. He has an afternoon nap now. Come on, let's have a coffee."

Violette enters the dim kitchen and pours coffee into a saucepan, which she puts on the hob.

"What's happened to you? You know he doesn't want to see you anymore."

He sits down heavily on a chair that creaks beneath him.

"I'm in trouble. Nowhere to go. I have to talk to him."

Violette says nothing. She puts the cups on the table, along with the sugar bowl, then lights a cigarette. She doesn't look at him, watching the coffee in the saucepan instead.

"What do you want?"

His voice makes them both jump. André turns towards Abel, who is leaning in the doorway, breathless and unsteady. His dark eyes shine deep in their sockets; the skin of his face, stretched tightly over his death's head, glistens greyly.

Violette pushes a chair towards him and he sits down, holding on to the table as he lowers himself. He closes his eyes for a long

356

moment, and slowly gets his breath back. His face is waxy.

"It's you in the paper, isn't it? Darlac's trying to frame you for his own dirty business, right? So what do you plan to do now? Hide here? You're up shit creek, and you want me and Violette to join you for a paddle? Is that it?"

"Just for a few days. Just enough time to . . ."

"Enough time to what?"

Abel makes a hand gesture to Violette. She gets up, grabs a cup, and pours him some coffee. He takes small mouthfuls, coughs a bit, pulls a face, then blows on the cup. He shrugs, and looks André in the eye.

"I'm all out of time. I'll soon be finished with all this. Anyway, you know what I think about you, about what you've done. But I'm not going to die leaving a bloke on the run to the mercy of the streets, especially not when it's Darlac who's hunting him. There's a spare room upstairs. Move your stuff in. You don't owe me anything. I'll still have plenty of cash left when I'm dead. You can even take the car if you want."

"Thank you, Abel. I—"

"Skip the pleasantries. I don't even know why I'm doing it. Maybe just as a way of hanging on a bit longer. Because the past is all I have. Anyway, I think it'll make Violette happy."

The woman offers a tired smile. She puts her hand on André's forearm. The silence holds the three of them together, punctuated by Abel's ragged breathing. André jumps when Abel's chair legs scrape the tiles and he stands up, remaining immobile for a moment, leaning on the table, blinking and shaking his head, as if he were having a dizzy spell. Then he turns slowly to the door and sets off unsteadily, holding on until he reaches the table. They hear his feet shuffling through the hallway then the soft creak of a leather chair. André shoots a concerned glance at Violette, who reassures him with a pout and a flurry of batted eyelashes.

"He's going to read a bit, then he'll fall asleep."

"And you?"

"What about me?"

"What are you doing?"

"I'm with him. It's my life. I was always with him. What I went through before doesn't count. That wasn't living."

"Can you really do that? Cut your life in two, I mean, and get rid of the bad bits? Forget them completely?"

The woman picks up a sugar cube and soaks it in the bottom of her cup, then nibbles it.

"I don't think you ever forget anything. You just end up not thinking about it anymore . . . Well . . . Let's just say that it no longer weighs so much in the bag you carry around. I don't know how to put it. I think you have to put something else in the bag. Or maybe it's like salt: you have to soak the bag in water so the salt that burns you is slowly dissolved."

She falls silent, watches him. André can't bear the intensity of her gaze and looks away. He tries to think about what she's said. He wonders what river might be able to absorb the salt that inflames his wounds.

"It's as if I was dead and I came back to life. I remember the evening when I came back to myself. I didn't know where I was. There was Abel sleeping on a chair, and I was scared because I thought they were the ones who had . . . And then I recognised him and it all came back to me: the doctor, the pain in my stomach . . . Abel woke up and he said, 'How are you feeling? Are you hungry?' I replied, 'Yes, a little bit.' 'Don't move. I'll be back,' he said, as if I might be about to escape through the window or start cleaning the house. He got up and I heard him fiddling about somewhere in the kitchen. He came back soon afterwards with a tray containing two plates of overcooked noodles and some cold roast pork. And he spread some pâté on bread for me. I cried so much, I felt better. And that was it – everything started again that day. We never spoke about it after that."

She smiles and nods. Her eyes gleam. She stands up suddenly, rubbing her hands on her apron.

"I'll show you to your room and give you some sheets."

In the living room, Abel is asleep, mouth open, a detective novel open in his lap. His chest rises softly, at peace. André can't help seeing a dead man, despite the small patches of colour that have returned to his face.

The room smells of lavender and polish. It overlooks the small green garden, which is starting to turn blue in the twilight. He and Violette make the bed and André sniffs deeply at the scent of the clean sheets as he always has since he first slept in a real bed again, in Paris, after his return. Sleeping in this smell is one of the best moments of the day. He says this to Violette. She felt something similar after Abel removed the sheets in which she'd sweated, bled and slept like a corpse and replaced them with clean ones. These little things that no-one pays attention to in everyday life. Little scraps of happiness.

During dinner, Abel asks André: "What was it like, over there?" Violette stares reprovingly at him, sighs, stands up and clears away the bread and the bowl of vegetables to show her disagreement, then sits down again, putting a pack of cigarettes on the table and leaning forward to listen to André.

So André tells them. Sitting up straight against the back of his chair. For more than two hours, he tells them what he has never told anyone before. What no-one has ever asked him before. The things he has only ever confided to his notebooks. The things that fill his nightmares and his memories. And then Paris, his comrades, the need to live, to learn how to do it again. And also, sometimes – often – his tiredness with life. Hélène, who danced in the ruins. He talks about Olga and how he was unworthy of her. Olga lying sick in his arms and then dying in the terror of the gas chambers.

He stops speaking. Waits for the screaming to stop, the images to leave his mind. Violette holds a hand to her mouth.

Olga: he should have loved her better than he did. Maybe he didn't love her at all. He lives with the pain of this deficient love. He uses words like love and cherish, words that people usually only speak out loud cautiously, almost apologetically, as if they were saying something embarrassing.

He talks about Daniel, whom he didn't recognise at first when he went to see him at the garage to get that motorbike fixed. He remembers the little boy's hand in his when they would walk through the streets every day. He opens his hand and shows it to Violette and Abel as if a trace of the child might have remained there, like a mark.

Violette and Abel listen in silence. She gets up once to make coffee, but returns to sit down while the coffee pot burbles quietly beside her. Abel does not move, does not even blink. Sometimes he nods or shakes his head gently, to show his horror or his dismay. Exhaustion, it seems, does not dare drag him away from André's story.

"It's late, isn't it?" says André after a moment. "I keep talking and talking . . ."

"No, it's fine," says Abel. "It's not that late."

André pours himself a large glass of water. He cannot remember ever having talked this much.

Abel stands up. He holds out his hand to him.

"Can you help me?"

André holds him up. They walk through the hallway. The bedroom is at the end. Abel weighs nothing. Close to him like this, André can hear his rapid, whistling breath. He helps him to sit down in a wicker chair.

"You O.K.?"

Abel nods, sucking air through his mouth, trying to get his breath back.

"I misjudged you," he says. "What I said was unfair. Everything has changed so much. And you and I have changed too . . ."

"Don't worry about that. You should get some rest. We'll talk about it later, if you want."

Abel nods, then closes his eyes. He leans back against the seat of his chair, which creaks softly. André goes back to say goodnight to Violette. He finds her sitting at the table. Her cup of coffee has grown cold. She looks up at him with red eyes and smiles and gives a little wave.

"Everything alright?" he asks.

"No, but we'll muddle through anyway. See you tomorrow."

26

Madame is lying on the sofa. Bare feet, houndstooth jodhpurs, gold-buttoned blouse. She is reading a magazine and does not look up when Darlac enters the living room without a word and walks over to the sideboard, where he puts away his pistol, as he does every evening. He eyeballs his wife, who stretches out her arm to take a cigarette and light it, and he goes out to the entrance hall to take off his jacket then returns and loosens his tie and unbuttons his waistcoat. He cannot smell anything cooking, so he goes to look in the kitchen. Everything there is in its place, gleaming cleanly, and he sighs with pleasure at this reassuring display of order.

"Aren't we eating tonight?"

"It's already cooked. I did it yesterday. *Salmis de palombes.*"

The voice rises from behind the magazine and those Sophia Loren cat-eyes.

"Where's Elise?"

"At a friend's house. They're revising for their history exam."

"Which friend?"

Madame sighs.

"Hélène. De Taillac. The judge, you know?"

"What time is she coming home?"

He sits in a chair opposite her. She is still lying down, still reading the magazine, so still that he can barely even see her chest move as she breathes.

"How long have you had me followed?"

She tosses the magazine on the coffee table and stubs out her cigarette. Stares at him. Green eyes, or golden. Lips slightly parted. In the space below the collar of her blouse, he glimpses the slender joint of her clavicle, a strap of her bra. No make-up. Darlac is suddenly reminded how beautiful this woman is. He tries to remember how long he has hated her this much.

"What are you talking about?"

"I was followed, last Tuesday. Some bloke on a motorbike."

She continues staring at him while she sits up and folds her arms.

Darlac feels connections clicking into place. The air around him seems to thicken and it costs him an effort to keep breathing, not to rush at her and force her to speak.

"I have not had you followed."

"You've had Elise followed since she was attacked by that man."

"That's different. I never gave an order to have you followed or protected."

All of a sudden, he thinks that Laborde might have put in place extra surveillance in an attempt to catch him out, but he rejects this idea. A cop on a motorbike: he doesn't believe it. Particularly for this case.

"And why don't I have the right to any protection? After all, this man could attack me, couldn't he?"

"Where did he follow you to?"

"The cemetery. I went to lay flowers on Mother's grave."

"What was he like?"

"He was wearing a helmet, goggles, a grey jacket. Does that help? Could you stop treating me like an idiot? I saw he was a cop at first glance."

"He's not a cop."

She leaps to her feet and is about to storm from the room.

"Oh, stop being such a drama queen. Sit down. Let me explain."

He speaks without raising his voice. Without moving. Without anger. Madame turns to look at him, surprised. She sits down, lights another cigarette, exhales the smoke nervously. Her eyes look grey now and she blinks furiously.

"How's Willy?"

Annette Darlac looks away. Her eyes roam the room like a frightened sparrow, unsure where to land, then return, trembling, to her husband's steady gaze. She cannot think of anything to say. Apart from "Please, have mercy!" But she cannot even summon the courage to say that.

"Why are . . . ?"

She leans back in her seat and lifts her hand to her mouth.

"Why what? What do you think? I've known for a long time. Ever since he came back with his mother in '51 and you found him that house in Blanquefort. I was wondering why you were so determined to get your driving licence, and then to have your own car . . . So, I dug around, and I found out the truth. Hauptmann Wilhelm Müller left half his face and body in Stalingrad. In '49, his father died and left him everything; he liquidated his assets, then came here so he could grow old close to his daughter. And as he doesn't want her to see him in the state he's in, I know that two or three times a year you take him with you in the car and park on the street so he can watch her walk past on her way home from school. That's all I know. And that's why I'm sure that the bloke who followed you was not one of ours. Cos I don't want every cop in town to know that my wife – that Kraut whore – is cheating on me with a fairground freak. You understand now?"

"And you said nothing about it all this time?"

Her eyes brimming with tears, her voice choked.

"I wanted to see how you'd react. Caught in the trap. Cornered. Like a rat in a cage. I watch you all the time, you know that? Playing your role of the perfect wife, the cordon-bleu cook, the irreproachable housewife, the attentive mother. I don't know how you keep it up. Maybe you think you're resisting me . . . But it must hurt like hell, and that's enough for me. I know you're paying for what you've done, that you're punishing yourself more than I ever could. It amused me to watch you acting in this farce, imagining that I believed it all."

364

He speaks to her in a confidential tone, sitting comfortably in his chair, never taking his eyes off her, almost smiling. She turns her head to right and left, slowly, as if she were watching the slow-motion collapse of a building or the interminable fall of a figure thrown from an aeroplane.

"And now?"

"I'm going to catch the bastard who attacked Elise, who burned Odette and Emile alive, not to mention the girl who was staying with them. That's the man who followed you. The same one who killed Inspecteur Mazeau and his wife. His name is Jean Delbos. Tomorrow you're going to look at photos of motorbikes so you can identify his. As soon as we've located him, we'll arrest him. I'll arrest him."

"I wasn't talking about that."

"So what do you want to talk about? Tell me . . ."

The sound of the front door opening. Elise. Soon she will call out "Hello! It's me!" and throw her satchel on the floor. Darlac listens to the usual noises of her arrival and his heart beats a little harder, as it always does when she comes home. He knows that there will be a brief interlude in the dreary shit of his daily life; a few minutes' respite, before the girl falls into line with the routine order of family life, before her bitch of a mother catches her in her net once again and puts out that little flame. In this moment he feels capable of love and tenderness, even compassion. It seems to him – Albert Darlac – that a window is opening in his life, making such a transformation possible. He has moments of grace, the commis-saire, during which he feels he might rise above it all, weightless and radiant.

The girl's voice pronounces the ritual phrase and he gets up to kiss her and to hold her body against his for a few seconds, to steal that little pleasure, the secret that makes him shiver.

She accepts his embrace, then pushes him gently away without answering his questions about her history revision so she can kiss her mother too. The two of them share tender words, their voices smiling. Quiet, complicit laughter.

Darlac watches them, sick with jealousy. The spell is broken. He tastes that familiar bitter flavour again – that vile snot coating the back of his throat – and when they both look over at him with the same strange smile, he is struck by their resemblance, by the identical masks of beauty and irony turned towards him, a double vision that disturbs him because he no longer knows what he should love or hate. So he picks up his jacket and goes outside for a moment, standing on the pavement in front of the door to catch his breath, as if he had been diving without a snorkel to the depths of the sea, lured by sirens.

Later, after eating in a noisy, filthy café on place Saint-Michel full of chatty Spaniards and vagabonds, each slumped amid breadcrumbs with a bottle of red, he hangs around in the bars where Francis is a regular, but none of the barmen have seen him in the last three days and some of the owners seem hardly to remember his existence. As most of them don't know who is asking about him, they prefer not to say anything. Francis Gelos is not the sort of man you talk about behind his back, because everyone knows that, however pleasant and affable he seems, he can quickly be transformed into a vile bastard, a living nightmare. As for the few who recognise Commissaire Darlac, they offer him a little pick-me-up and grimace helplessly: "Sorry, I haven't seen him. Actually, I was just thinking that it was unusual." They do not want to hurt anyone, remaining polite and jovial, the two-faced smart-arses. Chatting about the weather, Darlac feels women rub themselves against him, feels the pressure of their breasts on his back as they sidle their way through the crowd at the bar to place an order. Sometimes the owner will wink at him: "A new one, Monsieur Darlac. Not bad, is she? She's one of Untel's." So the cop turns to look at the woman as she moves away, ogling her body, waiting for her to sit down so he can check out her face, then sighing. No, definitely not. None of them. Whores or otherwise – not that he sees what difference it makes – none of them have been able to entrance him the way Annette did in '44, the first time he saw her. He is filled with rage at the idea of this irreplaceable illumination. A star, now dead, that had outshone every other celestial body forever, leaving the universe a black void. He drains his glass and leaves without a word.

"There's another one we don't see at all anymore: Jeff, you know, the fat one. What's happened to him?"

It is Pascal Faget, A.K.A. Youyou, the owner of Le Tropical, a private club for V.I.P.s, who poses the question. Queer down to the roots of his hair, which he dyes chestnut brown for some unfathomable reason. Why not red or blond? Darlac stares at him over the champagne flute, a foot from his face, moisturised, bronzed and smoothed by Max Factor, and he sniffs his heavy perfume, the same crap the queer uses on his arse after he's been given a good seeing-to, to mask the other smells. He wants to smash his ugly face in, but this bloke is like a Who's Who of Bordeaux: he knows everyone and who they're fucking too, knows every bedroom anecdote – from the most harmless affairs to the most sordid crimes – involving the city's bosses, the wealthiest wine merchants, politicians, prostitutes, drag queens. Cops too, for that matter. Poofters, paedos, sessions with whips and chains, voyeurs, sex addicts, rich pervs, religious pervs, fetishists, sodomites (in the closet or out of it), cocksuckers, arselickers, panty-eaters . . . Youyou had an inexhaustible supply of dirt. Darlac knows perfectly well that Le Tropical's owner does not tell him everything, but what he does tell him enables the commissaire to have a good hundred honest and respectable citizens in his pocket, just in case.

"And you know what they're saying?"

Youyou leans his thick lips close to Darlac's face.

"That he was eliminated because he messed around too much."

Darlac puts his glass down. Swallows his mouthful of champagne. Tries to appear indifferent and amused, creating an asymmetrical web of wrinkles across his face.

"What do you mean, he messed around too much? Who said that?"

"Oh, no-one in particular. It's just a rumour doing the rounds. Well, I mean, you know perfectly well that . . . he does blokes now and again. And he's not exactly discreet about it."

Of course Darlac knows. That and the rest . . . Jeff was no prude . . . Guided only by his drives and instincts. A militiaman during the Occupation, an occasional hatchet man afterwards, he was also a robber, a rapist, a dealer. Hunting dog, guard dog, and attack dog. You had to keep him close to you, on a short leash. But he was faithful. Like a stray mutt that's been rescued: gratitude in his guts, knowing full well that his master has saved him from the doghouse or a lethal injection. Men went looking for him after the Liberation, guns in hand, to present him with the bill for his arrests, his interrogations, his pillaging during the war. For men of his kind, everything was permitted, and he didn't stint himself. Including the ones that no-one ever found out about. Resistance fighters who vanished as they were catching a train or while riding a bike on a country road, or just some nobody coming out of a secret dance and being welcomed by the butts of militiamen's rifles . . . Their bodies never found. Darlac had paid for his escape to Morocco on a passenger– cargo ship where Jeff had his run of cabin boys during the trip. He had to wait until people had forgotten him. Partly that would be solved by the sudden amnesia of those who wanted him dead, but he also had to wait for the country's vague desire for purification to wear itself out, and for the bastards to become a useful commodity again. He stayed out there nearly three years. First job: assistant in an ironmongery run by a Jew. You couldn't make it up. After that, he ran a bar in Tangiers: a happy time that he often talked about with fondness and regret. But he had to flee again, because the father of an eleven-year-old boy stirred up the city to cut off his balls and shove them down his throat. So sensitive, those Arabs . . . and what prudes!

"So he got killed by some bloke he knocked around?"

"That's what I heard . . . But you knew him well, didn't you? Haven't you heard anything?"

"He probably had to go on the run. It happens sometimes. I'm not worried. I'm sure we'll see him again before long."

Youyou lifts his glass of fizz and invites Darlac to do the same.

"I can't say I miss him, personally. Anyway, I'd never let him have me. Not my type!"

A roar of dirty laughter as he drinks; the golden liquid runs down his chin. He pours himself more champagne. It foams too much and overflows the glass. He hands the bottle to Darlac, but the cop refuses, turning his back and giving a cursory wave.

He walks, slightly groggy, incapable of thinking about anything, then, coming out on the Allées de Tourny, he stops to contemplate the view of the Grand Théâtre: a boring and arrogant building, he thinks, perfect for this sad, spineless city. He starts walking again, more quickly now, up the cours de l'Intendance to pick up his car. His mind is filled with images of Mazeau's and Jeff's bodies, tangled up in their sandy hole the way he'd seen them after being thrown in there by Francis, but found by a hunting dog or a rubber-tapper and soon afterwards laid out – monstrous, half-eaten by the quicklime – on the coroner's table. Or dug up by gendarmes after a tip-off. If that pansy Faget is starting to go on about it, then other people must know, or think they know, or suspect. Which means the corpses will soon be discovered. Which is definitely not good news.

Back at home, in the darkness of the entrance hall, in that familiar odour of waxed floorboards and stone, he stands motionless for a moment, breathing fast, then bolts the door, leaning on it with all his weight, as if taking shelter from the nightmare which is starting to pursue him. Francis. He has to find that son of a bitch and shut him up for good.

27

Sergent Castel walks at the head of a column of thirty men who are climbing the path up to the village. Meyran is behind him, lugging the radio set. Daniel comes next, his loaded Garand in his hands. He listens to the quiet tramping of the men's feet, their panting breath, the intermittent jingling of their straps and harnesses. The rest of the platoon is going up the other side, commanded by the new lieutenant who was sent here after the death of Vrignon. Caunègre, that's his name. He was near Constantine, on the general staff of a battalion. The hill stands out starkly against the pale eastern sky. Thickets of bushes, slouching roofs, lopsided shacks. The houses are huddled together in blue shade. Two or three cocks crow loudly, apparently thrilled by the new morning. A smell of woodsmoke reaches the men and the cool wind blows over them and Daniel looks up at the transparent, straw-yellow sky, slowly turning blue.

Suddenly, two dogs surge from a field below, barking and growling furiously as they head straight for the sergent and Meyran. The sergent shoots the first in the head; it leaps backwards and falls on its side, its body shaken by convulsions. The second one turns back and jogs away, tail between its legs, so Daniel catches it in his sights and puts a bullet in its backside, then finishes it off after it collapses on the ground and lifts its head to howl. The other men whistle in admiration, and he hears a few compliments uttered in hushed tones. When they reach the dogs' corpses, Daniel and the sergent drag them over to the grass and throw them on their sides and the men stare at the two dead animals, their wounds, taking care not to walk in the blood that is already soaking into the dust.

Shouts and screams reach them from the village, woken by the gunshots, so the sergent orders them to run over to the first houses.

They spread out through the streets, yelling loudly, and break down doors and enter dark rooms where they can see nothing apart from the pale stain of a piece of clothing or the flickering red of a fire and they start bellowing like frightened blind men, kicking over tables, smashing chairs, shoving benches against walls, breaking shattering vases and jugs, stamping on plates as women and children scream. Daniel misses the step that separates the street from the hard earth floor and lands on his knees in the middle of a room where all is dark except for the gleam of a copper plate hung on the stone wall. Meyran and Baltard yell that they can't see a thing for fuck's sake, don't they even have windows in these shitholes? A shutter bangs and they get a better view of the miserable furniture, the stone sink, the hearth full of ashes and, above all, that woman and her four children who press tightly around her: two girls in their early teens and two younger boys who hide in their mother's skirts. One of them is hardly old enough to walk, dressed only in a dirty undershirt, his lower half naked, and he wails piteously so Meyran grabs him and lifts him up by his undershirt, carrying him across the room like a parcel and throwing him outside. The mother hangs onto his shoulders and he hits her in the face with the butt of his rifle. The woman falls to her knees, groaning, face bloody, and then walks over to her son who is moving his arms and legs confusedly, lying on his belly, as if he's trying to swim along the gravel path. The other boy and one of the girls rush over and they all start crying and shrieking around the little one, hugging each other close. Daniel is in the doorway. He hears a burst of sub-machine fire further off, the screaming of humans, the bleating of goats, the yapping of dogs, and he doesn't know what to do. He wants to unpin one of the grenades that hang from his kit and toss it into this hovel to blow it all up, to make it all stop, to leave nothing in the smoking ruins but silence and calm.

He doesn't move, the butt of his rifle wedged under his armpit, and he sees Soler kicking the mother and the children, screaming at them to get up – "On your feet, bitch!" – while inside the shack Baltard grabs the other girl by her hair and shoves her onto a straw mattress, lying on top of her as he sniggers and snorts and struggles with his belt buckle. The girl fights back, hammering her fists into the man's ribs as he crushes her with his weight.

"Jesus, stop it!" he shouts at Baltard. "We're not animals!"

"They are though! This is how they like to be fucked while their men are out in the brush, killing our friends! Don't bloody start with me!"

"What's going on?" Meyran asks.

"Baltard's being a dick. You tell him!"

Meyran enters the house and bursts out laughing. He asks Baltard if he'd like a hand, and Baltard says they can share, so he starts unbuckling his belt too and jumps on the girl to hold her arms above her head.

"You watch the door. We're gonna be a few minutes!"

Daniel yells at them to stop, to calm down, but they tell him to fuck off and now he can't see anything in the darkness of the shack but a lumpy, moaning mass topped by the black mass of the girl's hair. He looks away, sickened, and sees the woman and her children still grouped around the little boy. He decides to walk over to them and order them to get up. But as they don't even seem to hear him over the noise of their moaning, he fires a shot in the air. They stand up then, one after another, still whimpering, and the mother holds her little boy in her arms, cradling his bruised, swollen face against her neck, letting his limbs dangle listlessly over her chest, and whispering words of consolation and pleading into his ears, between sobs.

He pushes them in front of him with the barrel of his gun, and when he hears the girl screaming from inside the house he has to aim it at them to stop them going back inside for her, and now he starts yelling too, hurling insults at them, you little shits, you fucking bitch, move forward or I'll blow your fucking heads off, forgetting himself in his bellowing. He doesn't know if he should cry, from rage or grief, or if he should shoot this woman in the back just to feel the thrill of her broken in two, slammed forward by the impact. He walks behind those poor limping devils as if at the edge of a chasm, suffering from vertigo, and he has the feeling that the next step will send him into the void.

At the bottom of a long, wobbly staircase, ambushed by the cool night air, he comes out into a noisy square filled with the roar of voices: soldiers barking orders, the villagers crying, exchanging words of fear as they are lined up against a wall, watched by the single eye of a machine gun. Daniel pushes his prisoners towards the crowd of other villagers, but the woman goes up to Lieutenant Caunègre, showing him her child and repeating: "He is sick, he is sick, on ground he is sick!"

The lieutenant turns to Daniel. "What's wrong with her kid?"

"Nothing. He just banged his head when he fell. She's been screaming like that ever since."

"Go with the others!" Caunègre says to the woman. "We'll sort your kid out afterwards."

But the woman does not move. She holds out her son towards the lieutenant, and the child's legs pedal vaguely in the air.

"He is sick! Monsieur, he is sick!"

"Go with the others, I said. Fuck's sake, is she deaf or what?"

As the woman continues wailing, brandishing her son in his face, the lieutenant takes a step back.

"You want me to make him better, do you?"

Caunègre slowly removes his pistol from its holster, slides the breech into place and touches the end of the barrel to the child's forehead. He cocks the hammer. Daniel has stopped breathing. His hand tightens around the butt of his rifle. He stares at the Colt, held steady at the end of the officer's outstretched arm, and he notices that the square has gone silent, that every gaze is converged on the point of contact between the barrel of the gun and the child's forehead.

"Take three steps back and go with the others," says Caunègre in a hollow voice.

He does not blink, and the gun remains pressed against the kid's head. The woman continues to hold her child in front of the soldier, but she is no longer wailing; her mouth hangs open, but she has been struck dumb by terror, her voice vanished. Daniel stares at the lieutenant's finger on the trigger and it seems to him that its pressure is increasing. He has the impression that the hammer is moving imperceptibly towards the firing pin. He presses his rifle butt harder into his armpit, lifting it almost to his shoulder, ready to fire, the lieutenant less than two metres from him in his line of fire.

Three Sikorski helicopters pass over the village, heading east. Paratroop reinforcements sent to clean up the jebel, which the Legion has been searching since yesterday. The woman looks up at the choppers, then retreats, holding her child tight to her breast. Staggering, bent double, she joins the other villagers, then sits on the ground and cradles her son. Other fearful women, other feeble old people are brought to the square. There are maybe a hundred of them now. The oldest boy might be twelve or thirteen. Hunchbacked, frail.

The lieutenant holsters his pistol. He walks over to the villagers, hands on hips, and the N.C.O.s give orders to the men with shouts and gestures, and the men all aim their guns at the crowd.

"Three soldiers were killed by cowards, four days ago. You all know it. It happened about ten kilometres from here."

A caporal shoves an old man forward and tells him to translate. The villagers listen, impassive. Children weep and babble.

"We know that an armed group passes through here on a regular basis to pick up supplies. We know that all the men of this village have gone to the brush. We know you're helping the rebels and we hold you responsible for the deaths of our comrades."

He nods at the old man: translate. Women exchange words, start to argue.

"What are they saying?"

"That it's not true, what you say. They say the bandits haven't been here for a long time, and that their men were forced to go."

The women shout louder. They shake their fists or walk towards the soldiers, holding out their hands imploringly. The children whine. The lieutenant signals to the machine-gunner. The breech clicks into place. Everyone freezes at the sound of gunfire. A few men flinch. Above the crowd of villagers, mud-bricks explode in pieces that flutter down onto the children and women who have thrown themselves to the ground, covering them with grey dust.

Caunègre waits for the dust to settle and the people to get up.

"Understood? Shut your mouths or I'll shut them for you, permanently!"

The old man starts to translate. He speaks just as loud as the lieutenant, and sounds just as angry.

The lieutenant is about to add something, but a jeep and two G.M.C. trucks arrive in the square. Soldiers jump out, about twenty of them, and a capitaine emerges from the jeep. He walks towards Caunègre and salutes him. Legionnaires.

"So? What's happening?"

"We haven't found anything. So we're explaining to them what we're doing and what we're going to do."

"You're explaining to them?"

The capitaine laughs silently. He whistles to his men, who are standing close to the trucks, and signals them over.

"Look what we've found."

One of the trucks reverses, stopping close to the villagers. Three soldiers drop the tailgate and push out two men, hands tied behind their backs. They land on their knees, and a soldier prevents them getting up. Panting, they stare at the ground: faces swollen, lips split. Blood on their shirts and their trousers. Head wounds.

"They talked like concierges," says the capitaine. "They've got wives and kids here. You'll see."

He confronts the crowd and points at the two men.

"Where are the *fatmas* of these two heroes? They can come out and kiss them goodbye before we take them away."

The old man translates again, staring wide-eyed at the two men.

Several women are teary-eyed. Others hold their heads in their hands. The kids stare at the two *fellaghas* and blink furiously. But no-one moves.

Daniel is still close to Lieutenant Caunègre. He watches the prisoners, electrical wire cutting into their wrists, bare feet bleeding, dressed in rags, kneeling unsteadily on the pebbles. These are the first ones he has seen alive. He recalls the face of the machine-gunner that he shot last month, appearing almost abstract, so distant, in his scope, whereas his wounded body, afterwards, was merely that of a man down, seeking only to live a few minutes longer. So this was the enemy. So these were the men who had killed Lieutenant Vrignon and Charlin. And Giovanni. The ones who hide and fire at them, as if they were coconuts at a fairground. Lambs to the slaughter. But he shakes his head. He has trouble imagining either of these two aiming at a man and putting two bullets in his body. All he sees are two miserable wretches covered in blood and bruises, on their knees, perhaps watched by their wives and their kids.

The capitaine starts talking again, thumbs wedged in his belt.

"No? Nobody knows them? Are you sure?"

The people massed in front of the bullet-pocked wall stare at him, terrified. Daniel observes their faces, searching for the woman and children that he brought to this place. Suddenly he thinks about the girl, with Baltard and Meyran. He turns to looks at the soldiers, trying to spot them. Baltard is chatting with the machine-gunner. Smoking a cigarette. Laughing.

The pistol shot, fired in the back of the neck at point blank range, sends one of the *fells* to the ground. He falls like a heavy bag dropped from the back of a truck. Instantly his blood flows, meandering between pebbles, thick and bright. A woman throws herself on the corpse and screams, insulting or cursing the lieutenant in her language. The capitaine, still holding his pistol, leans over the woman:

"Why didn't you say anything, eh? Why? You think we've got time to waste? You think we're just messing around here? Your husband wasn't messing around when he fired at our men though, was he? Tell me whatever you want, I don't give a shit. You're the one in hell, you bitch!"

He stands up and points his gun at the other villagers, who are bunched tightly together, their eyes huge with terror.

"This is what happens when you don't obey, when you lie. When you kill French soldiers who are here to protect you from bandits and cut-throats. The men of this village killed three soldiers, so we're going to blow up twelve houses. Maybe you'll understand then. Maybe you can ask your husbands to rebuild them instead of hanging around with rebels!"

The old man shakes his head and speaks. Then he sits down and starts to weep. The woman is lying on the corpse and sobbing in silence.

"Over to you," says the capitaine to Caunègre. "We've still got work to do up there."

He waves his hand vaguely at the mountains to the east, then puts two fingers to his mouth and whistles. His men load the prisoner in the back of the truck and return to their vehicles. The convoy starts up and disappears in a cloud of dust before turning onto the main road.

Caunègre gathers the sergents and caporals while the men close ranks around the villagers. They need volunteers to blow up the houses. Twenty men step forward, pushing each other out of the way to be part of this mission. Daniel is one of them. He is chosen, with eleven others. A group of protectors will lock down the village just in case. Grenades, then fire. Just make sure it burns. No flame-throwers, unfortunately, but we'll manage. Sergent Castel reminds them of the safety instructions. Demonstration. Cover your arses until it explodes.

They are handed equipment, plenty of grenades. They joke around, talk about fireworks. A few of them weigh the dense, chequered objects in their hands, pretending to juggle them. Others check the pin, put their finger through the ring. They leave in groups of two or three. Daniel gets rid of the caporal by explaining that he needs to check something in one of the houses they visited earlier. The caporal shrugs. Whatever you want. Just be careful. He turns this way and that in the labyrinth of alleys before finding the shack where the young girl was raped. He dives into the darkness and the silence that suddenly chokes him and stands for a moment in the middle of the room, waiting for his eyes to adjust. Then he moves cautiously towards the place where the other two fucked the girl, and he shoots a look above the overturned table.

There she is. Eyes open, arms crossed. A corolla of black hair around her head. One breast is visible through a tear in her blouse. Her skirt has been hitched up her thighs. Her lips are cut and swollen. There's a bit of blood congealed at the corner of her mouth. Daniel walks up to her. He is covered with sweat, panting slightly. He crouches down next to her. She's not breathing. At first he doesn't dare touch her, then he places his fingertips on her neck to make sure she has no pulse. With the back of his hand he strokes her forehead, then closes her eyes, feeling the softness of her lashes on his skin. Nausea forces him to his feet and he runs outside to heave and spit up bile. The sun is up now, its horrific light filling the street.

He takes a few steps forward, staggering, and catches his breath, wiping away the tears that the vomiting forced from his eyes. Alone in the world, with orders to destroy it. The heat beats down on him and he shakes like an animal to rid himself of its weight. He tosses a grenade through the door of the neighbouring house. Hears it roll along the ground, hit a wall, feels the vibration in his back when it explodes, and sees scraps of cloth, bits of wood, a saucepan go flying. The thick dust falls quickly, and in the darkness he makes out a fireplace. He throws the second grenade like a *pétanque* ball, aiming it with a flick of the wrist, and it rebounds against some tools piled up in the hearth and gets stuck in the middle. The chimney pipe explodes and the roof collapses. He runs away and hears the fire roaring in the fallen thatch, and when he finds a shady corner where he can rest, he drinks long mouthfuls of lukewarm water from his flask and suddenly feels better. He is no longer trembling, and can finally breathe easily amid this smell of burning that rolls through the narrow streets in clouds of black smoke.

Gunshots. The howls of beaten dogs.

Further off, he hears men shouting. He turns around. The sounds are coming from a shack at the end of the street, one even more rickety-looking than the others, listing to one side, still vibrating from the kicks that have smashed down the door.

"Fuck me! There's more of 'em in here!"

Daniel rushes over, loading his rifle. It's the two Parisians, Olivier and Gérard. He asks them what they've seen, but they don't hear, and each of them unpins a grenade and throws it – the two grenades arcing in unison – into the shack. The Parisians dive for shelter, crouching behind a low mud-brick wall.

They hear shouts, a sudden commotion, and then the explosion, which blows out a wall and propels it into the middle of the street in jagged blocks. The roof slumps and the joists creak, on the verge of collapse, and it's almost as if the cloud of smoke and dust, thick and dense, even doughy, holds the roof up a few seconds longer.

The two soldiers, aiming their sub-machine guns at the shack, watch this happen with an air of surprise, as curious as naughty kids who have thrown a cat down a well and are waiting for it to climb back up. They are retreating, tripping over bits of rubble, when a figure suddenly bursts, groaning, from the black fog, then falls flat on its belly at their feet.

A woman. Her hair burns down to her scalp, which is blackened and covered with bloody swellings. She tries to crawl and the two soldiers recoil as if she might give them some vile disease, plague or leprosy, and continue pointing their weapons at this smoking body clothed in charred tatters.

Daniel takes aim at them, ordering them to walk backwards and put their guns down, and the Parisians stare at him uncomprehendingly. They don't move, but all three men turn their gaze back to the inside of the blasted shack where another woman can now be seen through the falling dust, collapsed against the back wall. Daniel can't see her face; at first he thinks her hair has fallen forward and is hanging over chin. So he moves closer but still sees no face, only something that resembles a scrunched-up ball of newspaper soaked with blood and other fluids. The woman's chest rises and falls in convulsive breaths. She hugs herself mechanically, as if she were cold. She does not scream. The only sound she makes is that wheezing, asthmatic rattle.

Lying on her lap is a little girl, possibly dead.

Daniel tightens his grip on the rifle and keeps the two frightened bastards in his line of fire, blurred figures in his scope. He has to tell them something, at least insult them, humiliate them, but no words come. All he knows is that he has five cartridges in the magazine of his gun so he's going to give them two each – the first in the belly, so they suffer, so they can still see what they've done, so they'll be capable of hearing anything he might try to tell them, if he can think of anything to say before he pulls the trigger again.

"Don't do that. Lower your rifle."

Sergent Castel's voice, behind him. And between his shoulder blades, something hard, prodding him gently.

"Lower your rifle. Don't force me to . . ."

Daniel lowers his gun, then throws it on the ground. He waits, arms dangling. The sun blazes down on him; he can feel it burning through his combat jacket, his cap.

Castel approaches the two Parisians and smashes each of them in the belly with the butt of his rifle.

"Twats. Fuck off out of here."

He says this without raising his voice. Then he kneels down next to the woman stretched out in the middle of the street. The Parisians flee, breathing heavily and groaning, both bent double. Olivier stops and pukes. His friend grabs him by the collar and they move shakily away.

The sergent examines the woman.

"Help me."

He and Daniel lay her on her side. One of her arms, stuck beneath her, is torn off at the elbow. Her blood is soaking the arid earth. Daniel can feel sweat running down his face, dripping from his nose and his chin. He has trouble sucking in the hot air that rises from the stony ground.

"What are we going to do?"

"Nothing. She's practically dead. Lost too much blood."

"What about the others?"

He follows Castel, who cautiously enters the ruined shack. The sergent stands still and silent in front of the woman with the destroyed face. Daniel sees his shoulders rise, his uniform soaked with sweat. Tears fill Daniel's eyes. At this moment, he wishes he could beg someone or something: a magician, a god. But there is nothing but the stench of burned gunpowder and the sound of the woman's wheezing.

"The kid's dead. As for the woman . . ."

"Can't we heal them?"

"Who? Her? Have you seen the state of her face? Do you want to save her life, or soothe your conscience? And if she survived, what would you tell her? That France was generous enough to let her live like this? You want to use your rifle, go ahead. Maybe she'll go to their heaven, cos they believe in that too, you know."

He glances up at the collapsed roof.

"Come on, let's get out of here, before this fucking thing falls on us."

He leaves, picks up Daniel's rifle, hands it to him, and then walks slowly back up the street. Daniel turns back to the faceless woman. He stops, loads a cartridge, shoulders his rifle. The devastated face trembles in his scope. Her chest is still moving. He can see a gold medallion glittering with each breath. A pearl necklace. Thirty metres. The woman's torso, topped by that mangled face, fills his viewfinder.

"Leave it," says Castel, who has come to a halt further up the road. "It's not your problem. Come on, let's go."

Daniel pulls the trigger. He watches the woman crumple, then fall to the side. The sergent has turned around and is waiting for him. Daniel jogs after him. Castel shakes his head.

"What was the point of that?"

Daniel does not reply. He doesn't know the answer. The tears that had risen to his eyes earlier now overflow. They reach the square, where the men are gathering. The caporals are calling out names; everyone is there. They leave the village amid the acrid smell of fire. Cocks crow, perhaps encircled by flames. Dogs bark or howl. As they move away, some of them turn around to stare at the columns of smoke that rise straight up into the peaceful sky. Daniel tries to work out the location of the raped girl's house, then the one where the corpses of the little girl and the faceless woman are lying. Ten metres ahead, he spots the two Parisians marching, heads down. He'd like to know what they're thinking at that moment. Maybe just about their girlfriends, or their parents. Mates from work. About their civilian life, so peaceful and sweet. Or maybe they're trying not to think about anything. He is connected to them. By the hatred and contempt he feels for them, by the blood that was spilled. He does not see Meyran or Baltard. Doesn't even turn around to look for them. He let them do it, after all. He didn't do anything to stop them, so what's the point?

When they reach the trucks, the men collapse onto the benches and drink water, sighing. All you can hear are flask lids being unscrewed. Afterwards they're on the road, dust flying, jolting along, backs aching, the heat, and the silence of these stunned, dazed men. The daily routine of war, stultifying and speechless.

Daniel tries to think. In fact, he goes through all the names and faces of the people he loves, remembering voices, the places where he lives and works. He thinks about the cold of the garage, about numb fingers, clumsy gestures. He clings to these mental buoys to stop himself sinking. Irène's face, her laugh. Knights climbing a steep path in a film. The shapes of their bodies, shot from behind, shaken by the jerky movements of their horses. For a few moments he is not there, and he feels himself existing again.

28

"It's between Trensacq and Sabres, in the Landes. I don't remember which *département*, but there's only one road, so you can only go straight anyway. You'll see the *gendarmerie* vans. Be quick. I'll wait for you there."

Commissaire Divisionnaire Laborde hangs up without adding anything and Darlac holds the phone to his ear as he stares at the arabesques on the living-room carpet beneath his feet as if trying to decipher the twisted, almost painful tangles of his thoughts. Finally he replaces the receiver on its cradle, then takes a few steps towards the sofa and strokes the leather seatback and looks all around the room's utterly familiar layout, the solid furniture, the antique lamps, the paintings on the walls: all these things he never takes any time to consider with any attention. And this bourgeois banality, in which he so often feels bored or enraged, suddenly appears to him as something priceless, and he is gripped with terror at the thought that all this might disappear as part of a general collapse or in a bottomless chasm that will open up, there, suddenly, without warning, between the divan and the matching chairs. For a moment he fears that the earthquake that is shaking him to his very core will spread throughout the entire house and swallow the little world of which he thinks himself the centre, everything he has accumulated, built, and fought to acquire in the course of his bitch of a life.

He is shaken from his frightened daze by the sound of a creak on the stairs, as Elise comes down to give him a quick peck on the cheek. The impalpable caress of her perfume washes over him and he watches her walk away with that same slight pang in his heart that he always feels. Then he grabs his hat, goes out into the rain without bothering to put it on, runs over to the car and throws everything onto the passenger seat before sitting down heavily behind the wheel.

He extricates himself from the slow-moving traffic, which seems somehow glued to the roads by the rain, and drives as fast as he can, sometimes bumper to bumper with stinking trucks that drown everything behind them in a cloud of filthy steam that obscures his windscreen in a grey haze, preventing him from seeing what is coming the other way and forcing him sometimes to make risky overtaking manoeuvres in the water-saturated air where *distances and dimensions are obliterated.*

He insults other vehicles and drivers, of course, thinking if only he had some heavy weaponry he could rid himself of these monstrous pests that block his way. Sometimes he yells in the car's dark interior, the enclosed space swallowing all echoes of the rage that submerges him just as the rain is flooding the earth, and he advances, deaf and blind, following Laborde's meticulous directions.

Not that he needs them. He could have gone back there just by retracing the grey paths engraved in his memory.

Because he cannot believe that a rubber-tapper found the bodies of Jeff and Inspecteur Mazeau in that hole, beneath that pine tree uprooted by a storm. Because it is impossible for him to believe that the rubber-tapper in question made an anonymous call to the gendarmerie to signal the discovery. Nor can he imagine that they would have been identified this quickly, since he and Francis had relieved the corpses of their papers.

Commissaire Albert Darlac does not believe in chance, never mind disturbing coincidences.

Francis, you son of a bitch. You betrayed me.

He realises he's arrived when the bitter fog that his hatred has generated around him suddenly dissolves.

Here, it is no longer raining. Some patches of blue sky, the June sunlight shining from the south. He sees the gendarmerie vans in the distance and forces himself to take deep breaths in order to calm

385

the pounding of his heart, gripping more tightly to the steering wheel to control the trembling of his hands. There are five or six other cars parked there. You'd think it was some high-ranking politician, out on a jaunt. He pulls over on a steep verge, in high grass, and walks quickly along the cambered road towards a copper having a smoke, leaning on a 403 estate. He introduces himself, and the cop stands up straight and stubs out his cigarette then gives him a vague military salute and tells Darlac to follow him. "It's not far," he says. "Over there, at the end of the firebreak."

Darlac bites his tongue to prevent himself saying that he knows. Always this reflex to put down underlings for their ignorance or their mediocrity.

Commissaire Divisionnaire Laborde sees him coming, but makes a show of continuing his discussion with a gendarmerie officer and two others in plain clothes. A bit further off, an orderly is guarding the hole. In the woods, other gendarmes are combing the ground as if searching for mushrooms.

Laborde finally moves towards him. Handshakes. Introductions. Desclaux, the commissaire from Dax, a tall, skinny four-eyes with a bony face who reminds Darlac of Crabos. The capitaine of the gendarmerie, Guillou, tall and broad-shouldered, and a young, scared-looking man: Monsieur Gérard, the sub-prefect. Darlac forgets these stooges' names as soon as he's heard them. He glances over at the hole, sees a spade leaning against a tuft of broom, and some objects placed on a khaki blanket.

"Come and see."

Laborde takes his arm and leads him towards the bodies. He doesn't dare pull away from the chief super's grip. Finally Laborde lets him go and he walks to the edge of the ditch. The bodies are mummified, tangled together beneath a greyish dust. Darlac tells them apart by their clothes; their dead faces look the same. He tries to remember Jeff's large, round face, but can't. Not that it makes much difference right now.

"We haven't moved them. But on one of them you can see a bullet hole in his jacket. There, you see? The rip."

Darlac leans over Jeff's corpse. Yep, that's where it entered, the bullet he shot in his heart. He remembers.

"We found this too. Just next to them."

Laborde shows him the contents of a wallet spread out on the khaki blanket.

"These are Inspecteur Mazeau's papers. There's even his police I.D. We don't know who the other bloke is. You wouldn't have any idea, would you? That big bloke, who must have been pretty fat?"

Darlac feels his heart start to race. He shakes his head, turns to the bodies again, tries to look absorbed like a good, conscientious cop.

"Why would I know?"

He speaks without looking at Laborde, practically turning his back on him, to conceal the pallor he can feel in his face.

"I thought you knew everyone. A good cop like you knows people whose existence we don't even suspect. He reminds me of Joseph Laclau – you know, fat Jeff? You know him well, don't you?"

"He's been useful to me. Especially against Crabos' team, who are now out of the business and not bothering anyone. But I haven't seen him for a while. I heard he left Bordeaux because of some scandal."

"Put his cock in one hole too many, did he?"

"That's what I heard. I haven't had time to check the story. That's how we kept him under control. I knew what he got up to . . . Problem is, if I'd taken him down, he'd have taken some of the top brass down with him."

Laborde nods. He looks thoughtful and puts a hand on Darlac's shoulder.

"That's the difficulty with our profession: all these shameful compromises we make with shits like that. As if the only way we can fight evil is with evil, if you know what I mean . . . But there's no such thing as a good cop who doesn't keep bad company, is there?"

He takes a pack of Gitanes from his pocket and offers one to Darlac, who refuses with a hand gesture.

"I don't know if it really is Jeff down there, but I know who did this. That's a pretty good start, isn't it? And he used to be part of my 'bad company' at one time too."

"Oh, the bloke who came back from the concentration camps? What's his name again?"

"Jean Delbos."

The gendarme capitaine walks over.

"They're going to move the bodies. We're finished here."

Laborde turns his back on Darlac and starts to speak with the officer. They exchange notes, talk about procedures, the prosecutor.

Darlac takes advantage of their conversation to move away. Gendarmes and ambulance men come over carrying two stretchers covered with thick canvas blankets. The young sub-prefect observes these comings and goings with a dazed look on his face, arms dangling at his sides. The Dax commissaire lights a cigarette and blows smoke out noisily as Darlac passes.

"It happens sometimes, round here."

Darlac turns towards him. The other cop stares at him from behind his glasses. Sharp face, sharp gaze.

"What?"

"Bodies in the woods. Hangings sometimes. In barns, in winter. They're not always suicides."

Darlac shrugs.

"Yeah, I suppose."

"One day we'll find one at the top of a pine tree."

"Find one what?"

"A body, hanging!"

Darlac looks up to the tops of the pines, twenty metres above them. The man from Dax smiles.

"You don't think that's funny? That's how we test the newbies round here. We tell them a story about someone hanged twenty metres above the ground. And we watch how they react. Some of them don't see the problem. We keep them in the office, typing and filing, cos they're not good for much else."

Darlac has no idea why this prick is telling him all this. He shrugs and walks away.

"By the way," he hears behind his back, "you looked up."

Darlac turns around.

"Are you all like this round here, or did I just get unlucky?"

The Dax super smiles slyly, cigarette in the corner of his mouth. Darlac has come across a man like this before, in court. He'd killed his parents and his sister with a billhook, in the Médoc, before running away into the marshes with his dog and his hunting rifle, and he smiled just like that when he was in the dock, like he was trying to be clever. Didn't even seem to understand where he was or what they wanted from him.

"I don't believe it personally, this story about a rubber-tapper finding stiffs at the bottom of a hole. Neither do the gendarmes, for that matter."

Darlac takes a step towards him. So . . . maybe he's not the simple crackpot he appears.

"And why's that?"

"Because this part of the forest isn't tapped. We checked. There's not a jar of resin within fifty acres of this spot. So what would this rubber-tapper be doing here?"

"What do you think?"

"Well, it's a poacher, innit? Rubber-tapper my arse! That bastard was shooting deer, I bet you anything!"

Darlac tries to work out if this man is completely nuts or if he's taking the piss. He stares into the grinning face, the eyes vigilant behind those glasses, and can't tell either way. Commissaire Divisionnaire Laborde signals Darlac over, while staring at him and walking towards him.

"Meeting in my office, first thing tomorrow. I'm going to put everyone on this Delbos. We have to arrest him as soon as possible. We've wasted too much time already."

He sounds out of breath as he speaks. Walking thirty metres in the sand seems to have got his ticker pounding. Darlac waits a few seconds for him to recover.

"Is that all?"

"Yes," Laborde breathes.

Darlac turns on his heels and walks away.

He knows Laborde is watching him. He only brought him here to observe his reactions. To plant a few banderillas in him. Laborde the crafty bullfighter, acting clumsy but hiding a collection of swords behind his red cape, ready to stab them deep in his back the first chance he gets.

The sun is shining on the forest now, awakening a few cicadas. June. Darlac couldn't care less about the coming summer or any other season, but he is surprised that it is already so late in the year. And the heat that hangs heavy over him now, as his feet twist on the soft, shifting ground, as his shoes fill with sand, only adds to his oppression, shining a white, burning light in his face.

In his office, the telephone rings as he arrives and he snatches it up. It's Molinier, one of the coppers he's assigned to watch over madame.

"So?"

"So, it's like you said: she went to Blanquefort. An old woman opened the door. Her aunt, you told us. She came back just afterwards. And your daughter got in five minutes ago. We're outside your place now. Apart from that, nothing to report. No tail, no motorbike, nothing. Just like yesterday."

"Alright, you can go. Nothing can happen to them at home."

He is about to hang up when he hears Molinier saying something.

"Oh yeah, just one more thing. It doesn't help us much, but at noon we had a bite to eat in a little bistro at the corner of your street. We were chatting with the owner, and he told us about a bloke on a motorbike who used to go there a couple of times a week, for about the last two months. Tall, skinny, not very talkative. Always sat near the window. And guess what? There's a good view of your house from that café. The owner had talked to this bloke quite a bit, seemed to like him. He always had a notebook and a biro with him and he would write things down. He hadn't been there in the last week."

Darlac forces himself to breathe slowly. This dick of a cop almost forgot to tell him! He's searching for a murderer, he finds one of his hideouts, and he doesn't even bother mentioning it. Jean Delbos was there, less than fifty metres away, for hours on end, watching them come and go. He tries to make some saliva. His mouth is dry.

"What else did he say?"

The commissaire is furious. He's going to summon this twat to his office and give him a piece of his mind.

"Nothing. He thought he was a writer. The bloke told him that he was writing a detective story."

"Go home. That'll be all for today."

He hangs up, and walks over to the window, as he always does. He looks up at the sky where the last clouds are fraying and dissolving in the sunlight, and trembles with rage at the idea that Delbos is still able to enjoy such a sight, safely hidden, somewhere in this fucking city, calculating his next move.

He spends the rest of the afternoon checking procedures, calls the prosecutor's department twice, chews out a lazy detective, smokes and goes to the bathroom three times to wash his clammy hands.

As he sits down and dries his damp fingers on his waistcoat, he is startled by the ringing of the telephone. He grabs the receiver.

Francis. Son of a bitch. What are you playing at when you've already lost? He gets his breath back, concentrates his attention on the file about two women found dead in their home. Mother and daughter. Murder-suicide.

"What happened to you? I was beginning to wonder . . ."

"I was in Lille. At my fucking mother's funeral."

Darlac raises his eyebrows. His face twists into a malicious grin.

"I didn't even know you had a mother."

"Everyone's got one."

Darlac listens to Francis breathing heavily on the end of the line.

"I'll tell you the story of my life, if you like. You'll enjoy that. Anyway, we need to talk."

"Dead right we do. I have some news for you."

"Oh really? What's that?"

Darlac's vision blurs. Tears run down his cheeks. Hatred can overflow, just like grief.

"I'll tell you when I see you. You'll enjoy that. Where shall we meet?"

"My place."

"What time?"

"Whenever you want. I'm here now, and I'm not going anywhere."

Nearly six. He leafs through two files – breaking and entering, unpaid bills – that can wait till tomorrow. He takes the pistol from its shoulder holster, plays with the breech, takes out the magazine, reinserts it. Click, clack. There is no point to this, except to use up some nervous energy, maybe to reassure himself. He holsters the gun under his arm again. He likes feeling its weight pulling gently on the strap. He takes a .30-calibre pistol from a drawer; he got it ages ago, from some loser. He does the same checks, then slides it into his pocket and leaves the office.

In the corridor he bumps into Carrère, who asks him if he's seen the bodies, if it really is Mazeau. Darlac puts on an appropriate face. Yeah, it was tough seeing a colleague in a state like that.

"We need to turn over every fucking stone in this city till we find that bloke, whatever-his-name-is. What did the chief say?"

"Meeting tomorrow morning in his office."

"Ah, finally, cos . . ."

Darlac checks his watch, although he knows perfectly well what time it is.

"I have to go. Need to meet someone."

He leaves, feeling Carrère's disappointed gaze on his back, and walks downstairs. Relieved, almost light-hearted. Then out to pick up his car.

Francis lives in a huge apartment on the first floor of a rundown building overlooking the place des Chartrons. He opens the door to him in shirtsleeves and slippers and hastily shakes his hand before preceding him into the living room, which looks like an antique dealer's backroom: cluttered with old furniture, lamps, trinkets, sombre-coloured paintings hung on the walls, some of them askew. Gifts, most of them, from Gestapo officers in cahoots with Cloos, the head of the requisitions department for Jewish goods, in return for Francis' help in tracking down Resistance networks. Some of them he took himself, in payment, from the empty apartments for which Darlac had keys.

Darlac tells him, as he often has before, that it's imprudent to keep this mess of objects, which could become compromising if the law ever decided to investigate what some might consider plunder, but Francis reassures him with the observation that the law would have difficulty investigating what the law itself made possible: in Bordeaux, as elsewhere, everyone keeps his mouth shut, pretending to forget the dead and ignoring the survivors. Sitting in a red velvet armchair with twisted feet, he adds, "That was the war. And it's over."

Darlac wishes he was more convinced of this. He sits across from him, on a loveseat that groans under his weight and gives way slightly. Francis leans over an inlaid coffee table. He picks up a bottle of wine and pours it into two tasting glasses. He turns the label for Darlac to see.

"Deuxième grand cru classé de Pauillac. 1937."

Darlac sniffs, closes his eyes, concentrates. Hunting the aromas. A cellar master once told him that people find the smells they want to find in a wine. That there was a whole range from which one could choose, proceeding by elimination. A bit like a copper who can't find any solid proof, so ends up fabricating evidence. Ever since then, Darlac has mistrusted wine buffs. He takes some in his mouth and rolls it around while Francis crudely shoves his nose in the glass then swallows a big mouthful as if quenching his thirst.

"Good, isn't it? I got two crates of six. A gift. So? What's this news you wanted to tell me?"

Darlac signals with his hand that the news can wait. This moment is important. He keeps his nose inside the glass a little longer, pretends to sniff, eyes closed, then drinks some more. It's true: it is good. He puts his glass down and leans back, watching Francis as he puts on a show of concentrating on his wine. He wants to coax him out, get him to talk about those ten days when he was nowhere to be found.

Darlac continues acting out the tasting ritual while he waits for the next move. Francis pours himself some more, and drinks it like it's Ribena. A silence falls between them, undisturbed even by sounds from outside. Darlac stands up, takes a few steps and plants himself in front of an eighteenth-century engraving of Bordeaux's port. He examines the details, trying to recognise the city amid this chaos of ships and boats of all kinds, of goods piled high on the bank that slopes down to the river.

"So?" he says finally. "You wanted to see me?"

The sound of a throat being cleared. The dull clink of a glass placed on the tabletop.

"Yeah ... My mother died, as I told you. Fucking bitch. An uncle called me to tell me she wanted to see me before she kicked the bucket, so I went over there. Roubaix – it's not exactly next door."

Darlac turns around to see his lying eyes. Yeah, right. Give me a sob story. Play your little violin. I've heard others, and more in tune than this one. A lie, a trap – trembling in the eyes, dulling their sparkle. I know about lies.

Francis' eyes shine and his breathing is shallower, his voice less steady. Darlac is no longer sure.

"You never mentioned her before. I thought you'd been an orphan for years."

"Well, for one thing, you're not the kind of bloke anyone would necessarily want to talk to about their mother. And for another, I'm not an orphan but I was something pretty similar: a welfare kid. She didn't want to take care of me anymore – too busy getting shagged – so she dumped me in a boarding school and then with some old people. But the bloke used to beat me up, so I got sent somewhere else. And so on. Ended up in borstal. And the rest is history! Now you know the sad story of my shitty life. Although I'm sure you knew it all anyway: you had me investigated, didn't you?"

"I didn't go back that far. All I knew was your legal antecedents. I couldn't care less about the rest. I'm not like one of those idiot lawyers who'll go digging around in nappy shit to find excuses for their clients' guilt. Childhood doesn't count. Everyone's too soft and too stupid when they're a kid. Afterwards we change, for better or worse, and that's all there is to it."

"Well, anyway . . . I wanted to know how I'd feel about it, after all these years . . . almost a lifetime."

Darlac sighs. He couldn't give a toss about this bitch and the moods and feelings of her son of a. Is this really Francis spouting all this womanish crap? Francis, who is bothered by nothing, about as sentimental as a dog of war? Francis, who he's seen kill two men with his bare hands? Francis, who has double-crossed him and is going to die, whatever crap he spouts.

"So?"

"So nothing. It got me down, going back there. But I didn't even recognise the old woman. And she didn't recognise me either. She opened her eyes, and she looked frightened. I went for a walk round the places I used to hang out when I was a kid, all those streets of brick houses, all that shit. You should never do that."

Darlac sits down again. He drinks some more wine, notices that he's hungry and that the wine is making him feel slightly ill. He watches Francis visibly unravelling and begins to guess how all this is going to end.

"Is that all you have to tell me? You said we needed to talk. I came. You're not going to start telling me about the first bike you stole, are you?"

"I'm leaving Bordeaux."

He says this in a rush, and finally meets Darlac's eyes. A gulf of silence opens up between them.

"And going where?"

"Paris. I've got a mate up there who's invested some money in a business for me. A bar for rich blokes, with a few girls for the evenings. Behind the Champs-Elysées."

An admiring grimace from Darlac.

"And what about your business here?"

"I've sold my share in the bistro. I'm going to sell the apartment. I've got takers for the furniture and all the shit in here. There are men coming tomorrow to close the deal. I'm taking two girls with me. The others can take care of themselves. I'm clearing out in two weeks."

Darlac doesn't know how he manages not to smash the coffee table into Francis' face. He pretends to read the label on the bottle of wine, then takes a deep breath so he'll be able to speak calmly.

"Why didn't you tell me before? We've come a long way together, haven't we?"

"Yeah, but now we're going our separate ways. Anyway, you're not exactly the sentimental type . . ."

Darlac feels the room spinning slowly around him.

"This is because of Jeff, isn't it? You didn't like me shooting him."

Francis shakes his head. He looks more assured again and his eyes shine with that murky sparkle that they always have under those heavy eyelids.

"Jeff was a congenital idiot. And uncontrollable sometimes, as you said. Except if you knew how to use him; then you had no complaints. But to kill him the way you did, so coldly like that . . . I didn't think you were capable of that. And yet you're a piece of shit, just like me and all the other pieces of shit round here in the police and the gangs, not to mention all those so-called nice, respectable people. They're all as bad as each other, without a doubt. You choose your sides so you'll get the least amount of shit. But I thought if you could do that, then you could kill me too as soon as I didn't fit into your plans. So I'd rather leave. I don't want to continue. I wouldn't even dare turn my back on you."

Darlac pours himself more wine without saying anything. Considers his options. Thinks of some hurtful words and then decides that words are pointless.

"I would never do that. How could I? How could you even think that? You think I'm some sort of mad killer? The kind of bastard who'd shoot you in the back? Have you ever seen me do that to anyone? Shit, if I didn't know you so well, I'd be insulted! But with you, it hurts . . . But anyway . . . As you say, I'm not the sentimental type; I'll leave all that shit to women and queers. I don't really know what a friend looks like, but when I think of that word, I see your face . . . You see? I'm getting soppy. I need to get a grip. But you're not just any Tom, Dick or Harry. And I'm not going to shit on the memories we share, everything we've been through together . . . Oh well . . . At least I'll have a place to crash when I go to Paris."

"The bar will always be open for you. And not just the bar. Wait till you see the girls we'll have there. Maybe you'll forgive me then . . ."

Francis gives a knowing smile to Darlac, who responds with a wink and lifts his glass to future fucks.

"Actually, Francis, you don't have anything to nibble with your wine, do you? We should at least celebrate this properly, even if I don't like to see you go."

Francis gets up and disappears into the kitchen. While he hears Francis preparing something, Darlac grabs a large cushion from a chair and puts it next to him, stroking its midnight-blue silk covering. Then he takes the .30 and slides a cartridge into the chamber. He coughs to cover up the sound of the breech clicking into place. He looks around, his eyes roaming this Aladdin's cave, this ridiculous heap of old valuables that Francis has insisted on accumulating like a rich man, but without the discernment forged by inheritance and a bourgeois education, otherwise known as good taste . . . A monkey hoarding bananas, living in its cage surrounded by his favourite fruit and its rotting peel.

Francis returns carrying a tray, on which Darlac can see a block of pâté, half a loaf of bread and two knives.

"This is all I have. I hope it'll do."

They spread the pâté on the bread. Darlac's mouth waters. He spears a mouthful of pâté with the point of his knife. Francis chats about the charcutier who made the pâté, the baker who baked the bread, then he picks up his glass of wine and his slice of bread and raises them, with the words: "Come on, no hard feelings. To your health! Oh, and what was the news you were going to tell me?"

"Actually, it was about Jeff. They found his and Mazeau's bodies. That's good, isn't it?"

"Why is it good?"

"It's what you wanted, no?"

"Why do you say that?"

"Because you called the fucking gendarmes to tell them where the bodies were, you twat, and you left Mazeau's papers close by. And I wouldn't be surprised if Jeff's were there too, even if they are forged."

The blood drains from Francis' face. He swallows drily. But he looks Darlac in the eyes, without blinking.

398

"No, not Jeff's."

"You know they'll identify him soon. Everyone thought he was in Belgium, cos that's what I told them. So who do you think this puts in the shit? Why did you do that?"

"To settle the score. So that Jeff would get a normal burial. And also because—"

Darlac grabs the cushion and throws himself at Francis, knocking over the chair, which slides along the wooden floor until it bangs into a sideboard, and presses the cushion against his face. But Francis struggles, his choked yells like the grunting of a pig, his hands clinging to Darlac's forearms so he has trouble freeing himself to get hold of his gun and press the trigger.

"You see, you fucking twat, I'm not shooting you in the back. There's no need."

It sounds like a firecracker. Darlac absorbs the recoil in his shoulder and feels something tear or tense up in his shoulder blade. He grimaces with pain, then stands up and contemplates Francis' corpse, sprawled in his chair, legs outstretched, hands on his belly, wine and pâté all over him. Darlac remains immobile, gun in hand, mind empty, in a daze. Instinctively, he starts looking for the empty cartridge case, and it's at that moment that the cushion slides then rolls over the dead man's legs as if down a slope, to the floor. Where the cushion was before, he can now see Francis' face: the bullet hole in his forehead, his half-open eyes, mouth gaping and full of blood, which overflows in a trickle down his chin. He can't see the back of his skull, but he knows what's there, so he turns away from the corpse, spots the cartridge case under a table and picks it up. Then he notices that he is still holding the pistol, and slowly puts it back in his pocket.

He wanders around the room, massaging his shoulder; he leans over various trinkets to examine them more closely; he hefts the glistening two kilograms of an ebony elephant in his hand, and traces with a fingertip the smoothness of its little ivory tusks. Then he sees a silver candelabrum, and uses his Zippo to light the candles. He watches for a moment as the small flames crackle and blacken, thinking about nothing except what he's doing at that moment, the way you try to protect yourself if you're crashing down a flight of stairs. After that, swaying slightly, he goes into the kitchen and turns on the gas to all the rings of the hob, and then he leaves. Suddenly he thinks about his fingerprints, curses himself mentally for such negligence, and painstakingly wipes every surface he's touched. You never know, with gas and flames . . .

On his way out, he carefully closes the front door, feeling sickened by the odour that is already spreading through the house. Outside, he fills his lungs with the city's damp, polluted air and feels better. He looks up at the grey sky, then walks quickly to his car.

29

Caunègre and Castel do not give the men time to breathe or take a drink from the water truck's tap; as soon as they're back at the station, they organise a weapons maintenance meeting. Disassembly, lubrication, ammo check. They warn them that the slightest error could take off their hand or half their face if there's an explosion. Load, cock, chamber clean. It should be as free of filth as your girl-friend's pussy, and it should slide just as easily too, so you've got work to do. If it jams when the shot's about to go off, not only will you look like a dickhead – you should be used to that by now – but there's a good chance you'll die like a dickhead too. A few men snigger; others keep their nose down close to the breech and apply themselves, spreading the strong-smelling grease over the steel mechanisms with their cloths, pressing down hard with the tip of an index finger. They're sitting at tables in the refectory, still completely covered in dust, throats dry, wiping the crusts from their eyes with the backs of their hands, coughing to relieve their soot-choked lungs, spitting out the little saliva they have. They can already smell the ragoût being made by the two clowns in the hot, dark little space that serves as a kitchen, who occasionally improvise strange stews and hashes based on the random supply of food, as a way of chang-ing the sometimes poisonous rations that the army provides. One of them was a bank teller in Le Mans, the other a chemist near Lyon. The first so short-sighted that he has trouble – as he puts it himself – seeing his own dick when he pisses, while the second has such terrible scoliosis that he's virtually a hunchback and has to remain seated most of the time. Both of them wonder what the hell they're doing there; they don't understand – and nor do the officers and N.C.O.s – why the draft board didn't exclude them. So they are hidden away as best they can be before being sent back to their mothers: kitchen work, cleaning toilets, laundry, minor repairs, because they would be more of a nuisance to the army dead than alive.

Daniel has lovingly polished his rifle, checked the cartridges one by one before reinserting them into the magazine, cleaned the lens of his scope with one of the embroidered handkerchiefs that Roselyne slipped into his suitcase at the last minute and that he brought with him so he could smell the scent of lavender that still clings to them. He quickly checks his M.A.S.-49, lingering over the wooden butt which is so scored and worn away that it almost looks like someone's been chewing it, then raises his hand to indicate to Lieutenant Caunègre that he has finished. The lieutenant comes over to him and hefts the Galand, examining the scope, then looking around the room.

"Fucking brilliant weapon, that. You can do anything you want with it. You could put a bullet up a mouse's arsehole if you wanted to."

Daniel nods, watching as the lieutenant checks the gun's balance, and thinks: But we're not firing at mice. He sees again the woman collapsed in the ruins of the house. In the scope, he had been able to make out the pattern on her dress; he could have counted the pearls on her necklace. He could see the blood glisten as it ran from her smashed-up face.

"I hear from Sergent Castel that you're pretty handy with a gun. You got the platoon out of the shit the other day by taking out a *fell* hidden two hundred metres away. Good work! I bet the paras don't have many shots as good as you."

Daniel looks up into the eyes of the man who is speaking to him, leaning over him, his face earth-coloured and shiny with sweat, eyes wide with exhaustion, but his mind is still outside the blown-up house. The woman abruptly vanished from his field of view and he had to search the shadows of the house to locate her collapsed body as it tipped over onto the ground, one of her arms still on her dead daughter as if to protect her.

"Thank you, lieutenant."

Caunègre puts the rifle down on the table and gives Daniel a mechanical smile. He looks like a politician on an election campaign.

"Dismissed," he says. "You can go and have a drink."

He continues his inspection, stopping a littler further off to look at an M.A.S. that has been taken to pieces.

Daniel picks up the Garand and shoulders it. He looks around the room, then sees the two Parisians at the other end, sitting next to each other as they clean their sub-machine guns. He gets them in his crosshairs, alters the focus and leans his elbows on the table. He centres the scope on Olivier, his head in close-up, like a film shot, looking down, concentrating on what he's doing, conscientious, perhaps a little anxious. He sees the sweat on his skin, his long lashes blinking quickly. The tip of his tongue sticking out between his lips. The face turns towards him and the eyes widen.

"What the hell are you doing?" Caunègre demands.

Daniel lowers the rifle, puts it down. The Parisian is still staring at him, from the other end of the table.

"There was something on the scope. I was just checking it, lieutenant."

"I said you could go. So clear off."

Daniel puts the rifle in its slipcover and leaves. The setting sun sprays gold over the black mass of an advancing storm cloud. Gusts of cooler air float around him. The caporal in charge of delivering the post whistles and waves a letter at him. Daniel recognises Irène's handwriting on the envelope. He tears it open.

She tells him what he already knows by heart: her life at university, the communist students, the war and how everyone talks about it, how no-one knows what De Gaulle is playing at. She received a long letter from Alain, now in Dakar, who told her about the heat, the smells, the dark bars and cold beer, fighting with Englishmen, and the boatswain, who's a good man and maybe a former crook. Daniel recalls a film with Gérard Philipe that took place in searing heat, and this bar in some godforsaken hole where men sweated and gave each other dirty looks in the thick air stirred up by a huge ceiling fan. Alain the globetrotter. He tries to imagine it: those bars, those faces, hotels where no-one can sleep because of the heat and the stinkbugs and the screaming of whores pushed around by drunkards, the alcohol, the girls' arms and their tired eyes. He makes his film, motionless in the yellow air, with the lightning flashing and the thunder rumbling far off in that charcoal-grey cloud that is rising above him. A dark, slow film. Red and amber.

He should have gone with him. Climbed up that gangway behind Alain and the boatswain, hidden in a lifeboat, waited until the ship was in open sea before showing himself. Sure, they'd have put him down in the engines, amid the grease and the noise, in 120-degree heat, but when he went back up to the bridge, the wind and the sea spray would have cooled him down, cleaned him off, and later they would have offered him something else to do, anything, and he would have agreed so he could feel the massive swell of the ocean beneath his feet and see the edge of a continent heaving into view, the lights of a port, its swarming chaos. He would be in Hamburg or Tangiers right now, sitting in a taxi after asking the driver to take him to the parts of town that never sleep, and in his gut he would feel hunger and the exciting apprehension of the unknown. He lets these ready-made images flood his mind, the clichés amassed by those who don't know the truth, and who sometimes don't dare to find out.

Instead of which he is sitting on a bench, holding a letter written a week ago, his rifle leaning against him, and he trembles and then vomits between his feet at the idea of what he might have done and what he did, of what he might have been and what he's become. He spits bile in the dust that is turning his face into a hardened, earth-coloured mask, sticking to his eyelids as he wakes up in the morning and making his lungs wheeze.

He starts reading again, using the back of his hand to wipe away the tears brought on by vomiting.

I didn't want to tell you this because I didn't want to worry you or reopen old wounds, but in the end I think you have to know. Some cops came to our house two weeks ago to see Mum. They were aggressive, tried to intimidate her. One of them turned all the rooms upside down. He wasn't searching for anything, he just wanted to scare her. They said they were searching for your father. They said he wasn't dead, that he's come back to Bordeaux and he's killed people. Mum was shocked, and so was Dad. I've never seen them like that before. We talked about it until late at night and we don't know what to make of it. What do those creeps want? They even mentioned you being in Algeria. They said they would make your life more difficult there if my parents refused to talk. But the problem is they don't know anything! And your father was never really friends with them, as you know. They've told you about him before – he was a strange bloke. So watch out for those army bastards. Don't give them any excuse to make your life any harder than it already is . . .

I was sad to hear about the death of your friend Giovanni. They must be so rare, men like him, where you are.

Anyway . . . I wanted you to know. Our parents don't know that I've told you about this. They don't want you to worry, but there's no-one else I can talk to about these things. I miss you. We all do. We're counting the months until you get out of there, but for you every hour must seem like an eternity. Maybe the war will end more quickly, with De Gaulle. No-one knows, as I already said. Some people are afraid it'll turn into a dictatorship. Others, old comrades, claim it's all a ruse and he's already negotiating secretly with the F.L.N..

Take care of yourself. Come back soon. Your sister and your little comrade, Irène.

He rereads the letter. He doesn't understand. The images in his mind knock him off balance. His hand in that man's on a pavement, one morning. He tries to remember his face. Shoulders, a vague

405

outline, eyes turned towards him. His mother's voice. It all blurs together. Yes, his mummy: her smile, her hair. Her dark eyes. He tries to recall the day when. On the roof, suddenly. Don't move. He remembers that voice, whispering, urgent. Terrified. Don't say anything. Wait for us. He waits. He pees himself because he can't get his shorts unbuttoned; he's too scared of slipping down the tiles. He climbs up to the chimney and leans against it. Maybe he cries. Maybe he's scared. He can't remember. But he waits for them. Yes, he remembers that. He hears a few cars passing in the street below, hears people talking, windows opening, a caged bird singing. Mummy? Maybe he called for her, very softly. Little birds come to see him. They are freezing like him, feathers plumped. They flutter about near him and he talks to them in a quiet voice.

He walks towards the watchtower, looks up at the sentry standing near the machine gun. The man waves at him. How's it going? Fine. The man turns back, lights a cigarette. Daniel starts to cry. It happens just like that; a violent urge, like puking. He stifles his sobs, walks away, hides behind the water truck riddled with bullet holes.

He doesn't understand anything anymore. He cannot imagine his father coming back from the dead. The postcards of his memory are suddenly reshuffled, all those faded, time-stained images thrown down on the table, for a game whose rules he doesn't know. When the tears finally ebb and the spasms in his chest ease, he walks over to the refectory, watching his vast shadow, and wonders if it's really him that the setting sun is projecting onto the ground, or some other man. Or if he has, as they say, become a shadow of himself, a trace, a pale reflection of what he used to be.

In the middle of dinner, Caunègre stands up at the end of the table, in front of his mess tin filled with overcooked rice and meat of indeterminate provenance covered with a strong-smelling wine sauce. Castel does the same, and the men follow suit, but the lieutenant, with a paternal gesture, tells them to remain seated and he starts to talk about what happened today, what they had to do, what they will probably have to do again because they are at war here: yes, with all due respect to the politicians, it really is war they have been sent here to wage, to this country, to this province of our country, France, ravaged by armed gangs incapable of fighting fairly. He mentions the enemy's methods in this guerrilla war, this cowards' war, to which they must retaliate using the same methods, but without the barbarianism of that race who, were it not for France, would still be raising a few goats in barren fields. Without the throat-cutting, the mutilations, the disembowelments, the terror. Because that's not war, and even if things get dirty sometimes, it's important that they keep their hands clean.

"And your hands are clean, lads," he adds, showing them his own hands the way children do to their parents after they've washed them.

A few of the men look down at their fingers or ball their fists while others don't move, just stare at their stew going cold. Most of them look at the lieutenant, who is now resting both hands on the table like an orator or a teacher at his lectern, amid a silence broken only by the buzzing of flies.

Daniel, too, listens to Caunègre, and several times he meets his gaze as the officer sweeps his eyes over the men, sometimes seeming to speak directly to this one or that, although no-one can tell if he really sees those individuals or if he is just using a technique learned during officer training: how to address your men and establish your moral authority.

When the speech is over, they scrape clean their aluminium plates with metallic screeches that set their teeth on edge and loud chewing noises and then they stand up as soon as they've swallowed the last mouthful and go over to toss their dishes and cutlery into vast basins full of grease-curdled water, not even glancing at the poor dishwashers who throw soapflakes into that vile cold soup.

Daniel goes out into the warm night air and looks up at the vault of stars, touching Irène's letter which is folded in his chest pocket.

But the icy moonlight that rises in clouds above does not pick out any figure or show any path. It is a sky of indecipherable beauty, a sublime chaos, a phosphorescent mist that suddenly frightens him, as if it might crush him, choke him, dissolve him.

He remembers one night in the countryside just after the end of the war, sitting with Irène on a bench, looking up at the stars. The two of them were huddled close to Roselyne, who pointed out a few constellations that she knew, while they invented others: fantastical beasts, or strange faces, or flying saucers full of Martians, lights blinking as they moved closer. He remembers Irène asking if the Good Lord really was up there and where exactly and Roselyne telling them gently that there was nothing up there, only all those stars, but that it was already so beautiful, it was enough to fill the sky. Irène had squinted, examining the heavens more closely, and after a while she'd asked if that was where dead people went, so her mother had sighed and held them both even more tightly to her as she explained that each star was a memory and that the dead might be there and that all you had to do was think about them and the stars would shine. So stars are good then. In that case Mistigri is in a star and I can still see him. Yes. Even cats, my sweet. Even cats.

Daniel remembers how he had sat there alone after Irène and Roselyne had gone home and desperately searched for his parents' stars without finding them, because they were all the same. Perhaps he had called out to them, whispering their names, but the silence had been heavy, and him so small, until a dog had started barking endlessly somewhere in the distance.

And now here he is under the same mute stars, far from his childhood beliefs, in the same oppressive silence despite the racket of the lads getting drunk in the mess hall. The woman he killed that morning, attempting to put her out of that terrible agony, will rot underground in a darkness without stars. There is nothing beyond this material world that engulfs everything.

Then he goes off to drink with the others, because there's fuck-all else to do. He gorges himself on beer, he talks with men who laugh without knowing why or who take the piss out of him, saying why the long face you're not a fucking horse, telling him to stop being such a pansy you'll see your mother again, saying all this as they pat his back and open another can. He eyeballs the two Parisians, who are chatting at a table with the caporal, then he goes out to piss and there are four of them already, emptying their bladders, waving their cocks and talking shit: I'd have a wank, but I'm so sick of it, I'm going to end up with blisters on my palms. And they all laugh, and one of them – Daumas – laughs so hard that he pisses on his feet and swears and scratches at the ground like a dog when he's finished. And then Daniel goes back in the mess and dives through the hot, unbreathable smog that stinks of sweat and tobacco and he starts drinking like a fish again, pouring beers down into a bottomless hole, and the thought comes that a hole is exactly what he's become, an abyss that must be filled and drowned before he falls inside it.

All night long, the booze beats in his temples and he sweats it out through every pore in his skin. All night long, he is buffeted by a dizzying sleep that floats through his dreams until he is torn from them by nausea and he opens his eyes, unsure whether he needs to get up to puke. After a moment, he slips out of the dorm in his underwear to try to make himself puke, but all that comes out is a monstrous belch and a migraine that hits him smack in the head and rips his brain open like a bullet, so he stays there, bent double, hands on his thighs, almost falling, and he feels the cold night air on his sweat-soaked back and shivers as his entire body is chilled through.

When he goes back to bed, he curls up and counts the stabbing beats of the migraine ringing in his temples, seven, eight, nine, then falls asleep as abruptly as a boxer knocked to the canvas.

He is woken by the pale blue edge of dawn light creeping under the door. He lies in the darkness and listens to the others snoring or shifting on their beds or turning over with a mumbled groan. They're allowed an extra hour of sleep this morning, thank you, lieutenant. Then it's wash day. It's now or never. The idea has been planted there in his mind now, as impossible to ignore as the flag-pole in the middle of the square.

He gets up. Puts on his trousers and undershirt. Takes his camouflage jacket and his boonie hat.

"What are you doing?"

He does not turn to face the slurry voice.

"Nothing. Going for a piss."

He hears the man sigh then turn over, probably already asleep again.

He goes out into the cool air, into the light so pale it seems as if the sun is too shy to make an appearance. Eyes closed, he savours the breeze that is already stirring up dust. He walks around the outside of the mess hall and sits on the bench where he often goes at night, on an overhang that looks out over the valley. Pockets of mist cling to the treetops and hang between thickets. Cigarette. An American one. His migraine and nausea are gone, and he's hungry. He needs to eat, before. He waits there, letting his mind fill with confused thoughts that calm him down or make his heart pound. He dozes off at odd moments, swept away by a dream in which a couple have come to a train station to welcome the little boy he has become again, a kid who's been to war, who's killed a disfigured woman, a kid who recognises the faces of Maurice and Roselyne but not the people, who are his parents, his mum holding him in her arms, and the voices, the voices silent for so long are talking to him and the faces vanish so he no longer knows how old he is, his child-hood has gone, and it's at this moment of breathless disarray that he wakes, opening his eyes to the golden-brown beauty of the new dawn, as night flees the valley in ribbons of mist.

The smell of coffee reaches his nostrils and he decides to join the others. He eats stale bread soaked in sweetened coffee and a few biscuits, then drinks another bowl standing up outside the mess hall.

All morning, he pretends to be absorbed by the collar of the shirt he's rubbing, the sliver of soap that has slid to the bottom of the trough where the men do their laundry; he brushes, he rinses, he wrings, and the others do the same, sometimes talking about the kind, brave little woman who will soon be washing and ironing their shirts for them . . . The conversations don't get any dirtier than this, because there are too many hangovers bent over the task in hand. The men speak in low voices, concentrating, rubbing hard at the filth. But the odour of soap is perhaps too familiar. Suddenly it's as if they're all home again, in the ordinary days of peacetime.

Daniel notices that the door of the caporal vaguemestre– a man named Ledain – is ajar. He hasn't seen him come out, but he tries his luck anyway. Leaving the undershirt that he was scrubbing to soak in the murky water, he walks over to the building. The door is lopsided but robust, designed to be locked with a key. Daniel knocks. Calls out. No-one answers. He goes in and walks up to the little desk next to a window, opens the bottom drawer, finds the key, and shoves it in his pocket. He hasn't breathed for almost a minute. Ledain could arrive at any moment. He's a sneaky little fucker. He's been suspected of opening letters that he thinks are from women. No proof. But it seems like the kind of thing that slimy perv would do.

Outside, the circus continues. A few men start hanging their laundry on wire clotheslines that stretch across the refectory. Sergent Castel emerges from his lair, bare-chested, in shorts and espadrilles. He looks all around, sees Daniel, and observes him for quite a long time, one hand held over his eyes to shade them from the brutal sun, then he nods and Daniel salutes him, just in case, and Castel turns away, shaking his head and shrugging, maybe out of disappointment, or maybe because his head feels like a bag of pool balls clunking down a staircase.

Daniel finds his things where he hid them, under the front seat of the jeep, folded inside his dirty shirt, tied up in haste. The engine roars straight into life. He knows the jeep is in good shape: he helped change the oil the other day. A nice strong motor. And the tank is three-quarters full.

"Hey!" yells the man on top of the watchtower.

Daniel waves to him without turning around, then begins his manoeuvre. He is facing the gate, flanked by sandbags. The engine purrs smoothly. When he looks up at the watchtower, he no longer sees the sentry, who probably couldn't care less about this jeep or the bloke driving it. He puts it into gear and leaves the enclosure, driving slowly, and descends the steep little ramp that leads to the road with his foot off the accelerator. When he reaches the road, which is wider, he steps on the pedal, opens his mouth wide and swallows the air that blows into his face, and lets loose a yell, then another one, as if he wants the mountains and their rocks to hear him, then he sits back more comfortably in the seat and pulls his hat down firmly on his head so it won't fly off. He finds a pair of goggles hanging on the gearstick, so he puts them on, well aware that they make him look like some loony just escaped from an asylum, which is pretty much the case: an asylum that breeds insanity on a mass scale, crazed killers, sexual obsessives, silent idiots and dazed pissheads; an asylum that takes their soul and returns them soiled, crumpled, stinking, shrunken, like a shirt smeared with all the shit from their body, covered with sweat and blood and vomit and piss and then dragged through the mud, their soul reduced to a tattered uniform stained with all this human vileness.

He drives as fast as he can, feeling an intoxicated freedom in his chest, swollen like a stifled sob, a freedom he has never known before. They could stop him at the next crossroads and throw him in jail, but they'll never be able to catch him again. They will never be able to steal what fills his heart.

He drives like this for three hours, alone in the empty landscape, like the war's last survivor. No peasants, no carts, no roadblocks.

412

He sees smoke rising from a few chimneys in distant villages. On a curve of the road overlooking the valley, he stops and cuts the engine. He gets out of the jeep and it seems to him that the two or three steps he takes are his first. He has never felt so clearly, starkly aware of being upright and moving forward. The hot wind blows around his solid, firmly planted legs. Daniel shuffles the soles of his boots on the pebbly ground.

The wind blows silence into his ears. Whispers the peace of the world. The sky is a harsh blue, like a painted window. The steep-sided valley is a hotchpotch of blinding slabs of light and caverns still filled with darkness. He opens up the dirty shirt and takes out his little frame, then unfolds it and captures the landscape in a long, slow panorama, and suddenly each stone, the slightest trace of shadow, starts to vibrate and he has the impression that everything is beginning to bake gently under the sun in a silent quivering.

He ends his shot and catches his breath. He is surprised by the width of the frame, the depth of field. He realises that he has become used to the magnification of the rifle scope. For weeks now, he has looked for and seen nothing but targets. He stands there a moment longer on this outcrop and tries to think about all this, but suddenly becomes aware that time is passing and that he needs to reach the city as soon as possible, before they start searching for him.

He weaves through the agitation of the city at this hour, just before the shops close until the evening. He passes other jeeps, trucks with three or four soldiers slumped in the back. With his hat pulled down over his ears and his motorbike goggles, his filthy undershirt gaping under his arms, he imagines people will take him for some fierce warrior, returned from the jebel to enjoy his leave. He recalls the thirty men in a *commando de chasse*[35] that spent one

35 A French military unit created during the Algerian War to carry out counter-guerrilla operations, each unit consisting of about a hundred harkis – Muslim Algerian loyalists – commanded by about twenty officers and N.C.O.s from the French gendarmerie.

night at the base: armed to the teeth, some of them dressed in rags and each in his own style, wearing parachute jump boots. They looked more like a gang of highway robbers than a unit of the French army. The officer who commanded them, an unshaved capitaine wearing a scarf on his head like a pirate, wore no emblem or stripes. He never gave orders. His platoon acted like he did, as one, showing neither weariness nor zeal. Those men really stuck together. They sat apart and ate their Muslim rations – which everyone knew to be less disgusting than the regular ones – and they all slept in a half-collapsed building that was generally used as a garage, then left at dawn, without a word, after drinking gallons of coffee in the mess hall.

He likes the idea that all those dickheads could believe that. He abandons the jeep two blocks from the barracks where they came before to pick up supplies. He puts on his shirt and lets it hang out so he looks as little as possible like a soldier. But his canvas walking shoes, his baggy combat trousers, all that beige and khaki make it obvious that he is walking armed through the street in the middle of this indifferent but lively and colourful crowd, scattered with red dresses and white shirts.

He walks back to the café where he ate with Giovanni that day, remembering the way as he goes, then turns into the Arab part of town. Hundreds of eyes staring at him; he can feel them on his back. Dark, wide, frightened eyes. Voices whispering as he passes. Words spat in front of him. Insults, he is sure. He wishes he could tell them. Tell them how much he deserves their insults. And ask them the price of redemption for what he's done. Four kids follow him, jabbering away, and they ask him where he's going and laughingly explain that the army's not this way. And he smiles, says he knows, thank you, and he ups his pace, until a sharp voice echoes down the street and sends the kids running off amid peals of laughter.

He wanders lost for nearly an hour before he spots the carpenter's shop and recognises the corner of the street where Autin lives.

He knocks at the door and looks around as Giovanni did, but can see nothing at the end of this shadowy alley but the constant toing and froing of passers-by in the sunlight, can hear nothing but the shouts and laughs of children, the frenzied songs of caged birds, the whine of a saw from the carpenter's workshop. He jumps when the bolt slams and almost recoils in the glare of the professor's eyes when they stare at him, hostile or reproachful, weighing him up with a frown as he notices the dishevelled uniform. Say something. Find the right words. Daniel senses that the door is about to close.

"Giovanni is dead."

"Come in. Don't stay there."

Autin buries his hands in his pockets and leans against the wall.

"How did it happen?"

"It was on the road, the day we came to see you. An ambush. The lieutenant died too. And another bloke who was in the jeep at the head of the convoy. Giovanni took two bullets in his belly. The new lieutenant and the sergent told me they couldn't do anything to save him at the hospital."

Autin sighs. Shakes his head. He regards Daniel sadly.

"Did you come here to tell me that? And anyway, how did you get here? You're not dressed properly, are you?"

"I ran away. Stole a jeep. I'm not going back there. That's it."

"What do you mean, that's it? Just like that, on a sudden impulse? You decide you've had enough so you run away?"

"Yes, monsieur. I'm deserting. Giovanni was going to. He realised a long time ago."

"It was different, with Giovanni."

"I know. He'd been instructed. He was intelligent. And he had ideas, the right ones. Not like me. I thought it'd be like . . . I don't know . . . a sort of adventure. I didn't want to hear what they told me at home, I just let them talk, thinking I had to go and see it for myself."

"And what did you see?"

Daniel thinks of a verse that Giovanni often cited: *And at times*

I have seen what man thought he saw. He can't remember who wrote that. He wouldn't be able to explain it, but he thinks now he can understand it.

"It's difficult to describe. It's . . ."

"It's war. What did you expect when you came here?"

"Nothing. I didn't expect anything. But I didn't think I'd do what I've done. I could never have imagined that."

He's short of breath. His chest is being crushed by a giant hand.

"Come on. You should eat something. You'll think more clearly afterwards."

They cross the patio and enter the kitchen. Autin goes into a pantry and emerges with a plate full of dates, a loaf of bread, a bowl of black olives. From a cool box he takes a piece of cheese and a bottle of water. He grabs a glass and a plate from the stone sink.

"Help yourself. I've already eaten."

Daniel sits at the end of the table and Autin sits facing him and lights a cigarette. He eats a few dates, two or three olives. Autin picks up the bread and cuts a thick slice, then pushes the cheese towards him.

"Eat, I said. You have to eat."

Daniel fills his glass with water and drinks it straight down. He takes some cheese, chews a bit of bread, swallows it with difficulty.

"So?" Autin says.

"So, I can't take it anymore. I have to get out of here."

"Do you understand what you're saying?"

Daniel takes the pack of army cigarettes from his pocket and lights one. Autin hands him a pack of American cigarettes.

"Have one of these. Stop smoking that shit."

Daniel stubs out his Gauloise and lights one of Autin's cigarettes.

"Yes," he says, blowing smoke up at the ceiling. "I understand. I've become a murderer. I don't know where I am anymore, who I am. We slaughter people. All these poor squaddies getting shot to bits, and for what? For those fucking colonists? For all those *pied-noir* bastards who treat Arabs like dogs? To keep Algeria? My parents and my sister were right. They told me to stay right out of it, to hide in an office somewhere because it wasn't my war, because you don't make war against a people. And yet I did everything I could to see combat."

"And what did you do, in combat?"

"As soon as they put a rifle in my hands, I loved it. I put my heart into it. The instructors couldn't believe it. And when they gave me a rifle with a scope, I thought it was amazing."

"When you're shooting at cardboard targets, why not? It's just like a funfair, I suppose. Except that, one day, you have a human being in your crosshairs."

Daniel tells him. About the first ambush, the death of Declerck, the terrified men, lying on the ground to escape the machine-gun fire. Then the stampede up the hill with the sergent, then the *fell* hidden in bushes taking potshots at his mates. The pleasure of framing him in his scope, the electric charge that ran through his body as he squeezed the trigger. The badly wounded man, the sergeant finishing him off. The congratulations of the others, and the condemnation of Giovanni. The sensation that he was becoming someone important. The lieutenant's handshake.

Daniel speaks in a hollow voice, staring down at the table. Autin listens without moving. He holds a cigarette between his fingers, unlit.

The water-truck convoy and the second ambush and the lieutenant dying with his leg ripped off, Giovanni lying in a pool of his own blood in the back of the half-track, the fear, the *fell*'s corpse almost cut in two by a burst of .50-calibre gunfire, the hatred and the nausea when faced with this display of guts and the man's wide-eyed expression: Daniel tells him everything. The retaliatory operation against the village suspected of harbouring rebels who'd killed three of our men. He tells him about the grenades tossed into the houses, the girl raped and killed by those two bastards, the desire he felt to put a bullet in each of their heads because killing was becoming a sort of reflex, a solution worth considering. He also tells him about the woman with the destroyed face and how he finished her off, that head without any eyes or nose or mouth, only blood and scraps of hanging skin, and that death rattle rising from the back of her throat as if the flesh itself were groaning. He doesn't stop talking, doesn't even pause for breath, his face covered with sweat, dripping down onto his thighs, staring emptily, blindly, his gaze turned inwards, to his remembrances, to the pitiless darkness where the film of his memory is projected: yes, I pressed the trigger and I saw her fall sideways, and in that moment it seemed like the right thing to do because the harm was already done, but the problem is that in war the harm is always already done. It's like when a fence around a pillaged garden has been smashed down – from then on, it enables anyone to enter and to continue the theft and destruction. In war, everything is permitted, and I don't want to permit myself everything. I can't. Do you understand?

He sneaks a glance at Autin, but sees only the glistening stupefaction in his eyes and instantly dives back into his vision and his monologue, realising that it is the first time he has talked about all this and that it's doing him good, even as it tears at his soul and his guts, a bit like in the films when a man rips out an arrow that's stuck in his own chest: you see him suffering, gritting his teeth, sweat streaming down his face, then suddenly relaxing when the Apache dart is removed and almost fainting before rediscovering his indestructible heroic calm. This is the first time he's been able to find the words to describe this fuck-up, this hornet's nest . . . yes, that's it, a hornet's nest: the more you struggle, the more it injects its venom, to the point that your body and soul are saturated with pain and they become anaesthetised. He feels as if he is emptying himself, and little by little he slumps deeper into his chair, until he is slouching like an old man under the initially impassive eyes of this cold man who seems to have seen and heard everything before but whose gaze now is wavering, turning away from this young soldier to search for some mysterious reference point on the white wall across from him, a sign perhaps, and finally he lifts the cigarette to his mouth and lights it.

He smokes for a moment in silence, observing Daniel through narrowed eyes, perhaps because of the smoke or perhaps because of some instinctive mistrust. Either way, it is clear that he's thinking, calculating, and when Daniel fills a glass with water he holds out his own so that Daniel can fill that too, then he stubs out his cigarette in the ashtray, blowing smoke through his nostrils in two plumes that disperse instantly.

"I'll see what I can do. You can start by washing because you stink, then I'll give you some civilian clothes. Tonight Chadia will take you to some people. You can't stay here. From now on, you do not go out in the street without permission. You want to desert: I don't know how we're going to manage this, but from this point on you are under our protection and you have to obey our orders. It could take days or weeks before we find a way of getting you out of here. It's very rare that soldiers decide to do this. It would have been difficult even for Giovanni, who was a comrade, but we'd started to test out a network, so we'll see. Remember, if you fuck up, dozens of comrades will die. You do not have the right to put their lives in danger. When an Algerian militant is arrested, he's tortured. Did you know that? Here, the Gestapo is in power. So stay calm or we'll leave you outside a gendarmerie. Got it?"

Daniel nods. He says thank you, thank you, in a hoarse voice, his throat tight.

"Don't worry," says Autin. "It'll be O.K. It takes a lot of courage to do what you've done. And to talk like that."

The man smiles. This is the first time Daniel has seen him smile. Suddenly he feels as if he can breathe more easily.

30

Within a week, I had found a job and a place to live. My savings wouldn't have lasted long anyway, and I needed a quiet place where I could take refuge and an occupation to prevent me going mad by thinking constantly about the sole reason I had returned to Bordeaux: to make Darlac suffer as I had suffered. I knew it was impossible, but I thought if I went over every conceivable way of torturing a human being, I would eventually find one that seemed more or less appropriate.

The apartment was tiny and dark but clean. It was a second-floor flat, overlooking the cours de l'Yser. On the floor below me was a sad, pale Spanish washerwoman who worked all day, constantly coming and going from her home to the cellar where she boiled water in the washtubs that filled the stairwell with the odours of soap and bleach from morning to night. We were the only ones in that damp, leprous building. On the first day – because she was the one who had the keys and who opened the apartment up for me – she offered to clean and iron my laundry. She proposed a price so low that I wondered how many tons of laundry she must have to wash in a week in order to scrape a living. Her name was Madame Mendez; her husband had died during the Civil War and she'd had to take refuge in France with her sister. Her black hair, held back by a headband, was always gathered up in a compact little bun. She wore black from head to foot. The only colour she allowed herself was a violet shawl that she wore over her shoulders when it was cold in the mornings, when I would see her sometimes dragging her feet as she transported the day's first load of dirty laundry.

Mazeau almost choked at the other end of the line when I told him who I was and he finally accepted the proof of my identity that I provided. Oh yes, he remembered me. He had a good memory for names and faces, which was a useful quality in a cop. He too thought I had disappeared in the camps. That was the word he used: disappeared. Then he stopped talking and there was an embarrassed silence during which I imagine he thought about the long procession of the dead that I had, to his amazement, somehow escaped. Behind him though, I could hear the usual hum of an office: voices speaking, doors creaking, typewriters clattering.

When I told him I was calling on behalf of Abel, he cleared his throat. "We have to talk somewhere private," he said. I imagined him peering left and right in case one of his colleagues was spying on the conversation and already calculating what he might gain from this new source of trouble. He seemed about as safe to me as a steep, shaky old staircase.

We met in a packed café opposite the station. I recognised him easily amid the crowd of departing travellers, civilians and soldiers, the roar of conversations and the fog of cigarette smoke. He was pretending to read a newspaper and kept staring around with his suspicious, shifty light blue eyes, and he looked almost exactly as I remembered him: a pale, almost transparent man, his chestnut hair parted to the left in a ruler-straight line. When I approached his table and pulled the chair towards me so I could sit down, he lowered his newspaper and looked at me with surprise, maybe with hostility. I introduced myself, but the stupor did not leave his face even as he gave me his damp, warm hand to shake. He stammered that he hadn't recognised me, apologising as he stared at me, perhaps trying to determine what exactly it was about me that had changed. Then he relaxed and leaned back in his seat.

He asked me how I was, what I'd been doing all these years, since '45. I gave him the short version. I'd started living again, and that had taken a while. He nodded. He could understand that, after what I'd been through. He mentioned two or three people he knew who'd come back from the camps and were still unable to forget all that.

"Who said anything about forgetting?" I asked. "Who would want to? Who would be capable of it?"

From the empty way he stared at me, I realised that he did not understand. I ordered a coffee from the waiter who was walking past us, while Mazeau recovered his composure.

Unsure how to broach the subject, I began by talking about Abel: the man he had been and the one he'd become, sick and exhausted and bitter. About my sadness at seeing him in that state. Mazeau just nodded and made a few mournful comments: the usual clichés about the passing of time, which he must have thought were quite profound because he pronounced them in a croaky voice, staring vaguely into space and concluding with a hand gesture filled with fatalism.

Then he kept his silence, pretending to look around at the hustle and bustle of the café. He avoided my eye, concentrating instead on his empty cup or the little spoon that he turned in his fingers. I could tell he was afraid of what I was about to say. I'm sure he would have given almost anything to have me change my mind and suddenly leave, or for some unexpected incident – a train crash, a car accident – that would oblige him to run off.

"I came back to settle a few old scores," I told him.

I talked like the pen-pusher I was.

Mazeau looked up at me, round-eyed and frowning. He slowly rubbed his hands together.

"What scores? With who?"

When I pronounced Darlac's name, he glanced over at the next table, as if frightened that the three squaddies practically falling asleep over their beers might have heard, and he signalled me to shut up. I spoke more quietly so he would calm down and listen to me, and I explained that I wanted to know where to find him, but that I also wanted to know about all his friends, his relatives, about anything that might have helped him survive the great purge. I didn't tell him what I planned to do, because at that moment I didn't know myself. I merely led him to believe that I wanted to bring charges against Darlac, denounce this collaborator who had ended up as a commissaire.

He smiled and finally met my gaze.

"All cops were collaborators, for the simple reason that they were obeying orders and they were scared, just like everyone else. Scared of their bosses, of the Krauts, of some colleagues. Some were more zealous than others; some hated the Jews and communists, even if they didn't really know why, and wanted to eliminate them, and that was enough to motivate them. There was Poinsot and his team, the S.A.P.[36], but they got what was coming to them during the Liberation. And then there was the majority of cops, who just did what they were told to do, without asking too many questions. A few others, like Darlac, used the situation to make money. He was in cahoots with the gangs back then, and they'd plunder apartments left empty after the round-ups. He was also in league with the Kraut officers who took care of all that. Everyone knew, but no-one said anything. That's what it was like. There were only a few of us who tried to do good, to save our honour, if that was possible. Commissaire Laborde was another. But there were only about twenty of us at most. Most of the cops in authority now were also in authority during the Occupation. They'd have had to fire three-quarters of the Bordeaux police to purge all those shits. And that's what you want to hit out at? They'll come down on you like a ton of bricks. Forget it. You're too small and too weak to take them on, and anyway you've already suffered enough."

"Yeah, but they haven't. That's the whole problem."

He shrugged. He seemed genuinely saddened by my obstinacy.

"If you insist . . . I'll get your information for you. After all, if you manage to bring down Darlac, I certainly won't be complaining."

We agreed to meet in the same place the following week. He left first and I saw him watch the street before opening the door. I thought he was exaggerating a bit, but what he'd told me about the police corresponded to what I already knew, and to what I'd suspected at the time, back when I didn't want to face the truth, when I felt protected by Darlac, who told me not to move, to stay aloof from all that so me and my wife and kid

36 The S.A.P.: Section des Affaires Politiques (Political Affairs Section). The Bordeaux equivalent of the Gestapo, led by Commissaire Poinsot.

would remain sheltered from the coming storm.

I sat there for a while thinking again about my blindness, my coward-
ice. Wondering if the fact of looking evil in its face was going to give me
my sight back, now it was too late.

When we next saw each other, Mazeau gave me a rundown of the powers
at play, as he put it. Cops and gangsters. Rival groups in the underworld,
enemy factions in the police force. Prostitution, gambling, fencing stolen
goods. A few armed robberies, a bit of drug-dealing. Simmering post-
war resentments among the coppers. With Darlac, the city's best policeman, as a dishonest peacemaker, the puppeteer-in-chief. Holding some
by their balls, others by the throat. One name kept recurring: Penot.
Gabriel Penot. Gaby to his friends. He had been assistant detective in
Poinsot's special unit, the jobless cousin of one of his deputies. One of
those losers who do a bit of black-market dealing and have their fingers
stuck in various pies, and whose parents had fixed him up with his cop
cousin in order to keep him out of prison. So lazy and incompetent that
even his cousin kept him away from any important missions. He acted as
a messenger boy between the department and the Germans. Maybe he
doled out a few beatings during interrogations: he was capable of that
and, like the other thugs, took a certain pleasure from it. He almost
enrolled in the militia, but must have decided that was too risky, given
that, by late '43, the tide was starting to turn. He did help them out
though, offloading seizures of food intended for the black market, or
anything he could get his hands on during arrests: money, jewellery,
objects of value. But he covered his arse by acting discreetly and using
fake identities. So much so that when the Liberation came, the investiga-
tors in charge of purging the police had passed him over due to a lack of
evidence: after all, there were tens of thousands of low-ranking stooges
like him all over the country. He did six months in prison, then had his
case dismissed. The rumour was that, in '47, in exchange for certain
services rendered during the Occupation, Darlac had put money into
the bar on rue de Pas-Saint-Georges that Penot had bought on the

spotted in places. I would go there for a drink after work, about one o'clock; it was close to my office. The local craftsmen went there to eat lunch, and there were a few dazed-looking drunkards hanging around. Penot presided behind his cash register, a cigarette permanently planted in the corner of his mouth, while a waitress did all the work. During the afternoons I never saw him wipe a glass or pour a beer or make a coffee. He would chat with a customer or read Sud-Ouest or Ciné Revue or Match or stare through the windows at people passing in the street.

He was a short man with very dark hair, swept back and held in place with Brylcreem. His eyes, ever alert, burned feverishly in that bony face. The first time I went, I felt his eyes follow me until I sat down then return to me at regular intervals during the hour I remained there.

In the evenings, the clientele changed. Two or three girls would sit on bar stools, drinking Cinzano and smoking. Men would go up to them and have whispered conversations which were sometimes brief and sometimes slightly longer – here, this is for mademoiselle – and which would end with the two of them leaving together. Often, the woman went first, the man following three metres behind in case they were seen together. I enjoyed watching the goings-on of all these johns, some of them straightforward, approaching the girl directly, others trying to be more discreet or cunning and leaning on the bar to order something first. Then they would greet the girl with a nod and sip their wine while pretending to stare vacantly into the large mirror behind the shelves filled with bottles, before finally deciding to make their approach, smiling smarmily. The girls didn't bat an eyelid. They would look at their clients indifferently, even though you had the sense that they were weighing the man up while he chatted them up. Other than that, when there were no men there to bother them, they talked among themselves or chatted with the waiter, a skinny young bloke that everyone called Jeannot. Sometimes they would greet a new arrival, often one of those men in a raincoat and fedora straight out of a Hollywood film, or a tough bloke in a cap and sheepskin coat who would enter with a "good cheap, and that the two had remained on good terms ever since. It was also said that Penot's brother, a creep who fucked kids, had been rescued from some very deep shit in '50, by the good graces of Albert Darlac.

I listened as Mazeau told me all this in a monotone voice, and I suspected that he was enjoying the picture he was painting of the city transformed into a jungle ruled by predators, a permanent twilight where human filth was given free rein. He talked to me like a biology teacher during a dissection: blasé, effortlessly superior to their naïve students, all sickened by the sight of the gaping corpse. But he was forgetting where I'd come back from. The depths of night I had journeyed to. He couldn't possibly know or even imagine the ghost-filled darkness I carried around with me. Listening to him, I saw it again: Olga walking down the platform, swept along by the crowd, supported by an old woman. I saw her turn around, trying to see me one last time, before she vanished out of sight and everything was lost.

It was then, at that very moment, that I knew what I was going to do. I was going to eliminate a few of these bastards who'd been his friends or simply his acquaintances and wait for his cop's brain to realise that something was circling him, drawing closer. I had to attack his kid, who had nothing to do with any of this, because I wanted to scare him. I wanted him to be frightened every time he walked in the street. I wanted him to sleep badly, to look under his bed before he got in it. It was a good plan, but I didn't know if I'd be able to execute it; at times I felt as if I were a silly little kid, dreaming up a simplistic film script.

Gaby Penot. I managed to gather my thoughts and my will around this name. I didn't know how to go after him. He would be the first. I had to find a way to approach him. I hoped an idea would come to me, that my resolve would help me to act.

I became a regular in his café. It was large, dark, old-fashione Penot had kept the décor and furniture as they were, changing or a few windows and giving the walls a fresh coat of paint. The bencl sagged, the chairs were often rickety, the large wall mirrors w *evening" for the whole bar.*

All these people seemed to know each other. Sometimes they pretended not to greet each other, just exchanging looks, or signals, talking around a table for ten minutes then suddenly separating and ignoring each other for the rest of the evening, or abruptly leaving the café.

One night, Darlac came in. My heart stopped beating for several endless seconds, then started banging so hard that I could hardly breathe. He was with a broad-shouldered bloke, built like a docker, whom Penot called Francis. They congratulated each other and had a drink, joking in lowered voices. Darlac casually observed the room, as cops always do. I felt his gaze on me and looked up, my heart in my throat, but he had already moved on and was helping himself to water from a carafe on the table. I realised the mistake I had made, coming here: if he recognised me, my whole stupid plan would be screwed. I had changed, of course. Violette had had difficulty placing me. Mazeau would never have identified me if I hadn't introduced myself to him after first talking to him on the phone. But Darlac was another breed altogether: a bloodhound, or maybe a wolf, whose senses are all sharpened by the hunt for their prey, because their survival depends upon it. And then there were all the nights we had spent together, staying up until we were exhausted. That intimacy between us that marks familiar memories. If he didn't recognise me, it was probably because I was dead and only a few of my companions in purgatory could see me.

When he left, half an hour later, he said goodbye only to a girl who was being chatted up by a bloke near the door, and when he walked out onto the street, without turning around, I breathed in and felt as if my lungs were filled with pure oxygen.

I couldn't go on like that. I would go there at lunchtimes mostly and would sometimes order the plat du jour, and Penot ended up replying to my "hello" when I went in. In the evenings I would go in for an aperitif, but I could tell that my presence was out of place, could feel the boss's eyes resting heavily on me. I was going to end up making them suspi-

427

cious; he might talk to Darlac about me, and then I would have no chance of remaining invisible in his eyes. So I had to find a way to justify my regular visits to the bar.

From that day on, I got into the habit of always carrying a knife. It was a flick-knife and, when the blade opened, the noise it made gave me a shudder of cruel pleasure. It had been a present from a man I knew in Paris. Maybe I'll tell that story another day. Anyway, I knew I couldn't afford to hesitate any longer. I couldn't keep postponing it.

One evening I stayed until closing. I got there later than usual and left about eleven, with the last customers. Then I hid in a doorway to watch, and I saw Penot and Jeannot, the waiter, switch off the lights and lower the metal shutter. They went their separate ways without a word and Penot walked off down the street. He stopped to light a cigarette, then walked more quickly towards the cours d'Alsace-et-Lorraine. I gripped the knife in my hand at the bottom of my pocket, and I followed him, almost staggering. The two coffees I'd drunk were sloshing around in my belly and I'm not sure how I managed to avoid puking between two parked cars, because I could feel my blood beating in my stomach as if someone was repeatedly punching me. It was raining, and the splashing of the water drowned out the sounds of our footsteps in the empty streets. He turned into rue de la Rousselle and it was so dark there that I almost lost him from view. I heard the click of a key in a lock and I saw his figure illuminated by the light from a corridor before it disappeared. I kept walking until I reached that door so I could see what number it was: 30.

Suddenly I was no longer afraid. I noticed that the rain was streaming over me, icy on my neck, and that my shoes were soaked like mops. I savoured all that cold water as if it was washing away my cowardice.

I killed him the next day.

I didn't sleep that night. I thought about my whole life, about those I thought I loved, and those I should have cherished. Faces, voices, paraded through my mind. The dead and the living. But mostly the dead. They crowded into my room. Devastated faces, corpselike shadows, friends from long ago smiling and laughing. I felt possessed by a fever that made me shiver with cold in my bed. Once, in Paris, I smoked opium, and I believe the sensation was almost identical: a flood of images and sounds experienced in a half-sleep that was by turns oppressive and weightlessly floating. I wished Olga could come and sit on the bed with me; I wished I could take her hand, speak to her again. I searched the darkness for Hélène's figure, wanting to know if she was still strong enough to dance. I spoke to the shadows I thought I could see with a very clear sensation of going insane.

I waited half an hour opposite his house, hidden in the shadows of a porch. I was trembling with cold and exhaustion. Maybe with fear. I saw Penot arrive, a black, hunched figure, the collar of his raincoat pulled up. I let him open the door of his building and turn on the light.

"Gaby?"

He turned around, startled, but I couldn't see his face. Only the steam of his breath in the pale brightness of the corridor. Grabbing him by the collar, I pushed him backwards and stabbed the knife into his belly through the thick layers of his clothing, not knowing if the blade had entered his flesh or become embedded in wool and cotton. So I pulled the knife out and Penot took advantage of this to grab my throat. He started to squeeze it with his sharp fingers, but I managed to get him in the face. I saw the blade slice through almost his entire cheek and felt it hit something hard. I pushed harder and Penot fell back so suddenly, arms flapping, that I let go of the knife and saw it planted under his cheekbone. He fell on his arse and screamed. I don't know if he only started screaming then, but that was when I first heard it. Dark, glistening blood was pouring from his wound and I could see his eyes, open wide and trying desperately to see me – to recognise me, I suppose. He fell onto his side, holding his stomach, then his hand rose to his face and I was afraid he would take the knife and use it against me, so I rushed at him, grabbing my flick-knife in spite of his hand gripping my arm, and I stabbed the blade into his throat and felt the warmth of blood on my hand. I saw it spray out and tried to avoid it by leaping to the side,

429

then I stepped back towards the door, watching Penot as he tried to stop the bleeding as he lay back on the first few steps of the staircase. From up- stairs someone yelled, threatening to call the police. "Gaby, is that you?"

I went out into the street and I ran to the cours Victor-Hugo, then I slowed down to a walk in case a patrolling cop should happen to notice some bloke running alone on an empty street, particularly as I still had the knife on me and as, in the gleam of the street lights, I could see that I was covered with blood up to my elbows.

Only when I got back home did I wonder whether Penot was actually dead. I'd heard about neck wounds before and I knew that you would normally die from them in a matter of minutes, but there are always exceptional cases, strange miracles: blokes who survive after losing half the blood in their body – because it just wasn't their time, as people say – or whose wound stops bleeding, for one reason or another. For a brief moment I hoped that the neighbour I had heard yelling from upstairs had managed to save his life while they waited for the ambulance to arrive. I felt relieved at the idea that I had not really killed him after all, since he was still alive when I left. I was reasoning like a four-year-old kid who thinks he can repair the broken vase by sticking it back together with his spit or can erase what he's done by hiding the shattered pieces at the bottom of a rubbish bin.

I had killed a man. His blood had stained my sleeves, it was clotting between my fingers. I had seen the terror and surprise in his eyes. I got completely undressed and began to wash myself in cold water, shivering in a daze. I no longer knew why I had done it. I felt neither guilt nor pride, only a sort of self-disgust and such contempt for the man I had killed that he no longer existed to me except as a bled corpse, a carcass. Even his past as an evil, torturing bastard no longer mattered, as if he'd been purged of it by the fatal haemorrhage. As I rubbed soap on my skin, I tried to convince myself that this murder was part of a methodical plan intended to worry and then terrify Darlac, to make him lose his mind, but the truth was I could no longer find any logic in my act. I had no explanation for it at all.

So I lay down on my bed and fell straight asleep, crushed by the weight of all these questions.

The next morning, I felt peaceful and well-rested. No nightmare had woken me. Perhaps because, from that point on, I was doomed to flounder in a bad dream that never ended.

31

He waited eight days in that apartment in the company of a widow, Lydia Mourgues, who put him up in a sort of white-walled cell, lit by a dormer window that overlooked an alleyway, though all he could see of it was the bare-brick wall of the house opposite. A man who introduced himself as Ahmed had brought him here after a long confab with Robert Autin. It was the hour of the siesta, the streets were empty and the man walked quickly, without a w ord, without looking at him, Daniel five metres behind him in line with the instructions Autin gave him before his departure. Ahmed seemed unconcerned whether the young Frenchman was following him or not. Sometimes he would suddenly disappear around a street corner or would vanish from sight in a narrow, meandering passage between two houses and Daniel was surprised to spot his slender figure, absorbed by the shadows, creeping along the walls like a large cat.

Ahmed had knocked at a large studded door and had then slipped away without a goodbye or a backwards glance.

The widow Mourgues had welcomed him warmly, planting two loud kisses on his cheeks, holding him tight to her large chest, then had led him to what was to be his room: an iron bed, a small table, a chair. It smelt of bleach and lavender. Toilets are here. Bathroom next to it. My husband fitted it just before his heart attack. Here's the kitchen. And that's the living room.

Don't look out of the window. Don't sing. Don't speak loudly, in case the neighbours hear you. They're not here this afternoon, but they'll be back in the evening. In the absence of the mistress of the house, don't move about. Stay sitting or lying so the floorboards don't creak. Two hours, no more than that: I just have to do the shopping. She gave him these safety instructions while pouring him mint tea and a large glass of water so cold that he thought his teeth might shatter when they came in contact with it. She spoke softly, as if someone were listening with an ear to the wall. Then she turned on the radio and songs filled the kitchen, waking the five canaries in their cage near the window, who immediately started trilling loudly.

"I hope I won't have to keep you here too long because it's dangerous, having a deserter in the house like this. And the neighbours are bound to notice something eventually. They were Pétainists during the war, those scum . . . and they're even worse now. Always listening at doors, following me around. Thankfully she's a bit deaf and he's a boozer. It sends him to sleep about eight every night, unless they start a shouting match. He hits her sometimes. He knows my husband was a communist, and that I agreed with him of course. So we despise each other, especially with what's happening at the moment. And as neither of us is going anywhere . . ."

Eight days, and he counted every hour. He watched each day pass through the window in the imperceptible movements of light and shadow on the façades of the buildings on the other side of the narrow street, the movement of the splashes of sunlight that fell on the floorboards then slid furtively up the walls until they faded and then died away, returning the wallpaper to its naturally dull grey colour. He watched the sky pale in the cool of the morning then turn a harsher blue in the siesta hour when the widow went into her bedroom to sleep. Daniel rediscovered his mania for framing everything in his iron rectangle. Masses, volumes, colours. He examined with surprise these abstract fragments of his daily life, which was diminished by boredom. He yearned to draw, to take photographs.

Eight days spent trying to kill time. One morning, before going out to the market, Madame Mourgues had handed him a worn old book that smelt of dust and mould. The illustrated cover showed a sort of musketeer, with a feather in his hat, sword-fighting with two men. *Le Capitan.* Michel Zévaco. He sat down and opened the grimoire.

The next day, he ran behind the son of the Hunchback in the moats of Caylus Castle. He would have killed Peyrolles with his bare hands. The rough, porous paper smelt of the old days. Daniel lost himself in the alleys, evaded the traps set by the hateful conspirators. Galloped. Crossed swords with ten ferocious but stupid assassins, his back to the wall.

The days passed slowly. He shuddered every time the gates banged in the street or someone knocked at the door downstairs. The widow would stop what she was doing then, listen closely, and shake her head. "It's nothing," she would say.

Daniel wondered how she could be sure. "I have an ear for disasters. When my husband died, I heard him fall, even though I was out in the courtyard hanging up laundry. I knew straight away. I still hear him, every day. There are times when I think it would be better to be deaf." So he put his trust in those ears capable of hearing misfortune knocking at the door, or doom walking down the street.

At night, in the heat that took its time to escape through the open window, he found himself assailed by memories and their obsessive questions as if at the centre of a swarm of mosquitoes, kept awake by their wearying whine.

He had lived this incomplete life, without *them*, saved from a deep well at the bottom of which they had remained, often leaning over this abyss to see their faces, sometimes indistinct, mingled with the reflections of black water, and to hear the distant echo of their voices distorted by the depths of time, and he clung to the well's edge until he was in pain, until he was bleeding, sometimes tempted to let himself fall so he could rejoin them. But he was never sure if he would be able to find them again because that darkness was so impenetrable and fathomless.

And his father was rising up from this vertiginous hole, perhaps soaked and dirty and swollen with water from having being down there so long, and Daniel could not help seeing him as a monster suddenly returned from the land of the dead, a vile corpse like the ones he sometimes saw in horror films which he would go to watch with Alain at the Comeac or the Gallia, the two specialist cinemas on rue Sainte-Catherine. He didn't know what to do with this news. He felt neither joy nor nostalgia, only a curiosity that pricked his heart in odd moments. And why his father, after all? What about her? He buried his face in the pillow, seeking a cooler surface, and he held that soft, gentle thing tight against him, calling out to it softly.

He had been to war. He had liked it, often. He had killed, and afterwards been haunted by the images of his victims. He had thought himself a man as he crossed limits he had never known existed, had let himself be soiled by the ambient squalor, and now he called out for his mother as he hugged a pillow. He hated himself for this, despised himself for this, for being a murderer with such apparent sensibilities, and wondered who he really was: a child or a lost soldier? He couldn't find the words to express all this. He wished Irène was there to help him name what was circling in his mind like a creaking merry-go-round full of leering riders and dead faces.

Certain mornings he saw the sky turn pale and could not tell if he had slept or not, suspended in his fog of too-fleeting memories and impossible questions. Then he would sink into a heavy sleep where the shadows would slowly disperse.

Eight days.

One Tuesday morning, Madame Mourgues came back with a plumber. From one of the two bags he was carrying, he took out a pair of overalls and handed them to Daniel. The plumber's name was Youssef.

"You're going. Get your things."

The widow helped Daniel gather his few possessions, which she squeezed into a small black bag. She added *Le Vicomte de Bragelonne*.

"For the journey," she said. Then she folded up a thousand-franc note and slipped it into his pocket. He protested, but she told him he would need it more than her, then she held him close in her arms and warned him to be careful.

On the stairs, they passed the neighbour and greeted him, and the neighbour turned to watch them go, but as they were talking about a busted tap and a U-bend that had to be changed, paying no attention to him, he finally went back to his apartment. The street was swarming with people, and they pushed their way through the crowd with their bags. A shaky old van, grey with dust, was waiting for them, driven by the man called Ahmed. Without a word, he took Daniel to the bus station, eyes riveted to the rear-view mirror, face wet with sweat, features tensed, a muscle pulsing beneath the skin of his jaw. At the station, he handed Daniel an envelope containing a fake one-week leave on compassionate grounds (death of father), from the general staff of the Ninth R.I. The stamps, the colonel's signature: these were real. Ahmed explained all this to him without looking at him.

"And that's your flight ticket. Don't lose it, or you're fucked. You should have plenty of time: we erred on the side of caution, even if there's a roadblock check on the road or on your way into Algiers."

Daniel thanked him, but Ahmed shook his head and silenced him with a hand gesture.

"We're doing this out of friendship for Robert, even if it's risky. He was very insistent. We don't get involved in this sort of thing. Deserters, that's a French issue, a military issue. We have enough problems of our own. If it had been down to me, I'd have made you go back to your unit, even if it meant going to jail. I don't care. What difference does it make whether you desert or not? There could be a hundred of you, or a thousand, and it still wouldn't matter."

Suddenly he stopped speaking and looked away. The conversation was over.

Daniel got out of the van and crossed the street without turning around. He saw Ahmed's van melt into traffic, then he stopped on the pavement, under a tree, stunned by the noise and the heat. He entered the station concourse, which echoed with the hubbub of voices and the din of engines. There was a little kiosk there, selling newspapers and cigarettes. He bought a packet of American cigarettes, breaking into the note given him by the widow Mourgues, and he smoked a cigarette. He felt almost light-hearted, and strong, and perhaps happy to be there, at this moment in time, in war-torn Algeria, in the middle of this buzzing crowd on the main concourse.

Half an hour later, he left the last suburbs of the city behind.

That evening he arrived at Orly around midnight and passed without difficulty through two security checks conducted by cops armed with sub-machine guns. One of them, who had stripes on his shoulder, gave him a military salute when Daniel showed his fake leave form. Then he left the airport, and the coolness of the air felt good.

He woke up as the train was slowing with a deafening rumble on the iron bridge over the Garonne. A dreamless sleep broken by stops in stations, faces glimpsed on platforms, vague movements in the carriage, departures, encumbered arrivals, polite murmurs.

It is afternoon. He blinks in the soft sunlight, sees a pastel blue sky. He is drenched with sweat and when he stands up he feels his shirt stick to the back of the seat. As soon as he is out on the platform, he almost runs, and then weaves his way through the crowds trailing in the underground passage. In the arrivals hall, he goes through without looking at the people waiting and scans the door where the travellers appear. Finally, he walks out into the square, under the glass roof, and his heart contracts. He feels like walking, letting the streets swallow him up. He thinks about going to the garage and greeting Norbert and Claude – it's very close by – if only to see the looks on their faces, hear the surprise in their voices, smell the odour of petrol and oil and grease. He wants to fill himself in one go with everything he would find there, and the images and sensations overwhelm him, but finally his footsteps lead him to the bus stop where the number 1 is waiting and he gets on and buys his ticket from the driver then looks at the people seated in rows with the impression that they have not moved in months, as if they were waiting for him, as if nothing had happened.

The city starts to move around him and the streets and the façades of houses glide past in the June sunlight: all this greyness, softening the light, he left it behind in the middle of a charcoal winter, and he realises that he is instinctively searching for the whiteness, the harsh glare of the sun, the implacable blue of the sky, the dazzle that so often, over there, had made him blink and squint in spite of his sunglasses, made him lower the sides of his hat towards the stone path where he walked. He wishes the sun would burn down on this city to rid it of its grey crust, the way it beat down on the landscapes of Algeria, bringing them to life. He feels as if he has gone from a colour film to a black-and-white documentary, and he misses the depth of the shadows, the blinding three-dimension-ality of the brightness, and he knows that he will never see even the most banal things the way he did before; he knows he will always be searching for that luminous cruelty that scrapes away at the sleeping shades to make the colours blaze and shout.

He feels guilty about this regret, this frustration. He doesn't really understand what he is missing in the moment of his return to his life and his city. He does not understand that what surrounds him is the peace of a country at war. The warehouses on the docks, the huge moored ships with their forecastles shining incongruously bright, the endless trains moving slowly past: all this background detail, which he has moved past all his life, as something immutable, could be razed by bombardments and he wouldn't be remotely surprised. He watches those trucks manoeuvring, those men at work, bare-chested, cigarettes in the corners of their mouths, with the curiosity of a visitor to the zoo or an exile returning home after years away. With the avidity of a blind man recovering his sight.

Once the bus has crossed the swing bridge and passed the wet docks and is moving past the warehouses and factories in this narrow street lined with grey walls, it rumbles and vibrates over the cobbles and Daniel doesn't know if he is trembling because he's entering his neighbourhood or if it's the uneven road surface shaking him as if to rouse him from his reverie. He stands up to request his stop, and hangs onto the pole as the bus brakes and he is pushed forward and the vehicle judders to a halt. He jumps down onto the pavement and stays standing there, breathless and covered with sweat. His street is a little further on. The sun chases him, forcing him to cross the street and walk quickly, his bag hanging on his back. Low houses, roses climbing over fences, geraniums on window ledges. Kids playing, on bikes and makeshift carts, laughing and yelling.

He knocks and almost instantly the door opens and Roselyne recoils, moaning, the back of her hand over her mouth, eyes wide, staggering slightly, and Daniel is afraid she will fall so he drops his bag and takes her in his arms and hugs her and hugs her and she surrenders to this crushing strength and finally says, "Let me look at you."

She looks at him without a word. Her eyes are full of tears that do not fall. "I'm not going to cry," she says. Then: "Come on.". And she leads him down the corridor to the kitchen and opens the fridge and takes out a pitcher of water, takes a large glass from a cupboard. He sits down and drinks the water in one go. She grabs a handful of cherries and starts to eat them, leaning on the sink, never taking her eyes off Daniel, who smooths the wax cloth with the flat of his hand then looks up at her. She is holding the cherry stones in the hollow of her palm. She smiles.

"I deserted. They're probably searching for me."

Roselyne says nothing. As if she hasn't heard or hasn't understood.

"You're alive," she says. "You came back from that war alive.

439

Like Maurice, who came back one day out of the blue."

She sits down next to him and takes his hands in hers.

"We were so scared. All the time."

She shakes her head, and the tears finally fall. Daniel holds her against him and they stay like that without moving for a while, until their cheeks have dried and their hearts stopped racing.

Then Roselyne gently frees herself and looks him in the eyes and strokes his cheek.

"You'll have to hide, again."

He shakes his head. He wants to tell her that nothing is the same, but he gives up because tiredness falls on him like a net, along with the heat that has suddenly risen here. He feels weepy. His head is heavy.

"I'm going to sleep for a bit," he says. "Excuse me."

She insists on taking his bag and places it at the foot of his bed. Daniel opens the shutters and cracks open the window. He looks out at the shady garden. Pigeons cooing. The hum of traffic, further off, in rue Achard. He falls asleep straight away amid these peaceful sounds.

*

He feels Irène's gaze on him and it hurts. She is on the other side of the table in her white blouse, hair pulled back in a sort of lopsided bun, and she smokes and pours herself more coffee, watching him as he talks with the parents. They talk about everything and nothing: the latest news of the quarter, weddings, pregnancies, births, deaths. Roselyne and Maurice talk constantly, eyes and voices smiling.

"The Courrier boy," says Maurice, "you know, the one who was working at the S.A.F.T.? Jean-Bernard? Well, he stayed there, in Algeria. They found out two weeks ago. The funeral was Tuesday. They don't hang around repatriating the bodies. How long is that slaughter going to continue, for God's sake? What are they waiting for?"

Daniel purses his lips. He doesn't know. And the little he learned over there, he won't say. So Irène watches him as he plays dumb, as if she can glimpse, around him or in his eyes, the glow of his obstinate silence like a hidden fire.

He talked earlier, a bit. He told them about his life over there, at the station, the trips to the city, the patrols. The ambush, and Giovanni's death. He did not tell them about the destroyed bodies, the spilled guts, the blood. "It wasn't pretty," was all he said. Maurice nodded: "I saw a few, in my time." He did not tell them about the rifle with the scope, the iridescent light flickering through the viewfinder, the copper face hidden in emerald leaves.

Irène stares at him constantly. When he meets her gaze he smiles at her, but she does not respond. She looks shocked: mouth half open, seeming to breathe more quickly at times. He does not feel the same closeness between them. When she kissed him, after she came home, in the bedroom, he sensed her body pulling back from his embrace. A new kind of modesty. A question has haunted him ever since that moment: who is this other that has come between them?

They also talk about his father. About the cops who are searching for him for crimes he has committed. Jean Delbos a murderer? It's ludicrous. There's something else going on here. Roselyne and Maurice speak cautiously, do not judge, doubt that such a man would transform into a criminal. Not after what he must have been through. They exchange worried or embarrassed glances and sometimes fall silent in the face of Daniel's muteness. He listens to what they tell him as if it's a detective story, some dark, tragic Yank film with faceless actors. He would like to feel something other than this curiosity that has gradually taken over him, the way a nephew might feel about the return of a globe-trotting uncle.

"What do you think about all this?" Maurice finally asks.

Daniel shrugs. Irène continues to stare at him, immobile except for the smoke from her cigarette that flutters up in capricious curls.

"I don't know," he says.

Roselyne puts her hand on his arm and Irène stands up to clear the table. Daniel stands up too.

"I'm tired. I need to get some sleep."

32

The doctor stayed late last night, listening through his stethoscope as he bent over Abel's body, searching, probably, for some sign of life in that pain-riddled skeleton which seems always on the verge of sinking into the sheets, of dissolving there and disappearing. There is the heart, which beats crazily like a lone madman deep in a collapsed mine, and then stops, hoping to be rescued perhaps, before starting its disordered pounding again – 140 or 150 bpm – making this bag of skin and bones hot to the touch, burning hot. The hands and legs move sometimes and the eyes open and look around questioningly and close gently because the response is always the same. "He needs to go to hospital," says the doctor every day. Abel shakes his head, opens those terrible eyes, puts a hand on the doctor's sleeve and tries to cling to it: "No fucking hospitals. I want to die here. Stop bugging me with that." So the doctor shrugs, picks up the twig-thin wrist at the end of an arm too weak to lift itself, and nods, without even trying to hide the sadness of his smile.

Violette has learned to give injections, change drips. No nurses either. The last one, a snippy nun with pink rounded cheeks, treated Abel like a piece of meat, scolding each time she entered the room: "So how is he today? Has he made pee-pee? It's important to make pee-pee because that shows the kidneys are working, and as long as they're working . . ." She gave him injections without any attempt to diminish the pain, turned him over as if he were simply an object, sighed a lot and often grew impatient.

"Get rid of that old cow," Abel said to the doctor one evening. "Teach Violette instead. She'd do a better job."

Doctor Magnard agreed. He got hold of an I.V. drip, some

bottles, some vials of morphine. Violette prepares the syringes under the kitchen lamp, so she can see better.

André helps sometimes, especially with the toilet. Every morning, and during the day too, when necessary.

For a while now, he's dozed off watching the sun rise. He lets his dreams unravel inside his mind, the images fading to black. Every morning he needs this patience. Like waiting for a bathtub of dirty water to drain, leaving a film of filth that the day, life itself, will perhaps rinse clean. He listens to Violette, already busy downstairs. He knows that Abel is still of this world: she would come and tell him otherwise, even in the middle of the night, as they agreed. And so, slowly, he gets out of bed and dresses, inhaling the smell of coffee that rises up to him.

He has been here for a month, with Abel, who is dying, and Violette, who lives only for him. They have talked so much. In low voices, whispering sometimes, Abel short of breath, André going as far as he can in the brambles that cling to his legs. Violette close to them. She didn't say anything that she hadn't said before. She encouraged them with her questions, which left them thoughtful or forced a smile from them. "Good shot," said Abel. André shook his head, troubled. Of the past, all those lost years. They relived their lives through those leaps allowed by memory. I remember . . . Old suns shone again; recollected happiness made them roar with laughter once more.

As for the shadows, as for the night . . . André searched for the right words, tried comparisons, dismissing his attempts at saying things with a disillusioned sweep of the hand, and in the silence that fell over them Abel would fall asleep, exhausted, chest shaken by fast breathing. Other times, the figures from the past, the living and the dead, came and pressed around them, and then the little bedroom felt packed and Abel asked for the window to be opened: never mind the heat, he said, we're suffocating here, some air, quick, and he would collapse back onto his pillows to capture, mouth wide open, what little oxygen his half-eaten lungs could still absorb.

They put their memories in order, shared them sometimes, admitting their nostalgia, their regrets, their remorse, their inconsolable pain, and as time went by André felt his obsession with vengeance wilting as his words built the story of his life and finally allowed his hurt to cry out. He felt as if he were escaping a dark, silent cave and hearing what he had kept quiet about, seeing more clearly despite the blinding daylight. There was no consolation or relief though, in this enlightenment. His pain was there constantly, throbbing, like a toothache, with occasional darts of intolerable agony.

When André – from now on he is Jean again, for good, as he was before – wakes up every morning, after the dazed feeling left behind by his nightmares has dissipated, and feels the same bite in his guts, the same racing of his heart as he thinks of Darlac, of their corrupted friendship, of his betrayal, of his crime. He can still find any number of reasons to kill him, but he struggles to find the strength to do it. Getting dressed, he thinks of his two absent loves: Hélène on the dance floor, long legs and crazy hair, mouth half open as if she were hesitating between a scream and a smile; Olga walking in the distance, turning back to look for him without seeing him, scanning the crowd with her fever-bright eyes.

He smiles alone at their shadows and he looks at his hands, which can touch them no longer.

There's a knock at the door. Six in the morning, by his watch. This is just after he has heard two gates bang in the street. "Jean!" Violette calling him from the bottom of the staircase. The bag in the wardrobe. The notebooks are there. He shoves clothes in there, lifts it to his shoulder. Puts on a pair of espadrilles, trips over and falls to his knees by the window. Downstairs, they are hammering at the door. "Police! Open up!"

He jumps into the garden, lands on a concrete terrace. He can see nothing around him but high walls. Behind, inside the house, the sounds of doors slamming, furniture being tipped over. Through the open windows he hears yelling. Violette insulting the cops, their deep voices abusing her. André throws himself against a wall, gets a grip on the top, pulls himself up and swings over to the other side just as the French windows behind him are smashed by a shoulder-charge. He falls in the middle of a rose bed, his hands scratched, the strap of his bag caught by thorns, tearing off flowers as he pulls it free. He runs a few metres through this long, narrow garden and he feels something stuck in his ankle hampering his progress, and he has to remove the spiky branch hooked to the cloth of his trouser leg before stepping over another wall, at the back of the garden, between two palm trees, and slumping into a spruce pine hedge and rolling across a lawn and getting up and running towards a terrace where a man appears in front of a garden table with a coffee pot sitting on it. The man yells, out of surprise or fear, and André grabs him by his shirt collar and shoves him into the iron chairs where he collapses, and suddenly it's still the darkness of morning in this house cluttered with sombre furniture and the air thick with the smell of polish and coffee and cold ashes.

There is a large key in the lock and the door bangs loudly and then he's in the street. He goes right, slowing down when he loses an espadrille and has to put it back on while hopping. He can't hear anything now, and can't work out where he is because he has hardly left the house in the last month and the neighbourhood is unknown to him. Turning on the street corner, he sees the boulevard and its traffic. He stops running because he's exhausted: his legs tremble and his breathing is a painful wheeze; he has to cough and spit in the gutter. He starts walking again and rummages around in his pockets and his bag, in search of some cash – just a few coins so he can catch a bus – but he does not find anything, and realises he has left everything behind: his wallet, papers (real and false), money, and the pistol hidden under the mattress. He walks along the pavement, in the shade, beneath a summer sky so pure that he instinctively starts taking deep breaths, as if he could absorb it whole. He knows he is at their mercy now: tomorrow his photograph will be in the newspaper again and every cop in the city will be after him; every bar owner and every waiter and every hotel receptionist will have his picture on their counter, close to the telephone, ready to help the police.

He enters the labyrinth of streets, changing direction and sometimes doubling back in order to lose anyone who might be tailing him. And then he says to himself that they are not interested in following him anymore, because all he can lead them to is himself; what they want is to catch him and get rid of him, with a bullet in the head if need be, to avoid all questions, close the case and allow the newspaper to publish a front page with the headline DANGEROUS CRIMINAL SHOT BY POLICE AFTER AN EXCHANGE OF GUNFIRE, thereby selling more papers to all those people who like reading stories of blood and crime. He'd be found, without a doubt, pistol in hand, the barrel still smoking, the stink of burned gunpowder. Darlac would have a credible crime scene that no cop would dare denounce and no judge would question. He thinks about all this as he crosses the city, sticking to the edges of the pavements, imagining he could still escape them, inventing boltholes through which he might flee, unexpected hiding places, just as he used to when he was a kid playing cops and robbers in the playground.

No more shadows around him. Only the brutal reality of the city, the transparency of an indifferent summer morning. He is no longer being followed by the dead nor by his memories.

He crosses the city, heart in his throat whenever he hears a police siren or whenever a car slows down or stops in front of him. He watches figures reflected in shop windows, turns around, stops, scans the street in every direction. More than once he thinks about turning back and returning to Abel's house to attempt one final gesture, returning there by chance, attacking Darlac and grabbing his throat in the hope of finding some sort of blade to hand so he can slit it open up to his chin like he did with that scumbag Penot. He shivers at this thought: he can see himself, almost feel himself, covered with blood, kicked and punched by the other cops, beaten to death maybe, but he won't let go of the commissaire's twitching corpse until he himself sinks into unconsciousness, and it won't even matter because the satisfaction he feels will be absolute, and once he's accomplished that all his desires will drain away, even the desire to live . . . He realises that the conversations with Abel did not change anything. They calmed him at the time because death, prowling the room, stealing the sick man's breath every time it passed close, had forced him to lay down his weapons, had made his deepest hatreds and rawest griefs seem meaningless. At the edge of the abyss where Abel teetered, he didn't dare move. Too relieved not to fall into it again.

When André arrives within sight of the garage, Claude Mesplet is standing in front of the door, talking with a customer, close to a car with an open bonnet. He walks over and the mechanic sees him. Mesplet turns away and continues explaining to the customer that it should work now, then bangs shut the bonnet. The customer hands him some cash and gets in. The car moves away. It's almost noon and the street is hot, without a shadow to be seen.

"What do you want?"

Mesplet stands in front of him, hands in his overall pockets. Sleeves rolled up. Thick forearms, soiled with grease.

"The cops are after me. I was staying with a friend. They came this morning. I don't know where to go. I left everything back there. My papers, everything."

"You want money, is that it?"

Mesplet looks down at his grazed ankles, the bottom of his trouser legs stained with blood.

"No. Not money."

"Come in. It's hot out here."

They go into the garage. The apprentice is refitting a wheel.

He looks up, recognises André and smiles at him.

"How's the bike?"

"It's good. Runs like a dream."

Mesplet stands over the filthy sink and washes his hands.

"You can stop," he tells the apprentice, without turning around. "You got what you need?"

"Yeah, I'm fine. My mother made me lunch."

The boy goes to the office to fetch a small navy-blue bag and sits on a heap of tyres in a shady corner near the door.

The boss wipes his hands on a black-stained cloth. André leans against the side of a 403. Dizziness and nausea. Mesplet pretends not to notice how pale he is, nor the sweat running down his face.

"Let's sit down in there," he says.

They enter the glass-walled office, decorated with calendars advertising Motul, Cinzano, Dubonnet: happy motorists and pretty girls smile from their pages, holding glasses. Mesplet pulls a chair from under a desk covered with files and bills and pushes it towards André. He sits on a stool, then takes a bag from a nearby cupboard. The clinking of bottles inside.

"You'll have to make do with what I've got."

Bread, saucisson, tomato salad, cheese. They wash it down with wine mixed with water. André forces himself to swallow. He chews but it seems to get stuck in his cardboard-dry gullet. He remembers mess tins shared between three or four people after the camp was liberated, hesitant hands wiping the juices from the bottom of metal bowls. The rations the American soldiers secretly gave them in spite of orders not to overfeed the survivors. He starts shivering. Almost knocks his glass over when he puts it down.

"Are you cold?"

"It happens sometimes. It's nothing. It'll pass."

Winter. Rain, snow and wind. He feels as if he's back there now, in the same destitution, the same solitude. He thinks about Abel again, his frightening thinness, death pulsing under the skin of his belly like an unborn animal. He sees the fleshless bodies again. The comrades who couldn't get up, could hardly move, deaf to the words of freedom, of the end of the nightmare. And in their eyes it still shone, glassy and noxious, the glare of that unbearable dream. André is back there again. Sucked into the past by a whirlwind. The pain is the same, a pain he hasn't felt in years. The hunger less so. It grips him like a fever.

The mechanic gets up and grabs a bottle of cognac from an old sideboard cluttered with paperwork and spare parts. He pours some into a glass and gives it to André.

"Here. This'll warm you up a bit."

André swallows a mouthful, then coughs and spits. He feels a hot shudder run through his body and he clings to the chair to stop himself falling to the floor. Watching Mesplet through his tears, he catches his breath.

"We talked about you, me and Maurice and Roselyne. That cop Darlac, he's after you, and he went to their house. Came here too. For all those murders. Is it true you killed all those people like it says in the paper? Those collaborators, and that cop?"

"No . . . It's complicated. Anyway, what difference does it make to you?"

André does not have the strength to tell his story again. He gets to his feet. No longer cold. Able to stand.

"I'm going to leave now. Thanks for the food."

Claude Mesplet stands up too.

"Where will you go?"

"I don't know. I need to think."

He thinks that if he starts walking something will come to him, that it will all become clear. He wants to leave this office, this clammy, airless heat. Wants to feel air move over his face. In front of him, Mesplet hesitates, swaying heavily.

"I can't let you go like that. I've got a little flat upstairs. A bed, a sink. A scullery with a camping stove. It's clean. I lived there with my wife when I first took over the garage. I'll bring you some clothes and something to eat."

André looks into his eyes and the two men stare at each other, unblinking and silent, for several seconds.

"Why would you do that?"

"I don't know. Maybe cos you're Daniel's father, no matter what, and I don't want you to go to jail without being able to defend yourself. And also maybe cos you had your reasons for all that, that I can't understand. I've always been a bit heavy, a bit slow. I don't know . . . We talked about it with Maurice and Roselyne. They say what you're doing is up to you, cos of what you suffered, and we shouldn't judge you. And if Olga chose you, and she stayed with you till the end . . . well, you must be worth something . . . There, you see? I'm talking crap again."

He takes a key from a drawer and opens a door that is almost invisible, hidden behind a panel with tools and timing belts hanging from it.

The staircase is dark and cool. Mesplet opens the door to the apartment and a smell of dust and mouldy paper escapes instantly. The floorboards creak under their feet. It's a large room, with two windows overlooking the street. Thin strips of sunlight creep through the louvred shutters. A large bed, a table, three chairs.

"The toilet's downstairs, in the workshop. I'll bring you whatever you need in the afternoons. What do you reckon? If you want to think, you'll be better off here than in the streets like a tramp."

"Thank you. I won't bother you for long. Just enough time to make a decision."

André puts his bag on the mattress. Mesplet pushes open the shutters. Dust dancing in a flood of daylight. As the mechanic is about to leave, André asks him:

"Have you heard from Daniel?"

To start with, Mesplet shakes his head, looking down. Then he meets André's eyes.

"He came home last week. He deserted. He's in hiding. Like you."

The door closes, and André sits on the bed and stays there for some time, head in his hands, incapable of moving, convinced that he will never be able to stand up again, as if he's been chained to a wall. He can see that everything is coming to an end. He knows that this refuge will be his last. I'm going to have to die now, he thinks, and this resolution seems reasonable to him.

He lets himself fall to one side and thinks about his son. He can't summon any image of him, except the vague memory of a little boy with big dark eyes, always very serious-looking. His son, hiding somewhere in the city right now, just like him. His son, whom he can't approach without dragging the ghost of the boy's mother behind him. So he starts to cry. Softly at first, and then with deep sobs. He has not cried since the first night in the camp, after a man – an Italian – told him what had become of the women who arrived in the morning. Since then, nothing and no-one has been able to bring a single tear to his eyes. Even when he heard about Hélène's death. All he'd felt was that bitter tightening in his throat, which came over him sometimes, but which he quickly swallowed, turning away and taking huge gulps of air.

And now he's soaking this dusty mattress bawling like a kid because he doesn't want to die without holding in his arms, even if he pushes him away, the son he could have had.

33

Those two idiot detectives hesitate when faced with the woman standing in the hallway, arms outstretched to bar their way, but Commissaire Darlac pushes them past her and the cops are free to spread throughout the house while two guards stand watch in the street. He tells them to go upstairs and he drags the woman along with him, grabbing her shoulder by the light fabric of her dress and pulling so hard that the top buttons are torn off and her breasts are exposed as she falls to the floor, banging against the kitchen table and knocking over a chair. He tells her to shut her mouth, threatening her with his huge shovel-like hand. Another cop calls him from the living room. "Come and look." He says, "What?" in an irritated voice. Then, glancing at the woman in tears, collapsed on her chair, and judging that she is unlikely to try anything, he goes into the living room and finds that bed close to the window, with a man's gaunt face staring at him sadly from above the sheets, eyes ringed with sickness and death.

Darlac recognises Abel, and for a few seconds he forgets where he is and what's happening because at that very moment the two detectives yell from the floor above, shouting out the usual warnings and then saying, "Fuck it, that son of a bitch!". The commissaire rushes up to the bedroom and finds them gesticulating at the window, guns in hand. He chucks them out of there, ordering them to take a car and try to trap the fugitive in the parallel street, you fucking morons; he'll go through the gardens and come out on the other side. And call for reinforcements, for Christ's sake. And hurry the fuck up. The two coppers bound downstairs and he starts tearing through the contents of the wardrobe and the chest of drawers: a few clothes, bathroom towels, sheets and pillowcases. He lifts up the mattress – standard practice in these cases – and hits the jack-pot: a pistol, the one Delbos stole from Mazeau. Carefully picking it up with his handkerchief, he wraps it up and slips it into his pocket. In the drawer of the bedside table he finds a wallet with real and fake papers inside. He takes a good look at Delbos' face and wonders if he'd have recognised him had he walked past him in the street. "Now it's just you and me, you piece of shit." He goes back down-stairs and finds Violette plumping the pillows behind Abel's head. Inspecteur Lefranc is conscientiously, and very noisily, emptying the cupboards and sideboards. From time to time he breaks a plate or a glass, and each time he says "shit", the word barely audible above the racket he's making.

"Nothing here," he says, standing over the sink. "I'll take a look in the cellar."

The commissaire watches the woman as she lifts the sheet over the sick man's frail chest and smooths it flat with her palm.

"So it looks like I got here just in time."

Abel gently pushes Violette out of the way. He tries to lever him-self up on his elbows, but finally gives up and falls back into the softness of the pillows, eyes closed.

"No . . . You're too late. He got away and you'll never catch him. He's the one who'll get you."

He gets his breath back, has a brief coughing fit.

"That's not what I'm talking about. It makes no difference who finds who – it'll end the same way. He's not up to it. Anyway, if he really wanted to kill me, he'd have done it already, don't you think? I would never waste time like that: as soon as I get him in my sights, he's a dead man. But anyway . . . what I meant is that I got here just in time to see you still alive. That's my fault. I should have thought of it earlier. But for me, you were the last person Delbos could have gone to, given . . . After everything you told me the last time I saw you . . . All your big words . . . It's true Jean wasn't too happy about you flirting with Olga. Beautiful girl, wasn't she? Do you remember, or has your memory gone down the shitter with the rest of you? He used to tell me about it sometimes, the way you'd come on to her. You were a good-looking bloke back then, and a charmer too. You could sell water to a drowning man, remember?"

Abel lifts his arm then lets it fall again.

"Go away. Leave me in peace."

Violette bends over him because suddenly he is not moving at all anymore. She puts her hand on his chest and nods.

"Nothing in the cellar either, boss," says Lefranc.

The commissaire turns around with a look of contempt and signals him to button it.

"I have to call the doctor," says Violette. "He needs to come."

Darlac shakes his head.

"We can do better than that. He can go to the doctor. Lefranc! Call an ambulance."

Violette plants herself in front of him, her face at the level of his burly chest.

"But I've been looking after him for months. He wants to die here, not in hospital!"

"He's already unconscious. And once he's dead, why would he care where he is? You don't seem to understand: you were sheltering a criminal, you and Abel. Obstructing an investigation. Aiding and abetting. I kind of doubt whether Abel will be able to tell me much, but you . . . You're going to come with us and you're going to tell us everything. After that, the judge will decide. So what do you want to do? Let him die here or take him to hospital?"

Violette stares at him, mouth half-open. She looks stunned, uncomprehending. Abel's hand is still in hers. Then she makes a movement to which Darlac pays little attention and suddenly he sees her holding something in her fist and throwing herself at him. When he realises that she is trying to stab him with a syringe, a hot flush rises through him and he recoils, almost stumbling, then falls into a chair that slides backwards under him. He is poised to defend himself – legs bent, feet forward – but Lefranc smashes the butt of his pistol over the woman's head and she staggers sideways. A second blow on the temple knocks her out. Darlac kicks the syringe away as if it was a grenade or a venomous snake, then he calls out to the two guards:

"Take her to the station. I'll deal with her later."

The two cops lift the semi-conscious woman, her earlobe pouring with blood, and support her down the hallway, her bare feet dragging on the floor.

"What about him?" Lefranc asks.

"Wait for the ambulance and then go back to the station and get started with the paperwork. I'll get there as soon as I can."

Outside, he finds it easier to breathe. Relieved to get out of that house of death, with its smell of disinfectant and chamber pots. He gets in his car and calls his colleagues to find out what's happening. Nothing. Delbos has vanished. Four cars patrolling the area, and not a trace of Delbos. Shit. He tells them to forget it, then he has an idea. After this, he doesn't give a toss anymore. He can have Delbos when he wants him. All he has to do is arrest the son, who's deserted and must be hiding somewhere in Bordeaux, and he will have the father. Poor bastard is bound to be overcome by sentiment after all these years. He'll just have to use the press.

Soon he's out in the sticks. He hates all these fields, these trees and these hedges, these farmhouses covered with wisteria, these carts still pulled by horses. These dogs that attack the wheels of cars, these chickens that peck the grass by the side of the road. He can't stand this rustic straitjacket that stops the city expanding, although he knows that in twenty years it will all be gone. Drainage ditches everywhere, marshy expanses flooded throughout the winter and infested with mosquitoes during the summer, market gardens and watercress beds. He almost misses the little road to the left, braking and turning the steering wheel at the last moment, making the back tyres screech as they send up clouds of dust.

The house is more or less as he remembers it: long and low, white, at the edge of a wood planted with hundred-year-old oaks. He has never been inside. He knew that madame would come here. That Kraut she used to fuck during the war. Who gave her a child named Elise. Recognised at birth by Inspecteur Darlac, who was madly in love with that tall blonde who looked like she'd walked straight out of a Hollywood film. He thinks about that again, heating his anger to boiling point. He remembers all the lies she told him. Her insistence on passing her driving licence, on having her own car. For two years, he'd been completely taken in. And then, one day, a colleague named Gauthier in the secret service had taken him aside in a deserted office, looking embarrassed, and had spoken to him in a whisper as night fell outside and neither of them thought to turn on a lamp, or dared to do so. Of course, his colleague had told him all that as a friend. To warn him, to put him on his guard. He would keep the secret, naturally. He didn't know anything about the kid, but he knew the background of Hauptmann Wilhelm Müller: Bordeaux, then the Eastern Front, Stalingrad, where he lost half his face and a few other important parts of his body.

Albert Darlac walks along a high laurel hedge and puts his hand on the bolt of a black-painted iron gate. He walks up a driveway lined with blooming rose bushes that loom towards him with their large flowers and their thorny stems. He doesn't knock, because the door is not locked. He takes the handkerchief-wrapped pistol in his hand, sliding his index finger over the trigger and holding the gun against his thigh, arm dangling at his side.

He stops in the entrance hall that opens directly onto a living room still filled with bluish darkness due to the tall trees outside. He can hear classical music playing somewhere in the house. He doesn't recognise it. Violins, a symphony or a concerto . . . he knows nothing about all that stuff, couldn't care less. He can smell baking. To his right is a kitchen, with a cake on the table, in its tin. Still warm.

He examines the room: clean, tidy, perfectly ordinary. The smell of bleach. He jumps, sensing a presence behind him. A small, ageless woman holding a cloth in her hand asks him what he's doing there. Accent so thick you could cut it with a knife. She stands in the doorway, two metres away from him. She repeats her question in a louder, high-pitched voice, her eyes wrinkling and twisting with fear.

He shoots her in the face and she is thrown backwards, collapsing onto a coffee table between two chairs. He watches as she struggles, her arms twitching two or three times, then a long shudder runs up to her shoulders and she stops moving. There's a lot of blood pouring from the back of her head. Her eyes are wide open, in an expression of amazement.

He follows the sound of music, enters a corridor. The door is already open onto it, throwing a rectangle of light on the floor. The music stops and the silence halts Darlac as if he'd walked into a glass wall. He moves forward again, one step at a time, holding his gun out ahead of him, and in the doorway he spins to face a figure in a wheelchair, lit from behind, his back to Darlac, staring out of the window.

"I hope it wasn't too difficult."

The voice is composed, kindly. The accent, very light, gives a sweet harmony to his words. With a squeak of wheels, the man turns around.

"Most of all, I hope she didn't suffer. She's already suffered enough in her lifetime. In a certain way, you have brought to an end an ordeal that has gone on too long."

Darlac suddenly feels his heart stir. He is no longer sure that it's beating.

In front of him, barely three metres away, sits half a man, speaking like an actor in a sentimental film. In front of him is this wax statue that has melted down one side: only frozen drips remain, hastily pressed down over gaping wounds. In front of him is a body

458

that looks like it might have been run over by a train, carved up by a band saw, cauterised in red-hot fires and sewn back together with coarse string.

And it speaks. There is something human on the other side, a surviving Siamese twin still stuck to the corpse of its brother. Hauptmann Wilhelm Müller. Willy, to his friends.

Albert Darlac saw some smashed-up faces in '22, at a war memorial service. His twelve-year-old eyes had been riveted to those devastated mugs, despite his mother pinching his arm to make him stop staring. Back at the house, he had burst into sobs. Disfigured ghosts had haunted him for nights on end, robbing him of sleep. But here, now, at forty-eight years old, he is not sure he can understand what he's seeing. He cannot get his head around this reality. All he feels is a sad, sickened stupefaction. He can think of nothing to say. He wants to toss his pistol to the floor and leave this place. Oh well. He wouldn't be able to blame this one on Delbos anyway. Besides, that imbecile already has enough crimes to his name that he will go to the guillotine whatever.

"What do you intend to do?" Müller asks. "Someone already came, a few weeks ago, and pointed the same kind of gun at me. He didn't kill my mother though. He just spoke to me about you and Annette. And Elise of course. Then he left, as he had come, on a motorcycle. Do you know him?"

In Darlac's malfunctioning mind, the questions pile up like disused wagons on a railway siding. He tries to find words, air. He notices that he's trembling. Finally, he manages to speak:

"How did you recognise me?"

The lid of the man's single eye bats its long black lashes.

"You disappoint me. You. A gifted detective. Annette showed me photographs of you. I thought you were good-looking to start with. You were in love. You had a nice smile, holding the baby in your arms. I knew that Elise would be happy, that you would bring her up with good values."

He pauses to take a cigarette and a lighter from behind the gramophone.

"Do you smoke?"

Darlac shakes his head. He is no longer trembling. On the handkerchief, around the butt of the gun, he can feel the dampness of his sweat. He watches Müller take two drags with visible pleasure. Little by little, he recovers his spirits.

"For a long time, I trusted your nice-looking face and what Annette told me. It was difficult for me to check for myself, as you can see . . . And then, last year, she told me how much you torment her all the time because you are mad with jealousy over a ghost . . . Look at me. Look at what I've become. Look at the reason why you put her through such hell. Every day, every night. This constant slavery . . . Ever since I returned, more or less . . . For six years she kept silent about it, endured it without a word, without ever complaining. For the good of Elise. For my daughter. That is why I must not hate you or feel this desire to spit in your face. For her. So that something may be saved from this disaster. She is the only reason I have stayed alive. I should even thank you, but that is not why you are here, and I am not sure that good manners are appropriate between us."

The man speaks as if he's telling someone else's story. In an equable tone, with elegant restraint, with no hint of even the slightest emotion.

Darlac does not understand. He hears no anger, perceives no sadness, no distress in the words and attitude of this man. He does not feel he is in a position to understand, as if suddenly the man was speaking to him from a long way away, in a foreign language. He feels a vague unease, standing in front of this maimed flesh, of course. But above all, he cannot conceive how the man's mind has managed to barricade itself inside that destroyed fortress, nor in what state he has been able to survive, still capable of loving a slut and her bastard, and listening to that music without falling asleep, washed by his old mother. All of this is beyond Commissaire Darlac's comprehension. The man strikes him as the typical Franco-phile German officer, *korrekt*, cultivated. He used to see them smiling under their visors, standing straight in their boots, glasses in hand, surrounded by collaborators and gorgeous whores, in the drawing rooms of the prefecture or the mayor's office. He remembers that it didn't bother him much, at the time. He thought they had the style and elegance of victors, and that made it less bitter to accept the little arrangements and important services which he had resolved to render them. He had even shaken a few hands, like a well-raised child, bowing, straight-backed, to an affably smiling S.S. lieutenant as he stumbled through a few words in his tentative French, or to a Wehrmacht officer with greying temples. They had won the war against a nation of half-arsed yellow-bellied losers softened by too many paid holidays. That was simply the way it went.

Except that those bastards ended up losing. Destroyed. In shame and dishonour, with all the stuff about the camps. Woe to them! Darlac sometimes likes to package his morals in simple catch-phrases. No need to think too much.

He extends his arm and fires two bullets in the Kraut's chest. He didn't dare demolish what was left of his face. Müller is jolted back-wards by each impact, sending his wheelchair rolling into the wall behind him. In the seconds that pass as his arteries swell and his lungs fill with blood, he continues to stare unblinkingly at the cop, as if he is thinking of something to say, then he shakes his head and blinks, perhaps with contempt, and slumps over onto the maimed side of his body, with blood running from his mouth.

Darlac folds the handkerchief around the gun and exits the room, slightly dazed, as if he's just been through twelve rounds. He shivers as he sees the old woman's corpse, between the two chairs, then walks more quickly and leaves the house without another backward glance.

Outside, the sun beats down oppressively, almost knocking him to the ground. On the pavement he hesitates, working out where he is, then runs towards his car. The oven-like heat inside the vehicle forces him to breathe through his mouth as he winds down the windows, then he drives away, trying to get rid of the solid air that burns his face like hot wax.

34

Bad dreams pursue him to the point of total exhaustion. He falls asleep at eleven at night, but there are always the dead to wake him. The *fell* cut in half, the woman with the destroyed face, Giovanni twisting in pain around the bullets lodged in his guts. After that, sometimes until dawn, he tosses and turns in the warm sheets and once again he is trekking through the suffocating dust, under the vertical sunlight; he is with the others, and he can hear the slow footsteps of the column of men as they climb a path up the hillside.

Then a machine-gunner opens fire and they throw themselves to the ground and then he sees the face of the gunner in the cross-hairs of his scope, frowning, cheek almost touching the handle of his machine gun, face trembling in rhythm with the bursts of fire. Daniel squeezes the trigger but nothing happens or he sees the bullet leave, in slow motion, with a curving trajectory that never reaches its target. And while this is happening, he can hear men being hit all around him, their screams, their moans, their children's voices returned at the backs of their throats. Blood gushing between their hands.

In odd moments, shame grips him like a fever and he starts sweating as he thinks of the others who are still there, in that shit heap, the fear in their guts making them savage and stupid. He should feel happy to be away from all that, back with his loved ones, in his city. He should love the moments when Irène holds him tight to her and he feels her body through the light fabric of her summer dress. But he is only relieved, as if he had escaped the wreckage of a plane crash while others were still trapped inside it.

Most of all he is frightened by that other he left behind in Algeria, that twin brother, the double who emerged from him and who loved the war, who experienced every instant of those eight months as an adventure capable of imbuing life with meaning, who succumbed to the power conferred upon him by his weaponry, who surrendered to the dizzying spiral of violence and hatred, who tasted horror the way we might be pleasantly surprised by the sweetness of a cheese after first smelling its foul odour. On those paths, in the back of a half-track, staring into the scope of a rifle, he abandoned a soldier who looks so much like him that he struggles to tell the difference between them. Like a twin looking in the mirror every day and suddenly, one morning, no longer knowing if what he sees is his brother or his own reflection.

And he searches for the terrified child on a rooftop waiting for Mummy and Daddy to come and fetch him. And he can no longer tell if he really lived through that experience that has been told to him so many times that it has become like a tale of giants or dragons, something that seems harder to believe in with each passing year. And he misses that other little brother, perhaps stolen away by a dragon, perhaps dead.

He does not tell them any of this. He pretends to slip back into the calm flow of everyday life, in this peaceful summertime. From time to time, Maurice tries to get him to talk, making allusions, mentioning what he went through in '39–'40, hoping that Daniel will respond with confidences of his own, but nothing comes, apart from a few anecdotes, tales of drunkenness, Sergeant Castel with his soul still partly in Indochina, the wait for the post to arrive and be distributed, and then the city with its separate quarters, Europeans on one side, Arabs on the other, two worlds, two countries existing side by side. "Or one on top of the other," Irène suggests. Yes, that's it. One on top of the other, with a sandwich filling of meat and blood.

Of course, Roselyne and Maurice tell Daniel about the cop's visit, the return of his father to Bordeaux, the murders of which he's accused. Daniel listens to the fear in their voices, and the sadness too. Irène had written to him about it, but here, now, he has the impression of an old machine that everyone had thought irreparably broken, suddenly jerking back to life and threatening to crush in its gears anyone who gets too close to it.

After the war, sometimes the war continues. Silent, invisible. The past arrives at your door with the evil face of a bad cop; even the dead return. And not always the ones you hoped to see again.

One afternoon, despite Roselyne's fears, he takes the bus into town to see a film. He did not check the programme, so for a while he goes from one cinema to the next, looking at the posters and the photographs, and he devours those images – men in hats, blonde actresses, faces in chiaroscuro, galloping horses – with the avidity of a kid in a sweet shop. Finally he goes to the Rio to see *The Left Handed Gun*, knowing nothing about its director, a certain Arthur Penn, nor its lead actor – Paul Newman, a newcomer, whose picture Irène cut out from *Ciné Revue*, explaining that he was the best American actor of the moment. He prefers Gregory Peck. *Moby Dick* . . . Ahab . . . He remembers the spectral apparition of the cursed capitaine in the street, glimpsed through the window of the tavern where the sailors' songs suddenly fell silent, walking through gusts of rain amid flickers of lightning, and the sinister sound of his false leg made from a whale's jawbone . . . And that's without even mentioning the meeting with the Indian in the bed, all the stippled tattoos on his face, the peace pipe in his mouth. Gregory Peck and the scar on his cheek. All these characters marked, physically, by their fate: Quick Egg, Ahab, the whale itself, its skin pockmarked with broken harpoons from old battles.

So he chooses this Paul Newman. In the lobby, standing in front of the till, Daniel rediscovers his own path, which he had thought lost. From the till to the heavy doors of the projection room. In the gently sloping rows. The red chairs, the crimson curtain covering the screen. The whispers of people already in their seats, their heads silhouetted over the seat backs.

Algeria remains outside the door. Only the dream life enters here, even if it's a nightmare. The dreams of others, perfectly framed by the image. Day and night are often not real, and the people are followed by their shadows under the cold false sunlight of a trumped up moon. Even the dead get to their feet again afterwards, rubbing the dust from their hands on their suits. Tears sparkle more brightly and tremble for a long time on the eyelids' edge. Laughter sounds clearer.

He sinks into his seat, sighing with rapture. He hears the creak of the usherette's wicker basket and when he turns around, hand lifted, he sees a pretty brunette smiling at him.

Choc ice. Thank you, mademoiselle. The girl has a warm, husky voice, and she hands him his change with the tips of her cool fingers.

When the lights go down, a sob of happiness rises in his chest and sticks in his throat as the Warner Brothers ident appears. This is life. He lets himself be swept away by the whirlwind of challenges and gunshots, embraces and hatreds. He begins to understand why Irène is so taken by this Paul Newman, although he could do with a Gregory Peck figure to prevent him from getting into such trouble, an honest and straightforward bloke in a world of ruffians; not one of those old windbags, but a mature, handsome, solid man capable of telling him that his armed left hand will end up bringing him into harm's way.

He leaves the cinema, dazed in the heat of the street, and looks around him as if he has just got off a transcontinental flight. Then he hangs around for a while with his frame in his hand, isolating three windows on the façade of a building, a street corner where a man is waiting in the shade of an awning, following the trajectory of a passer-by, stopping at a mother on a porch talking to a child in a pushchair, and stories come to him, stories that would make wonderful films. But nothing, not even the sun, can lift the grey veil that covers the city, this blackness that oozes from its stones. There is always a little bit of winter here sticking to the buildings, to the roofs. Something oceanic; the cold glare of a stormy sky. He can no longer see this city the way he did before he left for Algeria. And maybe now he's seeing it the way it is: dark and damp, prone to flooding, at the mercy of the river and its mud, almost dissolved in the endless rains of November.

He decides to walk over to Irène's office: she works in a wine merchant's, calculating and checking customs receipts. He waits outside in the street that reeks of cork and cheap wine and sees women come out talking loudly, laughing, some of them pushing down on the pedals of rickety old bicycles and turning around to wave to each other before riding away towards the docks or the end of the street. When she sees him, she shakes her hair to give it more volume then runs towards him, her bag over her shoulder. When they kiss, a group of girls whistle in their direction.

"Don't worry. They always mess around like that."

"I'm not worried. They couldn't possibly know."

"No, they couldn't know."

As they walk to the bus shelter, they talk about the film he watched, the day she has spent in those dark, old-fashioned offices or on the docks sorting out paperwork and administrative procedures with customs employees.

"So . . . Paul Newman?"

Daniel purses his lips.

"All you can see are his eyes. He plays on them too much. It's like that's all they filmed. He's too handsome – it overshadows the film."

"Too handsome? Is that even possible?"

"Not for you, I'm sure."

She links arms with him.

"Oh, give over!"

In the bus, sitting face to face, they don't say anything. They watch the city pass through the windows, even though they've seen it a thousand times. The swing bridge is closed to let a ship pass into the wet dock. Daniel takes advantage of this to break the dense, invisible thing that has come between them. He takes Irène to the front of the bus to watch the slow movement of the monster that towers over them.

"So what about Alain? Where is he at the moment?"

There is a man leaning on the railing of the boat, smoking a cigarette and staring into space, or perhaps watching terra firma slide past beneath him. Other men are at work on the bridge, their voices audible. On the dockside, a lock-keeper in overalls walks at the same pace as the cargo ship, eyes fixed on the space separating metal hull from concrete edge.

"I don't know," Irène replies. "It's been a while since I heard from him."

When they sit down again, she looks him straight in his eyes.

"You've changed."

He shrugs, watching the ship's stern slowly move into the distance.

"No, I haven't. Why do you say that?"

"Because it's true. There are times when I don't even recognise you. Your face is the same, but it's like you're not really you anymore."

Don't tell her anything. Anyway, what could he tell her? He looks away. The bus starts up again.

"Oh, right. Like in *Invasion of the Body Snatchers*, by Don Siegel . . . We went to see that last year with Alain and Gilbert. It's just the same. Except I'm not from another planet."

"Don't make fun of me."

Irène speaks breathily, almost imploringly. He reaches out to touch her shoulder in apology, but she shies away from him and starts rummaging in her handbag.

When they get off the bus, Daniel catches her arm before she can cross the street.

"I remember a poem you told me once. I can't remember who it's by, but at one point it said: *And at times I have seen what man thought he saw.* Well, that's how I feel too."

She turns towards him and looks at him for a few seconds without saying anything, then she strokes his cheek with her hand. And it feels so good to him, because her hand is cool, and so soft. He would like to take this girl in his arms and kiss her, here and now, the way they do in films when nothing except the two characters seems to exist, when the entire world seems to rest on the axis they form, embracing tightly, indestructible. But Irène is already running frantically across the street so he follows her, watching her dress flutter around her legs.

As soon as they open the door, Daniel hears a conversation come to a sudden halt and a heavy silence falls in the kitchen. Sitting at the table, having an aperitif, are Roselyne and Maurice and Monsieur Mesplet. For a moment they look at each other without saying anything, as if embarrassed to find themselves in the same room, then Mesplet gets to his feet, saying:

"So, your boss doesn't even get a hello?"

They hug warmly, then exchange jokes about the disgusting army food. Not surprising you've lost weight, it suits you though, and you've got a tan too, you look very handsome like that. Maurice takes two glasses from a cupboard and fills them with muscat wine.

"Come on, let's drink to deserters and to peace!"

All five of them raise their glasses. They drink, and nibble peanuts.

Daniel watches them. He sees the wine in Roselyne's glass tremble slightly. She won't meet his eye; she seems to be staring vacantly into space. And the other two are speaking too loud, their laughter sounding false.

"How are things at the garage? How's Norbert?"

"Things are fine at the garage. No shortage of work anyway. Looking forward to having you back. And Norbert's making progress. He's getting pretty good now, so that helps a bit. When we have a lot on, I send for a cousin who comes in to give us a hand. So we get by."

Claude Mesplet falls silent and downs another mouthful of white.

"So, what about you? What are you going to do?"

"Wait for the war to end, I guess. I don't know."

"But you—"

"He's better off here than back there," Maurice interrupts. "After all, it might be over in a few months, who knows? Anyway, I think they've got better things to do than go after deserters, don't you?"

Nobody replies. Everyone stares into their glass or away from the table. Another silence. The sound of birds singing wildly through the open windows.

"You have to tell him, Claude," says Roselyne. "He needs to know."

Mesplet waves his hand in front of him. It's unclear whether the gesture is meant to silence Roselyne or to prevent his own mouth letting anything slip.

"What's going on?"

It's as if a grenade has just been unpinned in the room. Daniel hears it roll along the floor, waits for it to explode.

"Your father is staying with Claude," says Maurice. "He's hiding out in the flat above the garage. He's wanted by the cops, as you know. He escaped them the other day; he'd been staying with one of his old mates from before the war . . . Anyway, he didn't know where else to go. We thought you should know."

Claude clears his throat, has a drink to lubricate his voice.

"I didn't tell you this, but he came back last November. He brought his motorbike in to get repaired. You remember that man with the English bike? But I didn't want to see him, I almost threw him out when I realised who he was. The bike stayed in our garage for weeks before he came in to pick it up. He told me that seeing you had been enough for him, that he didn't dare speak to you, that he was ashamed . . . So I didn't tell you anything. And then what he's been doing, that vengeance . . . I didn't know what to think when articles about it began appearing in the paper. I talked about it with Maurice and Roselyne, but you were in Algeria, you had other things to worry about. But now he's asking after you. I think he's on his last legs, to be honest."

He's asking after you. Like some fucking ghost in a film. Daniel feels Irène's hand on his shoulder, the light pressure of her slender fingers. It seems to him that it is only thanks to this almost imperceptible, possibly magical touch that he is prevented from collapsing, because the room is spinning slowly around him now, swaying and rolling like the ship that took him to Algeria. Deep down, he knew this moment was coming, but he had kept pushing it back in his head. Too many other things to think about.

"What do you think of this?" he asks Roselyne.

She shakes her head. "I don't know . . ."

She examines the tablecloth, staring hard at it, then adds:

"You've been wondering about this for so long, thinking about it, asking us questions . . . Back when you were five, you used to ask about him – and about her – all the time. When they would come back, what had happened to them, how they were. And I . . . we . . . didn't know how to respond. We couldn't. You understand . . . I think, if you go to see him, at least you'll know. And then you can choose."

He watches them all, trying to decipher their gestures, their expressions. He looks at Irène, who bites her lower lip and looks down, head lowered, like a kid feeling guilty or embarrassed. He can no longer stand this silence, this glue paralysing them. He wants to scream insults at them, ugly things that will hurt them, so he leaves, slamming the door behind him, and out in the street, painted gold by the setting sun, he walks quickly, almost running, until he hears Irène shouting behind him, "Daniel, wait for me!" and those words send shivers of pleasure crawling all over his body, as if she had grabbed him by the elbow before kissing him full on the mouth.

471

He turns around and sees her coming towards him and never, ever has she looked so pretty, never has he felt this sure, and as soon as she is before him he will put his arms around her waist, pull her tight against him, put his lips to hers.

"What's the matter with you?"

She catches his arm and leads him further away, towards the too-bright sunlight, and she forces him to cross the street so they can find some shade and she pushes him against a wall, the collar of his polo shirt in her fist as though she's about to beat him up.

"What's the matter with you?" she repeats. "Shit, you have to talk now!"

"My father," he says. "My fucking father."

"Don't talk about him like that. I wrote to you about this. I told you he was back."

Tears. Daniel can't stop them falling. An acid knot in his throat. He coughs to get rid of it, tries to catch his breath. Irène runs her hand through his hair, down his cheek, to calm him, the way you would calm a child. The way she used to when they were little, in their hiding place, and he would cry because he was scared of shadows and memories.

"In Algeria, it all seemed so far away . . . It didn't make much difference to me that he was back. Even when we talked about it the other day. I didn't feel like it really concerned me. And then now, suddenly, with old Mesplet coming and saying all that, I don't know . . ."

"Maybe you have to go. Just to make sure. He must have changed. After everything that's happened. And so have you."

"He put me on the roof and he told me they'd come back to fetch me, him and Mum."

And there he is once again, in the clear, bright cold, among sparrows and robins. Trembling on the tiles, pissing his pants. Nibbling his bit of bread. Shivering. Almost falling asleep, tangled up in hazy dreams.

472

And then he doesn't know which of them, him or her, moves so close that their mouths are touching and then they are kissing like lovers, eyes closed. He no longer knows what is happening. Then they are walking home in silence, their two long shadows undulating over the uneven cobbles of the pavement. "I'll go tomorrow," he says before they go inside. "Tomorrow."

A sleepless night. The bedroom full of the living and the dead in the relentless heat. And as the early-morning breeze blows through the half-open window, he feels something a little like courage stir inside him.

35

One evening in December '44, I found Olga in tears. I thought she was going to cause another scene because I was late getting home. I'd done a bit of drinking and a bit of gambling, but not lost anything. I'd decided to quit while I was ahead. It was barely midnight, but I was content to go to bed early so I would feel fresh the next morning for work: I had to correct an account I'd dipped into the previous month before the boss did his end-of-year inventory and noticed.

Usually she would be in bed, and even if I knew she wasn't sleeping – either because I'd woken her or because she hadn't been able to fall asleep – she usually didn't move, remaining there with her back to me, and I liked to slide close to her and feel her warmth, and sometimes I would embrace her, wrapping my arm around her waist and falling asleep straight away like that, swearing to myself that I would never come home late again, would quit gambling, would stay with her and the kid. I must have made that promise a hundred times, while hugging my wife as she pretended to sleep. Occasionally I even whispered it to her. A hundred times I betrayed her.

A traitor to myself, my wife and my son.

She didn't say anything, just stared at me, breathing fast, almost panting. I asked her if Daniel was sick and she shrugged.

"No, Daniel's fine. Thank you for thinking of him."

"So what is it? Why aren't you in bed? It's cold, it's raining."

We could hear the patter of rain on the roof, the water gargling in the gutters. I remember all the details of that evening. They came back to me like a hammer blow to the head, later, in the camp, minute by minute, and for days they obsessed me to the point where I was incapable of thinking about anything else. She was wearing a grey sweater over her midnight-blue dress. And thick socks because it was so cold, because

we didn't have enough coal. Her black hair was down and would sometimes stick to her face because of the tears.

"Your friend Albert, the cop. He came."

I thought he must have warned her about the next round-up. I took
her in my arms but she pushed me away brusquely.

"Are they planning something else? When for?"

She looked at me contemptuously. She nodded slowly, her eyes
never leaving me, so I would understand just how much she despised me.

"No. Nothing like that. He just wanted to sleep with me."

"What? Say that again!"

I was speaking too loud, so she signalled me to be quiet. The kid was
asleep.

"Impossible. He's my friend. We've known each other for ten years.
He'd never do that."

"Your friend . . . A gambler, a swindler, a thief, a Nazi cop. That's
your friend. And on top of that, he wants to have it off with your wife
while you're out, your dear Inspecteur Darlac. God, you're pathetic.
You deserve a wife who'd cheat on you with that pig. You'd make a
wonderful cuckold, like those imbeciles in the films."

She said all of this in an even tone, her voice firm in spite of the tears
that kept rolling down her face. She was lying. She was just saying all
this to punish me for neglecting her, for gambling, maybe for cheating
on her with those girls one evening, even if I didn't think she could possibly know about that, not even suspect it. I felt sure that nothing had
really happened, that Darlac had come round to say hello, bringing a
cake or a toy for the kid, as he'd done several times before. He liked
women, I knew that, but I couldn't imagine that he would ever come on
to Olga. He was always telling me how lucky I was to have a wife like
her. He even wondered why I didn't spend more time with her instead
of hanging around in the back rooms of bars, gambling with all those
dropouts. He had managed to remove her from the lists of Jews and
protect us from the round-ups. That was surely the absolute proof of his
friendship towards me and the esteem or affection he felt for her. One

day he said to me, "At least this way there'll be two people who can be happy in the middle of all this shit. I'll protect that. You can count on me."

Clearly, Olga didn't understand. She had always hated and despised him. But I was the one who didn't understand.

"He pawed me. He put his filthy hands on me, that bastard. Here, and here. I had to defend myself, you understand?"

She touched her breasts, rubbed her crotch with her balled fists. It sickened me suddenly, seeing her do that. I thought it was indecent.

"So you're not going to do anything? You're just going to say, go ahead, dig in, you're my best mate, what's mine is yours? Is that how the two of you share your whores?"

I leaped at her and grabbed her throat. She cried out, so I hit her. A slap, and then a punch. She fell on the floor, knocking a chair over on her way down. I think I would have kept hitting her if Daniel hadn't come out of his bedroom in tears. I found myself between the two of them, weeping and screaming, and I stood there, above them both, but in reality I was the one on the ground, suddenly laid low. Powerless, stupid, ashamed. I held the boy in my arms and I knelt next to Olga, who was rubbing her ear where I'd hit her, blood flowing from her split lip. She didn't push me away when I tried to pull her towards me and for a moment the three of us stayed like that, them slowly controlling their sobs, me swallowing my shame and self-disgust the way you swallow some disgusting medicine, down to the last drop.

The next day, and during the days that followed, I searched all over town for Albert Darlac. I talked to every pimp, every loser, every black-market dealer, every collaborator and every cop I knew through him. None of those wretches had seen him in days and most of them seemed barely to remember me. As if I'd been nothing more than a silhouette beside him, a sort of cipher, an insubstantial stooge. I think it was perhaps then that I began to understand. I needed that. Hitting the woman I loved, scaring my son, and finding myself above the void, ready to send them both into it.

On the night of 10–11 January, there was a new round-up. Afterwards I found out that it was the last one on that scale. At that time, however, no-one knew which way the war would go. Of course, we'd heard about Stalingrad; through her friends, Olga followed all of that quite closely. But the Germans were not relaxing their grip here. They were making arrests, executing people, deporting them relentlessly, furious till the end. La Petite Gironde carried regular enthusiastic reports on the activities of the Gestapo and the French police against "terrorist" networks. Cops, French or Kraut, were everywhere.

Darlac never mentioned any of this. All he said was that what he did made him sick sometimes, but that he had to obey orders. It was his job. Anyway, as far as he was concerned, the war would have had to be won in '40; now we simply had to adapt to the situation. I didn't argue. I wanted to preserve our little life, for the three of us. The kid was born in October '39 and I swore we would protect him from the coming chaos. I hated the Krauts; I wanted them to be defeated; I knew they were coming but I didn't know when. I waited. And then I got into gambling, into girls. I needed those things to be able to breathe freely. It was thanks to them that I was able to love, to truly love Olga and Daniel. Olga became furious, for all these reasons. She should have hated me more than any other man. She should have thrown me out. And yet, since the day we had met, in '37, something held us together, an animal connection, an instinct. Explosions of happiness would regularly annihilate all the obstacles that cropped up between us, obstacles that should have kept us apart forever. I still don't understand it. We loved each other, in spite of what everyone else thought and said. And Daniel's arrival only strengthened that connection. We might fight and scream and tear at each other's throats like wolves, but we would still remain there for him, ready to kill anyone who threatened him. That was why Olga kept her friends at a distance, and why – after the arrests of hostages and Resistance fighters – they themselves let nothing slip about their activities. I never knew what they did and I preferred it that way.

As the rumour of a round-up had been circulating for a few days, they offered to hide us. But Olga refused because she didn't want to get them into trouble; they were already being monitored because they were communists. As for me, I curtly rejected their offers, assuring them that I had a friend in the police who would protect us. I remember the way they looked at me: with contempt, or with sadness. Their disappointed sighs. I remember the leaving the café where we had met and seeing their faces through the window all turned towards me.

On the fourteenth, at about half past seven in the morning, we heard cars stopping in the street and voices echoing, doors slamming, feet pounding up the stairs. They banged on the door so hard, it shook on its hinges. "Police! Open up!" We were eating breakfast. A sort of sweetened brown water for us – that ersatz coffee that was all we could get back then – and some milk for the kid. We used to dip the little bit of bread we had into our bowls. Olga had unearthed a few madeleines for Daniel.

She rushed into the bedroom with him and got him dressed in a thick sweater and a coat. She put a big woolly hat on his head and mittens on his hands.

"What are you doing?" I asked.

"I've arranged it with Maurice and Roselyne. They'll come to fetch him."

"What? What did you say?"

She didn't reply. The cops hammered at the door, yelling loudly. I told them my wife was just getting dressed. Two minutes. They seemed to calm down a bit and in that sudden silence we looked at each other, Olga and me, and we knew that our future was sealed now, that there was no going back. She wept as she got everything ready. She put some bread and saucisson in a paper bag. I took a flask from the sideboard and filled it with water. I looked at my son, who sat there motionless on his chair, looking so tiny with the hat pulled down to his eyes. He was playing with his mittened hands, silent and apparently indifferent, this kid who never normally stopped talking, who questioned us endlessly about everything.

"Go up on the roof. Sit right by to the chimney. They'll come in the morning. It's all arranged. Madame Dubuc will tell them."

The cops began banging at the door again. They warned us they would break the lock.

Olga picked Daniel up and looked into his eyes for several seconds as those bastards hammered at the door. Then she kissed him on his cheeks, on his eyes. She whispered unbearable words of love to him. I joined them and we hugged like that, the three of us together. The kid was moaning quietly. I could feel his tears on my neck.

I pulled him from his mother's arms and stood on a chair in the hallway so I could open the skylight that opened onto the roof. I lifted him up there, into the freezing cold, into the wind that was blowing that morning. I hoisted myself up halfway to tell him to sit close to the chimney because it would be warmer there. He crawled away from me and sat there holding his paper bag and his flask of water. I told him that bad men were coming to the house and that he had to hide and, most importantly, make no noise. I said we'd be back to fetch him very soon and that afterwards we'd go on the merry-go-round and eat barley sugar. He didn't move. He just nodded at everything I told him and as I went back down so I could close the skylight, I saw him waving goodbye to me with a little smile on his face.

Olga went to open the door, pretending to finish putting a sweater on. A cop came in and forced her back towards the table, threatening her with his pistol. Two others followed, both armed, and they started searching the apartment, opening drawers, removing pictures from the wall, throwing objects all over the floor. They found a few letters and postcards in a cupboard and looked through them before dropping them at their feet. When I asked them what they were looking for, they told me to shut my mouth. Within two minutes, they had turned the apartment upside down.

Olga shivered as she held her cardigan tightly around her.

"I don't understand," I said. "Call Inspecteur Darlac. He's a friend of mine."

I knew Darlac was behind all this, but still I tried to cling to this last illusion, the way you might grab a broken branch or a dead root as you slide into a hole.

The cop who had come in first, and who was keeping us at bay with his pistol, sniggered as he raised an eyebrow at his colleagues. They shook their heads and grinned like wolves.

"You should choose your friends more carefully."

After a while, they stopped searching the flat and stood motionless, all three of them, in the kitchen, looking at each other questioningly for a few seconds.

"And your son? Where's he?"

"Somewhere safe," said Olga. "With people in the countryside."

"What do you mean, somewhere safe?" a cop demanded. "Who gave you the right to do that?"

"Forget it," said the man who seemed to be their leader. "It doesn't matter. They're the ones we want. You have three minutes to pack a suitcase. Don't forget your papers."

"Where are you taking us?" I asked.

"Shut your face. Pack." Then, turning to Olga: "And you – you're a Jew? I don't want to know why you weren't on the list before. You are now. So here you go. For you."

He threw a yellow star on the table.

"Sew that on your coat. You should be grateful. I'm doing you a favour here."

Olga went to get her sewing bag and she quickly stitched the star to her coat while I filled a suitcase with clothes.

Three cars were waiting outside in the street, engines running. The air stank of exhaust fumes. Other cops were smoking on the pavement. One of them had a sub-machine gun strapped to his shoulder. They barely even glanced at us, just tossed their cigarettes on the ground and ushered us into two different cars. I tried to turn around in my seat to get a look at Olga, but a detective sitting next to me grunted at me not to move, not to give him any shit. We drove for five minutes through

Bordeaux. I no longer recognised anything. They might just as easily have been taking me through a foreign city. The cops wiped the condensation from the windows, but nothing I saw through the glass seemed to really exist, to evoke anything. I was already far away. Gone forever, perhaps.

They dropped us in front of what I took to be a church. The street was packed with police vans and trucks, with cops in fedoras and caps. Olga explained that this was the synagogue. I had never been here before. I knew vaguely that it was located here, had probably gone past it before without realising. We went into that noise. That murmur of human beings crammed into a small space. Children crying, people coughing, clearing throats. The occasional sound of a kid's laughter. Muttered conversations.

They took our names for their register, took our papers. Then a uniformed cop said: "Over there. Find yourselves a place and stay calm." A nun came to meet us and led us over to a mattress with a blanket.

"Are they taking us to Poland?" Olga asked.

"I don't know," said the nun. "I can't tell you anything. You must wait. They'll give you some food at lunchtime."

We sat down and for a long time we said nothing, just looked around us at the people lying or sitting, like us, staring into space, while others concentrated on trivial tasks: carefully folding a few old rags in a suitcase, cleaning a child's face with a damp handkerchief, arranging photographs in a wallet. Men walked silently through the aisles. I saw a swindler I knew, dressed in a coat that was too big for him. Our eyes met, and he turned away instantly.

After a little while I felt Olga shivering against me, so I got to my feet and helped her to do the same. We needed to walk to prevent the cold numbing us completely. She linked arms with me and we began to weave our way between the makeshift tents that people had set up on the floor. But the cold clung to our legs as if we were walking through water.

"I hope Maurice can get there quickly," said Olga, with a shudder.

I didn't reply because, beyond that hope, words no longer had any value.

We spent three days in that silent abyss where the few words we exchanged found no echo. We asked each other, "Are you cold? Are you hungry? Did you manage to use the toilet? You feel better now?" Animals, if they could talk, would probably express something similar with regard to their vital functions and their survival.

One afternoon another nun approached us with some bread and chocolate.

"Daniel is fine," she whispered. "Maurice says he's safe."

She smiled sadly then went over to a family with a daughter who had been suffering from a fever since the night before.

Olga and I hugged each other. We whispered sweet nothings that we hadn't said to each other in months. The next day, she started coughing.

Then they took us in their trains to their camps.

I wonder, now, if I ever really came back. Came back alive, I mean. In the months since I returned to Bordeaux, I have had the feeling that I am insubstantial, perceptible to no-one. I have been forgotten. Or buried, given up for dead in the clay of Poland or reduced to ashes. Scattered. Even my bones have no weight now. And nor does my soul. Once, in the Louvre, where Suzanne had taken me, I saw an Egyptian fresco show-ing a priest weighing a dead man's soul. What would he see if he put mine on the scale? I wasn't worth much before I was deported. They call us "good-for-nothings", men like me. During the months I was in the camp, I had time to try to work out my own worth. My value in weight. My body counted for less with each passing day, but did I have another value, over there, in my own eyes? How much does a soul cost? What price would the devil pay for one? For me, it varied between not much and dirt cheap. Later, in Paris, when I made an effort to live again, when I thought it would become easy, I realised one day that I was not worth the price of my suffering: a label stuck on me by the S.S. and deciphered by those around me. André Vaillant, former Auschwitz inmate. That was who I was, first of all. And I clung to this new identity in order to erase the old one. My memory, and my nightmares, were enough for me to know who I really was.

Only Hélène knew. Buried, like me, in our rubble, she waved her hand through the piles of ruins like those people who are trapped alive after earthquakes or landslides, waving to show rescuers that they are not dead but that they must be freed from what holds them down, what threatens to crush them. I think when she danced she was able to defeat this fatal weight. I think she only considered herself alive in those moments.

"Me? I dance." That was how she replied when I asked her how she was.

And me, so heavy and tired.

And now I am waiting for my son. I didn't recognise him in the young man I saw at Mesplet's garage. I could not manage to discern, in his face, the features of the little boy I put on the roof that day, or whom I took for rides on the merry-go-round or for walks in the park, where he would spend hours watching the rich kids playing with model boats in the ponds. He wept once, quietly, without anger, because he didn't have a beautiful boat like that. I promised him I would buy one for him and he started laughing and jumping while he held my hand, chatting away happily as he often used to. I remember his voice. His face is lost to me, but I can still hear his voice laughing in my memory. I never kept my promise.

I am waiting for him. He came back from Algeria. He deserted. What else could he do, apart from rebelling and shooting a few generals? I don't know if he will come. I hope he does. So I can hold him in my arms. Say my son, my boy, my little man. Like I used to, before. So I can say sorry for these old words from an old father, kept for so long in silence. How you've grown. Obviously. If only you knew how I've changed too.

I am waiting for him. No hope beyond that moment. Afterwards . . . we'll see.

36

"How could you let him get away? You've made a serious mistake, Darlac. Result: two more deaths. You had unlimited resources for this operation. Instead of which you go in with three men and only one car."

Commissaire Divisionnaire Laborde sucks at his pipe, which has gone out, and pretends to look through the report on his desk.

Darlac shrugs. Two more deaths. The Kraut and his mother. He remembers how, the night before, when Laborde called to inform them of the bodies that had been found that morning by the baker who came to present his weekly bill, madame fell onto the sofa and wept for an hour, slumped in her tears, sniffling and hiccupping, ugly at last, showing her true face – aged now, her features subsiding, her flesh soft and saggy – and how he had been happy to be able to hate her unreservedly now that he had found a chink in the fragile armour of her beauty.

If they were alone, he would grab Laborde by the back of his jacket and hang him on the coat rack, force him to swallow the glee with which he had, for the last quarter of an hour, been detailing the errors committed during the failed arrest of that bastard Jean Delbos. But there is another cop here, a bigwig down from Paris, Commissaire Belcher, a special envoy from the minister, who is concerned by the growing scale of this case. Nine murders in ten months; a notably determined and violent killer still at large: that's a lot for a city like Bordeaux, generally considered quite calm and orderly, the capital of political moderation, with a past marked by an efficient Gestapo and a formidable, much-feared secret police, a Resistance movement chopped into small factions, the Jews duly deported, and with a good proportion of bastards, traitors and

484

crooks, most of whom slipped through the net during the purge, and now led by that young, handsome mayor who looks like a vacuum-cleaner salesman, an irreproachable Resistance fighter, tasked by De Gaulle with transforming this whore back into a virgin, with cleaning up its snot-nosed brood of bourgeois hypocrites, wine merchants, cops and local journalists still happy at the end of their new leash. Nine murders that appear, seen from Paris, to carry the stench of the bad old days, as if someone had set to stirring up that marshy backwater with a big stick in order to bring everything up to the surface: the thick, heavy shit at the bottom, the stiffs, the trunks filled with secrets and accommodations, the suitcases overflowing with denunciations and plunder, the hastily falsified certificates of Resistance, the casually signed deportation orders.

A killer who is violent, determined and perhaps uniquely motivated. Who must be stopped urgently, by any means necessary. Whose motives must be kept quiet. Otherwise, if he continues his vendetta, there could be a serious risk to public order, particularly in these troubled times caused by the Algerian War.

Darlac mentally reviews his tourist brochure for the city with its gallery of rogues, because of course the memories are flowing now, the names echoing in his mind. Laborde and the Parisian are powerless against him. He is in control of the situation. All the ins and outs. They can go fuck themselves.

"All the same," insists Belcher, "I think you're treating this too lightly. Even if no-one's likely to come across this man, with a dangerous killer like this we must establish a more substantial police presence."

"I've caught blokes like this before with just two or three coppers, sometimes by chance. That's part of police work too, you know, or maybe you've forgotten? These sorts of things happen when you step out of your office occasionally. But so what? He has no money, no papers. He was practically barefoot when he got away. He has nowhere else to stay. Abel Mayou was his last possible refuge, and he's probably breathing his last in hospital at this very minute. I see that as a sign. It's time to go in for the kill. His other friends, or rather his wife's friends, refuse to have anything to do with him, cos of all his shady dealings before and during the Occupation. I'm keeping an eye on the garage where his son works; he's in Algeria at the moment. We're going to get this man, no doubt about it. It'll be wrapped up in a matter of days."

Belcher stands up, walks over to the window and looks up at the sky, hands in pockets. Without turning around, he says:

"This Delbos was your friend at one time, wasn't he? How can you explain his hatred of you?"

"All the people who made it back from the camps are a bit bonkers. They have trouble accepting what they went through, and sometimes they tend to blame any Tom, Dick or Harry for no good reason. I suppose it helps reduce their own guilt."

"Their guilt? Surely you're not . . . ?"

Belcher turns around and stares at Darlac with curiosity.

"You're not suggesting that they deserved what happened to them?"

Laborde and Belcher exchange a glance. Darlac suddenly feels himself cast in the role of a suspect, being grilled by two clowns. Keep your cards close to your chest. He feels his heart speed up a bit. He forces himself to calm down, unwind a little.

"No, of course not. But he must have thought that, being mates with a policeman, he'd be safe from what was happening at the time. He wasn't the kind of bloke who cared about politics. He was a bit of a gambler: horses, cards. He went to the same bars and clubs as me, and that's how we met. I got him out of a few scrapes, it's true. I liked him. He was intelligent, which made a nice change from the morons I was dealing with back then. His wife Olga was Jewish and a communist sympathiser. She was on the list, obviously. When they were arrested, he must have thought it was my fault, that I hadn't done anything to prevent it."

"Do you have a man outside that garage?" Laborde asks.

"Yes. I put two men there that evening. But there's been nothing. Anyway, I find it hard to imagine the boss sheltering him. He's not the forgiving kind. I think we just have to wait. I'm telling you: wait for him to fall into our hands."

Darlac watches these two fools who think they can order him around. He catches them exchanging another look, filled with irritation and collusion and for a second he wonders what exactly they know and are not saying.

"And that former German officer . . . Müller, is it? What's he even doing in France? You were talking about a man who was going after you, your friends, your family . . ."

"He came here in '49," Laborde interrupts. "We had him watched straight away. We heard about this wounded soldier crossing the border; given the way he looks, he was hardly likely to go unnoticed. He was from a family of industrialists who made a fortune during the war, like lots of others . . . When his father died, the mother sold her shares in the company and brought her son here so he could be close to his daughter, Elise, conceived with Madame Darlac in '42, before he left for the Eastern Front. He kept himself to himself, so we stopped the surveillance after a year. Madame Darlac used to visit him regularly, which was a way of keeping an eye on him, I suppose?"

Commissaire Divisionnaire Laborde turns to Darlac. He smiles. Pleased with himself. Darlac feels the skin on his face tighten, as if he dried off in the sun after swimming in the sea. So, those bastards knew a year before he did. They investigated him, they had his wife followed. Half the cops in the city must have known about it. He stands up and the other two watch him as he takes a few steps towards a metal locker with an old departmental schedule stuck to the door. He feels as if he is walking over a frayed rope bridge with crumbling wooden slats, suspended over a river full of crocodiles. His imagination never normally allows this kind of horrific fantasy, but he feels powerless to fight against the vertigo that has seized him, the vision that fills his mind. He punches the locker door, leaving a dent in the metal and making the whole thing vibrate for a few seconds. He grits his teeth as the pain rises through his arm, then wraps his grazed knuckles in his handkerchief and turns around, chest thrust out, acting tough.

"This all seems a bit disloyal to me."

This is all he can think to say, and instantly he feels pathetic. He's losing his grip. He looks at the door, filled with a sudden desire to get out of here as fast as he can, to grab his gun from the desk drawer and then come back for a proper discussion with these two bastards.

"Oh yeah," says Laborde. "Loyalty. I forgot how important that is to you. You . . ."

Commissaire Belcher claps his hands as if to calm down two kids who are about to start fighting.

"Commissaire Darlac, I have to make a report to the minister later today by telephone. This is still your investigation: what should I tell him? This case stinks. The Paris press is beginning to report on it. I need a deadline. For the moment I feel like this is one huge can of worms and it's better not to open it up. So unless you want me to get my can-opener out, tell me something I want to hear. And I need results. Understood?"

"Three days," says Darlac.

This seems like a good number to him. A prime number. The perfect balance of a triangle. He could have gone for seven too, but he doesn't need to recreate the world.

"In three days, I'll have him. If not, the minister will receive my letter of resignation. Is that what you want to hear?"

"There's no need for that."

"I think there is. Are we done?"

The other two exchange a look.

"Gentlemen . . ."

He leaves, taking care to close the door slowly. Out in the corridor, a current of cooler air makes him realise what a furnace he has just escaped. His shirt is soaked with cold sweat, sticking to his swollen belly, where he can feel his lunch still fermenting. As soon as he enters his office, he takes off his jacket and rolls up his shirtsleeves. Standing in front of the sink, he drinks from the tap, splashes water on his face, exhales, then coughs and spits and rinses his mouth again because he feels as if the mingled stench of their colognes and their sweat are stuck to his tongue and the back of his throat. In the speckled mirror he examines the drawn features of his face and thinks that, this time, maybe it really is over, that he should think about taking off. Sell his house and buy a place in Périgord, for instance, a small business, a newsagent's maybe, where he could see all the nobodies from the village file past every day, where he could listen to their secrets, hear all the local gossip, the slanders and scandals . . . He would be at the centre of the tiny local shit heap, watching them all eat their hearts out, and that would be great entertainment for him, all those malignant people, all that vileness, like a rural concentration of human nature. He also imagines himself with his arse parked on a riverbank, a fishing rod in his hand, or sitting by a hearth with a hellish fire blazing . . . Alone, of course. Or with a dog. A faithful companion, always happy to see him, obedient and sweet-natured. Madame and her daughter? Try as he might, he can find no place for them in the happiness he dreams up for himself beneath the yellowish lamp hung above the washbasin.

He remains for a moment in front of his reflection, not really looking at it, his hands still wet, burning pains in his stomach, attempting to project himself into the future the way you might try to spit as far as possible, and then the telephone rings.

"Someone to see you, commissaire."

"Who is it? What do they want?"

"Some kid. He says his name's Norbert and he wants to talk to you."

"I'll be down in a minute."

Life is good. You think it's nearly over, curled up at the end of a cul-de-sac like a dying dog, and suddenly up it gets and shakes itself off and starts barking again, full of vigour, as if nothing ever happened. The Dordogne can wait, and so can the fishing trips. I'll bury myself later. Right now I'm going to fuck them all and make them thank for me it. He grabs his gun from the drawer, puts on his jacket, tightens the knot of his tie and goes downstairs jauntily, like a young man.

Norbert is sitting on a bench facing the counter where two uniformed cops – an old fat one and a tall blond one who looks like a drunkard – are sweating as they give directions to two men, pointing out the floor and office number that they must report to. The boy stands up when he sees the commissaire, and Darlac grabs his arm and leads him outside. He takes him to a busy, noisy bar on rue Judaqueï.

Darlac orders a beer, Norbert a shandy. Beer is too strong, he says. This amuses Darlac. If you say so. Then he remembers the violent pisshead father and takes a better look at this boy with bluish, swollen eyes under his constantly frowning eyebrows, sipping his soft drink.

"So, you wanted to see me?"

Norbert lights a fag, blows the smoke up at the ceiling. Acting like a man.

"He came back. The boss is letting him stay in the flat above the garage."

Darlac knows what he means, but he wants to be sure. He downs half his beer in a single gulp and shakes his head to ward off the giddiness that is starting to numb his brain.

"Who came back?"

"Um . . . Daniel's father. Jean Delbos. You know, the one who brought a motorbike to be repaired back in November. He got there the day before yesterday, around noon. Didn't look too good. I take his food up sometimes. He doesn't say anything. Just lies on his bed and writes in a notebook."

"He writes? You think he'll be there for long?"

"No idea. Apparently he doesn't know where to go. But my boss never tells me much. Just the bare minimum."

Darlac just wants to know that he was right about this kid. Confirm his intuitions. Savour yet another victory over the weakness of men.

"Why did you decide to tell me? You don't owe me anything, after all."

"Yeah, I do, a bit. You kept your word. You brought my father in. That calmed him down for about three weeks and then it started up again, but I didn't dare come and disturb you for that. I hoped the chance would present itself. And that man, Daniel's father, I don't have any respect for him. If you have a son, you should look after him. He abandoned his. And I remember Daniel often talked about his parents, even though he barely remembers their faces. I mean, can you believe it? He didn't recognise his own father when he brought that bike to be repaired! How is that even possible?"

Darlac shakes his head, twists his face as if to say "beats me". He finds the boy so sincere, so touching, a little prince with greasy hands, that he wants to say something kind to him.

"Well, don't worry about your father: I'll take care of him. I'll see what I can do, but in a month or two you'll be rid of him, for a while at least, you and your mother. Enough time for her to change her life and for you to become a man. I won't forget what you've done."

The boy begins to shift about on his chair. He looks around as if afraid that someone might have heard them. Darlac knows this sort of embarrassed impatience. All informers are like that: they wallow in the denunciation, the details, and then after a moment they feel dirty, almost regretful. It's a bit like whores with morals: their virtue is like a small stone in their shoe, making them limp home every morning.

"One other thing: how do you get into his hideout?"

"Through the garage. There's a door that you can hardly see because there are shelves in front of it. You go up some stairs and it's there, on the first floor. But there's also a door to the street behind. Number 8, Passage Bardos. That's where the boss and his wife used to live. But no-one goes through there anymore. It's closed up."

"What do you mean, closed up?"

"I don't know . . . the shutters and all that . . . The boss kept the room where that man is pretty clean. There's a washbasin in there. But downstairs it must be full of mice and spiders, I reckon."

Darlac thinks about the two detectives staked out in the street. If Delbos goes out through the back, they could wait until retirement before they see him. A moment of doubt. Is it possible the garage owner and Delbos have some sort of trick planned that the kid doesn't know about?

"When was the last time you saw Delbos?"

"At noon. I took him up some food."

"And what time does the garage close?"

"About seven in the evening. Earlier sometimes."

Darlac checks his watch: ten past six. He gets up abruptly. He has to go. He's heard enough for today. Then Norbert slides something across the table. A large key. The cop pockets it and walks towards the exit. The boy follows him. He senses him on his heels and ups his pace. But the boy is still behind him. What's he doing, waiting for Darlac to sing him a lullaby? The cop turns around:

"What do you want?"

The words come out harsher than he meant them to, and the boy recoils almost imperceptibly, as if Darlac was about to hit him.

"Nothing, I . . . This is my turning here. Goodbye, monsieur."

Darlac watches him jog across the street, hands in his pockets, his little workman's bag slung over his shoulder. He thinks that the police works, in the end, because there are sad cases like that, overwhelmed by their own emotions. As if all the lazy suckers desperate for easy money were not enough! And then there are those who break the law because they don't know how to do otherwise at a given moment, because they're helpless, cornered, enraged, up shit creek, off their rockers, hypnotised by all that glitters. And also those who talk, betray, rat on their friends, for money or for vengeance or for no reason at all, because they are mad with jealousy, anger, hatred, love . . . Being a policeman is a job stuffed to the gills with feelings, in fact: good feelings and bad. And to be a cop you have to be a romantic, in a way: you must consider every possible passion, without actually feeling any of them. You have to stay safe in the shelter of your contempt for this human confusion, the way a soldier might lie flat on the ground to escape a burst of gunfire.

37

Abel died yesterday. Claude Mesplet called the hospital this morning. When I found out, I felt the tears well up in my eyes, then I slapped myself in the face to stop them falling – or to give them a good reason to fall – and my vision blurred and I felt so sad that I collapsed on the bed and lay there, motionless, unthinking, for maybe an hour. A real sadness. A child's sadness, inconsolable, immune to reason. I'd forgotten how it felt to be sad like that. I have been through states of despair, melancholy, the blues, whatever you want to call it, but I recall always trying to think, to fight the feeling, at least to put words to what I was experiencing, usually by writing in my notebooks. But this feeling of absolute solitude and suffering, this slow fall into a bottomless abyss, this inability to explain anything even to myself . . . I didn't know what it was.

I slept a bit. I sleep a lot here. I sleep and I write in this accounts book that Claude gave me. A twist of fate? A final settling-up? I have been writing in school exercise books since 1946, since I found the strength to do it, as a way of keeping a few beacons lit in my dark night, to help guide my memory. Since more or less the same date, I have kept records of my earnings and expenses, just to balance the books. It was my job, before. I always hated it. Hated my bosses: their obsession with profit, their natural propensity for fraud, their instinct for cheating. I think any boss, big or small, is a cheat who has managed not to get caught.

And now, the hour of reckoning has come and I write indifferently in the two columns as if profits and losses were cancelling each other out. Result: zero. Bankruptcy? No. Just nothing. A whole life, for nothing. I think that's how it will end. I don't know when, or where. But it will be soon, and not far away. Here, in this hovel above a roomful of broken-down cars. Or in Bordeaux, if I manage to escape Darlac. I cannot see beyond the next few days. Maybe the next few hours. I write. At least I will leave that behind me, if anyone ever wants to read what I've written.

My son, maybe. I left my other notebooks at Abel and Violette's house, and I feel more destitute, more naked than if I had fled without the clothes on my back. I'll get them to him via Mesplet, if he doesn't come to see me. I hope the cops haven't found them. But of course they have. Even now, they are probing the secrets of a killer, as the newspapers will put it. Of course they are. No way out. So, these lines . . . For you, Daniel. Reaching you across time and distance, if you decide not to come.

For the last three days there have been two cops sitting in a car down there, about fifty metres away, towards the train station. Claude spotted them almost straight away. They came that first evening. They must have found out I came here when I brought the bike to be fixed. They know my son works here. They realise it's probably the only place I could show up. Although I imagine there are cops sitting in cars outside Maurice and Roselyne's house too. Darlac knows all this, so he's cast his nets. I hope Daniel is well hidden, that they won't take him. I could get out of here, through the back door, and those idiot cops would never know. Mesplet would probably lend me a few francs. But where would I go? Paris? No, don't go back. Never go back. So I wait here and I write and I try to sleep. Imprisoned in myself.

"Don't go out in front. Take this key. It opens the door to number 8, Passage Bardos. You know where that is – I showed it to you once. Avoid rue Furtado: there are two cops waiting there, just for you. You'll need a torch. I haven't been in that house for two years now, so be careful where you put your feet, it's a huge mess in there. At the back there's a wooden staircase. Don't worry, it's not about to collapse. At the top there's a door. Go through that and you'll find your father."

Daniel takes the key and shoves it in his pocket.

"Thanks."

"I can come with you to keep an eye on the street, if you want."

"No. Maybe I won't have the balls to go through with it at the last moment. I'd better be alone for this."

Mesplet puts his hand on Daniel's shoulder.

"As you like. He's changed, you know."

"No, I don't know. I don't even know what he was like before."

He picks up his workman's bicycle, an old rust bucket with a bell that doesn't work. He had cleaned and oiled it that afternoon, dismantled it, checked the inner tubes and the tyres.

Roselyne brings him something to drink.

"Are you sure about this?"

"Yeah, I think so."

Later, in the mild night, Irène goes out with him to the pavement.

"Let me come with you. I won't say anything."

He doesn't reply. He mounts the bike.

"Daniel?"

She walks over to him and kisses him full on the mouth. She hugs him so tight he almost falls off, because he's let go of the handlebars.

"For afterwards," she says.

He rides calmly along the empty docks. Occasionally a car overtakes him, and each time he wonders where they are going, these people, at night. He has always wondered about things like that – where all these figures were coming from or going to, these figures he glimpsed or passed on the street, whom he watched or captured in his little metal frame, and he would imagine little stories for them, strange fates. Sometimes he thinks he should write books about all these people, giving them a past and a future.

He can't help staring at the moored ships. Always that curiosity when he sees an illuminated porthole, a silhouette on the bridge. Alain. Perhaps Daniel should have done what he did. But further off. Sumatra. Zanzibar. Djibouti. San Francisco. Anchorage. He barely even knows where these places are, has no idea what they're like. He's read a few books. Not enough. But those names resound in his mind like magical spells, powerful incantations heard whispered at the other end of the world, attracting madmen and dreamers. People always think I'll leave one day, later, there's plenty of time. And often they never do.

And then there is a woman's kiss, the softness of her hair against your cheek. And it feels good, close to her.

He lets his thoughts drift as far as possible from the man he is about to meet. Sometimes, when the reason for this nocturnal trip crosses his mind, a big shiver runs down his spine and his heart starts to pound in his chest.

He makes a large detour to arrive at the garage from behind, and leaves his bicycle about fifty metres from the street. It is dark and warm in this little alley and he hears something scurry through the gutter. Sweat starts to run down his face, down his back, and his short-sleeved shirt sticks to his skin. He switches on his torch because he can hardly even see his own feet. The moonless sky is no help at all. The streetlights on the neighbouring roads are choked by the night, illuminating nothing beyond themselves.

The key turns in the lock with a click. A hallway. Strips of paint peeled from the walls litter the floor. Daniel's feet crunch through cement dust, or maybe it's sand. The smell of mould, of old paper, saltpetre. Dead rats. His throat tightens in a little spasm of disgust, then he remembers three corpses swarming with wasps that he found during a patrol and the present seems less sickening. In the beam of torchlight he sees piles of chairs, a table on top of another, a sideboard with the doors wide open. A wooden crate filled with tools. He steps carefully through this jumble of objects and hears a stampede of mice under the floorboards.

Suddenly the stairs rise up before him, caught in the glare of the torch. He stops dead in front of the first step and looks up towards the landing where the staircase forks. Impossible to see any further in this darkness. He wishes a door would open, that some light would appear, but there is no illumination, no movement.

Of course, the steps creak under his feet. He senses that in the room upstairs a man he doesn't know is listening, and that he can hear the ferocious pounding of Daniel's heart too.

*

"My name is Jean Delbos and I am your father."

Hearing his son's footstep on the creaky staircase – it can only be him, because there is nothing sneaky about that slowness, it is merely shy and hesitant – he wonders what his first words will be. Or will he say "Hello, son" to reforge the connection, because Daniel knows who he is?

He can hardly breathe when he hears a knock at the door. He takes two steps forward, then stops. I'm not going to open it. Just leave all that well alone. What's the point? Olga. She would already be in her son's arms. Their son. And suddenly he is overwhelmed by tears and a moan escapes his mouth. How he wishes she could be there to live this moment. My little boy, come here so I can see you.

She is dead, her corpse gone in smoke up the chimneys of the crematorium at Auschwitz-Birkenau. There is no heaven, no place where souls can feel anything, caresses or vibrations in the air, no way of feeling joy or suffering. Everything is over, irreversibly so, and memory is merely an invocation without response to a fictional and incomplete hereafter. But he summons her image; the beauty of her smile, the warmth of her skin, the depth and sweetness of her gaze when she looked at him are here, with them both. Jean, my sweet darling, she used to say, in the early days of their marriage. Her voice. She would sing all the time.

He opens the door, his vision blurred by tears that he wipes away with the back of his hand, and all he can see is the blinding halo of torchlight and the figure standing before him, unmoving, indistinct as a ghost. He takes a step back, says, "Come in."

Daniel switches off the torch and stares at this tearful man. He closes the door behind him and walks forward and at that moment he wishes his heart would cease beating because it hurts, it's strangling him, choking him, and he feels as if he won't be able to say a single word.

"I'm Daniel."

He tries to catch his breath. He feels the sweat run down his back. The man wipes away his tears again and manages to smile.

"And I'm Jean. Your father. Even after all this time."

Daniel does not recognise this deeply wrinkled face. But the voice, yes. It hasn't changed. And that is how he recreates the image of the man who lifted him up in his arms and took him on the merry-go-round. He was a very tanned man, with good teeth. Always smiling. He sees him again now. He rubs his eyes, feeling suddenly weightless, the walls of the room spinning slowly around him.

"Are you alright? Do you want some water to drink?"

Daniel nods without looking at this frail, unsteady man, afraid to meet his gaze.

Jean walks over to a cupboard and takes out two glasses that he fills with water from the tap. He takes a few deep breaths while he does this, shakes his head, splashes water on his face. He comes back to Daniel and hands him a glass. He can see his son's face in this man's. Thinner and longer, of course. The eyes bigger, dark like his mother's. He wants to hold him. He can't bear to remain standing like this, a metre away from him.

Daniel drinks, staring into the bottom of the glass. He wishes he could leave. He doesn't know what to say and it disturbs him to stay here, before this man who has the same voice as his father, before this echo of the past. But he also wants the man to speak again so that everything can really come back, if that's possible.

"I don't recognise you. I can't. Only your voice. It's still like it was before, when you . . . When you took me to the fair and bought me doughnuts."

Jean smiles and the tears fall again from his eyes. He doesn't wipe them away this time.

"I'm sorry," he says. "It's completely stupid . . . I just can't stop. It's like a river, overflowing . . . I don't know, I'm just so . . . How can I say this . . . Happy, I suppose, but that's a stupid word, it doesn't mean anything . . . And I'm so ashamed too."

Daniel walks over and puts his hand on the man's shoulder, and Jean puts his on Daniel's arm, and then they hug, both of them relaxing. It is a sweet embrace, nothing manly about it: no pats on the back or hearty squeezes, just their bodies close together and each with their chin in the other's neck, but not daring to kiss because first they probably need to get a handle on the other's reality, their substantiality, to feel their breathing, hear them gulp as they swallow their emotions, balled up in a rough knot in their throats.

"Let's sit down," says Jean.

He takes a chair and invites Daniel to sit on the bed. Jean sits very straight-backed, and he wipes his cheeks again and rubs the last tears from his eyes. He is preparing to speak, to explain his embarrassment and his regrets and his sorrow, but Daniel speaks first.

"Everyone thought you . . . that you were dead, all this time."

"I thought I was dead too. Maybe I am, in a way."

"I don't understand. You're here, in front of me. I don't believe in ghosts."

"Me neither. And yet sometimes I feel sure they exist."

"And my mother? Is she a ghost?"

Daniel doesn't know where he found the strength to say that. How he scraped up enough air in his lungs to breathe those words.

"What happened to her?"

Jean stares at him, but what he sees is still Olga in the line of prisoners, held up by some woman, turning around to try and find him in the crowd, and not seeing him even though he was waving to her and calling out to her in spite of the S.S. guards screaming at him – at all the other men in the crowd who were gesticulating and yelling and crying and sometimes throwing themselves forward – to shut up, in spite of the S.S. beating them with the butts of their rifles or setting their dogs on them, the men falling to the frozen ground and curling up in a ball, no longer moving, their faces covered with blood.

After a while, he realises that he is telling his son what he has scarcely told a soul before.

"If we'd been able to see each other one last time, if we'd been able to look in each other's eyes, you understand . . . If I'd been able to tell her that I loved her, that she was the only one I ever loved . . . I don't know, I think that would have made things better for her. I even prayed to God, can you believe it? I even tried to talk to that thing, but apparently if you don't believe in him, he doesn't respond. Some old man told me that. And when you believe in God, you realise he's not there anymore. That he won't be there ever again. That's what this old Jew told me. He laughed as he said that, like he was telling a really good joke. God exists, he said, but he's never there, the bastard.

"But we talked all the time in the train carriage. For more than two days, the two of us huddled close, all of us crammed in together. I held her, leaning back against the wall so she could sleep a bit, just a few minutes. She was shivering with fever. I told her everything I hadn't taken the time to tell her in years. And we talked about you, and that was terrible, and sometimes we preferred not to say anything cos we would have gone mad."

Silence. The yellow light filtered through the filthy lampshade casts more shadow than brightness. They both slouch forward as they breathe, eyes lowered.

"Sometimes I can't remember her face," Daniel says. "I have to look at Roselyne's photos. But now, with your voice, loads of images are coming back to me. I'm glad you came back."

"Are you sure? Wasn't it simpler the way it was before? When I was really dead?"

"I prefer people to be alive."

Jean nods, pensive. My son is right. He is on the other side, in sunlight.

"Did you really kill those people?"

"Which people?"

"The ones in the newspaper."

"I killed some bastards. Friends of a cop I knew before the war. A cop I still hung around with during the Occupation, despite what was happening. When I let you and your mother down. His name is Albert Darlac. He promised to protect us, and then one day he just handed us over. I found a few of his friends, his relatives, and I killed them. That's why I came back, to start with. I thought it would be easy. But then there was that kid, at the bar. I don't know what she was doing there. She died in the fire. I didn't know what to do then. As for the others, Darlac must have been eliminating a few inconvenient witnesses and framed me for it."

"Is that true?"

Daniel immediately regrets asking this. Jean sits up, opens his hands in front of him.

"You're the only one who can believe me. I don't care about the others."

"That's not what I meant."

They fall silent again. Afraid of hurting each other with words.

Daniel looks at Jean. My father. He does not really understand what that means. This man makes him sad. He wishes he could love him. He's heard stuff before about blood ties being indissoluble, instinctive, almost animal, and now he can see that it's not true. There's that voice, of course, those echoes, those images coming back to life. Useless memories.

502

"Why didn't you come back to get me when the war ended?"

For years he's been asking himself the same question every day, and each time it is like a very fine needle puncturing his skin, creating an electric pain, deep and fleeting.

They jump to their feet when the door is suddenly flung open and bangs against the wall. Jean knocks his chair over backwards as he stands up and at first Daniel does not understand who this man is, entering the room with a pistol, a Colt like the ones the officers in Algeria carried. He is tall, wide, solidly built. He is wearing gloves, a pale sports jacket.

"Ah, shit! I bet I'm interrupting a family reunion, aren't I?"

Darlac points his gun at Daniel.

"You, lie on the floor. Face down, hands on your head. And do it quick, cos I'm in a bit of a rush."

He curses himself for not having thought to bring handcuffs. He wasn't expecting this little shit to be here too. Oh well, that's even better. Two for the price of one. The minister's special envoy will come in his pants with excitement. Inside his pocket, he handles Mazeau's .30.

Daniel obeys. He tries to remember the name of the cop his father was talking about. Darnac? Darlac. He wonders what his chances are of getting up and charging into this bastard before he has time to open fire. Slim to none.

"And you, grab that chair and sit your arse on it. Here. I want you both in my line of fire. And don't try anything."

Moving slowly, Jean picks up the chair, sets it upright, sits down on it.

"And now what are you going to do? Are you going to kill us? Make it look like I committed suicide and murdered my own son?"

"I don't know yet, but that's not a bad idea. Just shut your mouth and let me savour the moment. You are my best ever arrest, you know that? And no-one cares if you're alive or dead. I'll have caught the murderer of nine people. If this was America, I'd be on the covers of magazines for this, pistol in hand, smiling for the camera. Can you believe the irony? Why exactly did you come back? To kill those losers and scare me? What did you think was going to happen? What were you even avenging yourself for? That old business with the camps? I bought you a one-year reprieve. That's not too bad, is it? You thought you were on the right side cos you hung around with me and a few Kraut whores while your Jewish wife went on with her life as if everything was normal? How could you expect not to get wet when it was pissing down with rain, you dick? Jesus, how old were you? And now you come back to avenge yourself, like in a film? Look at you! You're fucked. I can kill you whenever I want, if I want, cos you screwed it up, as usual, by thinking that you're cleverer than everyone else."

Jean concentrates on the gun – on the single dark eye staring at him – in order not to look in Darlac's eyes. Between the firing pin and the cartridge primer, there remain ten to fifteen millimetres of space, in which is trapped everything he has been through, all his sufferings and hopes. He made every mistake possible. He even brought Daniel into this, and now his son is lying in the line of fire of this vile, crazy prick. Darlac is going to shoot, no matter what. He's going to kill him. He didn't think it would happen like this. So quickly. At the hands of this bastard. He'd have preferred to do it himself. Jump under the wheels of a train. He's thought about it often during the three days he's spent here, hearing the horns of the locomotives blaring from the station. He would probably have fucked that up too. Sliding at the last moment onto the ballast, or throwing himself off the wrong bridge, or onto the roof of a carriage. It's farcical, the way he can fuck everything up.

Daniel listens to the cop's sarcastic voice, discharging its venom. He thinks about getting up, creating a diversion, but Darlac is holding two guns and covering every possible angle. He would still have a hand free to shoot, even if he was thrown to the ground. And that type of man is never easily intimidated; that type of man always recovers, with some unsuspected back-up plan ready at a moment's notice, a secret weapon stashed up his sleeve. Daniel wonders if perhaps he isn't simply scared. Maybe because he looked into the cop's eyes and it was like staring into dead water, a toxic swamp waiting for you to move closer so it can suck you in. In Algeria, if he'd looked into the enemy's eyes, he would probably have thrown down his weapon instead of fighting, as he ended up doing.

A scraping noise of wood on wood, and then the sound of the overturned chair hitting the floor. Sudden yelling. Daniel gets to his feet and sees the two men rolling on the floorboards, Darlac's hands, a gun still in each, beating the air. A gunshot sends him to ground again and deafens him, leaving a painful buzzing in his ears. Next to the wall at the other end of the room, the two tangled bodies continue fighting. He gets up again amid the stink of gunpowder and charges, but suddenly Darlac frees himself and hits Jean in the face with the butt of a gun, then pulls backwards and aims at both of them. With the Colt, he fires twice in Jean's chest. Jean does not cry out. His body falls back against the skirting board. Then Daniel sees the cop raise his other huge fist, with the pistol pointing like a child's toy, and he feels a hammer blow to his shoulder that sends him flying. He falls to the floor, and when he tries to break his fall he feels as if he no longer has an arm and he rolls onto his side.

Darlac places the .30 in Jean's right hand, slides his index finger onto the trigger and squeezes. The bullet lodges in the wall above Daniel and a cloud of white dust puffs into the air. The cop stands for a moment in the middle of the room, staring at the two prone bodies, then goes over to Daniel as shouts echo in the street below, along with car doors banging. So he goes down the stairs leading to the garage, pushes open the creaking door, half-blocked by shelves covered in spare parts, and sees two figures waving torches and yelling, "Police! Don't move!" He tells them his name and rank, calls them twats and approaches them.

"Things turned ugly up there. I got here too late. He'd shot his son. I had to defend myself."

The two men grope around for a light switch, find one and silently stare at the cars gleaming under the 100-watt bulbs.

The street is packed with cops jumping out of vans and Peugeot 403s parked any which way across the pavement in the amber flashes of the rotating lights on their roofs. Commissaire Divisionnaire Laborde bursts into view, flanked by two detectives whom he immediately sends off to find out what's happening.

"So have you got what you wanted?" he asks Darlac. "Everyone dead?"

"I had to kill him. He threatened me with his gun. Anyway, it was two bullets or the guillotine. I prefer the first solution: it's neater, and it's cheaper for the taxpayer."

"That's not the only thing that costs the taxpayer."

Other cars arrive. The prefect. A bigwig from the mayor's office. Darlac has met them before at office meetings.

"So?" they ask, slapping Laborde on the back. "You got him?"

"He's dead, along with his son. Commissaire Darlac led the operation single-handed."

Laborde stresses the word "single-handed" and the prefect raises an eyebrow. All the same, he walks over to Darlac looking grave and solemn and shakes his hand.

"I don't know if it was done by the rules, but at least it's done. This city will be peaceful again. The police is honoured to have officers such as you in its ranks. Go ahead . . . go home to your wife. You've earned a few hours of rest. Don't you think, commissaire divisionnaire?"

Laborde nods. Darlac takes his leave of these good people, then walks over to his car amid congratulations, compliments and salutes. He shakes hands, gets his back slapped. "Jesus, say what you like, but . . . what a cop!" he hears someone say behind him. It has been a long time since he felt so at peace. In the warmth of the night, he breathes in with a feeling of perfect fulfilment. He daydreams about the cognac he will pour himself when he gets home. About the sweet sleepy feeling that will soon overcome him.

He drives with the windows down, smoking a cigarette. He feels the best he's felt in so long that he finds himself humming a popular song, one of those inane tunes that madame sings to herself in her kitchen as she cooks.

*

He is woken by the pain. Daniel is floating at first, then feels the weight of his body again. He is lying in an awkward position, his right cheek against the floorboards, his arm trapped under his ribcage, one knee bent. Just as he decides to move, a hand grabs his wounded shoulder, making him groan with pain. He turns over and lies on his back. The room is swarming with people. He tries to see where his father fell, but there is a forest of legs planted in front of the slumped body, which he can hardly make out at all. Above him, a bald, square-faced man stares dumbstruck.

"This one's alive!"

Pandemonium. Voices shouting. Four or five faces turn towards him, incredulous.

"He's been shot in the shoulder," says the cop crouched down next to him. "Call an ambulance. Tell Commissaire Divisionnaire Laborde."

He feels like he's nailed to the floor by his own weight, a bit like on those giant spin-dryers you see in funfairs where you're stuck to the wall by the speed at which the thing is revolving. He looks up at the dark ceiling, examining the random shapes of the yellowish halos cast by the lamp and tries to think about something. But the pain drives everything from his mind, leaving him feeling stupid, like so many pounds of lifeless meat. Through the open window he can see flashing lights, hear engines rumbling.

He comes to again when they put him on a stretcher. He asks the policemen who lift him up to wait and he turns sideways, leaning on his good arm, and stares at his father's body. There is no-one around it now, and he is able to see the face at rest, the marks of time seemingly faded, the mouth half-open as if he were about to say something in his sleep, and he remembers the man whose hand he held when they walked in the street, the man who smiled as he talked to him.

Later still, in the hospital lobby, his shoulder immobilised by bandages, he shivers with fever, feeling thirsty and desperately lonely. He wishes Maurice and Roselyne were there, to reassure him. He wishes Irène could give him something to drink and hold his hand. The feel of her cool fingers in his palm. Her lips near his.

A few words. He closes his eyes, lulled by these sweet thoughts.

Then the cop who's sitting by the foot of the bed looks up at him over his newspaper and asks if he's alright.

*

Commissaire Albert Darlac feels another wave of happiness as he closes the door of the house behind him. The air is cool. Through the open French window, a breeze blows in from the garden, bringing the scent of the jasmine that grows on the pergola. Madame is sitting in an armchair and reading by lamplight as a moth flutters around the bulb. What a charming sight. She is wearing a pair of Capri pants that show off her ankles and cling tightly to her legs, and a pale blue blouse with an open neckline. He contemplates the roundness of her breasts, feels the urge to see her naked. He wants her. It is sudden and brutal. Back in the good times – when *were* the good times? His memory is shot – he would have moved closed to her and slid his hand under the fabric, his fingers caressing her nipple as he buried his other hand between her parted thighs. She would lie back, moaning softly, and hold his hand firmly inside her secret warmth . . .

He pulls himself together, takes off his jacket, tosses his waist-coat onto the sofa as he walks over to the bar. Cognac. He pours a generous measure into a heavy glass that he holds in the palm of his hand. He sniffs it, takes a sip, then sits down. Sigh of pleasure. Silence and darkness.

"Elise not here?"

Madame shakes her head. He wasn't looking at her though, so he waits for her response, is about to repeat his question then decides not to bother: why should he care about his whore of a daughter, good only for turning him on with her cuddles or her distant attitude, depending on her mood. Soon all that will be over. He is going to put his life in order. During the last few months, he has done a good job of tidying up his mess: he got rid of a lot, it's true. But you can't go on living amid an accumulation of old stuff; you can't keep walking forever through the same old shit without it starting to stick to the soles of your shoes and to stink, making people turn as you pass.

Soon he will be a free man. He will file for divorce, because that slut went on seeing her Kraut for years without his knowledge – that's what he will say, and they'll believe him, and they'll look at that unworthy beauty caught up with the devil like some demonic creature, and she'll be like those women who are branded with red-hot pokers, their heads shaved while the good people jeer and spit at them. He is sure of his ground. He will request a transfer to Paris. Or no, maybe Marseille, because he likes the sensations and the strong smells. They owe him that, at least, after he rid Bordeaux of the worst killer the city has known since the war officially ended. So they can fuck off, his wife and daughter. Madame can start train-ing as a shorthand typist again and she'll get a job as a secretary in some office to make ends meet. She'll be fine: he can see her now, dispensing her favours to her boss. With a body like hers, she'll probably end up getting promoted and marrying some ambitious bureaucrat or being kept by an adulterous executive.

So here he is now, planning out his life. He who has always lived so determinedly in the present, forbidding himself to look backwards, mistrusting tomorrow, here he is now going soft over his prospects, thinking about his future. He puts that down to the alcohol that is starting to lure him into a sleepy bliss, punctuated with pornographic scenes: madame in every possible position, using and abusing her charms in the most diverse places, to the point where he wonders if – touching his rock-hard erection through the fabric of his trousers – he couldn't have her now: turn her over as he usually does so he won't have to see her face and smash into her without a word. Why not enjoy this little comfort, this right granted to him by marriage?

He hears her moving about in the kitchen and wonders what she could be doing in there. He is surprised that he didn't see her get up. He looks around as if he's just waking up from a dream and is reassured by the firm grip of his hand on the glass of cognac. He takes another sip.

She comes back into the living room. He sees her tall figure walking towards him, backlit by the light from the kitchen, and he is seized by the desire to touch her, to bend her over – here on the sofa, for instance – and take her. The thought makes him shiver.

He is surprised to see her standing firmly in front of him, arms dangling. He stares at the triangle at the top of her thighs emphasised by those skintight trousers, and thinks only of what is hiding behind that thin fabric.

He is surprised to hear the sound of her voice. "Why did you kill Willy? Why couldn't you leave him for me? I never asked you for anything."

He looks up and sees that she's crying. This surprises him too, because she spoke in a firm, strong voice.

He is surprised when she falls on him. He holds out his arms –

he is afraid of spilling his drink. He is about to yell at her, shit, what are you . . . then he feels a sharp pain in his chest and realises that his shirt is wet with blood, that it is soaking the top of his trousers, so he drops his glass in order to push his wife away but his arms have no strength and they fall back on her as if he was trying to hug her.

She lies on top of him, thrusting the knife in with all her strength. Her face is only centimetres from his. She looks as though she's about to kiss him or tear off his face with her teeth. She whispers, her jaw tensed, the words barely articulated.

"Look at me, you bastard. Look at me as you've never seen me before."

Albert Darlac does as she tells him and he has trouble recognising his wife, Annette, in the frozen mask that leans over him. And that impassive perfection scares him, really scares him, because it seems to him that she is not human and that he cannot control her, he who has always so shrewdly manipulated the mediocrities who surrounded him to his own advantage. He tries to speak, but the only sound that emerges from his open mouth is a groan of pain.

It is at this moment that she stands up and he sees that she is covered in blood: her hair tied back, impeccable as always, but her forearms red and glistening, her impassive face flooded with mascara trickling down her cheeks. He tries to pull out the knife plunged in him up to its hilt, but he can't find it because it is dark, and his vision is scattered with dazzling lights, and his arms no longer obey him.

On the chair across from him, leaning slightly forward, she looks at the wooden knife handle as it rises up and down in time with his breathing. In a whisper, she counts. One, two, three . . . On the eighth time, the knife handle rises then falls slowly and does not move again. And the woman wipes away her tears.

A New Library from MacLehose Press

This book is part of a new international library for literature in translation. MacLehose Press has become known for its wide-ranging list of bestselling European crime writers, eclectic non-fiction and winners of the Nobel and *Independent* Foreign Fiction prizes, and for the many awards given to our translators. In their own countries, our writers are celebrated as the very best.

With this library we mean to make the books you would not want to overlook harder to overlook. The landscape for literary fiction in translation is expanding; we will go on looking beyond our shores and making it possible for readers to share in the most exciting and most renowned international writers.

Join us on our journey to **READ THE WORLD**.

PUBLISHED IN 2017

1. *The President's Gardens* by Muhsin Al-Ramli
TRANSLATED FROM THE ARABIC BY LUKE LEAFGREN

2. *Belladonna* by Daša Drndić
TRANSLATED FROM THE CROATIAN BY CELIA HAWKESWORTH

3. *The Awkward Squad* by Sophie Hénaff
TRANSLATED FROM THE FRENCH BY SAM GORDON

4. *Vernon Subutex 1* by Virginie Despentes
TRANSLATED FROM THE FRENCH BY FRANK WYNNE

5. *Nevada Days* by Bernardo Atxaga
TRANSLATED FROM THE SPANISH BY MARGARET JULL COSTA

6. *After the War* by Hervé Le Corre
TRANSLATED FROM THE FRENCH BY SAM TAYLOR

7. *After the Winter* by Guadalupe Nettel
TRANSLATED FROM THE SPANISH BY ROSALIND HARVEY

8. *The House with the Stained-Glass Window* by Żanna Sło
TRANSLATED FROM THE POLISH BY ANTONIA LLOYD-JONES

www.maclehosepress.com